STRANGE GRACE

STRANGE GRACE

TESSA GRATTON

Margaret K. McElderry Books
New York London Toronto Sydney New Delhi

MARGARET K. McELDERRY BOOKS
An imprint of Simon & Schuster Children's Publishing Division
1230 Avenue of the Americas, New York, New York 10020
MARGARET K. McELDERRY BOOKS is a trademark of Simon & Schuster, Inc.
For information about special discounts for bulk purchases, please contact Simon & Schuster Special Sales at 1-866-506-1949 or business@simonandschuster.com.
The Simon & Schuster Speakers Bureau can bring authors to your live event. For more information or to book an event, contact the Simon & Schuster Speakers Bureau at 1-866-248-3049 or visit our website at www.simonspeakers.com.
Book design by Sonia Chaghatzbanian
The text for this book was set in Goudy Oldstyle.
Manufactured in the United States of America
First Edition
10 9 8 7 6 5 4 3 2 1
Library of Congress Cataloging-in-Publication Data
Names: Gratton, Tessa, author.
Title: Strange grace / Tessa Gratton.
Description: First edition. | New York : Margaret K. McElderry Books, [2018] | Summary: "Every seven years, the people of Three Graces send a sacrifice to the woods. The death of their 'best boy' ensures seven years free from disease, blight, and pain. But this year, the Slaughter Moon has risen early, and three, not one, will run into the forest as a sacrifice"—Provided by publisher.
Identifiers: LCCN 2017038908 | ISBN 9781534402089 (hardcover) ISBN 9781534402102 (eBook)
Subjects: | CYAC: Fantasy. | Human sacrifice—Fiction. | Devil—Fiction. | Witches—Fiction. | Forests and forestry—Fiction. | Villages—Fiction.
Classification: LCC PZ7.G77215 Stg 2018 | DDC [Fic]—dc23 LC record available at https://lccn.loc.gov/2017038908

To all the witches, harpies, saints, and sisters
who have made my life spectacular

The woods at night are full of awesome beings.
Listen carefully and you can hear them cry:
Love is strange and calls us to stranger things.

—Luke Hankins

❖ TEN YEARS AGO ❖

Branches scrape his cheek, hungry for his blood. Eyes wide, the boy pushes harder, shoving at the sharp, dry leaves, stomping through undergrowth and deadfall. The trees are an old-growth tangle of trip wire, a web of limbs and fingers and claws to snare him.

Behind the boy, the devil clicks his teeth.

I N THE VALLEY BEYOND THE FOREST, A BONFIRE BURNS on a hill: an orange beacon to oppose the silver moon, its flames flick and tremble like a pulse. It is the heart of the valley now, surrounded by weary folk who keep vigil until dawn. Men and women and children, too: They hold hands, they wander in sunwise circles, they pray, and they whisper the names of all the saints to come before this boy. *Bran*

Argall. Alun Crewe. Powell Ellis. John Heir. Col Sayer. Ian Pugh. Marc Argall. Mac Priddy. Stefan Argall. Marc Howell. John Couch. Tom Ellis. Trevor Pugh. Yale Sayer. Arthur Bowen. Owen Heir. Bran Upjohn. Evan Priddy. Griffin Sayer. Powell Parry. Taffy Sayer. Rhun Ellis. Ny Howell. Rhys Jones. Carey Morgan. And now this boy's name, again and again and again, an invocation: Baeddan Sayer. Baeddan Sayer. Baeddan Sayer.

Because of him, and all the saints before him, no illness plagues the valley; the sun and rain share the sky in perfect consideration for each other and for the growing land; death comes peacefully in old age; childbirth is only as dangerous and hard as pulling teeth, but no one has to pull teeth here. They made this bargain with the devil: Every seven years their best boy is sent into the forest from sundown to sunrise, on the night of the Slaughter Moon. He will live or die on his own mettle, and for his sacrifice the devil blesses Three Graces.

M AIRWEN GRACE IS SIX YEARS OLD. SHE STANDS with her mother, the witch, weaving thin rowan branches into a doll for her friend Haf, who was too afraid to hold vigil with the grown-ups. But Mairwen is also the daughter of a saint, a young man who died in the forest before she was born, and so Mairwen is not afraid. She keeps her dark sparrow eyes upon it, on that wall of darkness she knows so well. Her favorite game is to dash to the very edge, to stand where her bare toes brush against the first shadow. There she waits, at the line between valley and darkness, while the shadows shift and tremble, and she can hear the delicate clicking of teeth, the whispers of ghosts, and sometimes—sometimes!—the devil's laughter.

She imagines calling out to them, but her mother makes her swear not to, that she must never say her name where the forest can hear. *A Grace witch began this bargain with her heart*, her mother says, *and your heart could end it*. So Mairwen stands silent, listening—listening, a witch's first skill—to the voices of the dead and discarded.

Someday, she thinks as she crafts her doll. Someday she'll step inside and hunt down her father's bones.

A RTHUR COUCH IS SEVEN YEARS OLD, AND RAGE HE doesn't understand keeps him hot and awake and staring while the boy beside him slumps in sleepy reverie. For the first six years of his life his mother raised Arthur as a girl, called him Lyn, put him in dresses, braided his long blond hair, to save him from this devil's fate, to hide him away. He knew no better—none did—until an early summer day playing in the creek near the boneyard. All the little girls stripped and splashed, laughing until one girl screamed he was different.

Nobody blamed Arthur, who went to live with the Sayer clan and chose a name from the list of saints. His mother fled the valley, crying she hated the Devil's Forest and the devil's bargain and to have a son in Three Graces was to live in terrible fear. "You might as well already be dead," she told Arthur before leaving forever.

When Arthur glares at the forest, it's because he can't turn his glare at the men of Three Graces, who laughed yesterday when this small boy presented himself as a candidate for sainthood. "I'm small and fast and I can win," he insisted. "I'm not a coward." And the men kindly told him to wait another seven years, or perhaps fourteen. But the lord who comes down from his manor for the Slaughter Moon put a hand on Arthur's bony shoulder and said, "If you want to be a saint, Arthur Couch, learn to be the best. The best does not throw his life away for another's shame, or for anger or to prove anything."

Someday, Arthur thinks as he stares with burning blue eyes at the forest. Someday he'll run inside that forest and offer his heart to the devil.

R HUN SAYER IS THE NEW SAINT'S YOUNGEST COUSIN, yawning as he leans his brown arm atop Arthur Couch's shoulder. He's not worried, for this vigil is the same as all the vigils his mother and father and uncles and aunts and second cousins and the lord Sy Vaughn and the Pugh sisters and Braith Bowen the smith and every other person has ever told him about. Besides, his cousin Baeddan Sayer is the *best*. He's the fourth Sayer to be made a saint, more than in any other family since the beginning. They've got it in their bones. Two Sayer saints before now crawled out in the morning, two of only four survivors in more than two hundred years.

It bothers Arthur, and his friend Mairwen, too, but Rhun knows the forest and the sacrifice and the seven years of health and wealth are just the way life is. This night is terrible, but no *other* night is terrible.

And all those other nights the moon and stars light their valley with silver and boys can run and race and play and hunt with no fear. Broken fingers heal in days, blood never pours, infections burn out by sunrise, and you never lose your parents or baby cousins or even any of the fluffy puppies. Rhun understands that all the goodness in the valley is what makes the sacrifice worthwhile. He remembers Baeddan laughing yesterday, blotches of red in his cheeks from beer and wild dancing, petals falling through his thick dark hair as they fell from the saint's crown. Baeddan leaned down, clasped his hands on Rhun's cheeks, and said, "Look at everything I have! It is so good here."

Rhun's eyes droop, though he knows he should keep watching, keep waiting for the pink sunrise, for the first flash of his cousin's triumphant laughter. Arthur shrugs Rhun away, and so Rhun throws his whole arm around his burning friend. He smiles and smacks a kiss to Arthur's pale brow.

Someday, he thinks. Someday he'll be the fifth Sayer saint, not in seven years but maybe in fourteen, and until then he will love everything he has.

. . .

THE MOON SPREADS OVER THE SKY, STARS TILTING LIKE a slow-spinning skirt. It arcs from east to west, counting the hours. The people feed their bonfire.

Wind churns the black leaves of the forest. It hisses and whispers in the way of all forests, until a shriek breaks itself free. This is hours past midnight, the worst time, and the scream peels up the spine of every adult and freezes the blood of the children. They move nearer their fire, their prayers lifting stronger, edged with desperation.

Another scream, inhuman, and another.

Followed by cold laughter trembling up from the roots of the forest, frosting the dry winter grass.

ATOP THE HILL, MAIRWEN HOLDS HER ROWAN DOLL SO tightly a tiny arm snaps. Her mother sings a quiet song, a lullaby, and Mairwen wonders if her mother is thinking of that last vigil seven years ago, when Carey Morgan ran into the forest not knowing he was soon to be a father, and never came out again.

AT THE BONFIRE, ARTHUR'S CHEST RISES AND FALLS hard, as if he were the runner. He steps away from the heat, away from his friends and cousins, and nearer to the dark, panting forest.

. . .

R HUN WINCES AWAY FROM THE FIRST SLICE OF SUN-light. He realizes, though, what it means, and drops open his mouth. Others have noticed, too: his father and mother, and Aderyn Grace the witch, the sisters Pugh and the lord Vaughn. The name passes from mouth to mouth: *Baeddan Sayer. Baeddan Sayer.*

The people of Three Graces wait, though it is surely too late now. The Grace witch murmurs, *So the Slaughter Moon has set, and seven more years are ours.* They no longer feed the bonfire; it will burn itself out, and the ashes will go in winter gardens and soap.

As the sun lifts entirely over the mountains, transforming the sky in a bloody wash, Mairwen Grace walks slowly to the edge of the forest. Her mother reaches out but knows better than to say her daughter's name where the devil might hear.

Mairwen stops alone just where the light of dawn teases the first trees.

She stares into the dim and whispers the saint's name.

Nothing happens, and Mairwen throws the rowan doll as far as she can into the Devil's Forest.

L ATER, WHEN THE SUN FILLS THE VALLEY, A SHADOW stirs. It is a slinking thing, powerful and hungry. It lifts fingers of bone and root from the forest floor, cradling the tiny doll.

THE FIRST NIGHT

I t's a quiet, lovely day, like every day in Three Graces, except one of the horses is sick.

Mairwen Grace puts her hand to the beast's velvety lips and scrapes her fingers under his chin. She was coming from the boneyard, looping wide over the pasture hill to tease herself with the shadows reaching out from the Devil's Forest, when she saw the gray stallion shudder and lower his head to the stiff autumn grass. He did not tear a bite, nor nuzzle it, nor raise his head again. He only let his head hang and gave a great, racking cough.

She's never heard a horse cough, or even thought it possible. His flanks darken with sweat and the spirit has drained from his brown eyes. Worry sinks through her gut: Mairwen has known this herd all her sixteen years, and never have any of the sturdy, small horses been anything but the perfect image of health.

No one falls ill in Three Graces, because of the bargain.

Frowning, Mair leans her shoulder against the horse's

neck, cooing softly to calm the horse and herself. She gazes out at the forest. This near to winter, the leaves curl yellow and orange as far as her eyes can see, to the distant shoulders of mountains and hazy blue sky. Pockets of green remain, of fir and a few mighty oaks whose roots dig deep. Not a sound creeps out from the forest, not of bird nor beast.

It is a silent, strange wood, a crescent of dark shadows and ancient trees embracing the town of Three Graces like the pearl in the mouth of an oyster.

And in its deepest center, the Bone Tree rises higher than the rest, with barren branches, gray as a ghost. Every seven years a handful of leaves bloom just at the top, turning red as if some sky-giant has shed drops of blood. A warning that the next full moon will be the Slaughter Moon and one of the boys will become a saint. If they do not send a saint in for sacrifice, the bountiful magic that holds their valley healthy and strong will fade. *Then* sickness will come, harvests will fail, and babies will die.

But it has been only three years since the last Slaughter Moon.

Unease wraps fingers around Mairwen's spine. It draws her like a fish on a hook toward the forest. Her arm slips away from the horse and she sets down her basket of sun-bleached bones.

Her boots brush loudly against the grass as she picks down the long pasture slope toward the forest, eyes on the dark spaces beyond the first line of trees. Her breath thins and her heart beats faster.

Mairwen herself has never been sick, though she's felt the flush of nausea before. She thinks of the carcasses hanging in cages in the boneyard, of the buckets of macerating skeletons, all part of cleaning the bones to make magic charms and buttons and combs. She thinks of the tendons, blood, and offal, the vile residues and grease of her work. Sometimes the stench of rot gags her, sometimes it slips past the scarf tied about her face and curdles her stomach, but that sort of illness always passes when she finishes changing out the bucket water.

This is different.

The daughter of the Grace witch and the twenty-fifth saint of Three Graces, Mair has been raised to believe she's invincible, or at least special. A blessing and good luck charm. But a town like hers hardly needs additional blessings or luck, not when the bargain keeps everything in the valley healthy and good. So Mairwen pushes at everything. She skims her hands into the forest, and surrounds herself with bones. Although her mother, Aderyn, spends time teaching her the healing ways of the Grace witches, Mairwen is more interested in strangeness. In bone charms and dark edges, in crows and night-mice. In all the things the first Grace witch knew and loved. *The first learned the language of bats and beetles, sang with the midnight frogs,* Mairwen's mother used to whisper late at night, when Mair climbed onto her bed for stories about the long line of Grace witches.

At the final brink of sunshine, Mairwen stops.

Fingers of darkness slither over the trees, shadows where

none should be, moving in ways no shadows should move. She licks her lips to better taste the hollow breeze and touches her longest finger to the cool trunk of a tall oak tree. Her toes wiggle in her boots, and she steps forward, half in shadow, half in light. Her apron turns gray in the shade while the sun continues to warm her tangled cherry-bark hair.

"Hello," she says softly, but her voice carries through the dull first few feet of the forest. Wind blows, whispering back at her from the canopy above. From here she can see uneven rows of trees, some oak, some pole pines, chestnut, she thinks, and other grand, proud trees, their leaves curling orange and gold as fire. The ground is covered in leaves and pine needles, all grayish brown from decay. No undergrowth for a long stretch that ends in a snarl of rowan and hawthorn and weedy hedges.

She wishes to step inside. Longs to explore, to discover the forest's secrets. But her mother has said, again and again, *Grace witches do not return from the forest. We all hear the call, eventually, and walk inside forever. My mother did, and hers before that. You were born with the call, baby bird, because of your daddy, and must resist.*

Mairwen clenches her hands together. It does not seem right to ignore this yearning, but her mother has promised: *Someday, someday, baby bird.*

She listens carefully—a witch's first lesson, her mother has also said. A leaf falls, brown and torn. A cluster of white flowers shivers against a root, tiny as a handful of baby teeth.

She taps her own teeth gently together. Some evenings and other dawns she hears the creatures of the forest gnashing theirs. She's seen them: tiny black squirrels with hollow eyes; birds with hands and bloody beaks; larger shadows formed like people or mountain cats; shifting, see-through shadows. Monstrous because the magic of the bargain has made them so, Aderyn says. When the setting or rising sun paints the sky the pale colors, this threshold becomes impossible to see, and Mairwen likes to come here to find it with her touch, with her skin and mouth and the nervous flutter of eyelashes. Then she can hear them, the clicks and hisses, the rattling laughter that even in summertime sounds like empty winter branches and bones.

But not now, not when the sun is high behind her.

Now it is a tense, quiet forest. A promise.

Mairwen thought she knew exactly what that promise was. But one of the horses is sick. Something is wrong. Something has *changed*.

A laugh tumbles out of her, jagged and surprising. Nothing changes in Three Graces, not like this.

Whirling, she dashes up the hill to the poor horse. From her basket she draws a thin, curved bone, yellow and hard. A rib from a fox, as long as her forefinger. She braids it into the horse's mane, whispering a song for happiness and health. Hair, bone, and breath: life and death tied together and blessed, a perfect little charm. Then she takes off for her mother's house.

The golden grass of the pasture is nothing beneath her

sturdy boots, though bits of it cling to the short hem of her skirts. She's grown a handspan in the last year and her summer clothes make it plain. Her wrists stick out of her sleeves, too, and what used to be a bright blue bodice is faded and worn. At least her mother's handed-down square shawl fits: It's hard to outgrow a shawl. Mairwen is molded exactly after her mother, Aderyn Grace, in most ways: strong shoulders and round hips and capable hands; a ruddy face more interesting than pretty, but with a round little nose and bowed lips; eyes as plain brown as sparrow feathers under straight brows; cherry-bark hair that twists and annoys like brambles.

At the pasture wall, Mairwen climbs up to walk a measure along the top and delay the moment she arrives home. She'll tell her mother what she's found. This won't be her secret anymore. It will spiral out to the entire valley. Rhun will hear it.

If something is wrong with the bargain, what will happen to Rhun?

The wall stones are locked together by puzzling only, and so Mairwen treads lightly lest she set it all crumbling. She's been forbidden this game too many times, especially after her friend Haf fell off and broke her wrist when they were six. The bones healed in less than a week, of course. Now the rough stones wobble and tremble beneath her, but Mair can't bring herself to hop down. She's too exhilarated, too terrified and confused. Is this what the first Grace witch felt, Mair wonders, when she met the devil himself, when she gave him her heart?

Cool wind rushes across the fields, ruffling the grasses. As she grows more still, Mair can hear the tang of Braith Bowen's smith hammer, but no other sound from Three Graces finds her ears. Her back still turned against the northern Devil's Forest, she looks south down the gentle slope toward town with its gray and white cottages, thatched roofs, and muddy lanes. The central square is gilded with strewn hay, but the outer common gardens and smaller goat pastures hold green. Long tracts of land swarm with tiny figures that are her friends and cousins, their skirts tied up or shirts stripped away while they cut the last harvest. There the creek pours out of the foothills with the mill at its strongest straight. Beyond it all the herds of sheep spread up their mountain, guarded by children and rangy dogs. Smoke snakes up from chimneys in town, and from all the scattered farmhouses too. Long curls of it even mark the Sayer and Upjohn homesteads hidden beneath the gentler, kinder forest of their mountain.

And higher up still, Sy Vaughn's stone manor grips the mountainside like a hunting kite.

This is why she climbed the wall as a child: to see Three Graces mapped before her, to feel the warmth of recognition fill her lungs. To see her home, and its unchanging beauty, and imagine herself an intrinsic part, instead of somehow outside of it all for being a witch and a saint's daughter. Between the town and the forest, pulled in both directions so that she can never settle down.

She has climbed the wall with Rhun and Haf and Arthur

so many times. Rhun crows and spreads his arms as if to embrace the whole of it; Haf balances too carefully, compensating for her fear of falling again; Arthur walks easily, nose up, pretending not to check his steps, as if it all comes naturally to him, as if he were the best.

Where are the three of them? she wonders. Haf with her sisters, washing diapers and braiding baskets or hair or both, charging after chickens. Rhun in a field for the harvest, no doubt, in the center of all the people he can manage, laughing his hearty loud laugh that makes others mirror it. Arthur—alone, she assumes, with a cute sneer—hunting up the mountains to the south, determined to bring back a buck all on his own, or more in his brace of rabbits than any other hunter.

Or, because there's a sick horse, everything has changed, and she knows nothing of where her friends might be.

If something is wrong with the bargain, did her father die in vain? And Baeddan Sayer, and—

Mairwen jumps to the ground, catching herself with a hand on the earth.

Her mother's house is the farthest out of town in the north. Surrounded by a fence of logs and stone, the Grace house is two odd-shaped stories with a long wing for herbal work and a separate one-room workshop. One of the oldest local homes, its hearth is made of a single gray stone as long as a man, set down two hundred years ago by the first Graces to find themselves near the Devil's Forest. The upper level has been added twice, once for grandchildren and again after it burned down in Mairwen's great-grandmother's time. In the yard they keep chickens and three milk goats, and her mother's herb garden overgrows the rear field. A cluster of gooseberry bushes snarl over the wall near the front door.

Mair expects Aderyn to be in the yard where the herb-fire burns, stirring her iron pot for soap or charms or maybe just laundry, but instead angry steam hisses in waves where the abandoned pot has boiled over.

Just then a scream cuts through the pleasant groaning wind. It comes from inside the house.

She runs.

Her bones jar with every hard step as she careens down the slope, skirts tangled around her shins until she wrenches them up and sprints through the gate into the yard. The front door gapes open and Mair flies through, stopping abruptly in the dim entrance.

A single large room of pale daub and dark wood, dominated by the hearth and kitchen space, the bottom floor is usually full of neighbors at any time of day. But now every chair and bench has been haphazardly shoved to the sides of the room and piled atop the heavy dining table, leaving a wide space of only braided rugs. In the center, Aderyn Grace and her best friend, Hetty Pugh, support the pregnant Rhos Priddy between them as the younger mother-to-be grits her teeth and moans. The three women take slow steps around the rug. Rhos pants, then strains against the grip of the older women. Aderyn says, "You've got to keep moving, if you can, and we'll get you through this one and put some tea in you."

Hetty Pugh shoves black hair out of her face. "One foot, then the other, rosebud."

Rhos, four years older than Mairwen and only seven months into her first pregnancy, nods frantically, cheeks red, sweat darkening the sunshine curls around her face. Like the sweat turning that gray stallion black.

Mairwen hesitates, one hand on the doorframe, and reminds herself birth is difficult work even in Three Graces. She's heard the cries, boiled water, mopped up blood. It happens here often, for the Grace heritage makes their house with its ancient hearthstone a lucky place to be born. But this is too soon.

"Mother?" Mairwen finally says, as Rhos's breath evens out and the girl sags. Both Aderyn and Hetty turn sharply.

"Mair!" Hetty says. "Go to Nona Sayer and send her here. She might know something from outside the valley to help."

"What's happening?" Mairwen asks, still hovering.

Her mother slips an arm around Rhos's wide middle and leads the girl to one of the low rocking chairs. "Rhos is having some pains, is all," Aderyn says gently. Her dark eyes meet Mair's, and Mair feels the lie settle in her guts. But it's a lie for Rhos, not her. Aderyn soothes Rhos with tender fingers patting the girl's hair. Again Mairwen is reminded of the gray horse and her own ministrations.

Unlike Aderyn's unruffled surety, Hetty is furious. Her freckles stand out more than usual against bloodless white skin, taking years off the woman's thirty-odd.

20

Mair says as calmly as she can, "Mother, I need to speak with you," and Aderyn immediately gives Rhos over to Hetty and ushers Mairwen back into the yard.

"One of the horses is sick," Mair says in a gasp. "And this! What does it mean?"

"I can't know yet. Maybe nothing too much," Aderyn answers, wiping her brow. "Go for Nona, and then up the mountain to find out if Lord Sy is home from his summer travels yet, and tell him, and bring him down."

Mairwen goes in a swirl of skirts and tangle of fear.

R HUN SAYER PUTS DOWN HIS SCYTHE AND CROUCHES amid the cut barley. Sun beats down on his bare, broad shoulders, and sweat mixes with field dust and bits of seed to itch along his spine and behind his ears and where the buttons of his trousers rub his stomach. All around him men and women grunt and sing *"swing, child, swing"* to hold on to an even rhythm. This glinting haze only happens late in the afternoons on harvest days, when the lowering sun angles exactly to light up the dust tossed high from their work.

Everyone expects Rhun to stand wide, sigh happily, and grin, to declare this day has been a good day and maybe start a new song, something rapid and merry. A tongue twister or ask-and-answer. It's what he usually does, full of hard work and the promise of relief and hot meat and beer for dinner with his cousins and neighbors alive in the glare of low sunlight.

But Rhun isn't paying much heed to the haze or the chanting. He narrows his gaze onto the patch of dark, bent barley that he half sliced through. The stalks are spotted with pale freckles, ringed with blackening brown. He's never seen anything like it, but he knows in his gut this is blight. Not a thing to be blamed on beetles or grasshoppers, but disease. Like the pox that sometimes crawls through the valley, marking temporary scars on the young and old, and leaving relief behind in its wake, for here nobody dies of such things.

But some of this barley, Rhun thinks, is dead.

An unfamiliar frown pulls at his lips. Unease flickers behind it, and Rhun huffs out a breath. He needs to tell somebody, even if it's nothing but a strange outlier patch.

"Rhun? Y'all right?" It's Judith Heir, a woman five years older than him, as unused as the rest of them to a frown on the mouth of Rhun Sayer the Younger.

Rhun knows it, and smiles. He's a handsome boy, seventeen, with broad shoulders and the crooked nose that runs in his father's family, and the brown skin and odd carmine flecks in his eyes he got from his practical, cranky mother, Nona. Otherwise, he's symmetrical and large all around, wears whatever fits him and suits his day's task, and ties his black spiral curls into tails and clubs, never hiding his face. "Yeah, just got a crick in my shoulder," he says. For emphasis, he rolls his right shoulder dramatically, wincing. "I think I'll run and go get a salve from Aderyn Grace."

"Surely," Judith says, then mops her brow with her sleeve before hefting her scythe again.

Quickly, Rhun puts his fist around the base of some of the patchy barley and tugs it out of the earth. Hooking his scythe over a post, he strides for the witch's house, tapping dirt off the barley roots against his thigh as he goes.

Secrets are Rhun's least favorite thing in the world, for how they taint everything with a prickly combination of hope and fear, but he is certain that at least immediately, it's better to keep this discovery quiet. He'll find Mair and show her, get her take. Let her be fascinated as she always is with the rare and different, and pull him along with her enthusiasm.

Just the thought of her calms him: Mairwen Grace, the person he loves whom he is allowed to love.

Wind from the north blows in over the Devil's Forest. Rhun glances at the darkness cradled there, a horizon of black trees undulating under the wind like an angry ocean, with distant mountains behind. He pauses. The barley in his hand tingles, or perhaps that is a tickling unease in his palms, the urge to run, run, run.

Someday.

Rhun Sayer smiles a gentle, private smile, not performing anything but only for himself at the rightness of his future: Someday he'll stand at the top of the pasture hill with the entire town, beside a bonfire, wearing the saint's crown. And as the sun sets and the Slaughter Moon rises, he'll be the one to dive into the forest like his cousin, and run—and likely die—for the valley. For all this goodness.

The certainty of it comforts him as much as the thought of Mairwen did.

But the wind reaches him, chilling the sweat on Rhun's chest, and he realizes he left his shirt folded over the cart at the corner of the barley field. Awkward to knock on Aderyn Grace's door without it, so he shifts his path toward home instead.

I N A CLEARING OF AUTUMN TREES THAT GLOW UNDER the late sun like a soothing family fire, Arthur Couch pinches the edges of fur in his fingers, right at the cuts he made at the rear ankles, and with a firm jerk, strips the entire skin off the rabbit he snared and hung.

The tearing noise satisfies him, and the skin remains whole enough for several different uses. This rabbit died fast by his knife, not breaking its neck in the trap like many do, so the tiny neck bones should be intact enough for Mairwen.

A hot flush creeps up Arthur's pale ears at the thought of the last time he brought her bones. She tossed them into a large stinking barrel full of water and other small animal skeletons as if they weren't a gift, as if it didn't matter to her at all that it was him who brought them. He supposes it isn't terribly special to bring dead things to a witch.

Wind gusts high above him, bending the trees to loom over him like interested friends, but he hardly notices.

The problem is that he wants it to matter, wants to be special still, to her. He used to be. She used to laugh at his jibes and wicked jokes; her eyes used to sparkle when his burned; she used to race with him and care as much as he did which of them won. Rhun never cared—Rhun never *had* to care. He's so certainly the best boy, whatever he does is just what the best boy does, even if that's lose a footrace to Arthur Couch. But Mairwen cared passionately. She hissed when she lost. She dared Arthur to put his hand in the forest. She smirked when he wouldn't, yet.

It has been nearly three years since they've been comfortable enough together to be mean, and he misses it. He misses her with a simple ache that wakes him up at night. He doesn't know if he's in love with her or if he wants to set her on fire.

All he knows is *why* she stopped giving him her attention three years ago. Why things are tense with Rhun. Why he's even more of an outsider than he was before.

The answer is Rhun's secret, though, and Arthur tries to bury it deep.

But the only other thing that tugs regularly at Arthur's thoughts is the next Slaughter Moon. Four years away. Four more years before he can show them all, the whole valley, the town, that he is not some fool ruined by his mother, that he is no liar, not weak or soft. He can be as good as Rhun. He can be the best.

Arthur looks north, toward the Devil's Forest, though he can't see it. His heart beats hard and his hands fist. Arthur is a tall young man, and the sort of pale that burns in the sun. He's lanky and strong, with blond hair he saws off in chunks whenever he loses his temper. It hasn't been longer than his jawbone since he was eleven, and the ragged aspect ruins the pretty lines of his face exactly as he wishes. That rage burning in his blood keeps him skinny no matter what he eats, hollows out his cheeks to make his blue eyes too large, too cold. Always he carries enough knives for a seven-handed monster, as well as a woodsman's ax.

Suddenly Rhun Sayer bursts off the path from Three Graces, heading toward the Sayer homestead. Rhun sees Arthur and freezes, every handsome half-naked pound of him awkward and still as stone. Then he relaxes, forcing a smile that does not look forced. But Arthur can see it. See it and appreciate the effort, grateful at least they're still friends.

"Arthur! I'm getting a shirt and then going to find Mair. Do you want to come?"

Gesturing at the rabbit carcass, Arthur says, "I have to cut away the best flesh to save and bury this first."

Rhun grimaces. He's a hunter, sure, but he prefers roasting little creatures like this whole even if it ruins the bones. "I'll grab my shirt and meet you here."

But Arthur's eyes go to the clump of dying barley. "What's that for?"

Rhun taps the barley against his thigh again, then offers it to his friend.

Arthur stares, not reaching to take it. "What's wrong with it?"

"Disease, I think." Rhun angles the barley to better display the dark spots. "It was a clump of them."

Sucking in a breath so his teeth show, Arthur lifts his gaze to Rhun's. "A momentary blight? Something to pass?"

"Usually that just blows in and out overnight, doesn't kill. We'll find some waterlogged or bent with weariness, but always the grass stands up again under the full sun. Today was a good day. Not too much rain."

"This is different, then," Arthur murmurs.

"New," Rhun says in a hushed tone, wavering between awe and fear.

Unable to put his teeth away, Arthur smiles a rare, full-mouthed smile. "I like new things," Arthur says.

"Do you?"

The challenge slices away Arthur's smile and deadens the current between them. Arthur turns fully around and steps away. His shoulders roll as he works to sooth the tight knots pulling at his spine.

To make up for it, Rhun puts his hand on Arthur's back, firm and friendly, like any two young men might share. None of the tenderness Arthur is so afraid of.

Arthur nods, accepting the silent apology. Together they study the barley. Arthur touches the stiff yellow hairs falling around the rows of seeds. He can barely feel them against the rough pad of his finger. New is not anything they're much familiar with in Three Graces. Different is worse—he knows it from experience. From the boys who throw flowers at him still, ask if his mama took all his skirts with her when she ran away.

"Something must be wrong with the bargain," Arthur says with relish. He's waited for a flaw to reveal itself for ten entire years.

Rhun's whole face tightens. "Do you think so? I was going to ask Mair."

"If it's not a temporary blight—and you don't think it is—it has to be a problem with the devil."

Scratching at the back of his neck, Rhun looks in the direction of the Devil's Forest, through the rows of friendly trees. "Maybe because of what happened last time?"

Both boys remember the last Slaughter Moon clearly, three years ago. It was John Upjohn they blessed and followed in a snaking dance over the fields; John who was tall and lean and fast; John who they watched vanish into the black forest. The boys remember the vigil hours, the howls from the forest, staring from a safe distance, and Lace Upjohn, who clutched her son's tiny naming shirt to her chest as a protection charm, praying with Aderyn Grace and the sisters Pugh. They remember Mairwen as an ecstatic force between them, leaning up on her toes as if she'd be able to see farther if she were as tall as Rhun and Arthur. Grasping their shoulders in turn, back and forth. Arthur had fed off her energy, gritted his teeth impatiently; Rhun had put his arm around her waist to ground her, to comfort himself.

Too long past the harsh pink dawn John Upjohn did not emerge from the forest.

Mair had stepped forward first when she spied a sleek shadow spill from the trees. Then Rhun had seen it, and Arthur, too. Hope had pricked in Arthur's chest, blossoming sickly as he watched seventeen-year-old John crawl his way free, one of his hands torn off.

"I never thought much about it," Rhun says abruptly, avoiding Arthur's look. Arthur knows why; they'd not been overly concerned by Upjohn because of what happened between them so shortly after.

"Neither did I," Arthur admits. "But everybody will now, if this is . . ." He points at the barley.

Rhun takes a deep breath. Arthur can tell Rhun wants to touch him again, like he would touch Mair if she were present. For comfort, for reassurance. Just because he wants to. Rhun is the sort of person who needs contact with the people he loves, but he only ever avoids it around Arthur. One sign from Arthur and that will change, but Arthur doesn't give it.

Holding on to the barley with both hands, Rhun says, "It can't be broken. The bargain. We need it."

"You need it, you mean."

"No, I . . ."

Arthur huffs. "You can't fulfill your destiny if there's no bargain."

"That's not why. I . . . I don't want the troubles from outside our valley to come here. What we do is worth it. It's how we keep ourselves safe and well."

"Not you," Arthur points out. "You'll be dead, or so changed by your run you leave, like all the surviving saints before you."

Rhun shrugs uncomfortably. "Maybe it won't be me."

"It will be you," Arthur says bitterly.

The silence between them twists into brambles.

"Unless," Arthur says slowly, "unless something is wrong, actually wrong, and there's a chance to change it." The thought sparks fire at the base of Arthur's spine, and behind his eyes, a passion Arthur usually does not allow Rhun to see.

Rhun stares at Arthur's eyes, then mouth, then looks abruptly away.

"What if we could change it?" Arthur presses, ignoring the meaning of the glance.

"This is only one patch of diseased barley," Rhun insists.

Arthur slides him a disbelieving eye. "Only one patch," he repeats, hoping that maybe, *maybe*, in this sudden crack in the bargain there might be a place for his ambitions.

"We should take it to Mair," Rhun says.

"Yes." Arthur claps his hand on Rhun's bare shoulder and takes off, skinned carcass of his kill forgotten where it hangs in the tree.

RHUN FOLLOWS AFTER, WATCHING ARTHUR'S SLINK-ing walk, the sharp thrust of his arm as he shoves branches out of his path. His friend is prickly as a cat, just as prideful, just as dangerous, just as beautiful. As always, Rhun wishes he could convince Arthur he's good enough to do anything. He's known Arthur his whole life—known everybody in Three Graces as long—and liked him when he was a girl, and liked him more after the secret exploded and Arthur turned all jagged and lethal and determined to prove he was the manliest of men with sneers, loneliness, and a weapon in every hand. In any other valley, Arthur would be too pointy for his own good. Here he's tolerated because nobody is afraid his edges can do any harm.

If this is a break in the bargain and the valley is losing its safe magic, Rhun needs to find a way to fix it, so nothing bad can happen to Arthur. Or anybody. He'll find a way. That's what Sayers are for: keeping everyone safe. Rhun knows who he is and what he wants, so never questions why he's widely believed to be the best. And Rhun knows Arthur will never be chosen to run, will never be able to compete, because Arthur doesn't know anything about himself except what he is *not. The best can never be defined by what it's not,* he said to Arthur once. It did not go well.

As they push through the narrow footpath toward the Sayer homestead, the sun lowers enough to turn the air from bright orange to a gentle pink, dappled with warm shadows and the first evening birdsong. Woodsmoke finds Rhun's nose, and he can't hold on to the verge of fear any longer. The season is changing, and he loves it. He loves summer, too, and spring and winter, for every season brings different work and different things to laugh about. He sighs a great, happy sigh, loud enough Arthur hears it and glances back.

Arthur recognizes the expression on Rhun's face and puffs a laugh. "You're a fool," he says fondly.

"Everything will be all right," Rhun says. "And just as it's supposed to be. You'll see."

"I could take you more seriously if you had a shirt on."

Though it's Rhun's instinct to tease Arthur about how good Rhun knows his shoulders and chest look, he refrains, smiling a shrug instead.

Arthur's eyes narrow, and he nods, leading the way again. It's cooling, and it *is* a beautiful evening, but none of that matters when there's such a troubling note of uncertainty in the form of that diseased barley. It's amazing that Rhun, even gregarious, bighearted Rhun, could be so quickly distracted by nothing more than pretty autumn twilight.

The Sayer homestead consists of three stone buildings: a house, a barn, and a secondary house that's mostly kitchen and storage this generation. The main house has two full stories instead of only lofts, and a strong slate roof, but the others are thatched like the cottages down in the valley. A fenced-in lawn feeds their goats and gives a walk to the chickens, but all their horses are down in the valley with the rest until the winter sets in. It's quiet, as most of the Sayers are out helping with the harvest today. Only a thin trail of smoke slips up the chimney, trickling down to nothing as Arthur and Rhun arrive.

Together they step out of the forest into the flat yard just as a girl shoves out the front door and dashes around the back edge of the house to vanish again into the trees and farther up the mountain.

"Was that Mairwen?" Arthur asks.

"It looked like her hair," Rhun says, disappointed she didn't see them and stop. He starts on again, but Arthur hesitates, staring after Mairwen. Higher up the mountain from the Sayer homestead is only hunting and Lord Sy Vaughn. Mair is no hunter.

Rhun puts out his hand to open the front door, but his mother opens it first. She startles back at the sight of him, then shoulders past. "Get to town; see if you're needed," Nona Sayer instructs. Nona is as tall as all the Sayer men. To Rhun she passed her brown skin and coiling hair, and to her youngest the same plus a straighter nose. She was the first person from outside to settle in the valley in a generation, but since the bargain welcomed her, fast healing the bruises and starvation from her journey over the mountains, so did the people. She glares at Arthur, whom she took in when his mother ran off and his father refused him. "Same for you, boy."

"What's wrong?" Arthur asks, nicer than he'd have asked any other living person, because Nona always treats him like one of her rough-and-tumble boys.

Nona frowns at him, then at her actual son, measuring them up. "Rhos Priddy went into labor early, and Mairwen Grace claims a horse in the pasture is sick."

A thrill shoots through Arthur, but for Rhun the news sinks slow and firm into his guts. "Is it the devil? Did we do something wrong?" Rhun asks. *How can I fix it, Mama?* is the clear subtext.

She shakes her head. "Not you, Rhun, that's for certain. Go into town and keep folks calm. I'm going to Aderyn to help with the birthing, and we'll send word when we can.

Mairwen's off to fetch Lord Vaughn."

"What about me?" Arthur says. "I'm not good at keeping anyone calm."

"Try harder," Nona says, and that is that, for she swings her basket back into the crook of her elbow and hurries off to the north valley where the Grace house squats just a hill away from the Devil's Forest.

"Well, damn," Rhun murmurs.

"Try harder," Arthur spits.

Rhun lets the barley fall from his hand. It scatters over the green grass of the yard like a blight itself.

M AIRWEN GRACE HURRIES UP THE STEEPEST PATH to Lord Vaughn's manor, for it's also the quickest.

She knows the way, like everyone knows the way, though few have reason to visit. The Lords Vaughn often travel away from the valley, always returning for the Slaughter Moon, and sometimes for a regular winter, with trunks of books and expensive odds from the outside world. The current lord, Sy, is near thirty and unmarried. Mair has heard gossip he has a lover in the nearest city, but she is uninterested in a wedding that would force her out of her finery and into this primitive valley. Vaughn should find another, Mair thinks, or marry someone from Three Graces. The previous lord died just before John Upjohn's run, and so Sy has presided only over that one, and Mairwen isn't sure he has the experience to help if something is wrong with the bargain.

Mairwen clutches at roots and jutting boulders to keep her balance. Her palms are raw now, her arms ache, and her breath is harsh and cold in her throat. Mair heaves up around an uprooted tree that leans over the steep path. She's reached the level ground upon which the manor is built into the mountain—or from it, seemingly, for the gray stone bricks were carved from the cliff peak above them.

Mair rubs her hands down her skirt to clean them and taps her heel to her toe to knock excess dirt from her boot soles. Making her way to the wide front door with its iron gate, Mair thinks of three years ago, that night she sat with John Upjohn while he sweated through nightmares and, before the sun rose, Sy Vaughn came calling.

John was only eighteen, and she thirteen, gangly and passionate and thrilled to hold his head and arm while her mother worked to stanch the slowly bleeding wrist. They tied a tourniquet above his elbow and whispered together a song of healing that was fast and encouraging, but no more than a charm. Aderyn cleaned and bound the stump, then bound the entire arm to John's shivering chest, so the missing hand would've been higher than his pounding heart. All day they remained with him, dripping water and broth onto his lips, singing to him softly, drawing blessing triskeles on his arm. He slept the afternoon away, and into the night. Mairwen held him against her for hours, curled together on a nest of blankets near the wide hearthstone, staring as if she might see the impression of memories in his drawn skin, hear the devil's laughter in his harsh breathing, feel the chill of fear and exhilaration in the echoes of pain cut into his wince. She was desperate to know what he'd seen—had he seen her father's bones? Did he understand things about the forest she could not? Did he have answers for her? She longed to whisper her thoughts into his ear and wait for the response however it might come.

His strong body shook with nightmares; he cried hot, sticky tears; he held on to her with his remaining hand, clutching her ribs or twining his fingers in her tangled hair. She'd dozed, finally, cheek on John's shoulder. Her sleeping had been dreamless, a sleep of sweet exhaustion, but John's had been terrible. His feet twitched as if he'd never stopped running, and he panted hard.

The Grace door slammed opened and a dark figure strode in. John Upjohn woke with a cry, and Mairwen threw herself across him, between the saint and this new danger.

The figure wore a trailing black cloak with the cowl pulled around his face—if he had a face—and he stood leaning sideways, one gloved hand pressed to the blackened end of a walking stick that shone in the moonlight like a knife.

Mairwen said, "You will not take the rest of him, too, devil!"

Silence swept through the house, and the silvery moonlight cast everything gray but for the blood seeping through the bandage of John Upjohn's raw wrist.

The figure pushed back his cowl to reveal a square, pale face and curling brown hair. He said, "It is only Sy Vaughn, brave girl."

She relaxed slightly, but kept herself before John like a guardian spirit. "You can't have him either," she said.

And Sy Vaughn smiled, amusement tucked into the corners. He studied Mairwen Grace, thirteen and weedy and small, bent around the injured saint, staring at him with her mother's brown eyes. He stepped nearer, then crouched beside her. He tugged off his glove to touch her freckled cheek with a bare finger, and lowered his eyes to the saint.

John Upjohn lifted his chin with the last thread of his courage and said, "I survived."

"So you did, John. And I want you to know: My family has offered money to all the survivors, if you wish to leave the valley, if you find it too rough surviving still, this near the forest."

Mairwen knew this. She'd heard it from her mother, and knew all four survivors in the past two hundred years had taken the offer and left Three Graces forever, as if once a boy ran through the Devil's Forest, he could not be contained by the valley.

"No. You can't leave," she whispered.

And John agreed. "I'd drag the forest with me wherever I went. I feel it . . . too strongly."

"Here," Aderyn Grace said gently from her bedroom door, "you might never be happy. The memories, the nightmares . . ."

"I know," John said.

"That's not true." Mair turned and put her hands on his face. "There are cures for nightmares, and you're the best, John."

"I was."

Mair leaned up onto her knees. "You're the saint, always and forever. My father . . ." She could say no more, but John Upjohn seemed to understand.

"I'll try," he promised wearily, "for the daughter of Carey Morgan."

"None have survived and stayed," the lord said, studying not John, but Mairwen. She studied him back, staring at his face, warm and sunny even in these shadows.

"Please," she said, "let him stay."

With no word, the lord stood and went to Aderyn. Vaughn touched the back of Aderyn's hand. "Keep him alive, then, Grace witch," he said, and swept out.

Mairwen did not sleep again that night, though her mother refused to acknowledge anything odd had occurred, and John curled back again into the blanket nest, head tucked into Mairwen's warm embrace.

She can't help but think of it now, as she drags at the iron gate of the manor with all her weight, because it's three years since the last Slaughter Moon and the bargain is failing. The only change she knows of is John Upjohn both surviving and staying.

At her urging. At her plea.

And Rhun Sayer might pay the price of it, too soon.

The iron squeals open and she pounds on the cold wooden door with her fist. "Lord Vaughn!" she yells. "Are you here? You're needed! My mother, Aderyn Grace, sent me!"

Her words echo around the stone archway. Mair waits,

pressing her back to the door. The manor shelters her from wind, and she can see the southern edges of the sunset against the mountain slope, and far beyond it, the next mountain all green dark shadow and lightning-strike of white peak. Beyond that, she imagines another peak and another, in a long string of mountain range, or if she sends her thoughts even farther, the plains of farmland they're told lead to a vast river and the first of the great cities. Sometimes in the spring, a cart and horse makes its way along the narrow passages through these mountains to their valley, led by a trader who knows Lord Vaughn's name, and they tell stories of the cities and kings and vast church government. Less often, a person stumbles into Three Graces to stay, like Rhun's mother. Refugees or orphans or folk seeking they're never sure exactly what, until they land here. Even more rarely a person leaves, never to return.

Mairwen's mother says someday Arthur Couch will leave, because he burns too hot for Three Graces. But Mair suspects Arthur burns too hot for all the world. She can imagine him, though, far away from here, past those large mountains and surrounded by others to fight.

The thought of him gone sours her tongue.

It strikes her how quiet it is here at the lord's manor: unlike every step of the valley, where you can hear birdsong or the clang of Braith Bowen's hammer and anvil or complaining sheep at all times. Even at night, the wind seems to chitter and chat.

But here it's silent.

Perhaps Vaughn has not come home, because it's not supposed to be a saint year. Perhaps he reclines in an elegant city house, with oranges and fancy wine, with that lover of his, reading a book and not thinking at all that he's needed here four years early. But no—she saw smoke lift off his chimney this afternoon.

Against the small of her back, the handle twitches as someone on the other side unlocks it.

Whirling, she's ready when the door pushes out, and there stands the lord in elegant black with his face clear toward the sun. It catches his miscolored eyes, making them clear as glass.

Vaughn slides away to allow Mairwen entrance to the small foyer. She does, and he quickly shuts them into darkness. The only light comes from the hallway to her left, just a flicker of fire.

"Lord Vaughn," she says, offering an awkward curtsy.

"Mairwen Grace," he says, smooth and relaxed. "Welcome to my home."

He sweeps past her and leads her toward the firelight.

The hallway is broad enough for two abreast and built with no windows and the candle alcoves are empty. Some tapestries warm the walls, dark, bold floral patterns woven into them. Vaughn takes her past two closed doors and then down three shallow stairs into a warm room with wooden rafters and limewash to brighten the walls. The shutters on two tall windows are drawn, but a small fire burns in the great wide hearth she remembers from her visits with Aderyn. A wingback chair rests near the fire, surrounded by stacks of books, and she spies a small writing desk and an entire shelf of ink bottles and pens.

"Sit if you will," he instructs, pointing at a three-legged stool with a velvety cushion, then at a small sofa with gilded legs shaped like talons. She perches on the stool with her hands on her knees, glad not to feel uncomfortable or strange in his lovely room.

Vaughn sits in his wingback chair and stares at her. Still handsome, despite the oddness of his eyes: one dark brown and one gray. His long fingers curl around the green arms of the chair, adorned by only one ring: a silver band gripping three black gemstones.

She draws a breath and says, "There's a sick horse in the field and Rhos Priddy went into early labor. My mother sent me to fetch you, for it seems there's something wrong with the bargain."

He nods, resting back so his face half disappears in the shadow thrown by the wing of the chair. The fire crackles, and Mair hears her pulse suddenly in her ears, but nothing else.

"You aren't surprised! Did you know? Is that why you returned this year?"

"I come home nearly every year. It is difficult to stay away, knowing outside the valley anything might happen to me and I will not be healed."

"Oh." Mairwen tries to calm down. She nearly asks what

it's like, outside, but that is what Arthur would ask. If she truly wished to know, she'd have had answers from Nona Sayer years ago. Mairwen only cares what is deeper inside the valley.

Vaughn sighs. He said, "But I am not surprised. Not entirely."

Excitement pushes Mair to lean forward. "Why?"

"Because of John."

"He met the rules of the bargain."

"That we know of. No saint has done as he did, surviving but leaving a piece of himself in the forest."

"I can go into the forest, sir, and find what's gone wrong."

The lord's eyebrows lift and he smiles, which brings a sharpness to his cheeks and reminds Mairwen of someone, though she cannot think who.

"I'm not afraid," she says. Then puts fists upon her knees. "No, I am, but not more afraid than I am courageous enough to do it. And willing."

Vaughn reaches for the nearest pile of books without looking away from Mairwen and flips open the top book to reveal a hollow cutout. Nestled inside is a small curved pipe. The lord lifts it out and taps the mouthpiece to his lower lip, but doesn't move to fill or light it. "Being a witch does not mean you would be welcomed instead of torn to pieces within the first hour."

Mairwen says, "My father was Carey Morgan, the saint seventeen years ago. That will protect me."

His mouth opens and the tapping pipe stills. "From the devil?"

"I am not in danger of losing my heart like the first Grace," she lies.

"My God, you are something," Vaughn says eagerly.

Mairwen lifts her chin, feeling similarly eager. "I am the daughter of a saint and the Grace witch. Who better to discover what's gone wrong than me? What good is it to have been born as I am if not for this?"

"No," Vaughn says.

"Sir!" Mairwen leaps to her feet.

"You would risk breaking the bargain further, or entirely? Then what? Rhos Priddy's baby dies, and maybe Rhos, too— afterward famine and plague for all?"

"But . . ." She trails off, heart pounding, because if she can do nothing, then it will all fall upon the saint's shoulders.

"Wait with the town." Vaughn slowly stands. He uses his pipe to touch her chest, just over her heart. "Return to your mother, Mairwen Grace, and tell her, and all of Three Graces, we must wait for morning before acting. If something is wrong with the bargain, surely there will be blood on the branches at dawn and we will have a Slaughter Moon early. Please, Mairwen."

She wants to say no, to swear instead that she'll go into the forest tonight, because she needs to do it and always has needed to. Because an early Slaughter Moon means Rhun will run now instead of years from now, and she wasted all this time playing and stalling.

But in this dark room, with the lord's eyes so near to her own, and smelling tobacco smoke tinged with something bitter, she can't. Her tongue freezes, and her fingers hide themselves in the folds of her skirt, because she remembers saying the same to Lord Vaughn, to keep John Upjohn. *Please.* She had a hold on him then, and now in return, he holds her, too.

ARTHUR'S VERSION OF TRYING HARDER IS TO LEAN against the outer wall of the church, where it faces the town square, and carefully keep from glaring.

The square of Three Graces was built nearly two hundred years ago, before the first saint went into the forest: Instead of a central well, a stone fire pit of gray and white bricks spirals like a summer storm in a circle twenty paces across. The rest of the open space is grassy and strewn with hay, stretching from the stone church at the north to the Royal Barrel in the south, with the oldest pale stone houses butting their front doors right up to the edge. Those doors are painted bright colors, no two the same, and the window shutters to match. Wooden charms and horsehair blessings hang upon lintels welcoming saints to the square, and the bonfire circle is often chalked with similar charms and prayers. Arthur stares at one, a spiky white triangle crossed with the word "hail." It's Mairwen's writing.

His eyes drift up and up the line of their mountain, to the winking red windows of Sy Vaughn's manor. What is she doing up there? Did she go to fetch the lord? Surely he's not home.

Rhun laughs a few paces away, clapping Darro Parry's shoulder. The old man nods, frown fading.

When Arthur and Rhun arrived an hour ago, only a few folks wandered in the square, caught by furtive glances and the tension of the wind on their way home from the fields, or before ducking into the Royal Barrel for a pint. There were other patches of blight discovered, and a rumor about Rhos Priddy and her early baby. Arthur scowled and said, "At least we know how to fix it," but Rhun had yet to acknowledge anything was broken. He moved among the growing crowd, assuring and telling jokes, being himself, and in his wake the tension eased like a loosening braid.

At least half the town is crushed into the square by the time the sun is set. Arthur has kept his eyes on the brightening moon, nearly full. It appeared before dusk, hazy and pale against the sheer blue evening; it now glows with promise. Two nights to come is the fullest moon. Will it be a Slaughter Moon?

That is the question everyone asks with covert glances and fidgeting hands.

As he watches the people, Arthur slowly realizes what is putting him on edge—at least, more on edge than is usual.

Men have clustered around men and women around women.

And here Arthur leans alone.

In Three Graces everyone sows the fields, everyone

harvests, but beyond that, most work is divided into men's work and women's. Men hunt. Women sew. Men prepare meat and repair thatching. Women care for homes, gardens, and families. Men make what needs to be made, from beer and barrels to wheels and shoes. There are exceptions: Braith Bowen learned his smithing from his mother and grandmother, and Brian Dee and Ifan Ellsworth compete for the best herb garden. In the evenings there are usually more men gossiping in the pub and more women and girls laughing and sharing tips around private cottage fires. Nobody knows as well as Arthur that there are things for men and things for women. But it's not usually so obvious as it is tonight. When the town gathers here for marriages or memorials, for celebrating the end of harvest or first planting, when Three Graces comes together for joy, all mingle. Men and women, boys and girls, woven together as they eat and tease one another, as they cheer on the celebration or flirt.

Arthur feels a sneer curl his mouth and doesn't put it away. It may well be that men and boys should be drawn naturally to some things and women to others, but what is not natural is the way this fear tonight, the way this tension of wondering if someone will die, if someone will run early into the Devil's Forest, puts everyone into a very strict location that is either with men, or with women. Nothing in between.

On a night like this, a person can only be one thing or the other, no matter how it compromises the truth to choose a side.

He should join the men. But he still remembers the laughter ten years ago, gentle though it may have been, when he'd volunteered to run. Seven years old and furious and frightened, and the men had laughed.

They didn't laugh at him anymore, but they didn't like him much, either.

"Your face will stick that way," Mairwen says, a perennial comment.

Startled, Arthur clenches his jaw, then smoothly turns to her. He won't give her the satisfaction of having surprised him. "What does Vaughn say?"

She lifts her chin and, instead of answering him alone, marches into the center of the square. Lifting her hands, she calls out, "Everyone!"

"Mair," Rhun says, waving in relief. Everyone looks to her, making space where she stands so more can see, as there is nothing for her to stand on.

"Vaughn says we wait for the morning," Mairwen yells. "Either all this illness will pass as always, or blood will appear on the Bone Tree, and we will have our Slaughter Moon in two nights."

She makes to leave, having said what she came to say, and Arthur smiles tightly at her naïveté when Rhun catches her elbow and murmurs something clearly remonstrative. Mair's lips curdle into a frown and she shrugs.

"I don't know," she says belligerently. But she looks around.

You're supposed to be the Grace witch, Arthur thinks,

shaking his head. He laughs a little to himself, meanly, and joins them.

"What?" she asks.

Arthur turns his back to the crowd so none see him suggest, "Tell the story, Mair."

It's how the Slaughter Moon rituals begin, always. The Grace witch recounts the tale. It should calm the crowd to give them familiarity to cling to. *Tradition.*

Mair's eyes widen in acceptance and she calls out, "All three sisters were named Grace!"

Rhun appears with a bench, Haf Lewis carrying the other end of it. The two lift her up. She steadies herself with a hand on Rhun's shoulder, though it should be Arthur's—he's the taller boy.

Mairwen says again, "All three sisters were named Grace.

"One after the other," she tells the town, "the daughters were born to a desperate mother, and named Grace by their terrible father, only to be swaddled out of the cottage under the pretense of sudden death. They were smuggled thirty miles away to be raised by their widowed aunt and never seen by their father. For seventeen years the three girls lived with their aunt in peace: The eldest Grace was tall and lovely, preferring her garden to the world; the middle Grace was strong and enjoyed running and climbing most of all; the youngest Grace was never satisfied, for she had a curious nature. When she was fifteen, the youngest wandered far from home, searching for peace. But it was this valley she discovered instead. Secure on all sides by grand mountains, home to wild ponies and several happy goats, with a small creek flowing through and a deep forest, the youngest Grace was amazed no people lived there yet. She felt as though her heart belonged in the dark forest and that inside it she would discover great secrets and the answers her heart desired. But in her travels she'd grown wise enough to know she needed her family to keep her grounded. And so the youngest Grace returned for her aunt and sisters. She persuaded them with a handful of never-dying flowers from the edge of the forest and a branch that would not break. The three Graces came to the valley and made a home.

"Others soon joined them, as if the sisters' loving presence had opened doors through the mountains, and settlers were beckoned through, from all corners of the world, all kinds and looks of folk who sought safety or peace or merely to satisfy their curiosity. The town grew in size, pressing against the walls of the valley, and especially the dark woods to the north. When her roots had grown deep into the village, the youngest Grace ventured into the forest, drawn by the shifting shadows and a dream she frequently had, wherein she stood in a grove of yellow spring flowers, beside an ancient white tree, and smiled as though she had never been so happy.

"She explored the forest and met the devil who resided there: She saw his form to be beautiful, as mysterious as the night, as elegant as reaching oak trees, and dangerous enough to sink through her heart. The youngest Grace fell in love with him. She brought her sisters to the edge and said, 'Here is an old god of the forest. I love him and I will make him my husband.'

"But her sisters screamed, for they saw a horned devil with black eyes and claws, whose fine legs were covered with rough fur and whose feet were cloven. They saw a monster, not the god their sister loved.

"Her sisters tried to convince her to stay with them, or to flee the valley again, because this devil could not be trusted. But the youngest Grace knew the forest and understood the land, and so, too, did she believe her devil was a piece of the forest, dangerous only as the world is dangerous, monstrous only as is the lion or crow or any human. She said, 'Sisters, I love him, and if you love me, you will trust me. He knows magic, and has taught it to me. I will teach it, in turn, to you. We will make our valley strong and perfect, so that no harm touches any of our neighbors or friends.'

"'Impossible,' her sisters replied. 'There is no magic so strong.'

"And then the devil spoke, in a voice like summer and birdsong, thick around his sharp teeth, 'Oh, but there is. It is the magic of life and death, hearts and heart-roots, stars and decay. We will bind ourselves together, your sister and I, and ever after Three Graces will be our children, and blessed. For all of time your fields will bear fruit, your mountain abound with meat, the rains be gentle, and no plague come upon you.' The devil smiled and continued. 'But when the Slaughter Moon rises, you will send the best of your sons to my forest. Willing he must come, and ready to fight. My demons and spirits will harry and torment him; they will hunt him and try to feast upon his bones. Either this son will fall, never to be seen again in this world or the next, mine for all time, or if he proves himself brave and strong enough to survive until dawn, he shall return to his home and family, to live long with the bounty of his sacrifice.'"

Mairwen stops.

She can't seem to help herself: She glances straight at Rhun Sayer. But Rhun's eyes watch the crowd, earnest and willing them to listen.

It's Arthur who meets her gaze.

Arthur thought he was a little girl when he heard this story first, and with the other little girls played out the tale again and again. He'd liked being the middle sister, the one with the ax. Mairwen, when she played at all, insisted on playing the devil. They'd used the story to scare themselves: Haf as the youngest Grace would lean toward the edge of the forest, so that Mair the devil could pretend to appear out of it. Haf always screamed, and Mair insisted they hold hands, and kiss, and that was the part Haf didn't mind, swooning over herself as if wildly in love with Mair the devil.

He can't hear the story now without remembering the exact moment he'd been forced to realize he wasn't a sister; he wasn't one of the girls. He'd *liked* who he was. He'd fit in and had friends, worn skirts and been happy. Then all of that was taken away.

It makes him feel like a monster, like the devil, to miss being a girl.

The witch tears her gaze off Arthur and finishes. "The sisters hesitated, but the youngest smiled so brightly they finally agreed, for it was a miraculous promise. The youngest Grace and the devil married, striking the bargain together. The youngest Grace went inside the forest and never returned, her heart affixed to the center, bleeding so the Bone Tree bled, binding every generation of folk in Three Graces to note the rising of the Slaughter Moon and send the best of our sons to face the Devil's Forest."

Though the story is fraught and bloody, as it ends, the entire town seems to sigh in relief. This they know. This they understand. The rules and origin.

At least, Arthur thinks as he holds out his hand to help Mairwen down, they believe they understand. Not many in Three Graces have ever had their world shifted under their feet like this. But Arthur has. Twice.

To his surprise, Mair touches his hand briefly to hop down from the bench. Arthur says for her alone, "You won't sleep tonight. Neither will I. I'll be stalking that moon, and the blood on the Bone Tree."

It's an invitation, but Mairwen purses her lips. "I'll be doing everything I can tonight to keep Rhos Priddy and her baby alive, Arthur Couch."

With that, she swirls away and dashes off, leaving Arthur with a feeling of censure, as if she meant to put him in his place.

The problem is Arthur has never *had* a place in Three Graces. Not since he was seven years old.

Just like sickness and blight, like torrential rain and sudden death, Arthur does not belong.

He shudders like a flickering candle flame, wishing he knew where to stand, or how to make himself into an inferno.

THE SECOND NIGHT

For most of his seventeen years, Rhun Sayer has slept soundly, waking with the sun or just before it along with his brother and cousins and parents, joined them all in a raucous breakfast before they parted ways to hunt or plant or harvest, to chop wood or run with the dogs. As the oldest of his brothers and with his closest cousin Brac married now, and Arthur in the barn loft, Rhun sleeps alone in a narrow room just off the kitchen. It's always warm from the rear wall of the hearth, and only a trunk of cast-off clothes and a small bed fits, though he's hammered nails into the wall from which to hang scarves and boots laced together and a small basket for his few prized possessions. But after standing restless in Three Graces last night with the villagers after Mairwen left, wishing he could lean on Arthur, and waiting to hear that Rhos's babe was finally born, a little girl, but weak and refusing to cry . . . after such tidings, Rhun did not sleep well at all.

He wakes before dawn, before his mother or father stirs

up the fire, and can't relax. So he pulls on boots and trousers and jerkin, only half tucks in his shirt, grabs his bow and quiver, and slips quietly out of the house. Instead of darting up the mountain to hunt, he turns on the path toward town. A starry sky bathes Three Graces in calm silver light, and the wind is still.

Rhun doesn't allow himself to glance toward the Devil's Forest. Even in this light, if there's blood on the Bone Tree he'll see it. And if there's blood, there will be a sacrifice. Rhun will run; he'll do it. He's always known his sainthood would come.

But he expected more time.

He walks slowly toward the whitewashed cottages and thatched roofs gray in the predawn, letting his chest tighten as it's wished to ever since he discovered the blighted barley. Something like pain wraps his ribs, and he feels light-headed as he goes quietly past the sleeping bakery and the pub into the center of town. He walks along the spiral of chalked blessings.

Aderyn Grace herself—and more often lately her daughter—does the chalking on Sundays as part of what's become the weekly ritual for town since the last circuit priest abandoned them when they refused to abandon their devil, during Rhun's grandfather's boyhood. Now every Sunday the women bake bread to be shared in the church, and the men bring a special brew of wine from casks hidden from the sun in the dugout of the Royal Barrel. Together they sing old prayer songs while the witches do the chalking, while children play and weave charms from grass and flowers. It's an informal spirituality the townsfolk have built together, managing to perform their own marriages and baptisms and final rites with an eye and prayer toward God, hoping he hasn't renounced them for the pagan practice of the Slaughter Moon.

Rhun never worries, because his grandmother told him God loves and is love, and had been willing to sacrifice a son to the world because of love. Was that not the very same heart of the bargain? She said, *God is with us every time we send a boy into that forest, because we do it for love. And that boy, our saint, becomes a piece of God.*

It makes him smile as he crosses the town center, thinking of her. She died a few years ago, and the funeral had been here, and it had been merry. Gatherings in Three Graces tended toward merry, even wakes and funerals, for nobody is taken before their time. Until now. It is not Rhun's time, and yet . . .

The weight of it hangs on his shoulders.

His sigh puffs in the air, though it shouldn't be cold enough. Rhun turns a slow circle, looking at the buildings, and remembers dancing at his cousin Brac's wedding last spring, everyone laughing and happy. Remembers the last night ten years ago, before his cousin Baeddan went into the forest, and Baeddan was glorious. *It is so good here!*

The pain in Rhun's chest, he tells himself, is love.

He loves Three Graces, the people and the land, and he'll run early to keep them safe.

A few dim stars wink directly above him as those in the east are defeated by the dawn, and Rhun knows he can't put it off: He turns his face toward the Devil's Forest and takes the first step just as a singsong wail slithers out of the Bowen house. Rhun immediately alters course.

The chimney of the smithy smokes thinly, and he hears no rush of bellows or hammering yet. But through the open shutters of the house trails little Genny's cry, and he goes through the rear gate and into the house without knocking. Braith stands over his two-year-old daughter with his mouth open, eyes pinched, and his large sooty hands out like tree branches.

"All right, Braith?" Rhun asks.

"My wife is . . . sick." The mid-aged smith drops his hands to his sides. "Head just aching, she says, and I'd just fired up the . . ."

"Oh no," Rhun says, but puts on a smile as he bends to Genny. The little girl is half out of her smock, with the armhole knotted about her braid. Tears stick to her lashes and pink cheeks, and dark purple jam paints her mouth in wide strokes. "Come on, sunlight," Rhun murmurs. "Let's get ready for the day."

Genny clings with sticky hands to Rhun's trousers.

"You take care of Liza," Rhun says. "I'll keep Genny with me for the morning."

Braith Bowen stares a moment at Rhun and his only daughter, lines cutting at his mouth. He unties his heavy smith's apron and keeps on watching as Rhun calmly plucks

Genny off the dusty floor and puts her on the table, as he washes the child and sings a song about noses and eyes and mouths and keeping them clean for the saints to kiss. He kisses Genny's nose and eyes and mouth after each rhyme, with a delicate smack. Then he tickles her knees and ribs, wiggling the smock into its proper place.

Rhun glances at the tired face of the smith. "We'll be all right, Braith. It'll be good for me, too, to have Genny to look after until . . ."

"Until we know," Braith says.

Rhun nods, eyes darting toward the north window and the lightening sky.

Braith touches his daughter's hair, then Rhun's shoulder, and disappears through the door toward the back bedroom of his cottage.

Rhun picks up his song again, changing it to one of the harvest tunes. He teases the child that he'll slice off her hair with a scythe if it doesn't get combed once a week, *slice* like the barley, *slice* like the wheat, *slice* like the butcher cutting his meat. And Rhun chops his teeth lightly at Genny's chubby fingers. He gets her hair unknotted and braided in a rope, then hefts the babe onto his hip and takes her outside, where the square remains empty, but he can see more smoke lifting out of the chimneys as the folk get up and started for the day. Are others sick? Have the goats dried up or milk gone sour? What new pieces of the bargain have fallen apart today?

The two-year-old kicks, knocking her heels on Rhun's

thigh. "Let's walk out to the pasture, shall we?" he says, snuggling her close. "See the horses?"

"Horses!" she repeats.

As he carries her out of town, he sings again, about walking and trotting and galloping a pony, varying his own gait according to the song, until Genny laughs so bright the pain around Rhun's chest lifts away just enough.

D AWN IS NOT YET MORE THAN A LINE OF SILVER IN the eastern sky when Mairwen arrives again at the pasture hill nearest the Devil's Forest. As expected, she hardly slept the night before, taking turns with Nona Sayer to care for Rhos and the tiny babe. They swaddled the girl and warmed her, massaged her and kept constant eye that she breathed, using what little knowledge Nona remembered from keeping puppy runts alive as a girl. Water boiled over the fire all night while Aderyn worked with Rhos to get her milk flowing, though by the time Rhos finally wept herself to sleep there'd been no success. Finally, Aderyn sent Mair up to her loft, but she'd only dozed, too focused on the tiny gasping breath of the baby to sleep, wishing she'd defied Lord Vaughn and her mother to go into the forest. Nona Sayer confided that without the bargain, Rhos's baby would certainly die.

Finally Mairwen got up, got dressed, and creaked down the ladder to the kitchen. She stirred up the fire so it would warm the room before the other women woke, then took a boiled egg from the basket, and her mother's old leather coat from the peg beside the door.

She crunches through the dying grass to the horse pasture, peeling her egg as she goes and scattering the shell behind, whispering tiny blessings to the grass. Stars sparkle crisply in the chilled air, and no clouds mar the diamond sky. To her right, the far horizon bends silver where in less than an hour the sun will rise. By the time she reaches the stone wall around the pasture, she's finished her egg, and pauses to swipe a handful of wild dill to chew.

The horses huddle in the valley, opposite the forest slope. Two mares pop their long faces up to snicker at Mairwen. She shushes them, searching for the gray who was sick yesterday; he kneels alone, head low.

As she reaches the crest of the hill to gaze down at the woods, it surprises her to realize she's not the earliest riser. Someone stands below her, at the very edge of the Devil's Forest, near the ugly tree the children call the Witch's Hand. Its lightning-scarred branches crawl up against the midnight green of the forest itself, streaked with white ash and decorated with a number of red blessings tied there by brave—or foolish—children. They dare each other to do it: to ready a charm against the devil and walk up to the wrecked tree and stand there long enough to tie up their blessing. No matter what they spy creeping in the deep shadows of the forest, no matter what shrieks they hear or the chill of demon breath trickling down their spines.

They'd all been eight when Dar Priddy challenged Rhun

to hang a blessing, and Mair heard from Haf that the boys were sending someone out. Haf had tittered how brave it was to make such a gift, and the Parry sisters giggled nervously that it was always boys doing it; wouldn't it be grand for one of their own to be so brave? Mairwen, just to be contrary, said it was meaningless courage because nothing came of those blessings, so why not save bravery for an act that mattered? Bryn Parry sniffed and told her sister obviously Mair was just afraid and using her awful logic to make her fear sound sensible.

Of course, Mairwen was not afraid of the forest, and so it was easy to walk up to the Witch's Hand at the same time as Rhun Sayer and convince him there was no good cause to leave a blessing.

When she came up behind him that dawn, Rhun had been trembling and tense. At her footsteps he whirled around, ax in one hand and limp red ribbon in the other. "Mairwen Grace!" he squeaked, backing up to knock into the trunk of the tree. Its branches rattled overhead, and Mair pressed her tongue to the roof of her mouth, looking wide-eyed at Rhun, who was no taller than her then, but only a boy with big hair and a crooked nose too large for his face. She put her fists on her hips and said, "Better to give that blessing to me than to a cursed tree like this, Rhun Sayer!"

His mouth fell open and he laughed.

Mairwen laughed, too.

She'd never paid him much attention before, though she

supposed she'd known him all her life. The cadence of his laughter had warmed her from the inside out.

But the noise of it carried well into the Devil's Forest, and a laugh echoed back at them, high and wicked enough to prick.

They leaped together, grasping hands, and ran up the long hill to the grazing horses, where their peers waited, jeering and wide-eyed, but shaking too, for they'd heard Rhun's laugh and the mirror of it from the forest.

The girls held out their arms to welcome Mairwen back, but skinny Arthur Couch had insisted, "It doesn't count if you don't tie the blessing on," holding his hand out for the ribbon. "I'll do it. Give it to me."

But Rhun tied his ribbon into the thicket of Mairwen's hair instead.

Now the young man standing before the Witch's Hand takes a low-hanging blessing in his fingers, gently tugging. But he doesn't untie it, only strokes it, and then lets his hand drop.

Arthur.

Mair feels a rush, both glad and annoyed to see him. It's a common blend of reactions to Arthur Couch. He's brash and bold, always pushing at her the way she pushes at the forest. Like a promise, and one she wants to keep. But because of Rhun, Mair refuses to love him.

She walks down the hill slowly but not too quietly. As if he knows it will be her, Arthur doesn't turn until she's just beside his shoulder. They look into the forest, caught in darkness before the sun rises. The shadows wait, still and black. A cold wind gusts out, slinking through the trees without touching them, without moving branches or leaves. Only the shadows shiver, rippling and expanding, reaching.

Glints of light draw Mairwen's eyes to the forest floor, to the shuffle of fallen leaves. Something moves beyond the thick black trunks, a weight of darkness. She steps toward it, fully into the shadow of the forest.

Arthur grabs her elbow. "What's wrong with you?" he asks.

A breeze shakes the naked branches nearest them. *We are so hungry*, the breath of the forest whispers.

Arthur makes a noise like a groan trapped in his chest and drags Mairwen several paces back. "Would you make it worse?" he snaps. "By going inside after some flitting shadow?"

Mair's chest aches with cold. She tries to fire herself up by saying, "Just because you're afraid to step inside, not all of us are."

His nostrils flare. "I am not afraid of the forest, but for my friend who'll be sent into it."

"Rhun won't die," she says, heart aching. Then she thinks of the saints who survive and leave, never returning to the valley because of all the horrible memories. So it's said. And John Upjohn, the only to remain, who is frail and haunted. Mairwen can't imagine Rhun so broken he begs the Grace witches to let him sleep at their hearth, shaking from nightmares. She has to imagine he's stronger, better—the best.

He can survive and thrive. She has to believe it, even knowing every mother and lover and friend must think the same of their saint. What else can she do? What else will she be *allowed* to do?

"I would run for him," Arthur insists.

"For yourself," she whispers back.

"For all of us."

Mairwen shakes her head, knowing the lie. Arthur doesn't care about saving the people of Three Graces, only proving to them that he can. Be the saint to erase the little girl who dogs him in his own memory worse than in the memory of the town.

"Don't try to be what you're not, Arthur," she says, knowing he'll take it badly.

Arthur digs his hands into his choppy pale hair, pulling hard. His elbows jut out at the lightening sky. But he says nothing. Mair clenches her teeth and turns away from him. She doesn't understand Arthur's anger, except that it always makes her angry too. Rhun says the two of them should be better friends. *You're both so pointy and strange and beautiful, my favorite people in the world.* But she won't forgive Arthur.

"Mairwen," he hisses, and she hears him unsheathe one of his knives.

Turning, she follows Arthur's gaze into the forest.

A deer picks its careful way over deadfall, sides heaving. Tiny antlers fork off its skull, catching the first hints of dawn light.

Blood drips from its mouth, from unnaturally sharp teeth

cutting out at terrible angles through its face. Vines wrap its delicate legs, and when it takes one more careful step, Mair can see talons—not tiny hooves.

It raises its head and looks straight at her with eyes the purple of crystal.

She steps forward, awed and excited.

The creature bellows, a low bleat of fury and pain, and charges.

Arthur leaps between it and Mairwen with no hesitation, knife out. He dodges its teeth and jams his long knife straight into its neck, hilt deep. The creature screams and bucks, clawing at Arthur as he twists. He hits the grass and rolls, coming up with a kick to its rear legs.

Mairwen has nothing but her body. She punches at it, connecting with the downy cheek, and when it whips its head furiously, nearly catching her with an antler, she scurries back, tripping up the hill. Arthur cuts again and again at its flank with his second knife.

The creature stumbles and falls onto its knees, howling. Arthur grabs his first knife and saws it free. There's sudden silence. It's dead.

Trembling, Mair starts forward. She grasps at Arthur's arm to help him to his feet. Together they stare down at the creature. Its antlers look more like winter branches, not bone, and its claws are black. Tiny purple violas bloom from its wounds and vines twist around its legs and torso—vines bursting from its own flesh, like ribs come to life to choke it.

Arthur wipes blood from his forehead. He's hurt, but not

badly. A shallow cut at his hairline, and Mairwen finds a slash in his jerkin that didn't reach flesh. His right forearm is bright red with blood. Purple blood from the deer splatters across his belly and neck and the right side of his face.

"We have to get rid of this," Arthur says.

"What, why?" Mair would prefer to study the body, to take its wooden antlers and investigate what its bones are made of. Nothing has come out of the forest before, that she knows. The birds never fly free, only scream in their tiny human voices. The scaly mice never scurry even an inch past the border, and no snakes emerge to find sun.

Arthur whispers the worst curse he can think of and shakes his head. "There was talk last night that John Upjohn did something wrong, that if the bargain is broken, it's because of him."

"He is a saint!"

"If people see this monster, they'll be even more afraid."

Mairwen looks at Arthur's burning pale eyes. "This isn't John's fault."

"But something is very wrong. This is unnatural, even for the Devil's Forest."

"Poor thing," she says, eyes dropping back to the malformed body of flesh and vines. Arthur is right: The bargain is broken, or so weakened it cannot even bind the monsters inside. "Let's roll it back across the threshold."

Arthur bends and grabs the neck and shoulders, grimacing at the torn mouth. Mair picks up the back end by the ankles, lifting and dragging.

It's not nearly as heavy as it should be. Like its insides have dried out or been eaten away.

They manage to heave it to the edge of the forest, where the rising sun still can't penetrate. On count of three they roll it fully into the shadows, then stand there panting, staring at its bulk, just hidden in the thick, rotting deadfall, less than a foot from the light.

A shuffle of tall pasture grass behind them warns them somebody's coming. Mair darts up the hill in time to see Rhun easily hop over the stone wall even with what appears to be little Genny Bowen in his arms. All Mair's urgency falls away at the sight of him. Rhun Sayer with a baby girl. She thinks of her father, Carey Morgan, the saint who went into the forest not knowing he had a daughter on the way. Rhun would be a wonderful father.

Mair makes some noise of sorrow as Arthur joins her. "*Damn*," he whispers, sad and furious and thinking the same thoughts as Mairwen.

But Rhun smiles at them, a boyish, wide smile, and lifts Genny's chubby hand to wave.

"Go to the creek and wash off your face," Mairwen says. "He, at least, should know."

She hesitates, then nods and trudges up toward Rhun, who says, "Morning." As if compelled by unseen forces, he steps close. Even with Genny between them, he kisses her.

It's such a welcome thing to Mairwen, who feels her heart quiet, her bones stop their anxious vibrations, as always when Rhun kisses her. She becomes rooted to the spot, like a trembling willow tree. Genny puts a warm hand on Mairwen's cheek.

"Kissing where the devil can see?" Arthur calls with poison in his tone.

They part, though Rhun remains intimately near. She slides Arthur a glare just as Rhun asks, "What happened?" with horror building in his tone. His brown cheeks are rough with a spotty young beard, his lips tight with strain.

"Hello, Genny," Mairwen says calmly, taking the baby.

"Arthur?" Rhun eyes the blood on Arthur's face.

"Mama is sick," the little girl tells Mairwen.

"Then it's good," Arthur says, pointing his hand north, "there's blood on the Bone Tree."

They all look, and there, rising from the deepest center of the forest, the Bone Tree spreads its barren branches and a scatter of red buds catch the sunrise like a scream.

"So," Rhun says, voice thick, and he can say no more.

Dread hardens inside Mairwen, like she swallowed old yellow bones.

It's Arthur who puts his hand flat and solidly on Rhun's shoulder, scowling at the bloody flowers. "Tomorrow night, then," he says.

B Y THE TIME THE FIRST OF THE TOWN ARRIVES, ARTHUR and Rhun have been to the creek and back, the former to wash and relate the brief morning's adventure to the latter. Mairwen holds Genny, both of them all awkward elbows, and she sings softly to the little girl. It's a song about the Bone Tree, about three little squirrels who try to make a nest in its branches and one by one grow wings, antlers, and fangs. Mairwen can't recall where she learned it—from her grandmother maybe—or if she made it up on her own during long hours cleaning bones to carve for combs and needles.

Fortunately, Genny seems to like it, and as the townsfolk gather, Mairwen sings it again, louder. They stare at her, this strange saint's daughter, including the Pugh sisters, the shepherds and bakers, the families who ask her blessing and those who think it strange she dances at the edges of shadows and boils bones despite her holy father. There's Gethin Couch, Arthur's father—and the town leatherworker—standing with some brewers and watching his son from the same distance as always. Lace Upjohn, who sent her son in last time. She must come closest to understanding how Mairwen feels. John himself isn't here. Devyn Argall arrives carrying a stool for Cat Dee, the oldest woman in town, to rest upon. Mair sees her friend Haf Lewis, a pretty girl with a rosy smile, tan cheeks, and sleek black braids, who does not think Mairwen is strange, only Mairwen.

Her voice fades, and Genny wiggles to be let down. Mairwen bends to set her on her stockinged feet, and the girl stumbles and rushes to her father, who's come with her mother cradled in his arms in order that both might see the scarlet leaves crowning the Bone Tree and know soon Liza Bowen will heal, because blood leaves are proof that the bargain can be re-formed with a new saint's run. Mairwen wishes she believed it. Something is wrong, so maybe everything is wrong. She looks for her mother, and finds the witch standing opposite in the crowd. Aderyn's mouth softens when she sees her daughter, and she beckons.

It's time for the first ritual to begin, and together the two witches go into the herd of horses and choose a healthy one. He's a dark roan, still young and strong, but with a son of his own to carry his qualities on so they won't lose the power from the herd. Aderyn turns him over to the rest of the women, who brush him to a shine and braid his mane and tail with red ribbons, put a wreath of thistle and holly around the beast's neck. Then the men anoint the horse's brow with a blessed salve, and each boy who might run approaches. One by one they grip the wreath, hard enough the pricking holly and rough thistle draw blood, and whisper their name into the horse's ear.

Mairwen gnashes her teeth. Her mother winds their hands together and murmurs, "You have a story for me, little bird. There's blood on your sleeve and a wail in your eyes."

"Not for here," she replies, leaning her arm into her mother's. *The devil is an old god of the forest,* her mother would whisper when she told the story only to Mairwen. That was the first line of the Grace witches' private version. *He was bold and powerful, beautiful and dangerous, but he loved the first Grace witch, and it was from that love the bargain blossomed. This valley is made on love, little bird. Find love. Seek it, always. That is where our power resides.*

"Morning, Mair," Haf whispers, coming up behind. Mair squeezes her mother's hand, then lets go and turns to her friend.

Haf's height barely surpasses Mairwen's shoulder, but the braided crown of her hair gives her a few more inches. Haf is nearly a year older than Mairwen, and engaged to Ifan Pugh, but most pin her the more youthful of the two girls because of her easy smile and tendency to forget what she's doing. But she never forgets things she's said or promised. She loves Mairwen for being brave, and because Haf understands that Mair's distraction and hunger for other things have nothing to do with any insufficiency of Haf's. That simple self-assurance made Mair fall in love with her right back. It was Mair who brokered the engagement with Ifan Pugh, eight years their elder, because he'd been too nervous to approach Haf. That alone turned Mair in his favor, for who but the truly besotted would be more afraid of Haf than of her?

Mairwen puts her arm around her friend's waist, weaving them even closer.

"Will it be Rhun?" Haf asks very quietly. Mair looks toward the boys lined up to whisper their names to the horse. There he is with Arthur, leaning against his shoulder like a comrade, like a boy with no care in the world despite the early Moon, despite the monster this morning, while Arthur seethes silently, jaw working. Beside him are Per Argall and the Parry cousins, and Bevan Heir: all boys between fifteen and twenty, offering themselves up to the town. But everyone knows who will be sent into the forest.

"He's the best," Mair whispers. Without even a goodbye word, she whirls away from Haf and strides south toward home.

She kicks at tall grass as she goes, taking satisfaction from the tiny golden seeds that scatter explosively. There must be a reason this happened, there must be a cause, and surely—surely—that cause is not John Upjohn. If something went wrong with his run, why did the bargain last these three years at all, and not simply collapse upon itself immediately after?

Mair grits her teeth and lines up her questions for Aderyn Grace.

Do you know what's wrong? Mustn't you, because you're the Grace witch?

Why can't I go inside, really? What is the magic in my heart or in my bones? I'm half saint!

Why did a monster try to escape?

How can I save Rhun Sayer?

Hardly noticing as she crosses the stone wall, barely checking her speed as she careens down the hill toward the Grace house, Mairwen seethes and sighs through her teeth, hating this uncertainty. Even Arthur knows what his role is today: apply to be the saint, with all the other potential runners. Haf knows, and all the villagers know: Ready the valley for a bonfire celebration tonight, with a feast and dancing and the ritual throwing of charms into the fire. Women and girls will bake and sweep. Men and young boys move tables and benches, spit a pig, carry heavy casks of beer.

Only Mairwen doesn't know. She's not the Grace witch yet, but more than just a girl.

The forest calls her. The Bone Tree calls her.

Why isn't she allowed to answer? Why isn't she allowed to *run*?

I would run for him, Arthur had said. Well, so would Mairwen. And she'd be sneakier and determined.

How could it possibly matter to the magic to sacrifice a boy instead of a girl?

But maybe the devil cares.

Mairwen slams through the short wooden gate into her mother's yard, and stops when she hears a startled grunt to her left.

It's John Upjohn, crouched inside their fence, half hidden beside the gooseberry bushes. He's twenty-one and lean, with watery green eyes and thin blond hair he keeps braided in a tail. The impression of being no more than a ghost is so familiar to Mair it's hard for her to believe the people who remember him lively and bold, before his run.

His left arm is tucked into a pocket specially sewn to the side of his coat to easily hold the stump of his wrist.

"Mairwen," he says, attempting normalcy.

"Oh, John!" She flings herself down beside him, but not touching him—she always waits for him to make contact. "Are you well? You weren't at the pasture with your mother."

John tilts his head, which is the nearest he comes to expressing unease. "Is there blood on the Bone Tree?"

"Yes." Mair does her best to keep her voice even, not let him hear her fury and confusion.

His wince is mighty, but lacking surprise.

"Will you tell me, finally, what happened to you in the forest?" she asks.

"I did not do this, Mairwen Grace," he answers with more ferocity than she's ever heard.

"Nor did I say you did," she snaps back, leaping to her feet. "This is new, John, an early Slaughter Moon for the first time in two hundred years. You can't be upset we want to know why, and you're the last person to be in the forest!"

The saint shuts his eyes and drags his hand down his face. It falls off his chin, turns to a fist, and slams into the grass beside his hip. "I'm sorry," he murmurs.

Carefully, Mairwen kneels. She breaks her own rule and touches his knee. "I've been a safe place for you for years, me and my mother. I don't mean for that to end today. I'm the one who's sorry."

They pose in silence for a few breaths, both inwardly focused. She thinks of the times he's brought his nightmares to her door, of holding tightly to his shoulders as he shakes. "Can you tell me anything, John?" Mair finally asks, soft as she can. "Did you see the devil? What is he like? How did you lose your hand? What is inside that forest? Is it beautiful?"

"Beautiful!" He frowns. "No."

It's a no that reverberates through all her questions. Mair wants to argue, but it's John Upjohn, the last saint, and she won't. Instead she turns to lean against the fence, where gooseberry brambles tangle in her hair.

"So much of it I only remember in my nightmares," he confesses.

Without looking at him, she asks, "Why have you stayed, if it's so hard? Not for me, surely."

"Thinking of leaving is even worse. I don't know how the other surviving saints left, even with the lord's help and money. A part of me never left that forest, not just my . . . not just . . . but at least here I'm . . . close to it. I have to stay close."

"Oh, John," she whispers, putting her shoulder against his.

"I shouldn't hide today. That will make things worse."

"You be yourself. You've done nothing wrong. I won't let anybody hurt you."

"I believe you," he whispers.

"I want to go into the forest," she whispers back. "To find out what changed. John, I feel like this is . . . an opportunity. An opening in the world that only I might fit through."

"No." John Upjohn pushes up onto one knee and grasps her shoulder. "Mairwen Grace," he says firmly, making her name an invocation. "Do not go inside. For me. You asked me to stay here three years ago, and I'm asking you to do the same now." Sweat beads at his hairline, though the morning is cold.

"I can handle it, John," she says resentfully.

His fingers tighten on her shoulder. "But you shouldn't have to. Nobody should have to."

"Rhun will have to. Why should he handle it alone?"

John pauses, and his eyes lower. Mair struggles to regulate her breathing, so she seems less upset, less desperate. "I'm sorry, Mairwen."

Frustration tightens her muscles and Mair has to dig her fingers into the grass, ripping fistfuls up by the roots.

ADERYN COMES ONCE THE MORNING RITUAL IS DONE, pauses at the sight of her daughter and the last saint leaning together in the yard. Mairwen leaps up and drags Aderyn inside, to the cool shade of their kitchen. "Mother, a deer charged out of the forest this morning, monstrous and misshapen. Arthur killed it and we rolled it back into the forest."

Lines pinch between Aderyn's dark brows. "That has not happened before."

"Something is *wrong*."

"There is nothing to do but let the Slaughter Moon run its course."

"Nothing! But we're witches."

"And we guard the bargain."

"But shouldn't we investigate? What if the devil is . . . is hurt? Or what if the first Grace's heart cannot bear the weight of the bargain any longer? Their love lasted two hundred years, which is a very long time."

"Not ever after," Aderyn said with a dry smile. "The magic promises the bargain will last so long as we send our saint to run."

"Every seven years," Mairwen cries, then quickly lowers her voice, glancing to the kitchen window. "It's only been three since John escaped."

Aderyn holds her daughter's shoulders, studying Mairwen for a long moment, until Mairwen licks her lips and her fingers twist into her skirt. Aderyn says, "But John is not the first saint to run back out of the forest, and this is new."

"So it must be something else. Something has changed! Don't we need to know what? Why can't I go inside? I'm strong. I'm fast. I—I'm not as strong and fast as Rhun, but I'm cunning." Mair knows she's pleading with her mother. Aderyn draws her toward the hearth, where they kneel together on the wide, dark stone.

"You cannot go inside, little bird. Of all people. Not because you're a girl, but because of the blood in your veins. I know you long for the forest. I know it calls you. But answering is not worth the peril. Your heart would be so much at risk."

Mairwen sinks, putting her cheek to her mother's thigh. She closes her eyes and listens—listens deeply—to the pitter-patter of her heart, quick and loud. Aderyn strokes the brambling curls as best one can. "Isn't it worth the risk?" Mairwen whispers.

"You're a Grace witch, not a saint. I've told you, we go inside and we do not return. Our hearts are tied to that Bone Tree, just as the heart of the youngest Grace sister was. Wait until you have lived a full life."

"Rhun hasn't."

"That is part of the sacrifice."

Making a fist in her mother's skirt, Mairwen says, "It is hard enough to think of Rhun dying if it gives us the seven years we're owed. But if it is only three years again? Or less? We cannot be sure his run will be enough, if we don't know what changed."

Her mother continues to pet Mair's head. "Have faith, and love, little bird. In the bargain, in our traditions. One cycle out of pace with the rest does not mean it all is worthless. You *are* strong, Mairwen, and what you do means something to this town. Show them how to be, how you can lead them after me. Not only for Three Graces, but for Rhun Sayer. Show him you will be strong when he runs."

"I love him. Will that be enough to save him?" Mair clutches her mother's knees, for how can she say such a thing when her mother lost her lover to the forest seventeen years ago?

But Aderyn teases at Mair's curls and says, "That boy loves widely and well. If love can protect anybody, it will protect Rhun Sayer."

"Too widely?" Mairwen unbends, panicked. "Too well?"

"Little bird, I'm not sure there is any such thing."

HAF LEWIS AND HER SISTER BREE ARRIVE TO BAKE FOR the bonfire that night, sending Aderyn on her way to check in with Rhos and the baby, back at the Priddy house.

Mair is glad to take her frustration out on dough, and her bread comes out tough.

Haf and her fifteen-year-old sister keep up a dialogue between them, enough the kitchen doesn't overwhelm with tension; they tease each other and compete to make the finest pinched pastries. Their fingers move fast, and their smiles match. The girls look everything of sisters, smooth black hair and round faces, bright eyes, though Bree's are a surprising green and her skin a rosy tan, evidence of three generations the Lewises have lived and married in Three Graces.

When Bree's best friend, Emma Parry, rushes in to drop off a bowl of sweet meat and grab more elderflower honey for the Pugh sisters, she knocks into Mair hard enough Mair retaliates by throwing a handful of flour and snaps, "Watch yourself!"

The powder scatters in Emma's blond hair, and she purses her lips, putting fists on her slight hips. "You should find a chance to go by the square, Mairwen," Emma says with false kindness. "The boys are building their bonfire, and I think Arthur Couch might be having a better time of it than Rhun Sayer."

"Oh," Bree says, "you should bless them, Mair, you should."

"She's probably *blessed* Rhun Sayer enough," Emma adds with a giggle.

Bree gasps, but Mairwen ignores it, striding to the pot on the fire to slop her spoon through the reducing gooseberry sauce. Emma says, "I mean . . ."

"I know what you mean," Mair says coldly. Truthfully, she likes being accused of such things. It's good for Rhun's reputation.

The girl dashes out of the cottage and Haf says, "She's only excited."

Mair's hand stills the spoon in the green sauce. A few more minutes will be enough. She needs to finish rolling out the dough. Or she can leave this to burn, to turn to sticky, ruined innards, and go back out to the pasture, be alone where she can't foul the town's customs with her thorns. This is too important, isn't it, to push at until it breaks?

She turns to face Haf and her sister, who stand beside the worn kitchen table with a pile of perfectly shaped pastries ready to be carried to the Priddy ovens. Bree's chin is down, her small fingers pinching dough around a spoonful of the candied venison Emma just left. Bree looks up at Mairwen from beneath her black brows, then glances quickly down again, biting her lip.

Mairwen hefts the pot of gooseberries off the fire and sets it on the hearth to cool. The stone is old and blue-gray, a single heavy boulder carved rectangular like an old pagan standing stone tipped onto its side. Possibly that is exactly its origin. She wipes her hands on her apron. "Do you think all this preparation matters? Shouldn't we be doing something else? Trying to find out what caused the change? What if it's something we all did?"

Haf tilts her head to consider. Not a wisp of her braided crown slips out of place. Afternoon sunlight streams through the western windows, highlighting clusters of drying herbs that dangle from the rafters, dull green and purple and yellow, and the limewashed walls are as bright as ever. It smells of tangy gooseberries and flour, fire and hot stone. Haf finally says, "Don't we have to go on with the bargain no matter what caused this change? I've never been sick in my life, nor lost a little brother or sister as a babe."

Bree's fingers twitch, ruining the arc of her pastry. Her braids are messy, falling to pieces, because for some unknowable younger sister's reason, she won't let Haf do the braiding for her. "Our grandma used to tell us stories about plague when we were bad," she says. "That your—your skin rots off and you get boils that weep blood until you cough up your own insides. She said if we didn't behave we'd be made to leave Three Graces and die of it."

"Oh, Bree," Haf says, exasperated.

Grimacing, Mairwen says, "That's terrible." She can't help imagining it, how horrible the smell would be, and the fear. "But I know why we have the bargain, why we send our saint into the forest. I understand the—the sacrifice part. Or I understand how it's supposed to work. But how can we do everything traditional, everything the same as always, when last time we did it all just like this and the bargain only lasted three years? How can our rituals matter? These pastries and our bonfire celebration matter, or tomorrow's blessing shirt? It seems useless to me if we don't know it will work again."

"What else can we do but try to fix it?" Haf says.

Mairwen scoffs. "We don't know which part is broken!"

But it's Bree who murmurs, "My mom says John's hand is the only different thing."

"That we know of," Mair says darkly, thinking of the monstrous deer. "And by the rules of the bargain, he did nothing wrong by surviving and leaving his hand behind."

"That we know of?" Haf suggests with a wince.

Mair grits her teeth, longing for the cold shade of the forest's edge. "Exactly. I want to know."

"But how could you discover it without risking *everything* breaking?"

"There's no rule keeping anybody from going into the forest any other night of the year. We just don't, because we're afraid of the devil."

Haf's eyes widen. "For good reason."

Bree says, "You can't."

"That's what everybody says," Mairwen cries.

"Maybe," Haf says softly, "try to find something you *can* do. That won't risk the saint, or the bargain."

"Like make pastries and bless the saint shirt. John had all those things."

"And John survived."

"The bargain didn't."

There's nowhere else to take the argument. Everything comes back to the same: Mairwen is not allowed to do anything useful. She'll make her own charms for Rhun, she thinks, to protect him.

When the pastries are all pinched, full of sweet meat and gooseberries, they load them into a basket, layered carefully with linen, and carry it toward town. Windows are flung open in the houses they pass; chatter and laughing spills out into the muddy lanes. Children run freer than usual, unleashed for the afternoon to play devils and saints or mirror the older boys' games of shooting and strength and balance. The tiniest Rees cousins have braided their hair together and gallop past, giggling and shrieking like a six-legged beast. Older boys dash after, arguing who will slay the red dragon of Grace Mount. Mair decides to shuck this dark, dour mood if she's able, as her mother suggested. For the runners.

As they approach the square they sense a shift in the air: still celebratory, but tenser, heavier. Haf says she'll deliver the pastries for baking and join Mair and Bree to watch the boys.

Five paces later Mairwen stops at the corner of the Royal Barrel. The bonfire is finished: dead branches piled against each other, stacked and leaning, twice times her height. Evergreen boughs decorate it like fur, and sprigs of thistle and rosemary and burdock, too. Fennel and leeks surround the base, some dried blooms and some bulbs, for prosperity and luck.

It's magnificent, and will burn for hours.

The runners cluster in the south curve of the square. They've hung the wreath from the stallion upon the bonfire wood. About an arm length wide, it suits as an archery target. All the boys hold their bows and use a communal quiver, though Mairwen recognizes the leather tooling as

Rhun's. Per Argall stands at the chalk line, aiming with very decent form for the youngest of them. Just fifteen last month. It seems half the boys already shot, and though all hit the target, none are too near the center, meaning Rhun has yet to shoot.

Per looses his arrow. It flutters past an evergreen sprig at the edge of the target and disappears into the pile. Beside Mair, Bree claps. As do the rest of the spectators scattered about the square, some chuckling at the bashful way Per flops his hair over his face. He'll never be a saint, Mair thinks.

His older brother shoots next, only marginally better, and then Rhun and Arthur Couch look to each other. Rhun shrugs one shoulder and smiles, stringing his bow in an easy motion. He takes an arrow, rubs the fletching down his cheek as he's wont to do, and notches it, aims, looses it casually, as if merely swiping a drink of beer. His arrow flies true and buries itself three fingers off the center of the wreath.

Mairwen can't help her prideful, tight smile.

Arthur steps up, six previous arrows waiting and only Rhun's to beat.

He takes more time than Rhun for his turn, relaxing into his pose gracefully instead of with Rhun's casual skill. Mairwen notes the rise of his shoulders and slow, slow fall as he sighs into the shoot.

The arrow hits true, a single finger off-center.

A loud cheer swirls around the square, led by Gethin Couch, and even Haf murmurs her amazement from beside

Mairwen. Rhun grins and claps Arthur around the shoulders, saying something merry but too quiet to hear from the edge. Mairwen smiles too, as Bree applauds, joining in with the rest of the boys, and the long arc of spectating men slapping their hands to their thighs. Too bad for Arthur all these tests aren't the real way saints are made. They're only a show, to bring all the candidates together and keep them out of trouble. Tradition.

"It could be him," Haf says, clutching the basket of pastries to her belly. Mairwen darts a sharp look to her friend. It sounds as though Haf means that to comfort Mair.

"Weren't you to take those to the bakery?" Mair asks.

Haf's mouth twitches and her fingers tighten on the basket's handle. "I forgot! Yes, of course I'll go." She laughs at herself, and knocks her shoulder into Mairwen's arm before skipping off. Bree nudges Mair too, and uses her chin to point across the square to Ifan Pugh, whose eyes track Haf's progress.

Mair can hardly take her own gaze off the boys, especially Rhun and Arthur as they organize a race, debating obstacles and directions. Men call suggestions from the sides, for hurdles and traps. Mairwen sweeps out, offering herself and Bree and Haf as race markers, to hold ribbons the boys will have to carry from one to the next as proof they've gone the whole way. It's set, and so they spend the rest of the daylight: playing games to echo the final night of the Slaughter Moon.

. . .

A S THE SUN SETS, ALL RETURN TO THE SQUARE, flushed and dirty. Rhun is hot with laughing and the race, trailing behind everyone as they chatter and argue over who won. Mairwen received a kiss from every boy who ran: gentlemanly hand and cheek kisses from Bevan Heir, the Argall brothers, and the Parry cousins. Arthur kissed her on the mouth, but swiftly and with a tight sneer that mirrored the shape of Mairwen's and left her breathless. Rhun picked her up by the ribs and kissed her long enough to make her smile again. So long it lost him the race.

Falling behind not from nerves or sorrow, but the weight of gladness for all he has, Rhun is the one to see John Upjohn walking a parallel path to town, and he angles his route to meet up with the saint.

John Upjohn is the only person in Three Graces who never smiles at Rhun, though Rhun's been told the saint has a sweet smile, with dimples on either side of his mouth. How Rhun would like to see that smile tonight. "John," he says, almost bashful.

"Rhun Sayer." Deep wrinkles pull at his eyes, as if John were twice his true age, and the corners are reddish, a sign of his poor sleeping. Mairwen has told Rhun that John still has nightmares, still sometimes comes to the Grace house in the middle of the night as if its hearthstone is the only thing that soothes him enough to rest. The saint is wearing the usual costume of a hunter: wool trousers and leather jerkin over a wool shirt, though he's without a hood tonight. His stubbed wrist is tucked into a shallow pocket in his jerkin, and in his only hand is a sprig of dried flowers for the bonfire.

They walk in silence, drawn toward the crowd in the square, to the flicker of torches already lit. Rhun worries his tongue at the back of his teeth, unsure how to make the saint smile. What to say on a night like this, to someone so haunted by it?

Two houses before they reach the square, it's John who stops. "I remember your cousin, ten years ago. I was only eleven, but I remember him, how bright and happy he was the night of his bonfire."

"I remember, too," Rhun says.

"It helped me during mine. To have that memory. I'm sorry you've got me and memories of me in the way."

"No!" Rhun reaches out and grips John's arm, to reassure him. "I'm not sorry."

The saint makes a smile that is more of a wince, no dimples anywhere. "You will be."

A chill grips Rhun's spine, but he shrugs it off as if fear is a choice. "It's what I'm for," he says.

"Is it?" John Upjohn shakes his head and pulls his stump out of its pocket. The sleeve of his shirt is tied off so there are no scars to see. "You can choose," he says finally, echoing Rhun's thoughts.

Rhun lets his hand slide away from the saint's shoulder. "It's worth it."

Expecting John to immediately agree is a mistake Rhun knew he was making even as he made it. When John slowly, reluctantly nods, Rhun apologizes: "I'm sorry. It must be impossible for you, tonight of all nights."

The saint smiles helplessly, and there they are: two long dimples making John's face more handsome for a moment before the smile falls away and John says, "You're facing your best and worst night, and apologizing to me. I'm the one who's sorry, Rhun Sayer. You're too good to survive it."

Unsurprised by the sentiment, only the bluntness of someone saying so aloud, Rhun lets his mouth fall open, and for a moment he's at a loss. His cousin was the best, and didn't live: Rhun never expected to be better than Baeddan. "I don't have to survive it, to fulfill the bargain. I just have to run."

"You should want to survive it, though." The haunted blue of John's eyes catches the last sunlight as he steps nearer to Rhun.

"I—I do," Rhun says, though he rarely has thought of any future past the night of his run. All his future thoughts have been of the four more years he was supposed to have between now and then. The moment the blood appeared on the Bone Tree this morning, Rhun's future vanished. He knows in his heart, in his gut, this is his second-to-last night.

"Good," John says sorrowfully, as if he knows Rhun doesn't mean it but can't bring himself to challenge it.

The saint and almost-saint pause together in the narrow cobbled alley, though Rhun is broader, with more bright tension in the way he stands, and John Upjohn holds himself as still as stone.

"I'll be all right, John," Rhun says, and though he hates lying nearly as much as he hates secrets, he adds, "I promise."

"Just remember," the saint says, moving away from Rhun, glancing back over his shoulder, "you must have something to focus on, besides the devil. Besides the run. Something outside, something . . . good. A person, or hope for yourself. Something to pull you back out."

"What did you hope for?" Rhun calls softly.

John lowers his head and holds out his arm with the missing hand. He doesn't answer.

Before Rhun can press, the saint hurries toward the village square.

THREE YEARS AGO, WHEN ARTHUR WAS NEARLY FIFteen, his best friend, Rhun, stopped them along the narrow deer path they'd been stalking along, and kissed him. The moment before, as he leaned in, Rhun's eyes were bright with happiness, so much so that Arthur started to smile back before he realized what was happening.

Then Rhun's mouth was on his, warm and soft, and Arthur stumbled away, his boots tangling in the spindly autumn grasses so he had to fling his hands back against a tree to catch himself. The bark scraped his palms, burning all the way up his arms to spark like fury in his skull.

Rhun laughed and grasped Arthur's shoulders. "Sorry. I didn't mean to startle you. I just—"

"Don't *touch* me," Arthur cried hoarsely and low.

"What?" Rhun pulled his hands back, shock widening his eyes.

Arthur shoved away from the tree, turning his back to Rhun. "I'm not a girl," he said.

"I know that?" Uncertainty put the question in Rhun's words.

All Arthur could see were crowns of flowers and petals catching fire, hear the laughter of boys and that pitying look in the eyes of men. He was shaking. He made his hands into fists. "Don't do that, ever. I'm not a girl."

Rhun couldn't help it; he reached out again. He was afraid and Arthur could see it in how his brow pulled into a solid black line. "I wanted you to know," awkward, fourteen-year-old Rhun said. "Next time it'll be me, and I wanted you to know."

"Next time?" Arthur's voice was pitched high with hysteria. "There can't be a next time!"

"The Slaughter Moon," Rhun whispered.

Arthur fell silent, though his chest heaved. Two days before that one, John Upjohn had charged out of the forest, so they had seven more years of bounty. He stared at Rhun, horrified still, and his lips burned. He wiped them roughly with the back of his hand, glaring at Rhun the whole time.

Rhun grimaced but didn't look away. "I know you're not a girl, Arthur. I only . . . want to kiss you anyway."

A wind blew golden-brown leaves between them and shook the bare branches overhead. They were still, both shorter than they'd soon be, and slimmer, but Arthur hadn't chopped off his hair in enough months it brushed the sharp cut of his shoulders in smoothing layers. The wind fluttered it against his neck where it tickled and itched.

"You can't," Arthur said, and added with vicious finality, "It's disgusting."

Rhun shook his head sadly, and the shape his mouth and crooked nose and dark eyes and strong jaw made all together was a shape of something Arthur couldn't understand. "There's nothing disgusting in our valley," Rhun said. "There can't be. Everything here is good and right."

"Not me," Arthur sneered, and tore away, stomping, then running, then racing through the cutting forest, up and up away from the valley, up to the mountain peaks, where there was nothing but rough heather and jutting chalk cliffs.

Next time is all Arthur can think of now, three years later, as in the final slash of daylight, Sy Vaughn and Aderyn Grace bring the torches to the pyre.

Together the young lord and the witch cry the names of the prospective runners, and together they light the blaze. Together they spill wine for the saints and for the devil, for God and his angels, for the king and the bishops, and for their grandmothers and grandfathers, until both bottles are splashed entirely onto the evergreen sprigs and thistle. Vaughn is like a holy saint himself, smiling and handsome, while Aderyn is dangerous and strong, her twisting curls tinged nearly red by the fire in her hand. They thrust their torches deep into the pyre. At first only the inside flames: burning hot, a pulsing heart inside the bonfire shell. Arthur knows that pulse too well.

Then evergreen boughs flash aflame, and everyone cheers. The thistles and smallest branches catch, and they cheer again.

As one by one the mothers of the potential runners walk or stride or creep to the fire and toss in their son's charm, the town falls quiet. The mothers stand side by side to watch the charms burn. Except Arthur's mother is gone, left a decade ago, and Nona Sayer can't cast his charm because she cast her own son's. Nobody thought of it, clearly, since nobody thought of Arthur Couch's potentiality really mattering at all. He lets his lips curl, even as Rhun knocks their shoulders together enthusiastically.

Mairwen darts out of the crowd suddenly, wrinkling her nose as if irritated. She makes big eyes at Arthur and shows him the bone charm in her hand. It's a string of teeth, all shapes and sizes, deer and rabbit and sharp mountain cat and small fox and goat and sheep. Someone says her name, and a few others say his, and Mairwen throws the teeth into the pyre with a violent thrust.

Arthur's entire body clenches and he bites his teeth together too hard, pretending to bite her, to kiss her with the same violence. Rhun's fingers dig into his shoulder, grounding him in just exactly the right kind of pain. Rhun knows. Rhun always knows.

Drums come out, and whistles and three fiddles. Women

bring the platters of pastries, to join the roasted pig that smoked and cooked all day long in a pit. There are cakes and pies, so much dripping meat, laughter and music, and the dancing begins when the moon rises.

This moon is nearly full, fat-bottomed and perfect: a spot of silver to compete with their roaring bonfire. That fire spits up red sparks against the black sky, so bright they consume the stars. But the moon beckons everyone to dance.

Arthur eats and drinks, dances with Haf Lewis and her sister, with Hetty Pugh, who stares narrowly and with amusement the entire time. He drinks more, snatching sips from his partners' cups, and an entire flagon from Braith Bowen the smith, and snaps morsels of food from offering fingers, for he *is* one of the prospective runners, even though everyone knows—*knows*, assumes, presumes—the saint will be Rhun. Only that scathing dick Alun Prichard asks Arthur to dance, bowing and calling him *Lyn*. Arthur grabs the front of the young man's shirt and drags them together. He bashes his head into Alun's nose, then thrusts him away.

The gasps of nearby dancers hiss into shrugs and head-shaking when they see it's only Arthur, as usual.

There are Mairwen and Rhun, dancing too closely. They spin and Mairwen clings to Rhun, dread widening her features. She suddenly stops dancing in the middle of the square, causing him to trip gracefully. She shakes her head and Rhun turns her right into Arthur's arms.

He catches her as she leans in. Arthur's short pale hair

spikes around his head, alight as a saint's halo, and his lips spread over his teeth. "Mairwen Grace," he says, unable to help himself, "rather dancing with me than Rhun Sayer."

Mairwen shrugs and spins. She skips and turns, lets her head fall back and her hair shake loose. The world spins, too, the bonfire blazes, the people around them laugh and dance, and Arthur cups her elbows, then her waist as they turn and turn. He pulls her closer, their bodies pressed into one, at the center of all this wild dancing, and the full moon streaks her tangled hair with ghostly light.

"I'm dancing with all the runners," she says.

"It *could* be me chosen," he whispers into her ear, and Mairwen laughs. She laughs so free and loud it draws heads and gazes around them. She puts her hands to Arthur's neck and smiles.

"I would rather it be you," she declares, laughing still. Sparks flash off the fire, making shapes more scattered than constellations, and dangerous as goblins.

Fury burns through Arthur and he jerks her closer, as if to slam his head into hers as he did to Alun Prichard.

"You'll have to cut your hair again," she whispers, "violent boy." She toys at the ragged tips with both hands, and his earlobes, too, causing him to shiver. Her touch leaves cold impressions, driving straight down to his loins. He tears away, shoving through the crowd, away from the fire and pulsing drums.

"I'm sorry," she calls from behind him as he reaches the churchyard and stops against the short stone wall of the little cemetery. He turns to her; she's lit from behind by the fire. Mairwen touches the wall to steady herself, and he realizes she's drunker than him.

"Don't be sorry," Arthur says.

"Arthur," she says, "I've never been so . . . out of sorts."

He doesn't move, a pale spirit against the dark cemetery beyond. Rough-cut stones marked with family names spread in uneven lines between the holy cross monument in the west and in the east the plain pillar memorial carved with the names of all the boys lost to the Devil's Forest in two hundred years. Arthur can't read the names from here, nor even see the shadow of them against the creamy stone, but he knows them, and knows the order. He recites them in his mind, to eradicate thoughts of her hands. The last name is *Baeddan Sayer*, carved ten years ago. How terrible will it feel to see Rhun's name there? To wait at dawn for *him* to never come home?

So lost in the sick thought is Arthur that he doesn't notice Mairwen until she's just beside him. He eyes her as his anger reignites, mingled now not only with desire, but worry and sorrow. A mess of sharp, contradictory emotions. He says, "Can you imagine my name there?"

Mair sits on the wall, clutching the corner of it tight enough to mark her palms. "I refuse to. Bad enough seeing my father's name."

Arthur glances at the memorial pillar, where he knows *Carey Morgan* is carved.

"If it were you," she whispers, and Arthur scoffs but seats himself beside her and hangs his head.

"If it were you," Mairwen begins again, "what would make you feel better tonight?"

He looks back toward the square, firelight awaking in his eyes, reflecting the fire in his heart. "Knowing what I had to fight for."

"You mean the town? All of this reminding you how good it is? The saint's shirt to carry with you as a—as a talisman of Three Graces?"

"No, stupid girl."

Her back straightens and she opens her mouth to snap and leave him, but Arthur says, "I mean *who* I had to fight for. Knowing she'd be there at dawn, waiting."

All Mairwen's breath rushes out.

"I'd survive it. I'm harder and faster than him," Arthur says. "I don't let anything hurt me and have no pity to slow me down. And of course I'm more expendable."

"No one is expendable," Mairwen answers ferociously.

Arthur kisses her. He kisses with his lips and teeth, hard and formidable, hands on her jaw and neck, dragging her closer. And Mairwen kisses him back. She flings her arms around him, shoving as much of herself against him as she can. His teeth drag at her lip. Her nails claw his scalp. These are not fresh or easy kisses.

Suddenly Mairwen pulls away with a cry, violent enough to stumble to the ground, landing on her hip.

She stares up at Arthur, who's on his feet, jaw clenched and a hand hovering near his mouth. Moonlight brightens her eyes, and her teeth glint between open lips. "Oh, no," she says. "Not now, not you, not tonight!"

It cuts hard into him, the abruptness and finality of her rejection. Angst twists in his stomach, leaving rope burns. But she's also right. Tonight is the night before the Slaughter Moon. Rhun's Slaughter Moon. He says, "Rhun told me . . . when he . . . kissed me . . ."

Mairwen scrubs at her mouth.

Arthur wants to drag her hands away, hurt her for it. He has to take deep breaths. He says in as calm a voice as he's able, "He told me he kissed me because he wanted me to know, before *next time*. His time. His moon."

"I know how Rhun feels," she hisses. "About me *and* you."

"Does he know how you feel?"

"I think everybody knows."

"I mean, does he *really* understand?" Arthur grinds his teeth together, hating everything in the entire world. "You love him too, and so you should . . . make sure he knows."

Her eyes sink to Arthur's mouth, and he forces his body still lest it catch fire again. "You should too," she whispers, then stands up and leaves him alone with the dead.

THE BONFIRE BLAZES UNTIL AFTER MIDNIGHT, AND though a handful of older women and their husbands remain to usher the embers and ashes into death, the square quiets. Mairwen strays farther and farther into the fields, tilting and a bit drunk, worried and reckless and cursing herself for kissing Arthur Couch. If love can protect Rhun, if that's all she can do, she must not divide her heart! Finally, she collapses onto the cold grass and stares up at the stars. They blur and blink, and Mair's mouth is still hot, her heart a mess.

She was in love with Arthur Couch for two minutes when they were children, when she found out her friend Lyn was not a girl after all, though she was still unsure how it should matter to her and their friends. Mair stared at Lyn as he became a boy, and she remembers clearly the look on his face when he chose what to do, which part of himself to cling to, which rules he'd allow to define him. But for a moment—a wild, mysterious moment—he'd been both a boy and a girl, and neither, and Mairwen had the eager idea that Lyn-Arthur could stand with her at the edge of the Devil's Forest.

That moment passed, that between space, that shadow where possibilities lived.

Arthur never stepped into it again. He chose the worst parts of boys, thinking they were the strongest when they were only the least *girl*. It made him hurt Rhun, and that Mairwen has no interest in forgiving.

Next time, she thinks as she lays on the cold ground, *next time*, as if Arthur passed along a sickness. This is Rhun's next time. She presses her hips back against the earth, puts her hands to her waist and slides them up along her bodice to her flattened breasts. Her eyes fall closed and she touches her lips.

Later Mairwen wakes up, chilly and light-headed. Glad her mother never bothers to worry when Mair forgets to sleep in her loft, she climbs to her feet, stretches all the way up to the sky, and turns toward the Sayer homestead. *Next time.*

She's thought of something she can do.

There is plenty Mairwen Grace knows about magic (*life and death and blessing between*), and plenty she knows about the bargain (*the devil is an old god of the forest, and a witch's heart is the heart of the spell*), and there is one way she can think to use magic and love to save Rhun Sayer.

Four hours before sunrise, the night is crisp and still, but bright as twilight thanks to the moon and stars casting silver over the rolling valley. Mairwen pauses at the vista before her: the pale stone houses of Three Graces shine like pieces of the moon itself; the spreading gray fields; thin smoke weaves up from chimneys and vanishes in the scatter of stars; their mountains wait dark and calm and strong.

It will never be the same without Rhun.

Rhun Sayer who's kind to everybody, who stops to help carry water or mend a torn doll, who is so good at reading his competition he always knows if he can get away with letting them win. He used to lift Mair up onto his shoulders so she could see over the crowd at the spring games, until she was too old for it to be proper, and he lifted little Bree Lewis instead. Rhun never drinks too much to walk straight and endures his cousins' teasing like an oak in an autumn storm. He forgives Arthur over and over again. Once Mairwen complained to Haf that he's overprotective of her, and Haf replied, *Not of you, of everybody.*

He was born a saint, and nobody in town doubts it.

Rhun himself never has.

He is so perfect, he's going to die.

She walks quickly at first, but shifts faster as her heartbeat picks up and she thinks of her intentions. Rhun can't be alone tonight. He must know how much she needs him, how much they all need him, alive and real, not a name on a cold memorial. Rhun deserves to know he's loved, more than—than Arthur, more than herself.

There are just enough moonbeams under the trees for her well-adjusted eyes to clearly see the way up the path. No light shines from the Sayer house, though a flicker of candle glow presses through the small window of their outbuilding. It's long as a barn, where the Sayers store hunting tools and weapons, and an odd collection of deadfall branches Rhun's grandfather used to make furniture. Mairwen sneaks toward the window and carefully widens the shutter gap to peer inside. Rhun's small brother Patrick sleeps on a pile of deerskins with Marc and Morcant Upjohn, and one other boy she can't recognize for how his features are blocked by sprawling hands. The four boys have feet on stomachs and heads under arms, layered like puppies. It means Rhun will be alone in the room he used to share with Arthur and Brac.

She goes to the main house, surprised to discover the front door open. But two of the Sayer deerhounds spread across the entryway like snoring furry shadows. Mair walks up slowly, and Saint Branwen lifts her bearded face.

"There, Bran," Mairwen says softly, and hears the thump of the dog's hairy tail. The other, Llew, stretches all four of his legs out straight, shivering with the release, but doesn't bother standing. He trusts Branwen, Mair thinks, as she scratches the dog's neck and behind her ears. She then steps carefully over both hounds in one large effort.

The house is dark, even the hearth banked down, and smells of ash and blessing thistle. She pauses to let her eyes adjust again. It won't do to knock into the broad table or stumble over a stool. Nona and Rhun the Elder bed upstairs, for Nona claimed the valley view from the second floor within days of arriving in Three Graces, and wouldn't give it up for convenience nor love.

The walls are hung with wooden saint blessings, gloriously pronged antlers, and a small painting of a grand lady Nona brought with her from the rest of the world. No bundles of drying herbs hang from this ceiling, though several heavy hooks bear pots and wooden spoons. The packed floor is covered with a few furred skins, and the furniture Rhun's grandfather made huddles in odd proportions because he rarely cut or carved his wood into regular forms. One arm of a chair might be longer than the other, but curved so gracefully it would insult the saints to trim it. The stools are smooth to sit on, but not square in shape or even circled.

As a whole, the home always strikes Mairwen as odd and

particular, but comfortable. She can imagine herself living inside it, when she imagines living inside any walls at all.

The door to Rhun's rear room is only a rectangle arch with a heavy wool blanket tied across. Mair skims her fingers down the coarse material, scratching slightly as a warning. She lifts the blanket aside and enters. Here, with only two high, narrow windows in the outer stone wall, she can barely see.

"Mairwen?"

She hears him moving in the darkest corner. Shadows shift, and there he is, standing off his low bed. "Rhun," she answers.

"What are you doing here?"

Mairwen takes the three steps necessary to put her against him. She peers up at his shadow-concealed face. Only the glints of eyes and teeth are visible. In reply, she lets go of her square shawl so it slithers off her shoulders and she unlaces her bodice. She takes a deep breath as her ribs are released from the gentle pressure and shrugs out of it. She unbuttons the waistband, then steps out of her skirt to stand in only her wool shirt and stockings, suddenly running hot with anticipation. Twisting her fingers together, she opens her mouth to speak, too aware of the brush of cloth against her breasts, the sharpening of her skin, the loose bramble of her hair a teasing pressure between her shoulder blades. Her belly quivers and pieces of her she usually ignores knot tight. All she's done is take off her outer layer of clothes.

Rhun does not need to be invited any louder.

He reaches for her, taking her hips in his hands. Mair touches his chest, realizing he's in even less than she: an old, worn pair of braies loose and threadbare and soft. She touches his skin and flattens her hands over his chest, dragging her palms over his dark nipples to his stomach. It's smooth and soft with a layer of bounty and health, rich as the earth, and she digs her fingers to find the hard, flexed muscle beneath.

Rhun shudders and does the same to her hips, and they grip each other too tightly.

"We're not supposed to do this," he says.

"Whatever the best boy does is right and good," she teases, his own frequent words, tilting her head up for a kiss. Their mouths come together lightly, touching quick. Rhun shakes his head, pushing her hips back and holding her an arm's length away. He says nothing.

Mair touches his mouth, then his waist again, and presses the heels of her hands to his hips. Her mouth is dry; she licks her lips, staring through the darkness at the curve toward his belly and the arc of skin vanishing beneath the laces of his braies. "Let me give you this to hold on to, to remember, so you know exactly what you have to come home to."

"Holy mother Mary," he breathes.

Mairwen smiles for how it sounds like her own name, even as she flushes. She knows what to do. Her mother made certain Mair knew her own body as soon as she started to bleed. She slides her hands flat along Rhun's worn waistband, but he grabs her again, pulling her against him, kissing hard. He takes her ribs, slides his hands up her back, down her arms, to her waist and hips and rear, a mess of desperate pulling. Mairwen sighs, lets her head fall back, arching against him. Rhun puts one arm full around her waist. His other hand draws up to her breast and hovers there, either unsure or reverent.

Mairwen is still, cool and calmer than she thinks she should be. "Rhun," she whispers, and he strangles some wordless answer, hand pressing her breast flat. She grabs for his neck, tugging onto her toes, and puts her mouth against his throat, where he tastes like smoke and salt. She will make a charm of these kisses: life, death, and blessing in between.

"Stop, Mair. Wait. Stop," he gasps, resisting her with his hands clenched in fists. "I can't." He pants between his words, but forces them out. "I can't. Mair, we have to—to stop."

She releases him and sits on the straw mattress. After a long moment, she says, "We don't *have* to stop, Rhun."

"We do, because . . . ," he whispers. He's a black pillar in the center of the small room, hands pressed together flatly as if in prayer.

She says, "I do love you. I've never said it to you, have I?"

His back is half turned away, but his shoulders slump and his head tilts to her. All his spiral hair flops down around his face. "I love you too, so much."

"Come here, then. Come here and—and just *do it*."

He crouches, one hand balanced on the packed-earth

floor. "It isn't because of you, because I don't want to—with you."

She slides off the bed to kneel beside him. His eyes are tight shut, his mouth in a line. She says, "Arthur. If it were him here, you'd do it."

Rhun lifts his dark eyes and shrugs helplessly.

"Oh, Rhun."

They bend together in silence for a long while. Frustration makes her feel brittle and sharp. Finally she says, "I'll go."

"No." He catches her hand. "Stay. I want you to stay. Even if he were here I'd . . . Oh God, I'd want you to stay too. Both of you. Maybe there is something wrong with me. Maybe I'm not the best."

The admittance of doubt freezes her heart. She blinks away sudden tears. It's so stupid, so unfair that this has been his burden for so long. "Don't let Arthur Couch make you question yourself, do you hear me? He's an idiot. He has everything, and pushes it away because of fear." She brushes springy hair back from Rhun's face, gathering it in her hands, and together they climb onto the straw mattress. Leaning against the rough wall, Rhun pulls her against him, his arm slung around her. She plays with the tips of his fingers, calloused from a thousand times plucking his bow.

Into the darkness, he says, "After all of this, will you promise me to take care of him?"

Mairwen hisses, clutching his hand. "You'll do it, because you'll live."

"Mair." He leans his head against hers.

"Arthur can take care of himself."

"Promise me."

"You promise me you'll live."

Rhun sighs. His eyes close.

Mairwen strokes a finger down his crooked nose. "Survive, and I'll marry Arthur to trap him here, and you can live with us, because I'm a witch and you're a saint and we can do whatever we want, and then you can spend the rest of your life seducing him. We'll fight all the time, but we'll be happy."

A laugh bubbles up Rhun's throat, popping light and merry. "And we'll never know who fathers your children, tying us all together even more."

"Oh, we'll know," Mairwen sneers. "Yours won't cause me any pain at all, and Arthur will only have daughters with hearts so hot they burn me the entire time they're cooking."

Rhun kisses her, slowly and shallowly, then kisses her nose and eyelids. "You should do that if I don't survive too."

Mairwen feels tears in her eyes again, angry tears for not knowing how to convince him he can't go into that forest expecting to die. He touches his nose to her neck, breathing long and slow and thin down her collarbone. It slides under her shirt and over her breasts and she clears her throat gently. In her normal, though quiet, voice, she says, "I wish I could go in with you."

He only laughs softly and whispers her name.

THE LAST NIGHT

Arthur wakes up with the sun, on his pallet in the loft of the Sayer barn. It's a small half room partitioned by old trunks and pieces of Rhun's grandfather's unfinished furniture. A square window faces northeast, though the tall pine trees on this side of the mountain block all but the most determined dawn rays. Other than weapons, Arthur has very little in the way of personal belongings.

Groggy from staying up most of the night with the other potential runners, he yawns and rubs his eyes. Their mood was too soft for his taste, all of them accepting their fate—or rather their lack of one. Rhun will be the saint.

Is it always so obvious? Arthur wonders. Did everyone know three years ago that John Upjohn would be the runner? Did they know it of Baeddan Sayer ten years ago? He casts his thoughts forward to the boys that will be teenagers in seven more years. Can he guess?

No. Arthur has no idea.

Hungry, he shoves off the quilt and pulls on a fresh shirt

and boots and a thin knitted sweater handed down from Rhun Senior. He quietly climbs down the ladder to his long leather hunting coat, then picks his way over Sayer cousins and one of the Argall brothers—Per, he thinks it was, who followed him here last night. Outside, he grabs the well bucket and hooks it onto its rope before plunging it down. The water is cold but not yet freezing, and refreshing on his face. He runs wet fingers through his hair, shakes his head, and sends the bucket down again for water to take inside to Nona Sayer.

The front door is ajar and he knocks it open further with his foot. Saint Branwen sniffs at his hip while Llew stretches his long legs exactly in the most way of Arthur's path.

Nona says, "Thanks for that; here's bread," and trades him the bucket for a hot crust. "Butter's out too, today, and ham."

He thanks her and spreads plentiful butter, sitting on one of the precarious three-legged stools while she pours the new water into her cauldron over the fire. "Rhun up?" he asks quietly.

"No." The tightening of her mouth in disapproval suggests to Arthur she's less happy with her son's fate than she ever let on before.

"I . . . ," he starts, but doesn't know how to show her any of his heart. It's never been necessary before: Nona took him in when his mother left and his father couldn't bear looking at him. She treated him hard but kindly, and doesn't expect any thanks, she's said often enough he believes her.

Nona faces her adopted son, studying him carefully enough as Arthur eats his entire breakfast under her stare. She's handsome and tall, with the same warm brown skin and same eyes as Rhun, but hers are tinged with displeasure, as if the world will always disappoint her. Probably that's why Arthur usually relaxes around her, feeling the same.

She says, "I'm glad to have to worry about only one of my sons tonight."

Rather angry than touched, Arthur rises to his full height. "You're so sure which one?"

Gesturing for him to lower his voice, Nona says, "No."

It stuns Arthur. He crosses his arms over his chest. "You think it might be me?"

"I doubt it, here in a place like Three Graces. Out in the rest of the world, though, you would be the one."

"Why?"

"The rest of the world appreciates ambition and fire."

"Not you, though. You chose this place, knowing both worlds."

Nona smiles her flat, no-nonsense smile. "It is a very good place, Arthur."

"No it's not. What kind of good place takes its best and throws it away?"

"We don't throw it away. It's a sacrifice. A hard one,

and don't you think otherwise. There's no power in throwing something away, only in giving something up."

Arthur clutches himself. "How can you do it? How can you just let this happen to Rhun?"

The older woman stares down her nose at him. "This is a better way than the way of the outside world."

"How?" Arthur hears the ache in his own voice, the pitch of pleading.

Nona sighs hard enough to blow down a straw house. "In the rest of the world, Arthur, bad things take you by surprise. They knock down your door when you're cooking dinner, they knock down your door when you're sleeping, or sometimes they don't even knock at all. You're worried about it all the time. If I raised my sons out there, this danger might have found Rhun years ago, or if he survived this long, it might find him any day in his future. But here in Three Graces, we throw the door open wide and say, 'Today is the day, trouble. Your only chance.'" She takes Arthur's wan face in her warm hands. "The dread today is hard, but the relief will be so much finer. I prefer to keep the devil on a schedule."

Arthur feels his fire calming—no, not calming, but settling in deep, like the hottest embers in the heart of a log. It makes sense to him, on a profound level, to choose such a thing. To invite trouble when you're ready for it. He is ready for it.

But nobody else can see.

Nona strokes her thumbs along her prickly almost-son's

temples, then lets her hands slide away from his face. "Go outside, boy, and I'll send Rhun along in a moment."

He obeys.

D AWN PASSES, AND NEITHER MAIRWEN NOR RHUN wake, having finally fallen hard and heavy into the first real sleep either have experienced in days. Mair wakes first, and suddenly. Something in the kitchen snapped her out of dull dreaming. The mattress crunches as she shifts and blinks against bright sunlight. She slowly stretches her arm around Rhun's chest, flexes her toes, rolls her neck, and snuggles deeper against him. His breath puffs the hair at the top of her head, and one of his arms curls around her waist, pinned beneath her.

She lays a hand over his heart. A few curled black hairs accent the shape of his muscles, and she traces their path below his collarbone and down his stomach. Rhun's hand around her tightens, and she stops moving, lifting her gaze to his still sleeping face. The sunlight gilds his short eyelashes, and an ache of fear clenches in her belly.

Swallowing it away as best she can, Mairwen glances around. Wool blankets hang on the walls to lessen the drafts from the old stone. The cream and gray brighten the entire room. He's tied blessings and bone amulets to one of them, on the eastern wall. A trunk set in the corner holds his few clothes beside the leather jerkin and hunting hood spread over a stool. His axes lean against the trunk, his bow and quiver, as well as pieces of unmade arrows on the floor, including three white feathers she brought him, salvaged from the body of a swan in the shambles.

The sunlight brings it all clear. Sunlight from those narrow south-facing windows. Mairwen jerks, clutching at Rhun, who wakes instantly.

"Mair?" he says thickly.

"It is *late*," she whispers.

Just then, the heavy blanket tied across Rhun's bedroom door snaps aside. His mother stands with her arms out majestically, a fierce glare shaping her entire face. "Idiot children! You're late, Rhun. Get up. Arthur's waiting outside to go with you. And you"—Nona sweeps her eyes down Mairwen's thinly covered body—"you're due at your mother's house to sew the saint shirt with the rest of us."

And Nona Sayer is gone again. The blanket falls hard behind her.

Rhun rolls out of bed swiftly. Mair grips the corner of the blanket, sticking it and her hands under her chin. As he strips off his braies, she stares, lips parted, at all his long lines. Rhun, naked as a babe, throws open the trunk and digs in. He holds up a wad of cloth. "I know I'll receive the saint's shirt this afternoon, but I should wear fresh underthings to run in, don't you think?"

Mairwen attempts a smile, though teasing is the last thing she wishes for today. "That's what you call fresh? Balled up in your trunk?"

Rhun laughs, lighthearted as the sun. Mair longs to lose

the weight on her chest too. When he stands, facing her and entirely naked crown to toes, it's her voice she loses instead. He steps into the woolen braies a leg at a time, smiling a promise at her, and straightens, tying them fast at his waist.

She slips out of the bed and kneels before him. She ties the soft braies at his knees, skimming her fingers against his calves. When she finishes she peers up, leaning back on her heels. She smiles bright and clean and with everything of bounty she can make it. None of her shadows, none of her bristling. "I'll help you with your stockings and the rest, too."

Together they dress him, in dark wool and leather, tying and buckling until he's fit to go into the forest. Mairwen slips the lacing of her bodice free and uses it to help him tie back his curls.

He kisses her mouth, and her heartbeat slows, regulating itself to the central rhythm of Three Graces: the Slaughter Moon, the bargain, the Bone Tree, and Rhun Sayer.

Rhun picks up her skirt and holds it open for her to get into, then buttons it for her. She pulls her bodice over her arms, but leaves it open on the front for lack of laces. Rhun wraps her square shawl over her shoulders, then finds her boots and helps her on with them.

From the kitchen, Nona Sayer roars, "Out, both of you, now!"

But Rhun takes Mairwen's hand. "When the saint comes for you tonight, will you dance with him?"

"You know I will," she says. With that, she gathers her

shawl across her undressed chest and ducks out of his room, wishing she could make herself the saint.

Nona leans against her uneven kitchen table, brow lifted expectantly. Mairwen thinks she should tell Nona that her son was *good* and broke no rules, even at the urging of the saint's own daughter, but all she does is hold herself tall. "Good morning," she says tightly as she leaves.

Nona Sayer snorts. "I'll catch up to you, girl."

Mairwen winces at the bright sunlight as she pushes out of the house and stands there, gazing down the slope of yard that ends in thick mountain woods. She can't see any of the valley from here—for that, one must be up on that coveted second story—but the mountain trees are colorful enough, full of jewel-toned leaves and rustling shadows. Overhead the sky is perfect blue with sheer clouds. The air's near balmy for so late in the season.

Several paces away Arthur Couch sits up from the grass. Leaves cling to his spiky blond hair. His look of surprise pinches as he sees her and stands slowly. "What are you doing here?"

Tightening her shawl around her, Mairwen clenches her jaw. "What do you think?"

"Dressed like that." Arthur bites out every word.

"Jealous?" she asks.

Arthur's lips part and he stares at her as if she's both completely right and completely wrong. Mair pushes past him and starts down the path.

"How could you?" Arthur calls, as if he has some claim to her.

She spins back around. "I was reminding him who he has to fight for, Arthur Couch!"

Instead of yelling back, or even sneering as she expected when she threw his own words in his face, the young man nods slowly, bobbing his head like a bird.

Her irritation melts, and Mairwen chews her bottom lip. But she has nothing else to say to Arthur. So she turns again, stomping through fallen leaves.

A hand grabs her elbow and swings her around. Arthur's flickering eyes gouge into hers. "He didn't let you, though, did he? *I* would have."

She shrugs. "That's only proof of what we both already know about the difference between you and Rhun Sayer."

"And *you* and Rhun Sayer," Arthur shoots back.

Mair's blood boils, and her cheeks flush hot, like Arthur infected her with his burning ulcer. "Fine, yes," she hisses. "We're neither of us as good as him, neither of us noble and bound to the promise of Three Graces. Is that what you want to hear? *It doesn't matter.* It's him who's going into the forest, him who'll face the devil. The men will choose him because he's everything a saint of this town is supposed to be: brave, strong, kind, generous, friendly! Noble and inno-cent, and not always angry and doubting like us. That's how it should be. If we didn't love him, it wouldn't be a sacri-fice." She jerks free of Arthur's touch. "You paint a smile on that sour face, and you don't let him see anything else. He doesn't need your frustration and doubts and denials. Do you understand me?"

"Yes," Arthur murmurs. He holds his hands away from her. "I understand you perfectly."

"Good. Because he *loves* you, and if he doubts he has reason to survive this night, it will be *your fault*."

This time, when Mairwen leaves, Arthur doesn't stop her.

Her wild heartbeat presses her home fast, and Nona doesn't manage to catch up with her after all.

R HUN'S MOTHER HANDS HIM A THICK SLICE OF BREAD slathered in butter, with strips of fried ham on top. "Here. Eat up. You'll need it."

He takes his first huge bite while Nona watches. "I've got to get to the Grace house," she says when he swallows. "I love you. I'll see you . . . tomorrow morning."

Before eating more, Rhun balances the bread precariously on the edge of the table and grabs Nona in a hug. It might be his last chance.

She returns it ferociously, but neither says more before she frees herself and leaves him.

Chewing slowly to savor the breakfast, Rhun shrugs his quiver on his shoulder and double-checks he's got his bow on his back and his long knife strapped to his thigh. The hilt of the knife is made of yellowish bone, smooth and warm under his thumb.

Outside, Rhun breathes deeply as he joins Arthur standing in the center of the yard. The sky is bright, the air warmer than he expected, and all the trees flicker their leaves at him. It's a beautiful last day.

Of course he shouldn't think that way, but he doesn't try hard to stop it. If he's learned nothing about himself, it's that he needs to be in the moment to truly appreciate it. Why pretend he might have more beautiful autumn days when he can embrace the promise of his fate and better love this *now*?

Arthur says, "Do you think this place would be prettier if it rained more often? So we had bad weather to compare with our good?"

Rhun laughs. "No. It rains exactly the right amount."

Giving him an angry look, Arthur starts toward the path up the mountain. But then, Arthur's looks are nearly always angry, so it can't touch Rhun's broad, winning mood. He hums as he goes after, striding longer than necessary, until he's far enough ahead of Arthur to turn backward and grin. "Keep up, man!"

Arthur says, "What's the point?"

"I want to be—I . . ." Rhun waits for his friend. "I'm glad to spend this day with you," he says.

"Oh." Arthur turns his head away as he catches up. His eyes widen in shock and panic as he takes in the trees around them, the golden-brown leaves and narrow deer path.

It dawns on Rhun this is very near the place he kissed Arthur three years ago. Fear tenses up his stomach and he swallows. He opens his mouth, but nothing pops in fast enough to fix it.

"I'm all right," Arthur says roughly. He won't meet

Rhun's gaze, but then suddenly he does: Arthur's blue eyes intense enough to curl Rhun's toes. "I'd run for you. Let me do it for you."

Rhun thinks, *This could be the last time we're alone. The last time I have a chance to say anything.* But then it sinks in what Arthur said. *Let me do it for you.*

"You can't do it for me," Rhun says. "It's mine to do."

Arthur's lips begin to curl, and Rhun leaps forward. "I don't mean you couldn't. I mean I won't let you. I won't let you die for me."

"Instead you die for me?" Arthur whispers. There's a thing so helpless in his face it takes all Rhun's willpower to keep himself from touching his friend. His crackling, frantic, beautiful friend. All the desire Mair teased out in him last night and this morning nearly bowls him over; he wants to just reach out and take something of Arthur for himself.

"I'm running, not dying," Rhun says.

Arthur winces rather elegantly. His choppy hair catches all the morning light, bursting like the sun itself. He reaches out in a jerking motion, and before Rhun can brace himself, puts his hand on Rhun's shoulder. It's always the other way around: Rhun touching Arthur, not this way, not from Arthur's choosing. "I don't want you to die," Arthur says. "I—I don't know what I would do."

"I don't want to either." He puts his hand over Arthur's, hoping for more and happy with this.

"Good. Then." Arthur withdraws his hand but doesn't

back away. His jaw clenches and he holds Rhun's gaze. "We should go up."

"Yes," Rhun says. He smiles, no longer trying to secret his heart away. This is perfect. This was perfect. He grins and hums to himself, ignoring Arthur's standard scornfully friendly laugh. He feels so light, so open, all the weight of worry and his lost four years gone, all the anxiety that something changed melted away. Rhun Sayer hikes up the mountain with his best friend at his side, knowing he kept the vow he made to himself and his cousin-saint Baeddan: to love everything he has.

MAIR ARRIVES HOME IN A FIT. EVERY FEW FEET SHE pauses to crouch and rip grass from the earth and throw it into the wind with all the force she can muster. When her house is in sight, she takes great seething breaths and tries to calm herself down. Smoke floats up from the front yard, and all the house windows are thrown open. As she approaches, she grips the shawl more tightly over her breasts. A surge of womanly laughter reminds her she'll have an audience, for the women already gather here to bless the saint shirt.

She sweeps around the northeast corner, walking proudly along the short wall toward the gooseberry bushes. More than a dozen women sit circled around her mother's fire, on chairs and stools dragged here from their own homes and from inside Mairwen's. They pass three bottles of wine among them, braiding ribbon charms and chattering enthusiastically. It's Martha Parry with the saint shirt in her lap: Woven of the finest gray wool, with perfect seams, already it bears the marks of several women in the form of embroidered flowers, tiny circles, spirals, and lightning shapes in every color of thread owned in Three Graces. Most of them collect on the chest, where they'll settle over Rhun's heart, but some arc like rainbows down one arm.

The conversation falls away as Mairwen stands there beside the tangled mass of gooseberries. Her mother rises from her place between Beth Pugh and her sister Hetty, whose mouth opens in a lazy grin when she meets Mairwen's gaze. Hetty pats back dark hair, and Mairwen inadvertently touches her own, which is more brambled than usual. Haf stares at her, eyes wide.

Aderyn beckons her daughter forward, and Mair hurries around the bushes to the front gate with as much dignity as a half-naked sixteen-year-old girl can when caught before her mother and aunts and cousins.

Hetty Pugh snorts loud. "Lazy girl, you've entirely missed breakfast."

Mairwen's tongue betrays her as she stops beside the fire, nearly in the exact center of the circle of women. She drops her shawl and cries, "It's the only thing I'm allowed to do! For him. Not go into the forest myself!"

Gasps come from where the youngest girls sit, gapemouthed on blankets spread over the grass. Each of them here for the first time to bless a saint shirt. Older women are shocked, amused, and some even approving—it *was* the saint's last chance, some must be thinking. Her mother's sharp eyes are full of worry. Hetty Pugh laughs bright and loud, and Haf giggles through her hands and murmurs Mairwen's name.

"This shirt is doing something," Aderyn says.

"It's not enough," Mairwen replies.

"Come inside and get yourself presentable," Aderyn says, more testy than most are used to hearing from her. She sweeps up and into the cottage. Mairwen follows—she needs new lacing for her bodice, after all—but glances back surprised when Hetty follows as well. Mairwen nearly crashes into her mother, stopped in the center of the cottage's ground floor.

"Hetty, close that behind you, please," Aderyn says, and Hetty shuts the house up. The women both study Mair. She feels their cool gazes like the pressure of fingers on her neck and arms and chest.

Hetty speaks first. "You're scaring the girl, Addie."

Aderyn presses her lips in a line. "Takes more to scare my daughter."

Mairwen says, "I wanted him to know he's loved. I wanted him to see my heart. Bind his here, so he'd come back to it."

The two older women share a glance, and Hetty says, "So his can't be bound to the forest."

Aderyn says, "That's dangerous magic."

Mair barely stops herself from flinging out her arms. "Why? To love a boy? To bind our hearts together? Sex isn't dangerous."

Her mother makes a disgruntled noise.

Hetty says, "I don't think your mama is ready to be a grandmama."

"I don't want him to die," Mairwen whispers. "He's so good and we need him here. I want him to grow old while I'm old."

Aderyn says, "What did you imagine before now? We've known, most of us, for years that Rhun would be the saint when it was his turn. He knows his heart so well, and he's never hidden from anyone that he believes he'll follow his cousin. Did you not think you would face this moment?"

"Eventually, I . . ." Mairwen shakes her head. "I had four more years. I didn't have to be afraid yet. It's too soon! The bargain is broken, or cheating us, and it's not worth Rhun's life."

"You never questioned whether the bargain is worth it before," Hetty says. "When it didn't threaten a boy you love."

Mair bites her bottom lip, gouging the skin hard enough to hurt. She sinks into a chair. "You're right, I feel it sharper now, but shouldn't I?"

Aderyn sighs and kneels at her daughter's chair. "It's true, when Carey Morgan died the valley's beauty lost some brightness to me. And when Rhun dies, you'll carry it with you. Every spring you'll feel it, an ache when the flowers bloom rainbows across our hills. When you taste our year's meat or sip the brews. You'll feel the pain, and that pain makes everything around it brighter. That is what the bargain is: death for life, a sacrifice that makes it all sweeter and sharper. Without it, how could we appreciate what we have? We love our saint, and he runs for us, and everyone here knows exactly how precious life is, and love itself. Everybody dies, Mairwen, but the saints of Three Graces die for a reason."

Mair grips her knees, bunching the fabric of her skirts too tight; she won't let herself be dissuaded. "Then what is the reason it came early this year? What did we do wrong with John Upjohn? He was the saint, and he ran. He survived. We met the terms of the bargain, didn't we?"

"As far as I know," Aderyn says, pushing to her feet again. "Have you eaten breakfast? There are leftover pastries."

"How can you not be curious? The devil owes us an explanation."

Hetty snorts, but Aderyn frowns hard. "First we must crown a saint and do our part, or Rhos's baby *will* die. After that we can try to understand."

Mairwen presses her knuckles into her eyes. She doesn't want Rhos's baby to die, but nor can she stand Rhun throwing his life away if there's something wrong. How can they not see it? "I have to do something. Can't you feel it? Something changed, and we shouldn't ignore it."

The Grace witch pinches her mouth in a thing nearing despair.

Leaping up, Mairwen makes to grab her mother's hands, but stops and draws a deep breath to show she can be calm. It evens out the pain in Aderyn's expression. Her mother says, "You know how to make charms."

"Yes." Mair tries not to sound too eager.

"Life, death, and blessing in between? That's the recipe."

"Always a balance of three pieces."

Hetty joins them, so they stand in an intimate triangle. But she says nothing, knowing already, Mairwen suspects.

"The bargain is a charm, but a very powerful one. Life, death, and blessing in between."

Mairwen sees it. "Life in the valley, death in the forest, and . . . we're the blessing in between. The Grace witches."

Aderyn touches Mair's cheek, sorrow in her eyes. "Our bloodline, our hearts, set originally by the youngest Grace, whose love and sacrifice started it all. We bind the saint. We anoint him with blood. A Grace witch."

Mair has always felt in between, been drawn to that edge of shadows, because her blood is already bound up in the charm. It's so simple. Except . . . "The saint doesn't always die. There's not always death in the forest, yet those four times before now, the bargain has held just the same for the seven expected years."

"What was the last charm you made, little bird?"

"A healing blessing for the sick horse."

"And how did you make it?"

"His living mane, a fox rib, and my song and breath."

"Nothing died for that death; it was only a piece of death, the promise of it." Aderyn smiles grimly.

"I see," Mairwen says, mostly meaning it.

"The saint must choose to die, but he does not need to truly die. But you cannot say those words to Rhun Sayer."

"Why?"

Hetty pushes her hair out of her eyes once again, lifting one brow. "If a saint knows he doesn't have to die, how can he choose to die? The one thing is paradoxical to the other."

Mairwen has nothing to say, only a smog of thoughts.

"You need food," her mother says, going for the bread basket hanging from a hook by the hearth. She digs in and pulls out a pastry so perfectly pinched it must be one of Bree Lewis's.

"Let me do it," Mairwen says. "I want to anoint the saint shirt with my blood and go up the mountain to crown the saint. It's the ritual. It's what the witches do, so let it be me!"

Aderyn pauses, pastry in hand. It has been her duty since her own mother passed it on. She looks to Hetty, and Hetty shrugs.

"Wait," Aderyn says, and vanishes into her bedroom.

Hetty Pugh wanders to Aderyn's kitchen table and begins picking at a spread of bowls filled with water to steep herbs. She dips a finger into one floating with wrinkled rose petals and tastes it. Unease ticks at Mairwen.

Her mother shoves aside the curtain separating her bedroom from the main cottage and emerges with a voluminous layer of blue and cream cloth folded over her arm.

A dress.

Mairwen touches her mouth to keep quiet her surge of hope.

Aderyn holds up the dress, handing one part to Hetty. It's a long bodice and overskirt, dyed indigo. Hetty spreads her arms to display the soft linen shift, embroidered at the cuffs and hem with delicate green vines Mair recognizes as her mother's own hand. The bodice has oversleeves that tie on and are slashed to display bursts of undyed silk.

It's too rich, too beautiful. "Mother," she breathes.

"I've been putting it together since last spring," Aderyn says briskly, brushing invisible dirt off the fine wool skirt. "There's stockings and ribbons, too, and a cream belt. A new shawl Hetty and Beth have woven for you. I was waiting for some fine boots Lord Vaughn helped me arrange to have made in the city, but you've grown so much these past months, and hardly fit yourself anymore." Aderyn purses her lips for a moment, eyeing her daughter's undone bodice. "It is a proper dress for a witch."

Mairwen throws her arms around her mother, crushing the dress between them.

The women help her out of her older clothes. Hetty brings the bowl of rosewater and tosses it across Mair's bare back, while Aderyn grabs a chunk of blessed thistle soap and scrubs. Mair only stands, arms up to hold her heavy hair off her neck, and takes it all, cold and hot in waves, embarrassed and thrilled to have her mother and Hetty washing *her* as if she's their peer. She closes her eyes and whispers Haf's name. Hetty goes to the door and snaps for the Lewis girl, returning with Haf hurrying at her heels. The girl asks no questions, but squeezes Mairwen's fingers as she holds bowls of water and oil.

The women braid and pin Mairwen's hair up. They clean

her fingernails and the backs of her knees, her elbows and hips and ears, and even wash her feet, then rub an oil Mair has never before smelled into her skin. The women's firm fingers work Mair's muscles and soothe her, until her head nods despite the cool air and her stiff pose standing with her arms up in the middle of her mother's house.

When they finish, they dress her in her long new shift, stockings, bodice, and overskirt. They tie on her sleeves, and the new shawl at her waist is of the softest cream wool she's ever known. Hetty puts a bracelet woven of her own and Aderyn's hair around Mairwen's wrist, whispering a blessing. Aderyn kisses her daughter and whispers, "All my strength is your strength. You are everything I am."

Then Aderyn Grace and Hetty Pugh leave the two girls alone in the sunny kitchen. Aderyn pauses before closing the cottage door. "Come out to bless this shirt when you're ready, Daughter."

Mairwen breathes with care. She smells thistle and rose and evergreen and pungent sage. Her skin tingles. She longs to find Rhun and show him how Hetty and Aderyn have made her into the Grace witch for his Slaughter Moon. It almost feels powerful enough to matter.

Haf takes both of Mairwen's hands and shakes her head wonderingly. "Mairwen, you look amazing, and seem so . . . ready."

"I hope this is how Rhun feels when the men are finished with him," she murmurs, drawing her friend nearer. She embraces Haf, touching her cheek to Haf's soft black hair.

This way, Haf can't see her face, or the tension pinching at her eyes. "When I put the shirt on him and lay the horse saint's head upon his like a crown, I pray he feels all their strength behind him."

Haf hugs tighter. "I hope it's enough."

"Rhun says he's ready, Haf. With me binding the charm . . . he can do it. Give himself up and also survive." *And then, if he has to leave the valley, I'll leave with him. So will Arthur*, she thinks.

But Haf says, "I meant enough for *you*."

"I love you, Haf Lewis." Mair wants to say it to everyone she loves today.

Haf kisses the corner of her mouth. "I love you too, Mairwen Grace."

When the girls emerge into the front yard, where the town's women remain circled about the fire, drinking and talking and sewing, there's a collective exclamation at Mairwen's new attire. She imagines it as armor. She lifts the shawl to show off the overskirt and holds out her arms and spins lightly until every woman is satisfied.

Mairwen's appearance relaxes Devyn Argall's shoulders and allows smiles to slide across the Perry sisters' mouths. They read the dress and Mair's face as proof: It will be Rhun Sayer, not their sons, sent into the forest.

It rankles her insides, and she holds their relief against them, thinking of Arthur's bitterness when he said, *I'd survive it.*

Joining the circle of women upon a stool so as not to

muss her dress, Mairwen nibbles at leftover cake from the bonfire as Haf kneels beside her. Bree and her friend Emma kneel with them, and as she waits her turn with the blessing shirt, Mair leans over to whisper to the three that yes, she spent the night with Rhun Sayer. Heat snakes up her neck and throat as she relates finding him half naked, kissing him, and her near begging, but then only sleeping at his side, nothing else. Emma sighs romantically, insisting Rhun must be the noblest man in all Three Graces, while Bree claims Per Argall would've acted the same. Haf says she knows her own Ifan Pugh would most certainly *not*.

Mairwen laughs as she's expected to, and presses her cheek to Haf's fine hair, remembering Arthur Couch say the same to her, as if he wanted *her* to hear it. She wishes Arthur were here with them, with the girls, to put his fire into the saint shirt where it could protect Rhun. Competing with the boys is a waste of his time. His power is more suited here, because he knows a thing about transformation. Or he *should*, if he'd admit it to himself.

When the blessing shirt comes to the girls, they let Mair take the lead. She touches the fine gray wool, imagining a ferocious lion or a quick rabbit to lend him strength or speed. But thinking of the Bone Tree, of the monster she and Arthur killed, thinking of the youngest, first Grace witch who fell in love with a beautiful devil, instead she chooses a deer, for the old god of the forest. Needles quick and sure, the four girls embroider it there at the shoulder. Em and Bree create tawny legs, Haf a sleek body, and Mairwen the crowning antlers. When they finish, Mair takes bright red thread and stitches a bloody heart to the stag's chest. She pricks her finger and anoints the heart with three drops of her blood.

Haf and her sister try not to frown at the dangerous addition, and Emma whispers, "It looks a bit like fire, doesn't it?" The girls each take a drink of wine, then pour the final sip into the earth.

I F THERE IS A PIECE OF THE SLAUGHTER MOON RITUAL Arthur Couch dreads deepest, it's the long afternoon fast and vigil each prospective boy is expected to keep in the rough terrain near Sy Vaughn's manor, alone—except for the company of his father.

Gethin Couch is as long and lanky as his son, with similar blond hair, but the rest of Arthur came from his mother. Gethin's got a hard jaw and a wide suntanned face, with soft green eyes, and his hands are stubby but talented with leather. He makes the best gloves in town, and any leather piece that requires detail work and dedication. Last year, the decade anniversary of his wife leaving Three Graces, he went through a carefully constructed un-marriage ritual with Aderyn Grace. It was the least they could do to help him move on, with no proof that Arthur's mother was alive or dead. Arthur had been invited, but he hadn't attended.

The two men sit three feet away from each other on a narrow outcropping of white chalk high on the mountain, entirely bared to the elements, for no trees grow so high and the scrubby heather and grasses offer no shelter even from the wind. Arthur stares out at the wide-open valley, eyes burning from the cold. He's supposed to be receiving advice and support from his father, but there are too many expectations wasted between them for Arthur to want such from Gethin.

He imagines the conversation Rhun and Rhun the Elder are sharing at the moment, and it relaxes him just enough to lean back against the rough mountain.

"Well, boy," Gethin Couch says, "your mother sure would be furious if she could see you now. Wish she could."

Arthur says nothing.

"I wager," Gethin continues, "she's counting the years, and expects you to be up in four more. If she's alive, she's still afraid and worrying about it somewhere. I hope it chokes her. Makes her look old and ugly before her time."

"I don't," Arthur says, remembering his mother's soft smile, and remembering too how terrible her mouth turned when she screamed at him, *You may as well already be dead.*

"Bah," his father says.

"We don't have to speak." Arthur has yet to truly look at his father; he's avoided the man for years, not finding any good reason to give thought or energy to somebody who turned him over to the Sayers without complaint. *Better he be raised around so many men and boys now,* was Gethin's excuse, said knowing Arthur listened.

"But you should know, son, I see what you've become.

You may not be the best, but there's no doubting you're as close as anyone with your temperament could get. Nothing she did hurt you."

Arthur closes his eyes. Every word pains him, infuriates him. Maybe this is why the potential runners are forced to fast alone with their fathers: It's no comfort, but a final test to discover what boy can withstand parental torture. "I don't need your approval," he says through his teeth.

"You have it anyway."

"Approve of this, then." Arthur stands up. "You're no father to me, and haven't been at least since my mother left, if you ever were before. You either were so blind and disinterested in a daughter you did not see what she did, or you agreed with her to do it, but blame her alone for all. So this is outside the spirit of the ritual. I'll see myself away."

He steps off the stone outcropping and skids down toward the path that leads back to Vaughn's manor. What a furious lie this valley is, he thinks. Perhaps the devil's bargain keeps sickness and death at bay, but it certainly doesn't make people good or keep families together.

Or perhaps it's only Arthur who thinks so. Everyone else is content and happy. Everyone else accepts the bargain and its restrictions. He's the one who doesn't belong, because his mother *did* ruin him. Who would he be now if he'd always been a boy? Would he be as good as Rhun?

Who would he be if he'd remained a girl?

A great wind blows at him, shifting him backward on the path: away from Vaughn, away from the valley. Arthur pauses and glances over his shoulder. The path pierces down that way, along a chalk ridge and toward the pass through the mountain, out to the rest of the world.

He could leave.

The thought sucks his breath away.

The rest of the world appreciates ambition and fire.

But Arthur knows too well what would be said of him here were he to leave. *Coward. Better off without him. Too hot for his own good.* Like they'd said of his mother. *Never belonged here.*

And if he goes now, he'll never know if Rhun survives. It would prey on him. *So,* he thinks bitterly, *perhaps I'll go the day after tomorrow.* When it's clear he's not needed, when Rhun can't give up the fight for not having him to come home to and Mairwen can't accuse him of being at fault for it. He could survive without them both. He could.

Arthur walks the path toward Sy Vaughn's manor, slow but sure, and when he arrives the lord is there alone, standing before a small fire built up in the center of the stone yard between the manor's gate and the tree line.

The late-afternoon sun is brutal, cutting every inch of Vaughn's attire bold and blacker than black should be in the daylight. It's a black that comes from outside the valley, where merchants have access to better dyes and more expensive techniques. Supple as a mountain cat's fur coat and glistening sleek, too. The lord's hair is loose, falling in russet curls around his cheeks and neck. His hands clasp behind his back. When the lord hears Arthur's bootstep, he turns. His eyes are black and gray—the left black, the right gray, or maybe that is only the way the sun hits half his face. He smiles with thin lips, and it occurs to Arthur that Lord Sy Vaughn is lovely. Striking and strong, sure, but also beautiful. Arthur wonders what it would have been like to have someone like this as a father, to protect and defend him when he was a child.

"Arthur Couch," Vaughn says calmly, gesturing for Arthur to join him. "Back so soon."

"That man has never been much of a father to me."

Vaughn nods, and something untwists inside Arthur just to be agreed with so simply and readily.

"I have a question for you," Vaughn says. He looks out over the valley, not at Arthur, and Arthur follows the young lord's gaze. From here they can see down the tops of the trees, across Three Graces and all the barley fields, tiny white spots of sheep, the rolling hills of the pastures, all the way to the dark Devil's Forest and there—there in the center, the pale Bone Tree with its scarlet crown.

"I'm listening," Arthur says when it becomes clear Vaughn is waiting for a response.

"Why didn't your mother take you with her?"

Arthur bares his teeth. "How should I know?"

Vaughn hums a single, low note of acknowledgment.

"She didn't want me. She wanted a daughter."

"It seemed to me that she wanted a child guaranteed to live."

"Then of course she didn't take me with her: I might've died a dozen ways outside the valley."

"Yes. I've seen many terrible ways for a child to die out in the world. But if I had a daughter, I think I would do anything to keep her safe, and if that failed, anything to remain with her."

"And if you'd had a son?" Arthur challenges.

Vaughn smiles again. "It would be an honor for him to be a saint."

"Someday maybe you'll find out if you're right. You'll have to marry and have an heir to take over this place."

"I suppose so. Any suggestions for a willing lady?"

Arthur waves his hands, aggravated with the turn of conversation. "I want to run, sir. I need to. Give this to me. Let it be me, not Rhun."

Vaughn's gray and brown eyes flick up and down Arthur's face. "You'll have your turn to plead your case shortly."

"Let me plead it now. I'm worthy—let me prove it. Show you. I can win this."

"Win?" Vaughn's eyebrows fly up, and he laughs softly. "Oh, Arthur Couch. There is no way to win. It is a sacrifice, not a game. It must be done for love."

"I can do it," he grinds out.

But the lord says, "No."

Arthur strides away with a frustrated cry. He crouches and his hunting coat flares around him exactly the way he remembers skirts billowing out. Putting his fists to his forehead, he seethes, trying to breathe evenly, trying to find an argument that will earn him the right to run tonight. To prove he's not more flawed than any other potential saint, including Rhun Sayer.

It occurs to him in a terrible flash that he could tell Sy Vaughn right now what he's kept secret for three years: Rhun Sayer is in love with a boy.

And in the next instant, a worse truth reveals itself to Arthur: He will never be the best, because he's not even good. No one good would ever, even momentarily, consider what he just considered.

He promised himself, ten years ago, to someday run into the forest and offer the devil his heart, but Arthur understands now that the devil ate his heart a long time ago.

A N HOUR BEFORE THE SUN SETS, ALL THE POTENTIAL runners, their fathers, and every man or boy in Three Graces older than thirteen gathers around the fire at Sy Vaughn's manor. Rhun's eyes are wide as he stares at the heavy blue sky overhead, taking in all he can. His father's eyes shine with unshed tears, but he smiles proudly, his arm around his son.

"You don't have to do this, son. Not for me, not for your mother. We're proud of you already," Rhun the Elder said, just before they returned to the manor.

But Rhun made this decision years ago.

"Where's Arthur?" he asks Lord Vaughn when he and the others step forward for the final choosing.

Vaughn says, "He returned to the valley, I suppose to lick his wounds."

Rhun glances toward Gethin Couch, who appears as surprised as everyone. He's never liked Arthur's father, which is as near to despising a person as Rhun can get. Rhun the Elder frowns apologetically at his son, for Rhun had asked if they might take Arthur with them on their afternoon fast and Rhun the Elder suggested it would be important for Arthur and Gethin to come to terms if Arthur was to have a chance at being the saint.

"I should get him," Rhun says, starting for the path, but a grumble from the collected men halts him.

"Stay," Lord Vaughn says. "Or forfeit your chance as Arthur Couch has."

Blowing air through his teeth, Rhun stays. He takes his place in the line of boys, sending them all a supportive smile. Per, and Darrick Argall, the Parry cousins, and Bevan Heir.

Vaughn removes a glass vial from his coat pocket and with great ceremony dumps it into the fire.

A gout of flame screams up, and the smoke turns as white as the moon, as white as the Bone Tree.

The signal to the women: We have begun.

Rhun breathes the smoke, finding it softer than he expected, comforting. His lighthearted mood remains, tinged only by wishing Arthur hadn't gone. But they had their moment in the woods this morning, and that is all Rhun needed. This is his time, his own moment to be what he's always been meant for.

Lord Vaughn calls, "Tell me, Per Argall, what makes you the best?"

Per clears his throat and says hesitantly, "I'm young and fast—the fastest. I . . . yes."

"Tell me, Bevan Heir, what makes you the best?" Vaughn asks.

Bevan, nineteen and thick in shoulder and head, says, "I have a plan, to alternate running with hiding. I can play this game with our devil, and make the night of the Slaughter Moon worthwhile."

And so Sy Vaughn calls on every potential runner to have their say. Darrick Argall claims to be the bravest and kindest. Ian Parry says he's practiced every day of his life. Marc Parry tells the men his mother has always known it, and dreamed he would be the saint, and he would like to be everything his mother dreams he can be.

When it is Rhun's turn to say what makes him the best, he shrugs and only offers, "Nothing but my heart, sir."

It is so earnestly done, the gathered men and boys nod along, and because Arthur is not present to sneer, nobody does.

THE GRACE WITCH ARRIVES IN A BEAUTIFUL BLUE AND cream dress, with a wreath of bones and yellow flowers around her neck, and a heavy horse skull cradled in her arms. Her cheeks are bright from the exertion of hiking here with the heavy thing, and bright from hope and fury and love.

She smells like a bitter salve she stirred under her mother's instruction, bled into, and with which she anointed herself.

Rhun waits at the fore with Sy Vaughn.

When she sees him, her lips part and she murmurs the litany of saints. "Bran Argall. Alun Crewe. Powell Ellis. John Heir. Col Sayer. Ian Pugh. Marc Argall. Mac Priddy. Stefan Argall. Marc Howell. John Couch. Tom Ellis. Trevor Pugh. Yale Sayer. Arthur Bowen. Owen Heir. Bran Upjohn. Evan Priddy. Griffin Sayer. Powell Parry. Taffy Sayer. Rhun Ellis. Ny Howell. Rhys Jones. Carey Morgan. Baeddan Sayer. John Upjohn."

Together, everyone says, "Rhun Sayer."

She sets the horse skull on the ground and unwraps the blessed and embroidered shirt. She glances up at Rhun, who, with the help of his father, removes jacket and shirt. The Grace witch steps forward and lifts the new shirt over his head. As he fills it out, she whispers his name again and again. The men join her, his name becoming an invocation, a hiss, a wind all its own.

The witch unties the wreath from her neck and wraps it around Rhun, then leans up onto her toes to kiss his mouth as she laces it at the back of his neck. Hidden in the flowers is the disarticulated jaw of the sacrificed horse. If the witch kisses the saint with a little more passion than usual, none make comment.

She unstoppers a metal box tied to her belt and smears her thumb in the dark ointment, then touches it to Rhun's lips and forehead. A bitter smell rises fresh.

Mairwen stands back, arms spread, full of nerves and fire. Rhun's father helps him back on with his coat and hunter's hood, but then Vaughn lifts the horse skull and sets it over the hood, hiding the last dark flash of Rhun's eyes from her. She pants in shallow gasps as the Parry cousins put a cape of horsehair over Rhun's shoulders, and Bevan Heir ties the tail so it spills like a crest down his back. Here Rhun is fierce and frightening, half man, half beast, and evening has arrived.

The horse skull grins down at her, one half of it caught in the burning light of the dying sun. Orange and pink bleed down that west-facing side, catching on the blocky teeth in the back of the skull. The light sharpens the long nasal bone into a dagger and blackens the eye cavities. The bottom jaw-bone hangs down from rope against Rhun's chest like a plate of armor, crushing some flowers in the wreath. He is hardly knowable, but she does know that leather jerkin, the deep oxblood of his hunting hood, his plain brown leather brac-ers. She knows those hands, and the thighs, too, wrapped in trousers, hiding the skin she touched and dressed herself only hours ago.

Mair's breath catches.

The saint steps to her and holds out his hand. The pale edge of the saint shirt peeks out from his jerkin. Her charm. The entire valley's charm. Mair finds his eyes, only a glint in the shifting shadows beneath the skull, and gives him the most meaningful glare she can. *Survive*, she mouths. *No matter what.*

Taking her by the waist, he tilts back his head so some rays of light can cut beneath the long skull and across his mouth. *I love you*, he mouths back.

Then Rhun tosses his head like a horse, prancing and spreading his arms. Inviting the Grace witch to join him.

He holds out his hand again and Mairwen takes it. Their fingers weave together, and Rhun leads her away.

TOGETHER, THE SAINT AND THE WITCH DANCE AND skip down the mountain, breathless. The men follow, murmuring his name, clapping their hands, Lord Vaughn joining at the end.

Together, the saint and the witch knock on every door in Three Graces, calling the town to join them too, to dance in a long, twisting line toward the Devil's Forest for the Slaughter Moon. Through houses and gardens, along cobbled alleys, through the square they weave, trailing a snake of people behind.

Around Three Graces in a sunwise circle they dance as the sun falls farther and farther, then to the pasture hill. Behind them everyone else yells and cheers, sings and weeps and prays as Rhun the saint leads them around and around the fire made by Aderyn Grace and the women, through bloody smoke where this stallion's organs burn. Mair and Rhun do not laugh or shriek with the rest.

The entire moon crawls free of the dark mountain horizon, and the saint stops.

The town pours around them into a massive crescent, a shield between them and Three Graces.

Together, Rhun and Mairwen face the forest.

It's a black wall, silent and forbidding, edged in pale moonlight.

The Bone Tree thrusts up from the center like a silver salmon leaping into the air. The ghostly crown is stark and compelling, missing every single scarlet leaf. They've all fallen during the day.

Rhun tightens his grip on Mair's hand, then releases it. With both strong hands, he lifts the skull crown off his head and sets it upon a staff rammed deep into the hill beside the bonfire. The skull settles there with a slow nod, one empty eye toward the forest, one toward the town.

Rhun Sayer the Elder walks to his son with a quiver and strung bow. He helps Rhun into them both, and his cousin Brac Sayer offers Rhun his axes, which he puts to his belt. Braith Bowen gives him a dagger for his boot.

That's all. Mair expected Arthur to give Rhun something, but she sees him nowhere.

A worm of disappointment eases through her guts. Where is he? He belongs here. With them.

Rhun glances at Mair, smiles bravely, and nods like the horse skull nodded. She readies herself to step forward just as a murmur ripples through the arc of townsfolk.

A dark figure dashes below them, from the direction of town, around the curve of the pasture hill.

Arthur Couch stands halfway between the Devil's Forest

and the crest of the hill where the bonfire blazes, where the horse saint's skull nods, where the people of Three Graces wait to offer their son to the sacrifice.

His spiky pale hair catches the last warm traces of daylight.

Mairwen's heart beats hard enough to thrust out of her chest and her toes tingle in her boots. Somebody whispers, "What is he doing?"

Arthur turns to face up the hill. His bow and quiver poke over his shoulder, and the glint of long knives mark his hips. He wears a black hunting hood, an old leather coat, trousers, and boots. Arthur puts both his hands out and waves madly at them all.

A strangled cry breaks from Aderyn Grace and Rhun grunts wordlessly.

Mairwen thinks Arthur looks coiled and sharp, dangerous and ready to face down the devil. She flexes her hands into fists and steps forward. Though she can't see his eyes clearly, she knows the moment Arthur fixes his attention on her. Her palms ache, and she feels hot, then cold, then terrified, because *Arthur doesn't have the shirt. He can't go in. He's not anointed.*

"But I'm the blessing in between," she whispers. Her blood. Her heart.

Behind Mairwen, a knowing, panicked look flashes in her mother's eyes. But Aderyn has never called her daughter's name where the devil might hear it.

Haf Lewis is not yet so wise, and when Mairwen leaps

forward, grabs one of Rhun's axes, and takes off down the hill, Haf screams her best friend's name.

Mairwen runs, thrusting hard against the skirt of her dress, gasping against the tightness of her bodice.

She pushes harder, boots thudding her heartbeat into the earth.

Her name becomes a cry behind her, a swarming prayer, as she careens downhill toward Arthur.

Their eyes meet for a flash, and she holds out her empty hand.

Arthur slaps his palm to hers, and together they run for the trees.

THE VIGIL

Haf Lewis has never been so afraid in her life.

Her best friend vanished into the forest only moments ago, and already a piece of her heart feels torn away.

Mairwen will survive, Haf tells herself. She's a Grace witch and the daughter of a saint. The forest won't take her. As long as Mair keeps running, keeps all her prickly pieces out like daggers, like a shield, she will survive until morning. She has to.

At the fore of the townspeople, Haf has a perfect view of the black wall of trees, of the shivering canopy lined with moonlight. She's gone out of her way to never imagine what hides beneath all those shadows, what monsters might swarm the roots of the Bone Tree. Hard enough to live so near it and listen to Mairwen wonder. If Haf let her nightmares loose, she'd run so far away from this valley she'd never find her way home again.

Beside her Rhun Sayer murmurs something she can't

quite hear. Eyes on the forest, he walks slowly but with absolute purpose down the pasture hill.

"Rhun," says Nona Sayer.

He acknowledges nothing, but continues on at the same pace until he's at the edge of the trees. He pauses, but doesn't look back over his shoulder, as if he knows looking back would hold him in place.

Rhun follows his friends into the Devil's Forest.

Haf understands, but it turns her heart even colder.

Conversation flares at her back, louder than the bonfire. Haf watches her shadow; flames cast it long and flickering and strange toward the forest. She swears she will not close her eyes until the sun appears. Lowering to kneel on the crisp grass, Haf arranges her skirt carefully around herself as a distraction. She'll need more than that, though, to make it the nine hours until dawn.

"Be calm," Lord Vaughn commands, and the fearful talk quiets.

"Our part of the bargain is intact," Aderyn Grace says, almost too softly. But they all hear.

Vaughn adds, "Hold vigil, as you—as we—always hold vigil. There is no more any of us can do. When the sun rises, we will see."

After a moment's pause, someone begins to recite the litany of saints.

One by one, the townspeople join in, until the prayer is a billowing cloud of hope lifting off the hill. Haf moves her lips along with the prayer, hands folded in her lap, eyes on the forest.

Her sister Bree brings her a mug of beer, but Haf waves it away. The beer would only make her tired. Hot tea would be better, or plain water, she thinks, though truly she hardly knows; Haf has never kept vigil before. Seventeen years ago she'd been a babe in arms. Ten years ago she left with her parents after the snake dance, after Baeddan Sayer ran in. She'd only been eight, and her mother easily convinced they should spend the night by their own hearth with little four-year-old Bree. Three years ago she tried to stand with Mairwen, but halfway through the night her eyes drooped heavy. She paced to stay awake, and pinched her cheeks, but several hours before dawn she fell asleep leaning against the pasture wall only to wake in sudden terror at the sight of John Upjohn's bloody wrist.

Haf pictures Mairwen covered in blood.

T*HE WIND INSIDE THE FOREST WHISPERS, GRACE, Grace, Grace.*

Mairwen, running, hears her name, and Arthur flings himself before her as if to protect her from ghosts. But the forest is everywhere around them: listening, stalking, laughing.

Grace, Grace, Grace, it says, and the tiny monsters chatter it, goblins and bobbing spirits, sharp-toothed birds and bone boys all revel in the sound of the name.

The devil bides his time, stretching his jaw in a massive, lazy yawn, crouched at the base of the Bone Tree. He will go after them soon.

Them. *It is an odd thing, but he smells more than a saint, and the forest is alive with that old name.*

H AF SITS SO STILL ONLY WISPS OF HER HAIR MOVE IN the breeze and the heat from the fire. Her braids are expertly crafted, and only a few long tendrils have fallen, exactly where Haf meant them to when she wove it up this afternoon. She wanted to look as pretty as Mairwen in the beautiful blue dress. Haf even daydreamed about her own wedding dress, nearly finished and folded in the trunk at the foot of her mother's bed. It's a warm summery green and embroidered, too, like Mair's, but without the rich silk sleeves. Haf had insisted on sewing loops and ribbons into the skirt so she could raise it to her calves after the ceremony, in order to dance all day and night with her family and friends and new husband. This spring, after the first bloom. Mairwen has to be there. In her heart, Haf feels absolutely certain she cannot ever marry without Mairwen to chalk blessings and kiss her cheek and find perfect delicate sparrow bones to weigh down the ends of her wedding veil.

A man's boot appears near her hip, worn and dark brown in the firelight. He kneels and touches her shoulder gently. Haf's eyes flicker to his—though the fire at his back turns him into a dark silhouette and fine features are impossible to determine, she knows it's Ifan. As if summoned by her slowly spiraling dread.

Not even this rare touch from her soon-to-be-husband comforts her.

She covers his hand with hers, though, curling her small fingers around his, and he accepts the invitation to sit with her.

"Are you warm enough?" he asks in his plain way. She nods quickly, shallow little nods highlighting her fear. She can't stop thinking about Mairwen hurt, bleeding—things she'd never imagined before. Mairwen in the devil's clutches, or forced to watch Rhun or Arthur or both of them die. She imagines the devil himself, like in the story: monstrous and strange, part forest creature, part man, with handsome eyes and face, but fangs and cloven hooves and horns.

How does anyone who loves the saint survive the vigil hours? she wonders. It would've been bad enough to hold Mair's hand all night long, both of them hoping after Rhun Sayer. Haf prepared for the past two days to be a solid force of friendship and love for Mair, prepared little stories she recalled of their childhood to distract her. She never thought to prepare *herself*.

*A*T FIRST RHUN MOVES FAST, TRACKING HIS FRIENDS *easily, for Mair's skirt tears and drags, leaving a path he could've followed as a child. Moonlight snakes through the* lattice of branches overhead, casting shadows in odd places. He tracks them to a deer path cutting through a scarlet hedge with thin leaves as red as blood and twice as tall as him. It emerges at a wide, shallow creek with an opposite bank of flat stones. The moon's reflection is a bright oval, a shivering fungus on the water.

It's too quiet. Besides the slow murmur of water and whispering breeze, Rhun hears nothing.

Fear seeps down his spine.

He crouches at the glint of water on stone—a footprint, a smear of wetness angling toward the wall of black trees. He jogs that way, eyes everywhere for further sign. There's a skid in the ground cover. Rhun heads deeper into the silent forest.

Behind him something snickers. He spins, notching an arrow. He draws it to his cheek and aims along his sight. Darkness, shadows on shadows. Columns of black trees.

The wind twists through the empty branches.

"Mairwen!" he yells. Silence swallows the name.

"Mairwen, Mairwen!" hiss back a hundred tiny voices, from every angle, all around. Above and below.

Rhun whirls, arrow aimed, left then right, sweeping upward in an arc.

He is alone.

He slides the arrow home in the quiver over his shoulder and moves on.

T HE MOON RISES.

Haf draws Ifan Pugh's hand to her cheek and

presses. A tear slips from her eye, smearing against his pale knuckles.

"Summertime," he whispers, a name he's called her once or twice, and wraps his arm around her. Haf wants nothing so much as to hide her face in his shoulder, let him be a shield between her and the fear and the forest. But she can't. She has to hold this vigil. Mairwen would, and Haf will be brave for her friend.

Around them the crowd shifts. Some keep warm by stomping, others walk wide circles around the pasture. Still others trade out with husbands or wives or sisters or fathers to watch little ones back home in the cottages. They talk softly when they talk at all, and though they do not eat, they sip beer and steep tea near the hot feet of the fire. Wind sings too sweetly through the valley, and the moon is too bright.

"Do you hold it against me, that I never was a true candidate?" Ifan asks, low in her ear.

Startled, she turns her head away from the forest. His eyes are inches from hers, tight at the corners and sad. She says, "No, oh no, I never."

He studies her for a moment. The tension relaxes a bit from his face. Firelight teases the wisps of dark hair framing his forehead, and the tip of his narrow nose. Haf has always liked to look at him, though she never was struck by any handsomeness or beauty. He is simply pleasant, and kind, and was hesitant enough to create a bit of attraction between them. Three years ago he was twenty-three, a bit too old to run, and the sainting before that he was six-teen, but while he competed with the others, he'd been as likely a saint as sweet Per Argall. From things her mother and aunts have said, Ifan was competent, just not invested. Unusual for a boy in Three Graces to not have an intense relationship with the sainthood. Haf has always liked unusual things—she is best friends with Mairwen Grace, after all.

"You are what you are," she whispers to him and, on a whim, kisses him.

His mouth is dry and cool, but he brings a hand up. His thumb presses just at the corner of her lips, and his fingers spread along her cheek and jaw, holding her carefully.

Faraway in the forest, a scream lifts out of the darkness.

Haf startles away, clamoring to her feet. Ifan joins her, as do a line of villagers, breath held all.

The scream dies away, and after her heart beats again, tiny black shadows dart up from the canopy, tilting like a furious flock of birds.

*A*RTHUR SPINS, PANTING. THE MARSH GLIMMERS *with tiny lights, teasing him. He hates being alone in this forest—harder to pretend he's not scared without Mairwen to lie to.*

Visions dance before him, moonlit and wavering, all rotting faces and leering, broken grins. His mother hangs by the neck from a bent tree, eyes open and caught on his. She laughs and hisses, "To be born a boy in Three Graces is to be as good as dead."

"Pretty girl," cries a ghastly demon, splashing up from the wet marsh. Its face is like his father's, its voice hot as Arthur's own.

He knows—he absolutely knows—this is a trick. The forest wants to drive him wild, confuse him, wear him out with fear.

"You're no saint," the forest spirits accuse him. "We taste it in your heart."

Bone boys giggle and the marsh lights wink in joining merriment. "No-saint, never-saint," says the voice of the devil.

"I could be," Arthur says, unable to resist any argument.

"Not you, not in that dress, not without even a mother to believe in you!"

Flowers pelt him from above, sticking to his cheeks and smelling like blood.

Arthur scrapes them off his skin and yells, "What I am is not for you to decide!"

S ILENCE FALLS HEAVY OVER THE VIGIL. THE BONFIRE snickers.

The moon continues to rise.

Haf thinks about Mairwen and Arthur and Rhun together, how she's never felt a nuisance to them or as if she didn't fit into their triad, though most would expect her to. Arthur told her that she should, but she's good at not being offended by Arthur Couch, because she was there the day they all realized Lyn Couch was a son of her mother, not a daughter, and she remembers the way his eyes teared and he tore at his hair. She remembers wondering about her own body, and talking with her mother about what makes boys and girls, and her mother's loose answers that never seemed to explain much of anything except pregnancy. She even remembers trying once to say so to Arthur, that there wasn't much difference, and Arthur's face turned red, his fists raised, and he followed with the scathing answer that of course a girl can't understand something that matters so much.

She suspects there's nothing that will crush Arthur down tonight, unless the devil calls Arthur a girl.

And Rhun Sayer is perfect, so perfect he's like Three Graces itself, not a person. Haf loves him the way she loves the valley, the way she loves springtime. Mair, after playing the messenger between Haf and Ifan for three weeks, in a game of proposals and passing compliments, had told Haf their courtship dance was ridiculous and she was grateful everyone simply assumed she and Rhun would marry some-day. (As if there would be no saint.) "But do you love him?" Haf asked, and Mair said, "I love him best because I love the part of him nobody else sees: that great, empowering sin of pride."

Oh, but Mairwen, so sharp and ferocious! She is proud as Rhun and hot as Arthur.

Haf hugs herself tightly.

The moon passes its peak, but hours still remain.

*T*HE SAINT, THE WITCH, AND THE ANGRY BOY CRASH *together again—finally!—relief and terror uniting them. Blood mars Mairwen's chin, Rhun limps, and Arthur is soaking cold and wet. They stare, standing in a triangle, and listen to the shuffle, crack, growl of the devil.*

"He's just behind me," Mairwen whispers, eyes wide with exhilaration.

*A*DERYN GRACE STANDS WITH HETTY PUGH, THEIR arms wound about each other, faces to the forest.

The Sayer clan is spread like a recalcitrant flock of sheep along the slope, huddled in twos and threes, hands clasped in prayer or just together, passing bottles of wine and whispering to each other.

There is Sy Vaughn at the fire, one boot up on a thick log. He watches the forest with a pinched brow, seeming so much older than he is.

John Upjohn stands alone, and if Mair were here she'd go to him, so that's what Haf does. She touches Ifan's hand to let him know. The grass swishes against her skirts as she walks, and there's frost on the tips of her boots. She says nothing as she joins John.

Cat Dee lists sleepily on her stool, and to Haf's surprise Gethin Couch paces in short lines back and forth, frowning so deep he probably will never smile again.

She sees her own family, her parents and two sisters, her cousin and nephews and nieces.

Soon after midnight, Haf realizes when the people of Three Graces recite the litany of saints, they've added not only Rhun's name, but Arthur's and Mairwen's as well.

It gives her a chill, so cold the tears might freeze in her eyes. Mairwen the witch can't die, but a saint could—that's what saints are for. She shakes her head, whispers, "No."

John Upjohn turns his haunted eyes to her. "I'd have them take my name out of it too," he says.

"I WON'T LET YOU DIE, RHUN SAYER."

"I don't want to die, Arthur Couch!" Rhun yells it with such violence he realizes it's true.

The devil laughs, fangs gleaming, and the boys run.

HAF DRINKS A BIT, FINALLY, AND WALKS TO KEEP HER limbs warm, clapping her hands together, snuggling deeper into her shawl. She lets Ifan stand behind her, chest against her shoulders and head, and put his arms around her. He holds tightly, fingers moving against her arms in a gentle massage, and she feels passion stretched between each movement. Haf told Mairwen this morning her Ifan wouldn't be so polite as Rhun had been if she showed up half naked in his bedroom, though it had mostly been a guess. She has a wild idea now to drag Ifan to a secluded meadow and try it, in Mair's honor. Her cheeks flush at the thought of grass against her bottom and Ifan's hands on her breasts, and so does her belly, so does the crook of her thighs, and she leans back into him, entirely aflame.

The forest is black and silent.

Haf hears her heartbeat thrumming in her ears.

The moon sinks.

*T*HE DEVIL HOLDS OUT A BROKEN ROWAN DOLL. "YOU *gave this to me."*

Mairwen gasps, blood on her mouth and under her nails: She sees through the devil, past mottled skin and terrible scowl, past thorns and scars and teeth, past years of torment and hunger, to what remains of his heart.

"I HOPE," IFAN SAYS SOFTLY, MOUTH AGAINST HAF'S tumbling crown of braids, "Rhos and her baby are well in the morning. I hope, because the Moon was early, that it does not matter three went into the forest."

She nods, crossing her arms over her chest in order to hold his hands.

The bonfire settles, and Haf settles too, into a daze of blurred memories and hopes as raw as starlight.

Wind blows out of the northern mountains. It raises a hiss from the forest, tossing leaves together, and the long white claws of the Bone Tree creak.

*R*HUN BURSTS INTO THE GROVE OF THE BONE TREE, *falls to his knees.*

The tree is a mammoth creature of striped bark, elegant, arcing branches, naked of leaves. The moonlight turns it silver, and it throbs and shifts like it's breathing. But that is not why he cannot look away.

Melded to the trunk are human bones. Femurs and vertebrae, narrow fingers reaching for him, delicate forearms, hips and sharp shoulder blades jutting out like butterfly wings. And black-eyed skulls, mouths gaping, woven to the tree by wormlike vines. One hangs at exactly Rhun's height, and he stares at its empty dead gaze.

Horror unlike any he's imagined sinks through the saint, and he trembles.

There are twenty-five skulls on the Bone Tree.

*I*N THE FINAL HOUR—SHE HOPES IT IS THE FINAL HOUR— Haf pinches her wrists to stay alert, to keep her attention bright as the lightening sky.

Her legs are stiff, her neck aches, and her eyes are burning and dry. Ifan cradles her hips, breathing evenly against her hair, relaxed as if he dozes even as he stands at her back. It brings to life a well of tenderness in her, though her brow is bent with anxiety, her heart hurts. She longs to walk nearer, to be right at the edge when the sun breaks in the east. Nearby, Aderyn Grace has put her knees and hands to the earth, fingers dug into the grass. The witch's back bends, her head lolls forward, and all her brambling dark hair—so like Mairwen's—falls as a veil. She's singing a soft song, a hymn it sounds like, with words like "God" and "mother" and "everlasting."

*T*HE DEVIL DANCES AS HE BINDS THE BOY TO THE *altar. So it goes, so it always, always goes: The devil has won and this heart belongs to the forest.*

THE MOON TOUCHES THE WESTERN HORIZON.

Haf looks right, where half the sky has painted itself pastel, where the stars are vanishing, and with them her fear. A solid, weighty thing grows in her chest, like hope but colder. The time comes, the moment, the answer to nearly ten hours of prayer.

The townsfolk keeping vigil stir and shift.

The sun reaches its fingers to the edge of the trees, casting pink light along the roots and trunks, destroying that liminal plane where Mair liked to tease and play. Every single person strains forward, stepping nearer, and every single person in the valley is surprised.

Arthur Couch emerges first: fitting as he was the first to vanish. He drags with him Rhun Sayer, limping and near-broken and barely able to stand. Rhun leans on Arthur as if Arthur is the only thing in the world keeping him alive.

A whimper of relief ricochets through the crowd, but they hesitate; they hardly move, waiting still, until there— just there, behind the boys, walking in as painful and slow a manner, comes Mairwen Grace in a ruined blue dress.

But she is not alone.

THE FIRST MORNING

Arthur has never been so exhausted in his entire life, but the light of dawn piercing his eyes like nails is a welcome pain. Sometime during the night, he stopped expecting to survive. That he has, that Rhun's weight pulls down at his aching shoulders as the two of them limp out of the Devil's Forest together, is a surprise.

He'll never admit that, though, not now that he's managed it, now that he spent the night running from the devil and emerged victorious. And his friends are alive too.

Never mind there are already pieces he can't recall, as if every dragging step out of the forest pulls him away from what happened. From what he did.

But the sun is a star rising in Arthur's chest: bright, pure, full of clarity. Arthur Couch knows who he is after last night.

Even if he doesn't quite remember why.

He winces as he steps fully into the sun, grips tighter around Rhun's waist as they pause in the warmth. Behind him the forest looms, and he hears Mairwen's shallow breathing, and the deeper, rattling breath of that thing Rhun would not leave without. It will cost them, Arthur knows somehow, but everything came with a price last night, and everything that comes next will have one too.

The bracelet on his wrist twists tighter, tiny thorns cutting his skin. It's magic, but he can't remember putting it on. Soon he's going to be extremely worried at his fading memory, but right now he's just bone-tired.

Clear morning sky stretches over the pasture, and there stand the villagers in clusters and lines, faces drawn, hopeful eyes wide on Arthur. He sees Haf Lewis first, ahead of the others, braid loose and mouth open in the start of a brilliant smile. He hears his name, and Rhun's and Mair's names, gasped and called in relief.

"Mom," Rhun whispers, leaning heavily against Arthur. He can't finish. Nona Sayer doesn't hear her son anyway.

She, and all the others, have turned in shock to the thing—man, monster, devil, Arthur doesn't know what to call it—they brought out with them.

Alis Sayer cries out, "Baeddan!" and lifts her skirt to run down the pasture slope toward the emerging saints.

Arthur has a nearly impossible time calling him *that*.

Baeddan Sayer, twenty-sixth saint of Three Graces.

Why can't Arthur remember anymore how Baeddan is still alive? After ten years.

The Bone Tree—it's something about the Bone Tree, and the bargain.

All Arthur remembers is that the story isn't true. The Grace witches made it all up.

Alis begins a stampede, and soon the four are surrounded by what seems like all of town, asking questions and pushing to be nearer, joyous and afraid, startled and loud. Arthur mutters into Rhun's ear, "The closest to these black trees most of these cowards have ever been."

Rhun shakes his head, weary, avoiding Arthur's gaze.

Arthur hisses out through clenched teeth. It hurts that Rhun refuses him. What happened?

Vines tighten around his arms, bending him back onto the altar. Arthur closes his eyes and knows this is worth it if Rhun lives. The devil presses down on his chest. Two of his ribs crack in a flash of pain and

When Arthur swallows, a bruise presses his throat. His side aches.

"Be careful," Mairwen says, loud and commanding, even from her bloody mouth, split at the lip from a terrible kiss. Arthur remembers that, too, just as suddenly: Mairwen kissing the devil. But not why her hair is no longer than her chin, cut off in chunks, worse and messier than his own. She steps around the creature Baeddan, protecting him though he's a head taller than she and nearly as broad as Rhun.

With his arm about Rhun's waist, Arthur can feel Rhun trembling; his knees are going to give out and Arthur very likely cannot hold him upright. What does Rhun remember?

Alis Sayer stares at what's become of her son.

Baeddan ran into the forest ten years ago—they all remember it. They remember a brilliant, strong young man more charming even than Rhun, and proud and handsome. This is a shadow of what he once was, but recognizable to those who knew him best: It's in the shape of Sayer eyes and crooked nose and jaw; it's in the bearing and way Baeddan raises his eyebrows in hope.

His mother hesitates. Her hands are out, reaching, but she doesn't touch him, even when Mairwen shifts to the side so she can.

Because Baeddan Sayer is as young as the night he ran in, but his skin is sallow, greenish and violet like bruises and death and the first signs of rot. Dark purple blood stripes his bare chest in many parallel furrows, like he put his own hands to his skin and clawed again and again. He wears the tattered remains of a leather coat and trousers, but is barefoot. His once-Sayer eyes are black through and through. Thorns grow out of his collarbones, hooked in two rows from his heart toward his shoulders. His knuckles are gnarled like tree bark. Antlers hide in his black hair, tangled and sharp, wrapping his skull in a crown.

Staring at Baeddan, Arthur knows, though he can't remember why, that Baeddan's skin is cold, that the lost twenty-sixth saint murmurs old lullabies like threats and sometimes screams and the entire Devil's Forest answers.

"What happened last night?" Hetty Pugh demands, looking furiously back and forth between the survivors. Aderyn

Grace is beside her, and there at the back of the crowd Lord Sy Vaughn waits, surprised.

Arthur barks a single laugh, but it hurts his throat and jars his cracked ribs. Rhun shakes his head, lowering it as if he is too tired to hold it upright any longer.

Mairwen puts her hand on Baeddan's chest, stroking the skin between ragged wounds, and says gently, "We ran, we faced the devil, and we rescued him who has been trapped in the forest for a decade."

Questions from everyone compete for their attention and the world tilts under Arthur's feet. He wonders if Mairwen remembers it, or is covering. Lying as a Grace witch is apparently born to do. He glances at Rhun to check the grayness of his cheeks and faint flutter of his lashes. Rhun releases him and steps forward.

Mairwen tries to speak again, asking for calm, attempting to take control of the situation, and beside her Baeddan lifts a hand to shade his eyes from the sun. He opens his mouth and says to his mother, "I'm so hungry," like a child's sad plea.

"Oh, baby," Alis Sayer says, falling forward against her transformed son. Tears stain her face, and soon Baeddan's blood, too, and the village presses closer. Some are laughing now, and calling up praise to God, pushing between Arthur and Rhun and Mairwen and Baeddan.

"Stop."

The order thrills through the villagers, from the certain voice of Sy Vaughn.

Quiet falls.

"This began," Vaughn says, arms still and outspread so his black cloak falls smooth as glass, "with illness and an unconventional Slaughter Moon. Before we celebrate, before we press too hard on these young people, we must assess the bargain."

Rhun slides a dark look at Arthur, then immediately walks up the pasture hill. His stride is less sure than usual, but he doesn't appear to be near fainting. Arthur looks to Mair, who meets his gaze with a stare of her own, and the two of them nod slowly together. Mairwen curls her fingers around Baeddan's wrist, and though he clearly wishes to stay with his mother, he does not venture a protest before going at Mair's side to join Arthur in following Rhun.

Three Graces follows behind.

As he climbs the hill, thighs straining, injured ribs aflame, Arthur begins to feel better. The pain diffuses like an old, angry bruise. It's working. The magic of the bargain. Whatever they did is working.

black, empty eye sockets stare out from the skulls, bound with snaking vines to the massive trunk, and shoulder blades, rib cages, all the bones forming the armor of the Bone Tree and

The sun is a burning disk in the east, warming the breeze; the smell of autumn ashes and bonfire and horse dung is as familiar as his own voice. Rhun is alive ahead of him, and the knowledge of it pulses in the binding on Arthur's wrist:

alive, alive, alive like a heartbeat. He senses Mairwen just behind and beside him, too, just as alive, just as connected. Their feet find a natural rhythm, and all three who ran into the forest walk across the hills of Three Graces at the same pace, tuned for the same song.

Baeddan Sayer clicks his sharp teeth in time with their stride.

Arthur is not afraid of anything, not even whatever it is he's forgotten. He survived. He's strong, and this morning he'll be whatever he makes himself.

Rhun leads them in a straightways path, not like the snaking dance twelve hours ago, but direct to the barley field, half razed and harvested. He arrows through the tall bearded grasses, ignoring how seeds shake loose. The sound is a rushing roar as Arthur and Mair go after, as all the town comes behind, boots and skirts transforming the barley into an angry sea.

Reaching the place where he stopped his work three days ago, Rhun bends with a muffled groan of pain. Arthur startles forward but stops himself, knowing better than to help Rhun right now. But he stands behind Rhun with his knee near his shoulder, so if Rhun chooses, he can lean in. He doesn't.

"Check on Rhos and her baby too, and that sick horse," Rhun says, rough and tired. "But the blight is gone." He stands with a handful of healthy barley, casting eyes out over the gathered crowd. "The blight is gone," he says again.

Sy Vaughn peers curiously at Rhun, and Arthur barely holds back a defensive sneer. Aderyn Grace says the ritual words: "So the Slaughter Moon has set, and seven more years are ours."

"Amen," Mairwen tells her mother, and the villagers repeat it fervently. Baeddan Sayer tries the word too, dragging it out into an awkward curse instead. Mair puts her fingers over his lips.

Rhun says, "It's not right."

"What do you mean, Rhun Sayer?" asks Vaughn. The people of Three Graces press close.

Mairwen answers, "It might not last, again. Because there's no . . ." She winces and shakes her head as if she can't remember. "Baeddan is here, and that means he didn't die, but nor did he, exactly, survive. But his bargain held seven full years. He was this, and trapped in the forest, but we still don't know why the Slaughter Moon happened fast now, after John Upjohn and—and—"

"We need rest," Arthur says. He meets Lord Vaughn's mismatched eyes and then looks around at everybody.

"Let's get these young men food and rest, and our young witch, too," Vaughn says, spreading a smile.

It's the usual way for the day after the run to go: The saint, if he survives, is taken home for rest and food, and when he's recovered the town will welcome him with a less desperate feast in the square. A thing to quietly honor him, an opportunity to give him gifts or ask for additional blessings. Last time, with John Upjohn, it had been more than a week before the saint agreed to do it, and then he only sat on a stool, rigid and silent, while the people ate around him and gave their gifts to his mother or Mairwen for safekeeping.

Arthur wonders what John Upjohn remembers about the devil.

"What happened inside the forest?" asks Per Argall.

"Tonight," Arthur says, wanting time first with only Mairwen and Rhun. He wants to know if they remember more than he does, or less.

Mair glances his way as the morning sun glints off the hair and thorns circling her wrist, and the small bone woven against the soft underside, right above her pulse. A similar delicate bone touches Arthur's own fluttering pulse, and one tied desperately to Rhun's as well. Where did these bones come from? He frowns.

"Yes," she agrees. "Tonight we'll be well enough, and tell our story."

All around their friends, neighbors, cousins, families smile with relief, clasping hands, congratulating them and declaring wondrous predictions for the years to come. Nona Sayer touches her boy's bloody brow, pats her hands against his curls, half tied back, half loose and flared in messy coils. She doesn't smile, but her relief is palpable. She reaches for Arthur then, and more firmly than ever wraps an arm around his neck.

Arthur grins and catches Rhun's hollow gaze, then Mairwen's wild one.

The bargain is bound, for now.

• • •

MAIRWEN REFUSES TO ALLOW HERSELF TO BE separated from any of the boys. No one argues with her, except her mother hugs her tight. "You should have me with you too, while you rest."

"No, Mother," Mair whispers. Aderyn smells like bonfire smoke and bitter flowers. Mairwen feels tears in her closed eyes. Her head throbs and her wrist, too, where the thorny binding pulls taught. After last night, she wants to sink into her mother's lap and confess all her fading memories before they're gone. But Baeddan is proof that the story the Grace witches tell is a lie, and Mair can't be sure her mother didn't know. Aderyn said the saint did not have to die, only choose to die, so perhaps this living monster Baeddan is exactly what her mother meant, and this was Rhun's true fate.

And what does Aderyn know about memory charms?

With a small sigh, Aderyn touches the ragged ends of Mairwen's chopped hair. "Will you tell me the story of this at least, daughter?"

"I did it myself," she says, anger dragging at her mouth because she can't quite remember why. A gift? A spell? There is hair in the bracelet on her wrist. "I'm sorry about the dress," she adds, glancing down at the stained, torn blue skirt of her gown. The bodice is streaked with drying blood—scarlet and violet both, splatter from all four of them.

blood sprays her chest and neck, and she screams, "Stop!" Arthur falls to his knees, the devil—no, Baeddan—behind him

Mair shudders, then turns it into a shake of her head. She winds her fingers through Baeddan's cold ones. He jerks his hand closed, too tight.

Nona Sayer leaves her hand on Rhun's shoulder. "I'd have my boys in my home."

"Mom," Rhun whispers. He takes her hand and kisses her palm, leaning his cheek against it. "I'm just going to rest, and I'd rather with people who . . ."

"Who know," Arthur finishes, when it's clear Rhun won't or can't.

It makes Mairwen search the crowd for John Upjohn. Does he know? Does he remember? Her heart grows thorns of anger sharp enough to make her gasp. Baeddan says, "No one knows," and bares his fangs for the first time.

The crowd gasps, even steady Nona Sayer.

Sy Vaughn says, "What a pitiful creature," with what sounds like true pity.

Then Baeddan moans and covers his eyes with his hands, digs his fingernails into the skin of his forehead and drags down, cutting.

"No," Mairwen says. "Stop."

He stops.

Mair turns her commanding gaze out across the people, using only her eyes to part the crowd until there's a path for her to take with the others. "We have earned our rest," she says to all. "Go hold your most beloved and give thanks the bargain is sealed. Tonight I will tell you our tale."

She holds her chin up as she leaves, Baeddan's hand in hers, sticky with blood. She does not look for any other individuals, not even Haf, whom she longs to see. That will be for later, when her vision does not waver, when her mouth does not ache even as it heals. Baeddan is her priority, Baeddan and the devil.

What happened to the old god of the forest?

It's her own voice in her mind, an echoing memory. She doesn't know what it means. All she knows is: She trusts Baeddan, and this bracelet she wears—she *made*—is somehow binding the bargain. For now.

The way home from the barley field is a narrow dirt path stepped through the sheep pasture by two hundred years of witches' feet, and Mairwen keeps her heritage at the fore of her thoughts as she leads Baeddan and Arthur and Rhun across it. She feels strings of blood drawing thickly through her veins, curling and spinning like tendrils of vines inside her. She trips. Baeddan catches her elbow in his cold hand and presses her against his scoured chest.

"Mair?" Arthur says with quiet urgency.

She waves him away, giving herself a moment to lean on Baeddan. Her temple feels aflame against his neck, the entire side of her that touches him cooling as if she stands in shade. That brings a smile to the corner of her mouth, for how she used to stand half in and half out of the forest, warm in the sun and cool in the shade. She brought the forest out with her, the heart of it, the forest devil, and so wherever she goes now with him, she'll have the shadows of the forest to block the sun.

The vines coiling through her blood slide smoother, calmer.

His breath rattles under her ear, and he touches his mouth to the crown of her head. Not like a kiss, more like a taste. Mair shivers and holds tighter to him. He is alive after ten years, and the heart of the bargain is a lie.

"Come on," Arthur mutters, pushing past the two of them. "I'm starving and Rhun is going to fall over."

Instead of arguing, Rhun only continues to walk, sliding Mairwen a worried glance. He includes his once-cousin too, and briefly his expression grows darker before he forcibly shutters it and passes.

The Grace house sits empty, thatching gilded by the morning sun, walls smooth and white and the windowsills and door recently painted a cheerful red. Rhun had helped with the painting. They'd worked beside each other to the smell of baking pie. Elderberry and apple, Rhun's favorite, and the only thanks he'd accept.

There are no baking smells now, but only the sharp scent of drying herbs as Rhun pushes through the door and holds it open for the others. Mair goes straight to the fire to wake it up, but the embers have died over the long night and she crouches to shove in more kindling. "Arthur?" she says, and he appears with his fire steel in hand.

Arthur obliges Mairwen to set a spark in the hearth. She busies herself gathering the kettle and tea leaves while he gets the flames going. Rhun drops an armful of logs from the stack across the kitchen at Arthur's feet, then goes to the loft ladder and climbs.

"Rhun, wait," Mairwen says.

"I'm tired."

"We have a few things to discuss before we sleep, and before we face town again."

"I can hear you." Rhun pulls himself up onto the loft and disappears against the sloping roof where Mairwen's bedding tucks.

Arthur's jaw clenches as he grinds his teeth, and Mairwen is moved to touch his cheek.

"Why did you do it? Why did you run in?" Mair asks, looking at Arthur over her shoulder. She is a piece of the wild forest: tangled vines of hair; beautiful dress torn and heavy at the hem with mud and water; insistent, dangerous eyes; lips parted; cheeks flushed. An ax loose in one hand like she's the vengeful spirit in a terrible story.

"Saving him is the only way to be better," he says.

"Better than him?" she whispers, shaking her head.

"Better than myself."

He wants to ask why she followed him, but Arthur knows. Mairwen Grace belongs here.

Mair and Arthur jerk apart. It had been *his* memory, but she remembers it now. Until she touched him, she'd forgotten the moment herself.

"Is this the same as the altar in the forest?" Baeddan asks before she can say anything to Arthur. The devil drops to his knees at the fire, hands spread wide against the massive hearthstone.

"Yes," Mairwen says, though she'd forgotten that, too.

Baeddan lays himself against the stone, his lips moving in a quiet song she can't quite hear. It's awkward to reach over him and hang the kettle, but she manages. "Will you get water, Arthur?" she asks. "We need to wash."

He goes outside, and Mair continues preparing a meal. She finds cheese and dry mutton, ignoring the strange ache in her bones and the dragging weight of blood in her veins. Her collarbone, too, blooms with bruising that seems to grow larger instead of healing. She needs to remain focused, to get through eating and cleaning, and they need to speak together, compare memories. However meager they might be.

Food spread on the table, she calls Rhun. He doesn't answer. She's about to climb up to fetch him when Arthur shoves the front door open and says angrily, "She won't go."

Startled, Mairwen meets Haf Lewis's wide eyes. She's carrying a bundle of clothes. Haf shakes her head helplessly, and her gaze sinks to Baeddan splayed like the sacrifice he was against the wide hearth. "Mairwen," she says, strained.

And Mairwen is before her in an instant. She throws her arms around Haf and Haf hugs back so very tightly. Arthur makes a disgusted sound and stomps past, sloshing the water in his bucket. But Mairwen doesn't care at all. Like this house, Haf is familiar.

· · ·

RHUN STARES UP AT THE THATCH FROM THE FLOOR OF the loft instead of the bedding. He's too filthy to touch quilts and the soft straw mattress. This slatted wooden floor is good enough.

Branches as thick as his wrist frame the roof into place, stripped of bark and polished a lovely rich brown. Layers of wheat-straw spread in bundles muffle sounds from outside, holding warmth in. Though most of the ceiling has been sealed with limewash, this section of the loft is uncovered thatch. It seems older for it, darker, full of tiny hidden secrets.

Below, Arthur argues with Mairwen over how long to steep tea and how thick she's spreading butter on bread and even over Haf Lewis being allowed to stay.

It should amuse Rhun and aggravate him, but he feels everything from a dull distance. Even Arthur's spikes.

Rhun closes his eyes and glimpses the dark forest: leaves flashing past, the splash of marshy water, flickering orange light. A white veil. Arthur's mouth open, gasping. Mairwen with—Mairwen with the . . . no, with Baeddan.

He opens his eyes to the thatching. He should still be in there. Cut to pieces and bound down by the devil, to fulfill the bargain.

Flinging an arm over his eyes, Rhun grimaces, wishing he could smile. His lips have forgotten the shape of happiness.

Even that melodramatic thought carves deeper into the empty cavern of his chest.

Everything Rhun believed in was a lie. Baeddan is alive, and Rhun feels betrayed. That wasn't the bargain. That wasn't what he was promised. Baeddan was supposed to be at peace, Rhun's fate should have been to die or live—that is what the saints agree to. That is the price. But he will not forget there are twenty-five skulls on the Bone Tree, and twenty-five saints before Baeddan.

Rhun closes his eyes.

Twenty-five pairs of black, empty eye sockets—

Arthur's fist out of nowhere, slams into Rhun's cheek—

Rhun can't remember, but—

He's crumbling.

Twenty-five. Nobody survived. There was never hope—Rhun doesn't understand how it's possible, when four saints ran back out of the forest, but he counted. Again and again. Twenty-five.

Mair backs away from the youngest skull, shaking her head. Her hair is short and ragged, her eyes wide and black. She's holding the devil's hand! "My father," she says, and—

Exhaustion and disappointment drag Rhun down, and this thing on his wrist stings and pulls. He'd rip it off if he weren't afraid of the consequences. To the valley, to Baeddan Sayer.

"Saint, saint! There you are!" the devil hisses. "I know that shirt and those bones and the glow of your skin and smile."

Rhun presses his arm into his eyes and allows himself a grimace. Tears smear on his cheeks, draining down his temples. He's not worried about his lack of memories, because all anyone needs to know about the Devil's Forest and the bargain is there's no surviving. There's no choice. There's no hope.

Baeddan was always doomed; so was Rhun.

It's gone silent below. Rhun rolls toward the ladder, startled to find Arthur perched there, watching him with a pitcher in one hand and a scrap of cloth tossed over his shoulder. Blood smears his chin. Blue hollows under his eyes turn them bright indigo. His mouth is half curved up, half bitter, and bloodless.

"Here's water," Arthur says, clunking the pitcher against the slatted floor. "To wash off the worst of the blood." He climbs the rest of the way up while Rhun scoots over, crouching so as not to knock his head or shoulders on the low ceiling.

But for the blood on his chin, Arthur seems clean already. He wears a too-large, fresh shirt that falls nearly to his knees, over fawn trousers, and is barefoot. He kneels and dips the cloth he brought into the pitcher. "Come on, Rhun. That back of yours is thrashed."

Rhun says, "You missed some on your chin."

Arthur swipes the cloth over his chin, pulling it away pink with blood. He lifts his eyebrows aggressively. "All right?"

"No," Rhun says, but they both know he doesn't mean the blood. He means, *Nothing will ever be all right again.*

A moment of silence squats between them.

Arthur touches Rhun's knee and they both feel the heat of it in the stinging bracelets tied around their wrists with hair and needle-thorns.

"I was afraid you wouldn't forgive me for running in here before you. For taking it away," Arthur whispers.

Deep in the forest, he huddles with Rhun beneath the roots of a tree tipped over a creek bed, and Rhun relishes the weight of Arthur's head on his shoulder, how Arthur doesn't pull away when Rhun touches his cheek to Arthur's hair. They're blinded by darkness, anxious to find Mairwen again, aching from bloody and bruised bodies. Rhun says, "I'll always forgive you. Haven't you figured that out?"

Rhun knocks Arthur's hand away.

A familiar sneer parts Arthur's mouth, the defensive one, the furious one, but he makes no comment.

"It's healed. Not thrashed," Rhun says. "My back."

"Are you really not going to let me do this?" Arthur is incredulous.

Rhun glowers.

"Fine, you jackass." Tossing the cloth on the floor with a snap, Arthur clamors back down the ladder. "Finish yourself and I'll throw up a shirt for you. Then you come down to eat so we can talk." His choppy blond hair vanishes below the loft ledge, and Rhun folds himself over his own lap. He laces his fingers behind his head. He has got to get it together.

A shirt flops up over the ledge, sleeve catching on the ladder. It's a pale-green shirt, thin and worn, but clean. Rhun strips his jerkin off—he lost his hunter's hood and doesn't remember when—and slowly peels his saint shirt away. It sticks to him, glued by blood, and tugs at his healing skin. Rhun angrily rips it free.

The tattered saint shirt lands in his lap in pieces.

Colorful embroidery decorates the sleeves, just along the top and near the shoulders. Flowers and lightning bolts, stars and an orange sun. And there is a stag sliced in three pieces by the devil's claws. It had a heart once, Rhun realizes. Just like he did.

MAIRWEN SMILES—A SMALL, GENUINE SMILE—AS Baeddan inspects a piece of cheese, then touches it delicately to his mouth. He nibbles, uncertain, before shoving it all in like a child. The fire flickers warmly behind him, and hot tea diffuses heat in her belly. Haf sits quietly beside her. Baeddan lifts his eyes, which have slowly taken a more human coloring, the black irises streaked and flecked with green. Green of spring and emerald green, the dark green of shadows and the green muck of a stagnant pond. His lashes are short and as black as his hair, vivid against the pale-purple skin fading to deathly bone-ivory and yellowish stains. Crescent wounds from his fingernails frame his brow, glinting with the rich purple of his blood. He smiles at her, a soft, hungry smile, and she can see the curve of his cat teeth. Her body thrills, and the thick blood in her veins pumps faster, smoother. Whatever else, Mairwen remembers that he belongs here. With her. Or she with him? Both of them in the forest? The details are sketchy, but the feeling is real: belonging, and the forest.

She wants to go back.

Beside the hearth, Baeddan touches his hand to his chest, curling his fingers to tear, but with their eyes locked, he doesn't do it. He only taps his forefinger at the hollow of his throat, *tap-tap*, *tap-tap*, with the beat of *her* heart. Mairwen leans nearer, drawn to the rhythm. She feels it dancing across her skin, pulsing in points of pain along her collarbone.

Sliding his hand lower, he cups his palm just over his heart, where on his chest are twenty-four small bones sewn into his flesh, and three seeping wounds.

Arthur thumps down the ladder and sweeps up the trousers and shirt and vest Haf brought from Braith Bowen for Rhun to change into. He throws it up in a messy ball, then turns to Mairwen and says rather viciously, "He has got to get on board."

Mair scrambles to her feet. She was supposed to be using this time to clean herself up too, not commune with the twenty-sixth saint. But Rhun is sliding down the ladder. "On board with what, Arthur?"

"With us! With what happened and with figuring out what to do about it."

"It was all a lie. That's what I remember." Rhun shoulders past him to the worn table and takes a hunk of bread. Before eating, he glances at Baeddan. "How is he—are you?"

he corrects himself. His face is drawn, splotchy with uneven stubble.

"Warm, cousin," Baeddan says. Then he laughs gently. The laugh nudges itself into a wilder grin that suddenly cuts off. Baeddan scowls. "Baeddan Sayer is my name."

Rhun stares at him, looking exhausted.

Baeddan hums a broken melody and takes Mairwen's wrist, drawing her down to sit beside him on the hearth. She's glad to, and presses near enough her hip touches his, and when he lifts his arm it's natural to tuck under it despite glowering disapproval from Arthur and uncertainty from Haf. She can't help it: Being near Baeddan is like being with the whole of herself. The call inside her quiets. The tension and longing she's lived with all her life has an answer. Because he is the forest now, somehow, the heart of it, and she is a Grace witch. Her heart always belonged to the forest.

Rhun sinks onto a bench, puts his elbows on the table, and begins picking apart his bread.

Arthur draws a breath to steady himself. "Tell me what you remember, Rhun, even if it doesn't matter."

"I remember running, fighting wolves—black and gray, bleeding purple. They were nearly dead, or like corpses risen to fight. And . . . I remember a stinking marsh with strange orange lights. You punched me, Arthur."

"What! I don't—"

"And I remember flashes of teeth and roaring, and it wasn't the devil stalking me; it was Baeddan. Laughing behind me, singing an old song about a bird?"

"I know that lullaby," Mairwen says. "I was singing it, not Baeddan."

Baeddan says, "I *am* the devil."

Mair curves her arm up to his face and strokes his jaw. "You're the saint. One of the saints of Three Graces. The bargain made you into this, tied your heart to the forest like . . ." She shakes her head. "Maybe. I'm not sure what happened. What the magic is." She lets her eyes drift toward the north window, as if she could see all the way to the forest.

"There were twenty-five skulls on the Bone Tree." It's Rhun, voice dark and dull.

Silence falls.

"My father," Mairwen says, reaching toward a skull. The youngest, white and yellowing, the bridge of its nose sharp as a dagger.

"We should burn it down," Arthur says. "The Bone Tree."

"Then anyone might die!" cried Haf, standing suddenly. "Babies!"

"Where did the four skulls come from, to make twenty-five," Mairwen asks, "if any saints survived and left our valley?"

Rhun says, "It's all a lie. The Grace witches tell a story to make us agree to run."

Mairwen meets his angry brown eyes, and a tremor of matching anger raises bumps along her forearms. Her mother, her mother, her mother. Except— "Maybe they've forgotten too. The Grace witches. My mother. We're forgetting.

Maybe . . ." She only wants her mother not to be a villain.

"Tell us your memories now, Arthur," Rhun says.

"Baeddan choking me. Ghosts like my family, taunting me. I remember a marsh, too, and—drowning. Running, but it's a blur, like a dream. And an altar, I think at the base of the Bone Tree."

"Yes!" cries Baeddan, "like this one." He smooths a hand along the hearthstone where he's sitting.

As if he'd not been interrupted, Arthur says, "And I remember Mairwen asking me why I ran into the forest at all, but I didn't until she touched me this morning. I remember hiding with you in that dry creek bed, since I grabbed your knee in the loft. We might remember more if we . . . do it again."

The look on Rhun's face is too easy to read. *Now you want to touch me*, he says without saying anything at all. Even Mairwen knows.

She says, "I remember Baeddan. And running—Arthur, you climbed a tree. Not the Bone Tree. I remember . . . birds. Tiny little bites. 'What happened to the old god of the forest?' I said that. I also said, 'We are the saints of Three Graces.'"

"I remember saying that, too!" Arthur stands suddenly, too excited to be calm. "*We are the saints.* We said it when we made the charm, I think."

Baeddan whispers, "It tasted so good."

They all stare at him for a moment of stunned silence.

"What did?" Mairwen asks carefully.

He touches his chest, and the three wounds beneath those other tiny bones sewn into his flesh.

the tip of the tiny blade pressed at the edge of the bone. "Are you ready?" she asked Baeddan, and the devil bared his teeth. She took a deep breath, and cut

Mairwen turns over her arm and stares at the knobby white bone tied to the bracelet. "It's a bone from John Upjohn's hand. And the rest are there . . ." She looks at Baeddan's mottled, scarred chest.

"Holy Mary," Arthur says, and Mairwen thinks she's never heard such reverence in his voice.

Rhun shoves the heels of his hands into his eyes.

Haf gasps. "Why did you do that?"

"I don't know," Mairwen says with a frown. Her breathing shifts as something near panic takes hold of her. She stares at the bracelet, narrowing her eyes. *Remember*, she orders herself. She is a Grace witch! She should remember.

"Why did we forget?" Rhun demands. "Why is that part of the bargain? Nobody ever told us that, did they! John should have. If he forgot too. Or is it—is it different for us?"

Mair thinks of John Upjohn and his haunted eyes, his nightmares. He remembers something, but maybe not all.

"We forget to keep the ones who run back out from telling us the truth," Arthur says as if it is obvious. "The four who survived, and John, if they'd told us they saw the previous saint, the story would have fallen apart."

"That's giving Three Graces plenty of credit. Assuming anyone would care," Rhun says. The bitterness turns Mair's stomach. It falls too hard and ugly from Rhun Sayer's lips.

Arthur glances at her, clearly just as worried about Rhun.

"It's also assuming," Mair says, "this is always what happens: A saint goes in, is bound to the forest, and becomes like Baeddan. Then they stalk the next saint, and that saint replaces the old *as* the devil? Unless they run out again."

Baeddan moans softly.

"The magic . . . works," Mair says, thinking, *Life, death, and blessing in between.*

"What do you remember, Baeddan?" Haf asks, then bites her lips as she watches him.

He touches a line of scarring that slides down his chest, ropy and purple. His head shakes in tiny fast motions. "The devil who chased me was the last saint, horned and vicious," he whispers. "I ran and ran, and then I was—chasing. I chased John Upjohn because he smelled right. His breath tasted like sacrifice. So did yours, Rhun Sayer." His claws cut into his flesh, and new violet blood blossoms. With the dull white of the bones sewn over his heart, his chest is like a meadow scattered with spring flowers.

Mairwen puts her hand on his.

Baeddan bares his sharp teeth and rolls up onto his feet quick enough Mairwen barely scrambles out of the way. He says, "The forest sang to me, lullabies and soothing hymns, and we made things together, creatures and—and new flowers. I tried. I tried to be what the forest needed, but I'm not good enough. I'm not—I don't remember, except! If I bound Rhun Sayer onto the altar slab, I would be free! My head on the Bone Tree with the rest of them, to make Rhun Sayer the devil in my place."

He pants, sweat glistening across his mottled forehead. "It's calling me," he moans.

"Baeddan," Mair soothes. "Baeddan Sayer."

Slowly, slowly Baeddan's lips lower over his teeth, and his brow smooths. He blinks again and again, shoulders drooping. "Baeddan Sayer," he whispers.

Mairwen holds on to his clammy shoulder and checks on Haf.

Her friend's cheeks are deep pink, but she's holding herself still. *Sorry*, she mouths.

"I feel it too," Rhun says. "Calling me. It wants me back."

It's on Mair's tongue to say she wants to go back inside the forest; maybe they'll remember if they go back inside.

Mairwen Grace.

Forest daughter.

She grips Baeddan's hand and sees a vision of Rhun, her Rhun, sliced open and bound to the Bone Tree's altar, vines piercing his wrists and thighs, twining through his rib cage, transforming him into a devil. It isn't a memory, but Baeddan moans again, and his hand under hers trembles.

Warmth hugs her wrist, and she sees Rhun's mouth twitch. Arthur clenches his jaw. They both feel it too, because of the charm binding them together.

She doesn't know how she made these or how much

time they have until the bargain breaks again, and she's dizzy suddenly. Her collarbone aches, her skull throbs, and blood drags through her veins slow and thick.

If she goes into the forest, all will be well.

Mairwen Grace.

She stands, distancing herself from Baeddan's touch, from all of them.

"It calls the survivors back," she whispers. "They leave the valley, maybe, but they come back. And they die. That must be what we realized in the forest. There is no surviving."

"No hope," Rhun adds. "I was a saint only to be slaughtered."

"I will make this right," Mairwen whispers. "I have to— lie down." She rushes into her mother's back bedroom.

Closing the door, she presses her back hard against it and digs her fingers into her chest exactly as Baeddan does. Her breath comes quickly and her collar aches and itches.

Her eyes fly open as her fingers push at the skin over her collarbone. Beneath the skin she feels small bumps, like her collarbone is growing hard boils. She walks her fingers along them, staring straight ahead at the fan of beautiful goose feathers hanging on the wall.

Baeddan has a row of thorns growing in short hooks from his collarbone.

Mairwen holds her hands before her, inspecting them.

The bracelet of hair and bone and thorns twists tightly around her wrist, stinging in a dozen places. But there's nothing obviously changed about her hands. Her fingernails are ragged and bluer than usual from being cold so many hours. She touches her face and hair, exploring with her fingers everything she can touch. She strips out of the bodice and overskirt, removes her shift and leggings, socks and boots until she's naked in her mother's room, shivering and running her hands everywhere, hunting for irregularities. All she finds are scabs and shallow scrapes from the night, mostly on her arms and neck and scalp, tiny bites, and the closing wounds created by invasive trees lifting her off her feet.

At her mother's trunk, she pulls out a long wool shirt and drags it on. She climbs into her mother's bed and huddles under the quilt, breathing deep of Aderyn's flower smell that's sunk into the pillow and mattress.

M AIRWEN LEAVES A VOID WHEN SHE DEPARTS. They stare at each other until Haf, very practically, sets more tea to cook and Rhun attacks some mutton, frowning.

Baeddan crouches at the hearthstone, hands dug through his hair and sharp thorns, humming to himself.

Arthur burns to say something to Rhun, to break him out of this dark mood, but Arthur's never been one for speeches or comfort. Especially not with Haf Lewis and the devil for witnesses. He focuses on not squirming, on staying where he is, when much of him would like to walk out that front door and burn it all down. Make the choice for all of them. Rhun's right: The bargain is a lie, and it shouldn't be remade. It should be ended. Three Graces should be forced to wake up.

Rhun says, "I'm going to sleep," and stands. Before climbing to the loft again, he crouches in front of the devil. "Baeddan, stay here. I don't know if you're tired too, but we have to rest. If you sleep, the bargain might—it might heal you too, if you can be healed."

"Yes, cousin," Baeddan says, putting a discolored hand on Rhun's knee.

Arthur thinks Rhun seems the elder of the two, the more weary. It breaks his heart and he *hates* it. He's filled with a longing to find some comfort for Rhun, sharper than it's ever been. For a breath, nothing matters except making Rhun Sayer smile. It's the bracelet—it has to be—binding them together, but when Rhun climbs the ladder, Arthur forces himself to ask Haf if she'll be all right, and at her affirmation, he follows Rhun.

His friend curls on the bedding with his back to the edge, dark hair a messy cloud of curls.

Arthur says, "We should go down and join Mair. I think we should all be together now. It'll make us stronger, heal faster. Remember more."

Rhun shakes his head.

Grumbling a sigh, Arthur sits next to the pile of mattress and quilts. He sniffs angrily. This is not a position he ever wanted to be in. He draws up his knees and props his arms over them, using his forearms as a place to lay his head. He waits, falling into a drowsy peace, until Rhun hasn't shifted or changed his breathing in several minutes.

Then Arthur carefully stretches out beside Rhun, back to back. He barely breathes, too aware of Rhun's body, angry about it, angry at himself for being angry, and finally falls asleep holding himself tense and straight.

*A*RTHUR RUNS HARD, LEAPING FALLEN LOGS AND *shoving through snapping branches, while the creatures dog his heels. He hunts for open ground to turn and fight, but there's no time, no place. A skeletal rat-boy jumps onto his back, ripping at his hood, and shrieks with laughter as he uses Arthur's hair like reins. Arthur flips one knife and slashes up at the tiny monster. His knife cuts, but the creature holds on. It slows Arthur, and other bone monsters claw at him.*

Grunting, he spins and slams backward into a tree, crushing the monster on his back. He's free for only a moment before another grabs his thigh. Arthur kicks, stabs downward with his long knife. The blade slides in too smoothly, and Arthur pops the rat-skull head off.

Laughter all around.

He runs again.

His pursuers are tiny and white, all knobby knees and elbows, some on two legs, others on four, with bloated stomachs, concave chests where the ribs press out like ladders. Their heads are the skulls of what they once were: rats and squirrels, owls, dogs, all with teeth and black hollow eyes. Some wear ragged capes of fur or feathers. They're all half rotted.

The darkness hides leaves and slippery deadfall, and it's all

Arthur can do to stay on his feet and ahead of them. He's no thought to direction, just getting away and leading them away from Mairwen.

His heel catches and he stumbles, drops a knife before impaling himself, and hits the ground hard. Rolling fast, he swipes with his remaining knife, bares his teeth, and growls. The bone creatures cackle like tiny ringing bells, clapping and dancing around him. One, fish-belly pale with a young deer skull, holds up the fallen knife, and then they swarm.

Arthur yells, tries to leap up, but they've got his legs, and two jump down from a tree onto his chest. It blows his breath away, and he struggles to suck more in again. He can't roll. He can't move. Then there's a cold blade at his neck, and the black, empty eye sockets of a raven skull.

This cannot be the end. He will not die here, so shortly into his run. He will not die by these damned tiny monsters.

But his head rings and his chest burns. They're tearing at his coat, tugging open ties to push it open and reveal his wool shirt. One whines something, like words.

Another answers, then another.

Arthur's breath is evening, though his heart pounds and his head aches. He still holds one knife in his left hand as he watches the bone creatures. They surround him, at least twenty, hissing and whispering to themselves. He has to risk it, or they'll bury him here.

In a single motion, he flings his knife up and slides to the side. Their knife at his throat cuts, but he barely feels it yet. His knife slashes the bone boy at his head and Arthur is free, grunting under the onslaught of grasping claws reaching for his arms and legs and chest. One has his hair. Arthur kicks with all his strength, sending more of them flying back.

Then he's up and about to run again, except the bone creatures scatter.

A part of him knows the most likely reason they fled is because something worse is coming, but he leans into a tree anyway, puts his arm against it and his forehead against his arm, and breathes deeply. Pain spreads in a perfect line across his neck, but the wound barely bleeds, he can breathe, and he can turn his head, so it's shallow.

Carefully, Arthur puts his back to the tree and looks around. He's alone, surrounded by gnarled black trees dripping sap that glints reddish in the moonlight. Like blood. But the smell in the air is floral and sweet. Arthur steps toward his dropped knife. It's caught between roots. His back aches from blossoming bruises, and he's amazed he hardly noticed the pitching, tangled ground while he was down on it. Jerking his knife free, he sheathes it, and the other. His quiver is cracked and useless, from slamming into that tree to remove the bone creature, or from his fall, he doesn't know. Taking out the handful of arrows, he tucks them into the back of his belt as best he can. It'll lose him time when he needs to draw them, but at least he'll have them. He backtracks slowly for a few minutes to find his bow if he can.

Too soon, he realizes it's impossible. This is only the way he believes he ran, and he's not sure when he lost the bow. It might be all the way back at that tree Mairwen climbed to orient them.

He doesn't say her name out loud, though he wants to, just to remind himself how it feels.

At a quiet noise to his left, Arthur spins, knife raised. He stares through the shadows, unblinking, as if the longer he stares the more likely he'll be able to see through the darkness to whatever shifted leaves.

A light flickers.

It moves like a living thing, like someone coming toward him through all the tangled forest with a small white candle.

Ducking behind a tree, Arthur keeps his gaze on the light.

Could it be Mairwen? Would she have been able to find fire? But she'd be louder, surely.

It grows nearer, growing in length: It's a figure in white, walking slowly, its entire body covered in a sheer white veil.

Around it the air is hazy, thickening into a lovely mist that reminds him of sunrise, when the low fields gather fog and dew spreads like diamonds across the valley.

It approaches him, and Arthur steps out from behind the tree.

The veiled figure pauses. Beneath the veil he can make out a lovely face, a woman's face. Or a girl. She's smiling. The veil falls to the tops of her white feet.

Arthur Couch, she whispers.

Her mouth does not move.

The whisper comes again, behind him. He whirls around: nothing.

When Arthur looks back, the veiled girl is gone.

*T*HE FOREST IS NOT WHAT RHUN EXPECTED. HE TRACKS Mairwen and Arthur on and on through the darkness, ignoring the whisper of movement all around him, the *occasional growl. And then—then come the footsteps.*

Hard, even thudding footsteps like heavy boots or massive paws.

It might be the devil.

Rhun moves faster. He keeps his breath even. He has to find Arthur and Mairwen before the devil does.

Unless this is the devil behind him, and Rhun can lead it away from his friends.

But how to know for certain?

He pauses when he realizes the path he was following diverges at the base of this wide yew tree: Arthur's long-stride prints smeared against undergrowth leading northwest; the broken twigs off a bush leading northeast where Mair and her skirts passed so destructively.

Shadows crawl toward him.

He follows Arthur, telling himself it's because he believes Mair is safer. The daughter of a witch and a saint, she can rely on her own power, but Arthur is vulnerable. Losing Arthur is a risk he doesn't know how to take.

The path leads far; Arthur was running, and there are tinier prints around his, some like tiny dogs, others cloven-hoofed but in a two-legged pattern, some clawed like birds. He finds a bow and lifts it off the muddy ground. It's Arthur's, and Rhun holds it tightly, teeth clenched. "Arthur?" he calls, unconcerned with attracting attention. Better the forest notice him than attack Arthur.

There is only silence in response. He tracks on, making little enough noise himself, eyes wide for flashes of color or movement, ears open, senses alert for shifting light or cold.

The trail ends in a small clearing, signs of scuffle apparent in gouged bark and crushed leaf litter. A smear of mud. A broken arrow. The trees are narrow and black here, dripping sap a thick reddish-brown color. It's more honey-like than the blood it resembles, and Rhun rubs his finger through it, pulling it away tacky and smelling like copper.

Scarlet catches his eye, on the forest floor.

Blood.

But not enough to stop Rhun's heart. Only a few speckles across a spill of oak leaves.

Rhun stalks the perimeter, noting where the tiny footprints gathered and scattered, where they head off without Arthur, directly toward where Rhun is fairly sure the Bone Tree waits. It's as if he can sense it, beating at the center of the forest. Part of him wants to follow that call, but Rhun rolls his shoulders, breaking the pull. He heads the other way through the dense undergrowth, hoping it's the right choice to continue finding signs of Arthur.

Soon moonlight wavers ahead of him, in a pattern he recognizes as water. He hears no trickle or stream, and assumes he's located a pond or such, wondering if he can drink it. Probably not, but he has a water skin strapped to his back.

It's not too long before the trees shrink and thin, growing like elegant needles out of long grass. Orange light flickers from the earth. He smells dankness and rot, and a low wind groans, bringing a tang of burning iron with it. Not a pond, but a marsh.

Rhun's boots sink into mud, and bright green grass clings to his calves with sticky fingers.

"Arthur!" he yells.

His voice rings out, then fades, leaving silence heavier than before.

A splash draws his attention, something large falling, and he dashes toward it, lifting his legs high to get through the muck.

It's Arthur, facedown, limp. Rhun grunts his panic and grabs his friend's shoulder, turning him over. Arthur's hair sticks across his face, his mouth open and full of water. His skin is clammy, waterlogged. He's not breathing.

"Arthur," Rhun says, slapping his cheek, digging a finger into his mouth to clear it, shaking him. There's nothing. No response. "Arthur!" he yells.

Water and mud suck at him, lapping as he splashes frantically.

He hears the echo of his own name, cried back at him from a long way.

It is Arthur's voice.

Rhun leaps up, the body rolling away from him, sinking, disappearing. He darts forward, searching the muck with his boots, crouching to dip his hands again and again in the water. The body is gone. It wasn't Arthur.

Relief and terror leave him a special kind of breathless.

"Arthur!" he cries again.

"Rhun!"

He moves toward the voice. At least he thinks he does. Sound echoes strangely in this marsh. The orange light disorients him and the shadows are not attached to what they should be. He stumbles into another body. His mother, Nona Sayer, drowned, too, her hand gray and open-palmed, eyes glazed and white as the moon. Rhun bares his teeth at it, steps over her, his heartbeat hurling through him, painful and hard. Here is Mairwen, and there his cousin Brac, and there—oh God—the little hands of Genny Bowen. His youngest brother, Elis. His town, his family and friends, dead and drowned. Rhun knows it's not real, but he can touch them, lift them, smell the dank death, even as the marsh glows, tuning their bodies into monstrous form.

"Arthur!" he yells.

"Rhun!"

He's nearer, and Rhun runs, kicking his heavy boots through the shallow water.

He sees Arthur across a stagnant stretch of marsh, spinning as though blind, attacking nothing, mouth bent in a ferocious grimace.

"Arthur," he says firmly, dashing for his friend. "Arthur, there's nothing here but me. It's Rhun."

Arthur lashes out, but Rhun blocks the strike, twisting around to catch Arthur's arms. They grapple, and Arthur shakes his head. "You're not real," he says desperately.

"I am. Arthur. I followed you in, tracked you. It's all right. You're all right."

"No. NO." Arthur shoves free. His cheeks are alive and pink with exhilaration, his blue eyes wild, blood streaked across his forehead and staining his wet hair. "I cannot afford to believe you. It's not worth my life to believe you."

Rhun reaches out again, helpless. "Arthur, please."

"I'm sorry, I can't." Arthur backs away, shaking, wincing. And staring Rhun up and down with such longing it breaks Rhun's heart.

He knows how to prove it, but also fears it, worried the answer will make everything worse. Fiery light surrounds them, as if they exist in the center of a bonfire. The dark water ruffles at their ankles. White faces of the drowned and deceased stare with hollow black eyes at Rhun. Everything he knows and loves dead, destroyed. His worst nightmare. He steps forward. Arthur waits. What does Arthur see? What fear?

And Rhun plunges in. He takes Arthur's face and kisses him.

He expects Arthur to jerk away, cry out and hit him, but believe him.

Instead Arthur melts nearer with a small cry of relief, kisses Rhun's jaw as he wraps his arms around him and hugs tightly enough to make them both shake. "Rhun," he says. "It's you."

T HE FOREST CLINGS TO MAIRWEN. ROOTS UNFURL from the mud to lap at her boots, and night-black flowers reach for her ankles. Invisible fingers press her cheeks and tug at her hair. Her sleeves tear and her dress, too, and she leaves a wake of blue wool, trailing behind her in fits and thready tangles.

"There, there," she murmurs to the forest, and hums a fragile melody. A lullaby about courting birds, a lark and a jay, who don't belong together but recognize each other's songs. Fewer roots curl up in her way and the trees drift and sway out of her path. Mair sings it softly, then louder, though she never thought much of her own singing. She repeats the refrain again and again as she slowly walks through the Devil's Forest, voice trembling. Not from fear, but from a growing pleasure. Everything she sees makes her think how right she was to come in here. She fits. Light and dark together, all angles and promises.

She finds herself in a copse of young dogwood trees, blooming their snowy flowers even now at harvest time. The petals draw moonlight like mirrors, and Mair breathes in the clean, bright perfume. These dogwood flowers would make a lovely crown, braided into her hair. With their cross-shaped blossoms, their pale-pink tones and bright-green centers, the tiny oval leaves. Blessing trees, these are called sometimes.

She makes certain her shawl is knotted tightly and shoves the handle of Rhun's ax into it for safekeeping. The head presses up against her back ribs. Humming her song under her breath, Mairwen walks over soft, long grass into the center of this dogwood copse. A warm breeze blows, shaking loose some white petals that float around her. Mair sits down.

Her skirt balloons around her, settling as gently as the blossoms. Here she belongs.

Plopping her hands into her lap, she allows herself a moment to mourn the beautiful indigo wool and skims a finger against the slits of silk in the sleeves. Arthur snapped at her, when they first ran inside, that her skirts would hold them back.

The warm breeze skimming through her tumbling braids reminds her of the sun, and she hopes Arthur is alive. Her jaw clenches. She makes fists in her lap.

"Why have you stopped singing?" a tiny voice asks.

Mairwen leaps up, trips on her skirt, and lands in an awkward crouch.

It's a woman the size of a sparrow, naked but for dowdy

brown bird wings folded loose against her back. Her eyes are black as a sparrow's too, her chin pointy, and her body slim, frail, with only a hint of breasts and hips. She stands an arm's length from Mairwen.

"I didn't realize anyone but the trees were listening," Mairwen replies, thinking to herself that honesty is the only path to take.

The bird woman smiles, her teeth like needles.

Mairwen gasps, suddenly imagining her own teeth growing long and sharp and special.

"We liked your singing," a different tiny voice calls, drawing Mair's attention up into the dogwood branches, where another bird woman perches, spreading her speckled wings.

"Yes, we did," several of them chorus at once.

From behind the petals, more emerge. They push aside the flowers, rubbing their cheeks to the soft petals, embracing them like friends. One bird woman jumps down, spreads her russet wings, and soars in a modest spiral around Mairwen's head.

The first bird woman ruffles her own wings and walks a few steps nearer Mairwen. "Yes, sing again. Sing about your birds."

"I should go," Mairwen says instead, standing slowly. "I have business to attend."

All the bird women frown. There must be nearly fifty of them, and though they're tiny, Mairwen doesn't relish the thought of a swarm of their needle teeth chewing at her.

"I need to find a friend of mine," she says.

"Don't go," says the first woman.

"Sing," says another.

"Sing!" repeat a dozen others, in a discordant harmony.

Mair opens her mouth to say no, but thinks there's no good reason not to give them another round. "The jaybird crowed his lonesome song," she sings, under her breath, backing away from the first bird woman. The flutter of wings behind her reminds Mairwen she's entirely surrounded. She can't remember the next line, though she sang it again and again just now.

A bird woman lands on her shoulder, wings brushing Mair's cheek. The woman grasps at her hair and the collar of her bodice. "Sing!" she shrieks into Mairwen's ear. The tiny teeth snap. "Daughter of the forest!"

"I—I cannot," Mair says firmly, "I need to find my friend. I must go."

The woman pulls hard at her hair, and three more dive at Mairwen's skirts and face.

She bats at them, tries to knock the woman off her shoulder, but the creatures cling to her hair.

"Then we shall have your fingers!"

"We shall have your toes!"

"We shall have your pretty eyes!"

"Or we shall have your song!"

Mairwen covers her face with her hands, jaw clenched at the ripping pain in her scalp. She hums the tune frantically, and the bird women cheer tiny cheers. At least four tangle in her hair, flying around, pulling at the curls, and one grips her ankle, no more than the weight of an apple against her foot. She feels one at her ear, tiny fingers tugging the lobe. Another—or two—take her left hand and grasp around her thumb and small finger. One settles against her breast, wings fluttering as fast as Mairwen's heart.

She hums, holds herself still, though her body trembles to run.

When the song comes around again and Mairwen falls silent, there's a second of peace and a soft sigh from the bird women.

"Sing!" one cries.

"Sing," begs another.

"No," Mairwen says. "I must find my friend."

Pain flares at her ear from a sharp bite, and then the bird women pull at her hair. They bite her fingers and Mairwen flings them away with a scream. She knocks at the woman on her shoulder as blood slips down her neck. "No!" she yells.

"Sing! Sing!"

"She tastes like a saint!"

"She tastes like the forest!"

"Sing for us, forest-girl saint!"

The demand echoes and swirls around her as the flock flies circles, darting in to scratch at Mair's skin, to grab curls and tear. She tries to run, but they dive at her face, swiping at her eyes and snapping at her lips. They drag back her hair, tearing her scalp. They giggle and shriek, tangling her hair in the dogwood branches. "Sing! Sing! Sing! Give us your voice, or give us your fingers and toes! Give us your eyes and give us your nose!"

"I am the daughter of a saint," she cries, holding herself still again, hands out and trembling, breathing too hard as the burn in her scalp and ache in her fingers and her ear gentles. "I am a Grace witch, and I already gave you a song!"

"WE WANT MORE!" they scream. "Stay with us all night! We will not let you go! You are ours, Grace witch!"

Mairwen opens her eyes. She has power here. They can taste

it. Bird women perch on her outstretched hands, showing her those needle teeth. Bird women crouch at her eye level on the dogwood branches, tearing at the blossoms as they long to tear at her skin. Bird women stand on the ground, surrounding her in circles and circles.

"I will give you something better than a song," she says. "Something that will last."

"Forever?"

"Songs last forever!"

"We love your song!"

Mairwen shakes her head, pulling painfully at the curls tangled all around her face and neck, stretched out to the dogwood branches like snarling vines. "I will give you all a piece of my hair."

The bird women stare with their blank, black eyes. They blink together.

"A strand of hair!" one of them sings: Mair has lost track of which was the first. "Yes!" sings another. "Hair! Braided and curled for us!"

"What lovely hair she has!"

Mairwen says, "Let me go, and I will sit. I will take my hair and give it to you until each of you has your own. But free me, and let me sit."

Several dive at her, fast enough she startles back, pulling hard at the tangles. They grab the ends of hair stuck in the trees, unwind it all with skill, unknotting and unbraiding, until Mairwen feels the last of it fall free.

She kneels with relief, surrounded by bird women darting

nearer, fluffing their wings and clicking their teeth.

Tears build in her eyes as she reaches for the ax tucked into her shawl. She places it on her lap and then braids all her thick, brambled hair. Grabbing it in one hand, she lifts the blade and before she can think, saws through with five rough, hard, slices.

Twice as many tears fall onto her skirt.

The bird women laugh and cheer. One flies up into Mairwen's face. Mair cries sadly, but the woman only licks up one fat, salty tear. "Oh!" the bird woman sings blissfully.

Another takes her place, and licks, then a third and a fourth. The fifth bird woman bites Mairwen's cheek, and Mairwen gasps, pushing them all away.

Her hair spills across her lap, dark as cherrywood, tangled and dirty with bits of bark and even a few snow-white dogwood blossoms. "Come," she murmurs over her sorrow-thick tongue. "For your nests or belts or charms."

The bird women dance to her, skipping or flying, some grasping small handfuls of curls, others holding out their arms for Mairwen to tie her hair around them like bracelets. They bat her gently with their wings, laughing and picking at one another, braiding the hair or flitting away with it.

Finally every last strand is gone. Seven of the bird women remain crouched with their wings flared like mantles around their bodies. Mairwen smooths her remaining hair off her face. It's too short to tie back, too short to be in her way. She chews her lip to keep back more tears, sad but annoyed with herself for such vain mourning. It's done, and the hair will grow back. She presses her hands to her knees. "I will go now," she says.

The bird women nod, and one, perhaps the very first one, says, "We will find your friend."

Mairwen says, "He is a terrible singer," though she can't remember if she'd ever heard Arthur sing. She realizes her hair is as choppy and short as his now.

The bird women titter, and all but the first fling themselves up into the air, flapping hard and vanishing into the night. The first says, "Follow me, Grace witch!" before darting off. Mairwen dashes after.

MAIRWEN WAKES FROM THE DREAM WITH HER hands fisted beneath her chin, stiff and cold.

The memory of the little bird women remains clear.

As does—

The bird woman flutters her wings and darts left, but before Mairwen can follow, a devil slides out of the shadows and in one swipe grabs the bird woman midair, shoving her into his mouth.

Mair reels back.

The devil grins, teeth bright and sharp; feathers spill past his lips, and she hears the crunch of bones.

"Pretty witch, you're no ghost or green girl," the devil says, spitting feathers from his mottled chin. He leaps forward and grabs Mairwen's head as fast as he snatched the bird woman. Mair's feet slip and

Baeddan.

Yawning, she slowly stretches beneath her mother's quilt,

feeling physically strong. She rolls out of bed. Her toes touch the wooden floor and she rolls on the balls of her feet.

The long shirt she slept in pulls strangely across her breasts and Mairwen touches her collar. Those small nubs press up against her skin now without her needing to explore. Mair's breath rushes out of her. She hopes there are no more obvious signs of change. She runs her tongue over her teeth; they feel normal. She inspects her hands again. Are her nails darker? Turning to talons or thorns?

Sliding her fingers through her hair, she searches for antlers and finds nothing but knots and tangles. From her mother's small table she retrieves a bone comb and quickly picks the tangles free. Blood and dirt remain crusted in her hair; she never did wash herself this morning.

An urge to rush out and wake Baeddan or Haf and confirm there's no change in the color of her eyes or the shape of her mouth grips her, but Mairwen remains calm, dressing in an old gray skirt of her mother's and a bodice missing several grommets that was waiting to be picked apart for reusing the stays. She looks like a beggar, she imagines, though she's never seen a beggar. She wraps a scarf around her neck, crosses it over her chest to tuck at her waist and conceal her collarbone as best she can. Then she carefully slips into the front of the cottage.

Baeddan curls by the fire, as much of his body as possible touching the hearthstone, huddled in his ragged leather coat and trousers. He is so still for a moment Mair fears he died—that bringing him out of the forest killed him. But his chest suddenly rises and holds, then slowly falls again. The same slow rhythm as her own breath. Relieved, she glances at Haf, dozing upright in a chair with her head lolled onto her chest. Her hands are loose in her lap, all of her limp and relaxed.

Letting go a long, slow sigh, Mairwen thinks about the dream, about the bird women and the snap of their teeth. *Daughter of the forest.* Was there something else? Yes, the feeling in that copse, as though she belonged there.

She does not belong here.

The bracelet on her wrist pinches. She needs to examine it more closely. And get out under the sky. Closer to the forest.

She considers waking Arthur and Rhun to bring them with her, but no. Let them sleep. Let them remember everything they can. They would only keep her away from the forest. After putting on her boots, she opens the front door and steps into the sunlight.

Mairwen sets her path toward her boneyard.

Beyond the horse pasture and directly east from her house, the shambles is a hollow between two hills where a young oak grows alone and sheltered from the wind. Mairwen hangs cages full of rotting skeletons in the oak so nature might help with the job of baring bones but no predators can make off with useful pieces. She has barrels of water for loosening the most stubborn flesh and tendons without the fire or heat that would soften bones and render them useless. It's filthy and reeking much of the time, but her grandmother dug drainage to send the refuse water spilling toward the

Devil's Forest and Mair had always assumed the hungry spirits enjoyed the snacks she sent them.

Mairwen keeps a stool and flagon of wine there, as well as tools for working bone into needles or knives, combs or fishhooks or charms, or even bowls if somebody brings her the right kind of intact skull.

No one sees Mairwen on her way, and it was unlikely they would, for the people of Three Graces have always avoided the shambles, viewing it as a witch's territory except for some of the braver children or hunters delivering bones.

She's going to have to confront her mother.

The afternoon breeze gently rocks the cages hanging from the oak limbs. Mair glances over the fenced pen she built herself three years ago to protect the slope where she sun-bleaches bones. Ribs and femurs from two deer are spread on an undyed piece of wool, nearly finished. They've been out all year, and are hardly discolored at all. The wool has been a partial success. Her grandmother used to lay bones out on rooftops for this, but the thatching or slate tiles always stained the bones on the underside.

Beside the fence is the burying ground, where she puts some carcasses deep in the soil with horse manure, to decompose slowly and safely, also in cages so the smallest bones aren't lost. It's safer than hanging if she wants to keep all the teeth.

Mairwen takes a deep breath.

It's been only three days since she was here last, but everything feels different.

Hunkering down on her stool, she puts her hand in her lap and examines the bracelet. She obviously built it in a hurry. Was she trying to bind the bargain? Or save Baeddan? All of it?

The bracelet is such a scraggly, ugly thing in the light of day. She flips open the tin box in which she keeps her tools and draws out a pair of tweezers. The delicate metal prongs allow her to pull on individual strands of hair, exploring the design while paying close attention to how she feels. How the magic trips and tingles against her skin and beneath it, tugging at the thick blood in her veins.

It appears to be her hair, and Rhun's and Arthur's, twined together into a dark muddle, black and gold and cherry-bark, wound with a needle-thorn vine. And knotted around the single knuckle bone from John Upjohn's hand.

Baeddan went into the forest ten years ago and was bound to the forest. Transformed. Seven years later the Slaughter Moon rose and John went in, but came back out. Only his hand remained, and Baeddan bound it to his own chest. Then the Slaughter Moon came only three years later.

If Mairwen thinks like a witch, thinks of what she's always known and what she's learned, leaving room for things she doesn't know or has forgotten, it makes sense to her that Baeddan's entire body would fuel the sacrifice seven years, and John's hand last only three.

Col Sayer, Marc Argall, Tom Ellis, and Griffin Sayer all lived through their Slaughter Moon, but there are twenty-five skulls on the Bone Tree. Someone died every seven years.

She can feel the call of the forest, a mingling of curiosity, longing, and desperation. Is that the reason for the memory charm? To draw the survivors back in? Will the mystery of it drive them inside, never to emerge again?

But Aderyn told her the saint does not have to die. Only choose to die.

Either Mairwen's mother lied, or was lied to in turn.

In the story—both the Grace witches' private story and the one they tell the town—the devil and the first Grace loved each other, and Grace gave her heart to the forest in order that the valley might thrive. The devil, in both, said only the run mattered.

Who lied first? The devil or the witches?

There's a gaping nothing in her mind's eye when she tries to make an answer: too specific a lack to be natural. She knew the answer, but she forgot it.

Frustration has her grinding her teeth. She should march back into the forest now. Straight to the Bone Tree. She's rested and ready.

A step on the grassy path hisses for her attention, and Mair glances up to discover John Upjohn standing at the shambles' threshold. She stares at him, feeling unwelcoming toward him for the first time.

John holds himself rigid, expressionless. A wool travel pack is slung over one shoulder and he's in a coat and sturdy new boots.

Mairwen stands. The tweezers fall to the ground.

"How could you?" he asks. His mouth barely moves.

"What?" She steps nearer him.

He flinches. "Bring that devil out of the forest. He *tormented* me. Chased behind me for hours, and . . ." John pinches his eyes shut and jerks his wrist free of the extra pocket in his coat.

Understanding brings fury to pinken her cheeks. "You remember him!"

John is barely breathing. Mair recognizes the tension boiling inside him from his midnight explosions at the Grace house door—John pounding, begging to be allowed inside to sleep on the hearthstone or with his head on Mairwen's lap. His nightmares compelled him to claw at his chest and shake and tremble, and while sleeping he reached with both hands, distressed not to be able to grasp anything in his left. He says, "Sometimes in my nightmares it was Baeddan, but I did not—I didn't think it was real. I thought it was an illusion to terrify me! Everything in my memories is mixed up." His mouth pulls into a grimace deep enough she can see his long dimples.

Mair takes John's elbows, pulling them closer. Sorrow and pity twist into something like love again, or the echo of it. "I'm sorry, John. My memories are all a scramble too."

The muscles of his jaw shift. "You always calmed me. You and that hearth in your house. When my nightmares were too much, when I was remembering too much, all I wanted was to go back into the forest. My dreams told me only the Bone

Tree could soothe me, make all this end. It was so terrible that first night after I ran, Mairwen. Only you calmed me. Anytime I decided the only thing to do was walk back inside, I could think of you, or hold your hand and . . . I could stay."

"John," she whispers. "I hear it. The forest. It's always called me."

"I want to leave the valley," John says.

"What!"

"I think Vaughn will give me the means, as his family has for all the—all the survivors. Maybe if I get far enough away the call will lose strength. Maybe I can sleep again."

"I don't think it will, John. But maybe I can help you. I—"

"You are not enough for me to stay. And I cannot—cannot!—remain while the devil that haunts my every moment lives and walks in this valley."

"Tell me what else you remember, John, and maybe I can put all the pieces together."

"Mairwen," he says. That's all.

She holds his gaze, memorizing the feathered lines at the corners of his eyes, the wisps of pale-blond hair falling out of the tail to frame his temples and tickle his jaw.

"I don't want to always be alone," he finally adds. "I have to go."

Lifting her wrist, she puts the bracelet between them, the delicate underside of her arm lifted to the sky. "John," she whispers. "Do you see this strange bone?"

It is shaped like a pebble, with five rounded corners, and white as the moon.

"I see it," he breathes.

"It is a bone from your hand."

John reels back, stumbling.

She reaches out, grabs at him, but he shies away.

"John, listen!" Mairwen speaks fast. "Baeddan has all of them, all the bones from your hand, sewn into the flesh of his chest, over his heart, binding you to him and to the forest—it was the most power from you he could take without keeping you, and why the bargain only lasted this long! Because your hand was powerful, but not powerful enough a sacrifice to burn for the whole seven years. Now the bargain is only held by my willpower, my little charm! It won't last even a season. Tell me what you remember, so we can understand what the bargain needs. So we can keep everyone safe. Even you."

He shakes his head, backing away, heels knocking pebbles and tufts of grass so he seems to trip and move like a gangly scarecrow brought to life. "I thought my hand would be on the tree."

"The Bone Tree?"

"Yes. It was covered in bones. Don't you remember that at least? It was the center of all my dreams, that wretched tree. Strung with skulls, rib cages, femurs, and vertebrae knotted together like a baby's mobile. And the altar among the huge white roots, embedded there snug and sound."

Mairwen nods slowly, remembering the skulls.

"The devil laughed as he tried to drag me to it, Mairwen. Baeddan Sayer laughing and singing a song I knew. My mother used to . . . and I—I thought to sing with him. He was so delighted I knew his song that he dropped me and I ran for the light."

"I won't let him near you," Mairwen says. She must convince him to stay. Whatever John thinks, Mairwen is the only thing keeping him out of the forest now. "I swear, John Upjohn, Baeddan Sayer will not bother you. I'm going to drag his memories out of him, too, and figure this out. Please stay. At least for a few days."

John is terrified; it's obvious in his tight eyes, the pull of his mouth. The tension in the leather pocket where he's shoved his stumped arm too hard. "A few days," he whispers.

"I swear I will find you answers," she says, leaning near enough to touch her forehead to his shoulder, and her mouth is near his collar, where on her own chest the thorns press up, hooking through her skin like sickles.

T HE CREATURE WHO WAS AND OCCASIONALLY STILL IS Baeddan Sayer hears the Grace witch leave her cottage. Like a puppy after a favorite ball, he pushes up and follows her outside, but instead of heading behind her to the shambles, his gaze turns southwest, toward Three Graces.

The whisper of the forest is a chittering in his ears, or in his mind, or both. He crushes his eyes closed, thumps his fists against his temples. "Baeddan Sayer," he says to himself, as clearly as she would. The name fills his chest, makes his tongue more human, and he takes a few halting steps toward town. "Baeddan Sayer," he says again, straightening his spine.

Along the sloping, grassy path he goes, called by the glinting white of cottages and smoke rising, rising, rising, against the too-bright sky. He can't remember his mother's face, though he knows he saw her, only a few hours ago. What was her name? Baeddan claws his chest, the pain sharpening his mind: Alis Sayer. Will she be in town, or up the mountain at the Sayer homestead? She spent most days with her sisters in town. Ha! Yes, he remembers that!

Also, Baeddan is hungry. His teeth cut against his lips, and he tastes his own blood, just a trickle. The sun is so warm across his back, through the ripped leather of his jacket.

And the Grace witch brought him out into it. Into the sun.

He smiles, oh, he smiles, broad and terrifying, thinking of her wildness, the taste of her mouth and her blood, the hot press of her fingers on his face, on his wrists, her warmth in the circle of his arms as they danced among the bobbing lights of merry ignis fatuus.

"You are no ghost or green girl," he says wonderingly, leaping forward to grasp her face. To peer at her crackling brown eyes, the shattered curls about her ears, the bloody scratches crusting along her jaw. At her lips, narrow and pink, wanting to eat her, to bury his face in her neck and discover her tenderest flesh. She looks as delicious as Grace.

"Release me!" she commands, and he does.

Just like that, no struggle, no anger. He obeys her as the forest obeys him.

"What are you?" Grace asks.

"The devil," he says.

Her eyes narrow. She reaches haltingly for his chest, to touch the furrows of blood there, the ropes of scabbing, the hard root-scars grown over his wounds. He reaches to touch her, too, and she snatches her hand away. "No you're not," she says, firm and certain.

Laughter drops from his mouth. "No I'm not!" he cries, gleeful.

"What are you? You look like my friend."

"Is your friend the Three Graces saint? I saw the moon rise. I know the saint is here, running, running, running. I'll find him, you know. Smell him out. They always smell like that. Like you, hmm."

Goose bumps lift along the girl's arms. She says, "I came in here alone."

The devil leans nearer, nose to her temple. He draws a long breath, sliding down her neck. He's so close his sharp antlers gently scrape her cheek. Did Grace come here alone? He doesn't remember. Should he?

"No," she says, though not to any real question.

"You're Grace," he replies, rumbling her name like a purr deep in his chest. She gasps. He can hear her heart beating off-kilter, and all around them the forest is a stage, full of eyes and hopes, making this moment into a dark spectacle.

"I'm a witch," she whispers. "What are you?"

He touches the skin at her neck, just over her bodice sleeves. She stares with wide eyes, as if he's as amazing a thing to her as she is to him. He skims fingers up her throat and to her jaw, and a hundred tiny shivers race down his spine and arms, tingling his palms. Her breath is cool as it breaks over him, musty and sweet, and he tilts her chin up.

"A saint," he says, and kisses her.

It's only a moment, lips on lips, but the devil tastes her heart. She wrenches away. "Baeddan Sayer!" she cries.

The creature pauses. He blinks. He puts the butts of his hands to his eyes and backs away. "My name," he whispers.

Wind hisses through the trees.

"You're Baeddan," she says. "You've been here ten years. You were the saint then."

"No, the saint is mine," he says, suddenly vicious, teeth bared. "I must find him and drag him to the Bone Tree! That is what I must do. Get my fingers around his bones. Not like his finger bones around my heart! Ha! Ha!"

"Baeddan Sayer, no. Listen to me."

He digs his fingers into his chest, under the tiny bones. "Say my name again," he pleads.

"Baeddan."

Clawing his skin, he drags his hands down. "Baeddan," he whispers.

Baeddan lifts his head and stares up at the sun until tears burn in his eyes. He can still cry.

He tries to recall the cadence of her heart, the rhythm of its song that was not the forest's song. He should have followed the witch. Not Grace, but Mairwen. Another Grace. But here he is, creeping toward town carefully enough to be aware he's trying not to be seen.

His bare feet crunch through the dry grass, unattached to the pull of the forest, the magic that used to flow through him strongly enough to plant flowers in his wake, to curl vines up around his ankles if he stood still for too long, that drew the eyes of the trees, the roots, all of it stretching toward him. His forest. His heart and his forest.

This land does not yearn for him. It is quiet, peaceful. He could stretch out and slumber as still as stone for years perhaps.

Baeddan takes a very deep breath and sighs it out.

The buildings of town are like boulders, he decides, slipping quietly around from the southeast to come upon them where there is no path. He easily climbs a yard wall, onto a side building, onto a thickly thatched roof, for he has not lost any of his unnatural strength.

People move below him, though not too many, for it is early afternoon and many still recuperate from the long vigil. He hears them stirring in their beds, murmuring quietly to one another, some walking about from home to pub or the chapel. The sounds comfort him, like long-lost lullabies. He hums along.

What did he used to be, he wonders, that this was all he needed?

The Devil's Forest is a shadow in the north, embracing the valley, calling him.

Baeddan stands tall at the crest of this house he's chosen, so the wind hits his sore chest and flaps the ends of his coat. The sun slithers through his hair, finding the antlers that circle his head, picking at the thorns grown from his collar, and transforming his mottled skin into something like a pearl, or unpolished amethyst, rough and beautiful.

Here in the sun, between the village at his feet and in view of the wicked Bone Tree, so far away and yet threaded through his heart, Baeddan feels wild and raw. Why did he not bring Mairwen Grace with him here, to hold his hand, to promise him this home again?

Spreading his arms, as if he is the embracing dark forest, as if he will hold Three Graces to his chest, protect it as he died to do, Baeddan whispers his name to himself.

In the center of the village, young Bree Lewis stares up at the devil from the spiral of cobblestones, thinking he's come on black wings, come to destroy them all now that he's free. She screams.

R HUN WAKES WITHOUT FUSS. ONLY AN OPENING OF eyes.

Arthur kissed him. In the forest. He remembers perfectly now.

Something opens inside his chest, and Rhun thinks, *I would have died for only that.*

There's heat and comfort at his back.

Slowly, it occurs to him that Arthur is stretched there, spine to spine; they lean together where the straw mattress sinks in the middle.

He sits carefully, sliding off the foot of the low mattress, and kneels there looking down at loose, sleeping Arthur Couch. How he used to long for such ease between them.

Arthur frowns, turning toward the warmth where Rhun's body used to be.

Rhun touches Arthur's ankle and feels the strength seep through his fingers again. No doubt this magic has connected their health and power not only to the bargain, but to each other. And somehow, Arthur doesn't seem to mind.

The Grace cottage is quiet, sunlight pressing through the tiny loft window, diffused all throughout the room below him. He picks up his boots and creeps down the ladder. Haf Lewis dozes in a chair; Baeddan Sayer is vanished from the hearth. Rhun drinks down the dregs of a cup of cold tea before ducking into the rear bedroom. Mairwen's ruined blue dress is in pieces on the floor, but Mair herself is gone.

Rhun goes outside to put on his boots. The borrowed trousers are slightly too long, so he tucks them in and swings his tattered hunting jacket over the new shirt. He scrubs at his face and pulls all his huge hair back, irritated to not have anything with which to tie it. It's a wild cloud against his shoulders. He pulls apart handfuls and braids them loosely. The texture and sweat and dried blood keep the strands stiffly woven when he lets go.

Stomping out of the yard and up the first hill, Rhun takes stock of the valley: It all seems lovely and well. He should be filled with satisfaction, should be glad and awed because no matter what else, he ran into the Devil's Forest four years before his time and survived.

But there's a secret at the heart of the bargain. A lie.

Rhun hates both secrets and lies.

"I should've set fire to the Bone Tree when I had the chance," Arthur says quietly behind him.

Rhun winces in the bright afternoon. "Maybe you tried and I didn't let you."

"That sounds about right." Arthur laughs.

Sighing hard enough to shrug his shoulders, Rhun turns to his friend, who stands several steps away, slouched on one hip, scowling and chewing his bottom lip. Arthur looks ridiculous in the too-large shirt. But good.

"We should go home and get our own clothes," Rhun says.

"I look so bad to you now?" Arthur spreads his arms out.

Rhun stares at him, at the sharp lines of his cheeks, his neck, the way the shirt presses to his ribs on the windy side and flutters on the other, at his spiky hair and bright blue eyes, at his mouth. He feels it still, but from that long distance where all his desires and needs and hopes live. He remembers the fork in the forest path and choosing to go after Arthur. "I think I died after all," he says, rough and simple.

"My God, Rhun," Arthur breathes. He closes the space

between them and grasps Rhun's shoulders, then his neck, thumbs pressed to Rhun's jaw.

"Get off him!" Rhun cries, tearing at Baeddan's hair and coat, ripping him off the fallen Arthur. Baeddan growls, and Arthur goes wild, knife up, sneering, and lurches forward again—

Rhun closes his eyes tightly, bowing his head, and Arthur puts his face nearer. "Rhun," he says. "You didn't die. You're here, with us. With me. Stop being dramatic."

It makes Rhun snort helpless laughter. Arthur lets go.

But there's a shimmer of tears in Rhun's eyes when he opens them. "I feel like it, though, Arthur. I feel lost. I should be telling Mairwen this. It's the sort of thing I would confess to her, not you. I always wanted you to think I was impervious to—to hurt. To damage. I wanted you to think you couldn't hurt me, no matter what, so you'd stay by my side."

Arthur hisses. "I'm such an ass. And a terrible friend."

He shakes his head. "I asked too much from you."

"No, never. You never did. It was just . . . love you wanted, Rhun. I thought giving it to you was weak, or made me weak at least. I'm the ass for holding it against you."

Rhun eyes Arthur, frowning. Why can't he remember what happened to change Arthur? It couldn't have merely been death. He'd give anything to remember. Rather remember Arthur than everything else that happened in the Devil's Forest.

The two young men—so much older today than yesterday—don't realize for a long moment that their breathing has aligned. Rhun lifts his right wrist, and Arthur mirrors him, until they hold the binding bracelets together, not quite touching but existing in the same tingling air, pressing warmth against each other. Wind shifts the golden grass around their ankles, murmuring along the rolling hills of the valley with the smell of smoke and clear winter ice. Arthur opens his hand and Rhun follows this time, and they put their palms together, sucking in air at the same time at the strange sensation dancing down their wrists along the lines of their veins.

"It's like a handfasting," Arthur says, but the scorn does not reach his eyes. His gaze hooks into Rhun's, and Rhun almost feels something. His breath hitches.

"You kissed me in the forest," Rhun whispers before he can stop himself.

Arthur startles, frowning. "I don't remember."

Despair is a thing Rhun never thought he'd become used to.

"But I *believe* you," Arthur continues ferociously. "I walked out of that forest alive, Rhun, and I feel that way. Alive. On fire. I'm not afraid of you anymore. I'm not afraid of anything."

"You weren't afraid of me."

Arthur eyes him, incredulous. "I was afraid of what you were, and what I thought I was."

Rhun shrugs one shoulder, feeling dull. "You've always been on fire."

And then here comes Mairwen, hurrying toward them in an ugly gray and brown outfit. Rhun thinks there must be something symbolic about none of them in their own clothes, like everything they were before is so changed nothing fits. It's Arthur who reaches his other hand to Mair, holding it out as she marches down the hill from the pasture, speeds up to skip and stumble, her own hand reaching until their fingers skim together. Rhun takes her other hand and reels back at the great clap of energy uniting them suddenly.

Their hands grip tighter, and Mairwen gasps, grimacing as if in pain. Between their feet the grass sprouts green, feathering with new spring seeds.

"Mair?" Rhun asks.

Arthur pulls her nearer, so the young men hold her between them, all three pairs of hands still clasped. She shakes her head hard, eyes shut, mouth tightly drawn. Rhun and Arthur share a fearful glance over her hair. Rhun shrugs. Arthur shakes his head slightly.

They wait, watching each other and watching her, watching the thin tracks of clouds stretching in from the west. Rhun is grounded, heels and toes firm to the earth, and it's good and right here with the two of them, hands held, even if everything outside their circle is broken and pockmarked with secrets.

—they climb together onto the crumbling altar, hands held, all of them trembling as the branches of the Bone Tree tremble overhead, and the skulls rattle, teeth clattering in nasty laughter—

Rhun grunts at the memory.

Mairwen's head falls back. Color returns to her lips. His own skin is over-warm, but pleasantly so. Like sunshine and laughter. There are three tiny purple flowers flaring teardrop petals at Mair's feet.

"Violas," Mairwen says, blinking, her eyes unfocused, then, "I have to ask Baeddan about the Bone Tree."

"Where *is* Baeddan?" Rhun asks, eyeing the pasture hill behind Mair, from which she came.

She frowns. "Inside?"

"No," Rhun says, and Arthur says, "He wasn't with you?"

"Oh no." Mairwen releases both of their hands and turns in a rather frantic circle. "Where would he go?"

Arthur snorts. "On a murderous rampage? Or skipping though the fields of sheep, singing old shepherd songs? Who can tell with that one?"

Rhun says, "Home."

T HEY SPLIT UP.
It's not the best idea, but worse to let Baeddan Sayer wander. Mair heads toward the forest, to loop around the northern edge of the valley in case Baeddan is being drawn to his more recent home; Rhun goes to the Sayer homestead; Arthur gets the rather short straw of searching Three Graces itself.

God, Arthur feels fiery, awake, fulfilled, even after only a few hours of sleep. The sunlight is clear, his eyes see far, and he's ready to act. Arthur came out of the Devil's Forest fearless. And that makes him powerful.

What I am is not for you to decide!

It's a revelation he wishes he'd had years ago.

As Arthur tromps through the grass, down around the barley fields, and skirts the edge of the sheep pastures, he smiles. There always was something wrong with this valley, and he knew it, even if he was wrong about the source. Three Graces is ruled by fear. Fear of death, illness, bad crops, too much rain! Fear of little girls, even, and saints. He remembers thinking only the Slaughter Moon reminds everyone of their place, two nights ago at the sacrifice feast. But it isn't the bargain. It's fear. Not of the devil, but fear of change. Fear of doing anything different that might cause a ripple and bring it all down. Fear of a little boy in a dress, because he didn't fit into the structure of town, the rules.

There was never anything wrong with Arthur.

Except his damn memory. He's angry he can't remember kissing Rhun in the forest. A wild thought crosses his mind—*You'll have to kiss him again, then*—and it terrifies Arthur, so he laughs.

A small group of girls—a couple of Howells and Bethy Ellis—head toward him from the edge of town. They pause to watch him, whispering behind their hands, and Bethy is sure to touch her lips flirtatiously. Arthur's smile turns a little too self-satisfied.

And then, around the corner from the last row of cottages comes Alun Prichard, calling out something to Taffy

Howell. He stops short at the sight of Arthur, though, gaping slightly before he sets his features in a knowing drawl. "Couch," he says, "borrowing a man's clothes from your daddy—or Rhun Sayer's daddy?"

It's Alun's usual sort of jibe, more ignorable than hurtful, but that never stopped Arthur from rising to meet the stupidity before.

Today something amazing happens: Arthur laughs. It fades into a rather condescending smile. "You, Alun, are the last thing that scares me anymore."

Confusion spreads on Alun's face, and one of the boys with him claps a hand on his shoulder, laughing with Arthur. Alun shrugs it off, and Bethy Ellis says, "Arthur's a saint now."

Because he can afford to, Arthur shakes his head. "No, that's only Rhun Sayer. I'm still just my mother's son." Nobody can change who he is except for himself, not any saint ritual, not an ignorant, terrified town, not a night spent in the forest, not a dress or a kiss. He steps nearer Alun. "My mother's son who can still beat you to bloody bruises if I want to, and who will say otherwise?"

A scream rips over the rooftops.

All the young people startle, turning toward it and the center of town.

Arthur is the fastest to react, still tuned in to danger, and he runs for the sound.

Shouldering through a crowd at the edge of the town square, he grits his teeth and hopes it's not Baeddan, though he knows better. More villagers push out of their houses around him, most not noticing who he is, which aggravates him. He elbows past two broad men blocking his way, ignoring the curse from the older one, and finds himself at the fore, surrounded by the worried, frightened, and drawn faces of his neighbors.

Baeddan crouches over streaks of ash and charcoal left from the bonfire celebration two nights ago. His bruised hands cover his face and his back is bowed as he bends over, making himself as small as possible. The tattered hem of his old cracking leather coat flares around him like a skirt. His shoulders are tense as he slowly rocks on the balls of his bare feet.

Arthur's seen this pose before, and if everyone shut up, he's certain they'd all hear Baeddan singing to himself, nonsense phrases and rhymes without finesse.

The devil crouches, muttering, and Arthur says, "It's not as frightening as I—"

The creature thrusts up, hissing through bared teeth at Arthur, who leaps back, long knife out. But Arthur's hand shakes—he's too tired, too sore, too furious! "Back off," he snarls, and the devil snaps his teeth at him, laughing.

"You'll run and run, but you can't outrun me, no-saint, never-saint, saintless, saint-free, saint saint saint—"

"Baeddan," Mair soothes. "Come away with me. Leave them. You don't need to chase them."

"He can chase me," Arthur snaps. "Welcome to try, devil."

"Ha!" The devil lashes out, ignoring the knife that slices his side, and catches his claws across Arthur's face.

Arthur strides forward and bends to one knee so he's at Baeddan's level. He was right; the devil is muttering softly to himself. "Baeddan Sayer," Arthur says softly but firmly, as Mair would. "Get up and come away with me."

"Not-saint, never-saint, is it you?" comes the singsong voice, muffled by his hands.

"It's Arthur Couch. Use my name as I have the courtesy to use yours."

"Courtesy!" The devil's broad shoulders shake with laughing.

It makes Arthur's mouth twitch with matching humor. He puts a hand on the devil's shoulder, unprepared for the spark that passes between them. The binding on his wrist tightens, stinging his raw skin. Arthur doesn't let go. The devil looks up with coal-black eyes, monstrous and lost.

"Why did you come here?" Arthur asks. "Let's go, to Mairwen."

"Yes, yes, Mairwen Grace, the Grace witch, where is she?" Baeddan whispers.

"Is it really Baeddan Sayer?" calls a woman.

Half the valley at least is here, and more arriving as word passes. There are the Lewises except for Haf—who might still be asleep at the Grace house—their youngest girl hiding her face in her mother's shoulder; Cat Dee propped on her grandson Pad's arm, too wrinkled to see straight; Sayer cousins and both Parry brothers, hungry as they stare at Arthur. The smith, the cooper, and all the butcher's family, and men spilling out of the pub. Including his father, Gethin Couch.

"Yes, it's Baeddan," Arthur says.

"Baeddan?" A different woman haltingly approaches. Effa Crewe, pretty and lithe, a decade or so older than Arthur. Under his hand, the devil growls low and longing.

Per Argall, who Arthur would not have credited with such pluck, calls out, "Tell us what happens in the forest, Arthur. How did you do this?"

Arthur stands, using the devil's shoulder for support. "I'd love to tell you, Per. But we'll wait for the others."

Lord Vaughn steps out of the crowd. He's with the men who came out of the pub. The lord is dressed simply in brown velvet that blends well with the garb of the men around him, and his brown hair curls reddish in the afternoon sun. He seems younger than before to Arthur. Or maybe Arthur feels older. "How is Rhun, and Mairwen, too?" the lord asks.

Arthur shrugs. "They'll be along. Tell you themselves."

Vaughn puts on a sympathetic face as his half-gray, half-brown gaze falls to Baeddan. "Poor creature, poor saint. We would like to hear your story."

Baeddan stands suddenly, staring at Vaughn, and Arthur almost thinks he'll attack, but then Baeddan only huffs and laughs gently to himself, then covers the tiny bones sewn into his flesh with his hand. Spinning, Baeddan dashes away, leaving Arthur stunned. It's not the exit he prefers, but Arthur takes off after the devil.

. . .

RHUN IS TOO FAR AWAY TO HEAR THE SCREAM, MORE than halfway up the wooded path to the Sayer home-stead. His legs feel strong and steady, his heartbeat firm, though he'd almost rather still be thrashed, too tired to face the day, face his family or any truth.

Leaves fall gently, yellow and orange, pieces of sunlight chipped out of the sky. He walks with his habitual stealth, though he experiences a sudden wild desire to crash off the path, make all the noise he can manage to ruin the peace-ful beauty of his home forest. Stopping, he forces himself to take several long, slow breaths. Autumn tastes sharp on his tongue, and the first freeze of winter tightens the back of his throat. *This place is worth fighting for*, he reminds himself. He has to believe that. The people are as earnest and honest as they were yesterday. As he was before he knew there was a lie at the heart of the forest. He had faith in the rituals, in the sainthood, in himself. He owes them that faith.

A sour smile turns his mouth. Arthur would say Rhun is the one owed, and Mairwen that he's given enough. But he was made the saint, given the burden of seeing the bar-gain completed, no matter how much of it was a lie. It was intended as an honor, and he embraced it as one. He can't let his little brothers down, at least, or his parents.

So Rhun Sayer tries to appreciate the golden atmosphere and merry birdsong, the tiny hints of life that were so absent in the Devil's Forest. He hums, but only the first several notes of different songs. He can't quite fall fully into one.

The front door of the Sayer house is open, smoke stream‐ing gracefully from the chimney. If it were all shut up, he'd be able to slip in and grab clothes, assuming Baeddan is nowhere to be found.

"—won't be long," his mother is saying when he steps up onto the wooden floor of the house, narrowing his eyes as they adjust to the combination of sparse sunlight and hot firelight.

Silence falls, and a woman gasps. There are four of them sitting around Nona Sayer's gouged kitchen table: Nona, his aunt Alis, Hetty Pugh, and Aderyn Grace. He has no idea what to say, and so remains quiet.

"Rhun, my God." Nona stands up from her mismatched chair, but comes no nearer to him; it isn't her way. Hetty smiles through the weariness scoured under her bright eyes, and Aderyn stares at him as if he's a ghost, though she is not the one most gutted by their return this morning. That is Alis Sayer, Baeddan's mother, who walks to Rhun and care‐fully puts her arms around his neck, hugging him so tightly she goes up onto her tiptoes. He hugs her back, lifting her slowly off her feet, giving what he can. "I'm sorry for the shock of it," he whispers to her.

"I'm sorry for nothing today," Alis whispers back, drop‐ping away from the embrace with shining eyes and a damp, pretty smile. She puts her hands to either side of his face and shakes her head happily. "My son is alive. How could I be anything but grateful?"

Rhun isn't certain how to answer without revealing too

much of the tortured existence he suspects Baeddan has suffered these ten long years. He nods.

Nona wipes her hands on her apron. "Tell us now, Rhun. Your mothers have been desperate for too long, and you shouldn't force us longer."

"Isn't it better," Aderyn Grace says carefully, "to tell us now, before the feast, when there are no children to be frightened?"

It's the only thing she could have said, perhaps, to solidify Rhun's determination not to share anything he knows, especially with her, before Mairwen has a chance. His jaw clenches, his fists, too. He says, "Children are the ones expected to give all to the bargain, expected to sacrifice their lives. I think the children deserve this story more than any of you ever could."

Aderyn pulls back, hands folding at her waist, and Hetty clicks her tongue. Alis Sayer touches her mouth, and her eyes drift shut to let a tear fall from each. Rhun's mother plants fists on her hips and says, "You've changed, son."

He rubs the binding on his wrist, relishing the sting. "I'm not a boy anymore, that's all. I understand some things I didn't before. About . . . people."

Nona turns an angry glance at the other women, then says to Rhun, "I hoped a valley like this would never teach you such a lesson."

"It was either this lesson, or death."

His mother's face slackens in shock, and Rhun feels only a small moment of shame.

"We're never promised innocence in this valley," Hetty Pugh says.

"Such a bargain would require an even steeper price," Aderyn agrees quietly, studying Rhun with a level, heavy regard. "Where is my daughter?"

"With Haf Lewis," he says, uninterested in revealing they lost Baeddan and split up to find him.

"Is she so changed as you?"

Rhun stares; he's not sure. The forest was always in Mairwen, he knows, but the night intensified her, purified her somehow. She is more herself than he thought was possible.

He says, "Mairwen is her truest self now. Maybe we all are."

T HE EDGE OF THE DEVIL'S FOREST SWELLS WITH SHADows, and Mairwen holds tighter to Haf Lewis's hand, stepping fully inside. Haf gasps but joins her, squeezing so tight their bones crunch together.

It feels right to enter the forest again. The air cools and ahead all is quiet. She remembers something warm and peaceful in the center. The altar.

rough gray stone is warm under her fingers. She avoids the dark streaks staining it, maybe from rain or old dead vines, maybe blood. Mairwen imagines laying herself down upon it and falling into a long, relaxing sleep. She's so tired, and this bed would welcome her bones. Her heart. It doesn't frighten her, though perhaps it should. A breeze rattles the thorns and dry leaves tossed over the surface of the altar. Dawn arrives soon. An hour or less. Beyond the altar, the Bone Tree is beautiful: white as the moon, layered with armor of bones. Half alive. She could make it fully alive.

"Mairwen Grace."

She lifts her head.

"I never thought to stand here," Haf whispers.

Mair transfers her grip to Haf's shoulder, hugging her friend. "There is an altar at the base of the Bone Tree just like the hearth at my mother's house, and if you touch it, it's warm, despite being hard granite. The warmth is the heart of the forest, and magic pulses out through the root system and canopy, the way our blood is in our fingers and toes."

"You make it sound like it's magic from a fairy tale."

"Oh, Haf." Mair looks into the forest, at the tall black trees and popping green undergrowth, the scatter of tiny white flowers, and every layer of shadows back and back and back. "This is all a fairy tale."

Haf wraps her arm around Mairwen's waist. "It's too real for that."

"We tell it as a story, the three Grace sisters and the devil. It's about falling in love with monsters and giving your heart up for your home. We tell it to the boys so they'll have it like a shield. We tell it to the entire town so none of us question the details of the bargain."

Wind blows the canopy overhead, littering them with tiny oval leaves, dry and brown and pale yellow, and Haf shudders, making an involuntary move to run back out into the sun.

Just then, the bruising ache along Mairwen's collarbones pulses, and she thinks she hears the creaking sound of branches growing and leaning in a harsh wind. Mair closes her eyes, focuses on the pain until it dissipates. What is she becoming?

beneath her sheer veil, the girl puts a finger to her lips for quiet

Mairwen closes her eyes, reaching out with her hand as if she can grasp the memory.

A tiny voice calls out *"Mairwen Grace!"* from deeper in the forest.

Haf startles, tugging away. "What was that? Who is in there?"

Mair walks forward, crunching over a bed of fallen leaves. It was not Baeddan, but a high, lovely voice, like a bird. She smiles. "Some bird women, I think, tiny creatures with sharp teeth. Be careful."

"Oh," murmurs Haf in awe.

"Mairwen Grace!"

Darting toward them from branch to branch is a drab sparrow woman. She flits and leaps in a stunted arc of flight. "Is that you, Mairwen Grace?"

"Hello, lovely," Mair calls, holding out a hand palm-up. The bird alights upon it, hands grasping at Mairwen's wrist.

Haf covers her mouth with her hands. "How wonderful

and terrifying," she says through pressed fingers.

"This is my friend Haf Lewis," Mairwen says.

The bird woman grins, displaying all her needle teeth. "Though she broke our forest, any friend of the Grace witch is a friend of mine." Then she stands, her bare feet tickling Mair's palm, and puts her hands to her waist, where a braid of red-brown hair circles her like a belt.

"It is an honor to meet you, Lady Sparrow." Haf even goes so far as to curtsy neatly.

The bird woman adores it. She whistles happily. "I like you. Do you sing?"

"Later," Mairwen says. "What do you mean, I broke your forest?"

"You stole our god and gave us none new!" the bird woman accuses.

"Your god?"

"The witches call him a devil!" She stretches her wings to their full expanse: near a foot, perhaps, if one is measuring generously.

"What happened to the old god of the forest?" Mairwen cries out.

The memory remains an echo of her voice, just the question, again and again.

Mairwen strokes the bird woman's long feathers, puzzling through what she knows. "Baeddan. The twenty-sixth saint, he stayed in the forest and . . . became the god. That's what we call the devil."

"It is uncomfortable in the forest today. Our heart needs a heart."

"My mother always said he was a god, not a devil," Mair says, glancing to Haf.

"Yes, yes, you understand, pretty girl, Grace witch. Oh, you are wise as you are beautiful." The bird woman offers a flirtatious, sneaky smile.

Mair draws the bird woman nearer to her breast. "How long has there been a devil in your forest, do you know?"

"The devil changes, again and again, new boys, new hearts, new songs."

"And before the devil, what then?"

The bird woman cocks her head, very like a bird. "There has always been a devil."

"Did . . . did the devil always change?" she asks carefully. "The first one, the old god?"

"No," the bird woman trills. "The old god left the heart tree, the tree at the heart of our forest, and everything was different."

Breathless, Mairwen holds the bird woman close, recalling Baeddan's taste for them, and strokes her long primary feathers. The rhythm of her petting meets the rhythm of her heartbeat, the rhythm of her breath and the itch across her chest. She feels it, too, in her fingers, and along her spine, and flushing over every inch of her skin. Changing her. Mair tosses the bird woman lightly up, and as the creature takes to flight, she crouches. Though Haf hums in confusion, Mairwen unlaces and knocks off her boots,

then places her bare feet against the earth of the forest. It's so cool and comforting her shoulders relax and she lets her head fall back.

The old god of the forest broke free of the Bone Tree. Mairwen would risk all their lives to wager that moment was the start of this bargain. The old god and the youngest Grace witch. The story says they loved each other, but can the story be trusted at all?

Mairwen Grace stands there, toes dug into the Devil's Forest, eyes shut, and the wind shakes her hair even as it shakes the canopy of autumn leaves. She is terrified, suddenly, and trying to bury the fear.

"Mairwen, I don't know what's happening," Haf murmurs.

Mair snaps her head up, looks down at her feet. Spring-green tendrils curl out of the dirt to tease at her toes and ankles, blooming even smaller star-shaped purple flowers.

S UNSET IS AN ELABORATE TRICK TONIGHT. WISPY clouds tumble along a horizon scratched with vibrant pink, and the sky is the rich purple that used to put Baeddan Sayer in mind of violas but now only reminds him of his blood.

He leans in the lee of the church, disappeared in shadows, awaiting the Grace witch.

Arthur Couch, tall and mean and bright as the morning star, runs interference for him, standing between Baeddan and the rest of the village, on one cocked hip and drinking

from a mug of wine. He offers some to Baeddan, who drinks it fast as water. The tartness lingers on his tongue as if the wine has a life of its own.

Baeddan cannot close his eyes, or all of this will vanish. He'll be back in the burning heart of the forest. The Bone Tree twisting all around him, tiny threads of roots piercing his ankles and wrists, penetrating the skin over his ribs, looping and winding through his bones in a ferocious agony. The forest ate his flesh and bones, spat him out as this thing, this devil with nonsense songs and lullabies looping in his imagination, faces and names confused together, and that great need pushing him on and on. The words find themselves, and he understands them, when he listens: *Find the saint, the saint, the saint. Find him.*

It's difficult, nearly impossible, for Baeddan to look at even Arthur Couch, who was not the saint, never the saint, and do anything besides strike. When Rhun Sayer arrives in the village square, dark and handsome in fresh, fitting clothes, the anointed saint, Baeddan cannot breathe for the compulsion racking his heart. He thrusts his fists into his eyes, grinding painfully until starbursts explode in the darkness, until he sees streaks and spots of white and blurred red.

The hiss and grind of the crowd talking, shifting, waiting, drinking, setting out food and dragging long tables into place, children yelling, running feet, all of it swarms together in a rush like the rush of blood in his ears, like a roaring wind blowing through the corrupted branches of the Bone Tree. It overwhelms him. He chews his own teeth, grinding, clicking,

clicking, oh yes—the click of teeth and tiny branches, the click of delicate hooves, *click, click, click*—

"Baeddan Sayer."

He shudders. Tendrils of forest magic tickle at his face.

"Baeddan," she says again. Mairwen Grace. He looks wildly at her, then snatches the scarf tied across her chest, dragging her nearer, and kisses her.

There come gasps and protestations from all around, but not from Mairwen, who allows it, who holds his face, thumbs stroking his temples. She is a piece of him, his heart, and Baeddan can breathe again, can think about things other than dragging the saint to the altar so his bones can be tied down, so his bones can be made the flesh of the forest. The Bone Tree rises in his mind, growing between them, lashing their hearts together.

The voice of the forest quiets.

She jerks back. Her eyes—oh, they are so many delicate brown shades, darkening together, blackening, he is sure.

His heart pounds. Mairwen Grace tightens the scarf crossed over her chest, tucking it more firmly around her waist.

She faces the village. "I am Mairwen Grace," she calls. "You all know my name, but so did the Devil's Forest. It knew me. It recognized me, for I have the blood of Grace witches and the blood of Carey Morgan, the twenty-fifth saint, running through my veins." Mairwen touches her mouth, bringing her fingers away with blood.

"Because of my blood, I was safe in the forest, and I found its secret."

Baeddan stands abruptly, knowing she means him. He bares his teeth, hungry.

Arthur Couch appears at his right, Rhun Sayer at his left. Each young man puts a hand on his shoulder, and Baeddan shivers at the flow of binding power between them all. It itches under his skin.

Mairwen continues. "We three found the Bone Tree, where Baeddan Sayer has survived these ten years, bound to the forest, the sacrifice we sanctified and sent inside to run and die. For that is the true destiny of the Three Graces saint: to become the forest devil until his seven years are up."

The crowd mutters and grumbles, staring at him, at Baeddan. They don't want to believe. Some point. Some make signs against evil.

"This is Baeddan Sayer, or what's left of him." Mairwen's voice is hot in his ears, and he sees flashes of who he was before: laughing, merry, dancing, a boy ready to face his destiny.

"What makes you the best, Baeddan Sayer?" the lord asks. Baeddan is the third boy to answer, and he has no idea what to say.

He shrugs and smiles his best charming smile. "I don't know if I am, my lord, but I know I'm willing to try, and die, for Three Graces. If that's what it takes."

"What's left of all of us," Baeddan sings quietly.

The Grace witch—his witch—glances back at him, then goes to the nearest bench and lifts one side, dragging it loudly across the cobblestones. She drops it and climbs onto it. Rhun moves immediately to her so she can balance with a hand on his shoulder. Around them, the faces of villagers stare wide-eyed as skulls, blanched and eager, frightened, excited, and hungry, hungry, hungry.

"Here is what I know," Mairwen says, putting her hands out. "We went into the forest, found Baeddan, and at the altar in the roots of the Bone Tree we made a charm to bind our bargain. I know the saints don't die immediately: They are bound to the tree, their hearts sacrificed to the heart of the forest. I know once there was a god of the forest, but that god is gone. Dead, or vanished, or fled, I cannot say. The story isn't the whole story."

"How long will your charm last?" says a bearded man wearing a dull yellow jacket.

Baeddan digs his strong fingers between two stones of the square.

"I don't know, but not long," Mairwen answers. "The forest has no heart."

Mairwen is a pillar of light standing over them all, the setting sun making a torch of her brambled hair. Her bare feet are streaked with dirt, and Baeddan understands why the two of them are the only people in Three Graces without footwear of any kind: *the forest, the forest, the forest.*

"We should let it end," Arthur Couch says. Baeddan agrees.

"We can't," calls a gangly woman with sprouting black hair.

"We shouldn't," responds the woman beside her—her

sister, Baeddan knows, but he cannot remember their names.

Arthur joins Mairwen on the bench. "Look at us. Three Graces never changes. We never change. So we don't live. This place might as well be dead! Nobody risks anything, but without risk, there's no life. If nothing burns, then *nothing burns.*"

"Burning hurts," calls Beth Pugh. Others nod around her, but plenty frown, plenty grip each other's hands and hold tight to their families.

"So does love," Arthur calls out in irritation.

"Since when do we listen to this boy?"

Baeddan doesn't see who calls it, but Arthur makes a dismissive hand gesture. "Since I ran into the Devil's Forest and survived, Dar."

"We live. We love," says the lord with the curling brown hair. "We know the risk of death, Arthur. It is possible to understand risk and danger without flinging oneself into it."

Arthur shakes his head. "It's a vicarious understanding. You understand through the saint, only that one night. Don't you all remember the tension, the anticipation last night? When else do you feel so deeply?"

Mairwen touches his arm. "There's more. The whole story should be told before we make choices."

"Do you remember the whole story?" Arthur asks. His irritability makes Baeddan laugh.

Aderyn Grace asks, "How did you bind the bargain, Mairwen?"

"Yes!"

"Tell us!"

Mairwen puts her right arm in the air. "This charm. Binding myself, Arthur, Rhun, to the Bone Tree."

"Does it mean the bargain can be met without losing one of our boys?" Alis Sayer asks, glancing at Baeddan.

"No." The tired voice is Rhun's. He doesn't join his friends on the bench, but merely shakes his head. "There are twenty-five skulls on the Bone Tree."

Gasps sound everywhere, and cries of shock.

Baeddan closes his eyes. His ribs ache, his fingers dig at the cobblestones. He grinds his jaw. "They're all dead!"

Those near enough to hear him fall silent.

"Baeddan?" It's Mairwen, leaning around him. She touches his temple.

"Don't you see? Don't you remember?" He clutches his head, backing away from them all. Baeddan shakes his head and bares his teeth again, eyes tightly shut. Their skulls laugh at him, twisted to the Bone Tree. He snarls, and shouting breaks out: questions and accusations, both hard and tremulous.

"Stop. Baeddan."

Mairwen catches his face again. Behind her is her mother.

Baeddan remembers Addie Grace, and as he stares at her bright brown eyes, her dark hair, her still hands and round hips, at the certainty in the shape of her mouth, he thinks of her when he was a boy. When she was sweeter and sadder, heavy with Carey Morgan's child.

Carey Morgan, the saint before him.

"Do you know, Addie?" Baeddan says in a growling voice he likes but hardly recognizes—it is the voice of the forest devil, the voice of the stalker, the killer, the monster bound to the Bone Tree. "I saw Carey Morgan last, when I ran, when I was your saint. He hunted me, green and sick yellow, horns on his head and claws and sharp teeth! He stalked behind me, one step at a time, teased me and scared me, and when it was nearly dawn he dragged me to the Bone Tree and . . ." Baeddan raises his arm, hand out like claws, as if he holds some large man by the neck. "Ah! He cut my chest open! And the forest grew out of me. Oh, it hurt, it hurt, and . . . he was . . ."

Mairwen puts her hands on his bare chest, smoothing down along the furrows of scabbing and old scars. "My father was alive until you took his place. You became the devil after him."

Sucking a ragged breath, Baeddan nods, and says it louder for all those listening. "He was alive until ten years ago. Carey Morgan lived as the forest devil until I took his place, and his bones were strapped to the Bone Tree, his skull hung with all the others!" Baeddan laughs, desperate, delighted. "All the others!"

"Is that how the bargain is kept?" Mairwen asks, as if she does not already know.

"Yes, yes. A sacrifice every seven years, a life to bind it to the Bone Tree, so the power roots into the land, spreading like a disease throughout the valley."

"How do you know?" asks Aderyn Grace.

"It's the only way. There must be a heart!"

Murmurs of uncertainty and disbelief scatter throughout the villagers. They've all turned to shadow as the sun vanishes, leaving only the pale glow of the creamy horizon.

"Aren't you the devil? Tricking us?" asks a young girl. Brave, though her chin lifts defiantly and her hands are clenched against fearful trembling. The small tawny girl who screamed at him from the square.

Baeddan shudders and crouches, hunkering down like the monster he looks. He gouges his chest with sharp nails and nods. "I am the devil, pretty girl, yes. Yes."

The girl keeps her brave face, and a boy as tan as she but taller and older, asks, "But sometimes the runner lives."

Other voices take up the protest.

"Some live!"

"John!"

"Col Sayer! Griffin!"

"Tom Ellis!"

"Marc Argall!"

"I don't know! I don't know!" Baeddan cries. "But someone dies. The saint dies, because the saint runs in anointed for the tree! It is how I knew John Upjohn and—and Rhun Sayer. They were already bound to the Bone Tree when they ran into the forest." Baeddan covers his eyes, then his ears, as the villagers ask a dozen questions. Rhun Sayer joins him, kneeling at his side. Rhun's shoulder touches his, and Baeddan grinds his fists into his ears.

· · ·

MAIRWEN IS ENERGIZED AND WILD, EYES TOO WIDE, unable to breathe through her nose, but only suck in air like she's tasting it all, needing the flavor of everything. The forest whispers her name again and again. She feels it like a thread of lightning from the thorns growing over her heart, down into her viscera.

She asks her mother to explain the charm to everyone: death, life, Grace witches in between; explain the blessing shirt and anointing. Aderyn does so, and it is little surprise to most folks, who've seen the Grace witches charm the square and sing blessings for their entire lives. The anointing oil is made from herbs collected from the edge of the forest, the fat and bones of the previous Slaughter Moon's horse sacrifice, and a drop of Grace witch blood. That is how she was taught by her mother, who was taught by her own mother, and back and back until the bloodline sprang from the elder two Grace witches.

"What else did your mother teach you, that isn't in the story?" Mair asks.

Her mother studies her, a familiar impatience on her face. "That the devil is a god, the old god of the forest, as you said, and that the saint goes in to keep the heart of the bargain strong. That all of us, our bloodline, are called into the forest finally, when it is our time to stay there. And . . . that a Grace witch can undo it all."

"I've always heard the call," Mairwen tells everyone. "Since I was a child. Because my father was already part of the forest. His heart."

"You risked undoing it all by going in," Aderyn says.

"If I hadn't, Rhun would be dead."

Nobody is willing to argue with that. Not yet.

But the town does argue over Baeddan's insistence that all the saints have died, even those who ran back out. They left the valley because their memories were too terrible, because they longed for further adventure, and would never, ever return without telling their families! Some say perhaps others died, strangers. Or it's the hearts of the Grace witches from the past two hundred years binding the charm in between saints. Or Baeddan is simply wrong—look at him, how broken he is. None agree. Lord Vaughn says he'll look through his family's books for information, but he doesn't know if it will help.

Without the old god to ask, Mairwen wonders if there's any way to know. Except to walk back inside. To remember. Her stomach churns as she listens to the voice of the forest in her mind and heart.

Mairwen Grace. Mairwen. Daughter of the forest.

The townsfolk ask her the same questions again and again, and she answers, again and again, though the answers never change. She doesn't remember enough for more.

She's starving, and as bread and meat are brought out, as rosemary potatoes fill the air with savory smells, Mair stands apart, breathing hard, not quite able to be a piece of the whole. Of all people, it's Arthur who takes Baeddan to the trough of meat and aids him in selecting a piece to devour. Arthur remains all sharp edges but seems less interested in stabbing people indiscriminately. Mairwen can't help but like it. Rhun stays beside her, solid and silent, unsmiling. She touches her shoulder to his. She shivers, but isn't cold.

"Hungry?" Rhun asks. Mair nods. He goes and brings back food and two knives with which they stab and eat potatoes and roast from the same bowl, shoulders together. Hot food in her belly, Mair feels less ephemeral.

Arthur and Baeddan sit together, devouring twice as much as Mairwen and Rhun, and Mair notices children are creeping nearer and nearer, especially the Sayer cousins. Baeddan eats with his hands, but carefully, eyeing the small boys and girls, occasionally showing them his teeth, even with meat in them. Arthur winces once or twice, and snaps something at the children. Baeddan snatches a hunk of bread from a little Crewe girl, who stares wide-eyed, then frowns at him and demands it be returned with a tiny, insistent white hand.

More Sayers cluster around as Baeddan and the girl negotiate, including his mother, Alis, who slides a hand through his dark hair. She jerks back, cupping her hand protectively, and Baeddan's father, Evan, inspects it. Baeddan himself hunches over, covers his ears, and again it's Arthur soothing him.

Rhun notices Mair stop eating, and takes the rest for himself. He eventually joins the Sayers around Baeddan, and Mairwen slips away, glad Rhun chose to seek out the comfort of his large family. She searches for Haf Lewis and finds her with her husband-to-be, Ifan Pugh, sharing a bowl of food too.

Ifan swallows awkwardly when Mair arrives, and balances his knife across the lip of the bowl in order to touch the back of Haf's neck.

Haf leans toward him, probably without realizing it, and Mairwen smiles very slightly. She says, "What do you think, Ifan? What happened to the surviving saints?"

"If you hadn't gone into the forest, I'd say your family drags them back in to that altar," he answers, and Haf gasps in the closest to fury she's capable of.

"Ifan Pugh!" she hisses.

He stands his ground silently.

"He's right," Mairwen says. "If it were me, at least I'd have all the answers."

She *is* the one receiving the most suspicious glances, the one apart tonight. If they only knew she was transforming, they wouldn't even listen. They'd assume she was corrupted by the forest at the very least.

Maybe she is.

Mairwen Grace has never felt more like a witch. But what to do about it? How to behave? What does she even *want* to do? Save the bargain, but also save the saints. It doesn't seem possible.

How does Aderyn fit in so smoothly? she wonders, looking for her mother. Aderyn the witch, husbandless mother, has never stood so apart as Mairwen has always done.

The best way to look for Aderyn has always been to look for Hetty Pugh's tall frame, and sure enough, the two women and Bethy, too, and Nona Sayer and Cat Dee stand together. Aderyn is staring back at Mairwen.

She starts for her mother without parting words with Haf and Ifan, but three steps on, she hears her name.

Rhos Priddy waits there in the torchlight, a bundle of baby quilt in her arms. Tiredness is plain in her eyes and poorly braided hair, but Rhos smiles prettily. "Thank you, Mairwen," she says, dropping one shoulder so Mair can see into the shadows of the bundle where Rhos's baby sleeps. "She's alive because of you. I know you're upset—everyone is upset—but I can't help not being so."

It warms tiny pockets of Mairwen's heart she hadn't realized had gone cold. Lips parting in awe, she touches a finger to the baby's nose, then one hairless eyebrow. The baby is so small, so soft. Mairwen thinks of those terrible hours rubbing her warm, touching thin cheeks and ignoring the sunken little eyes as best she could, and the gasping, choking breath.

"We did the right thing," she says quietly, and Rhos Priddy squeezes her elbow.

"Mairwen, may I have a moment?"

To her surprise, it's Lord Vaughn. He offers a soft, comforting glance for Rhos, who curtsies and goes. Vaughn gestures toward the cemetery wall, and Mairwen attends, studying the flash of torchlight in his paler eye. At the edge of the square, Vaughn says, "I hope you'll come help me look through my family books. You might see something I don't. Since you've been in the forest."

"I don't remember very much."

"Really?"

"Part of the charm, I think, is to make us all forget."

"But why?"

"If the saint survives, and remembers, he'll remember the face of his devil is the same as the last saint?"

Vaughn purses his lips. "Would that make a difference? Are you sure there isn't something else to forget?"

Mairwen closes her eyes and sees the girl in the white veil again. "Maybe. Ghosts or old spirits. The first Grace? There was a girl in a veil, and I don't know who else she might be. My imagination. Or myself, even."

The lord touches her shoulder. She remembers *him* suddenly, when she was a very small girl, picking yarrow at the base of the mountain. He helped her for a moment, crouched there, smiling at her as if she were the sun. Curling hair, young brown eyes.

It couldn't be him, twelve years ago: It was his father, the last Vaughn. Both eyes in her memory were brown. "What was your father like?" she asks.

Surprised, Vaughn hesitates. "My father?"

"He looked like you. Do I look like my father?"

The lord pinches the end of a curl at Mairwen's jaw. "His hair curled, too. He liked the forest. He wanted to go in. I remember that much."

"Were you at his ceremony?" Mair thinks Vaughn would have been thirteen or so then. Maybe old enough.

"Yes. I'm sorry you couldn't grow up with a father."

She closes her eyes. Tears are pricking at her lashes. "He was alive until I was seven years old. Until Baeddan went in. My father. I didn't know." What if she'd ignored everything and run inside as a child? Could she have saved her father as she saved Baeddan?

Baeddan is not yet saved, reminds a voice inside her head, snarling rather like Arthur.

"I must go," she says, and dashes off, out of the center of town and into the dark side streets heading north. A cold wind blows, chapping Mair's lips, and she sucks on them, tightening the scarf over her burning collarbone.

Mairwen Grace. Come home.

Daughter of the forest.

Mairwen slows down when she hears her name in a real voice behind her. Aderyn's voice. The moon is not yet risen, but the arc of the sky already fills with stars. Mair stops at the smaller pasture gate. Dozens of sheep huddle together.

She props herself against the fence as her mother catches up. Aderyn carries a long tallow candle, the flame protected by her cupped hand, and sticks the base of it to the gate post. She studies her daughter, frowning.

Finally, Aderyn says, "You're changed, Daughter."

"Rather a lot," Mair admits in a whisper.

Aderyn cups Mairwen's face, smoothing her thumbs along Mair's cheek. Her head tilts to the side, making Mairwen think of the bird women, but it's sorrow and loss adding weight to Aderyn's frown, not curiosity.

Her mother pulls Mair into a hug, and Mairwen returns

it, careful to hold her mother just away from her breast, where the thorns are ready to pierce her skin.

"May I examine that bracelet you showed everyone?" Aderyn asks as she draws away.

Mair puts her hand in her mother's, who angles it toward the candlelight. Aderyn leans over it, skims a finger against the tiny, sharp thorns.

The angry skin below heats up at the touch.

"This is well made," her mother says. "You must have been in a rush. What excellent balance, though. What is the death of the blessing? Your pain?" Aderyn's eyes lift to Mairwen's, curious and proud.

Mairwen nods. She wonders what color Carey Morgan's eyes were. When did her mother fall in love with him?

"You're sure you won't be trapped the way poor Baeddan Sayer is? Change like him? If he was the sacrifice, and now you three are, mightn't you turn into a creature like him?"

"Not yet," Mairwen says slowly.

"And John Upjohn's hand bones. My, what a gruesomely effective charm you've made, Daughter. I suppose I should not be surprised, given your love of the shambles."

Gently tugging her hand away, Mairwen frowns at her mother. The firelight pulls red from Aderyn's hair, just as it does her own, and flickers in the mirrors of their black pupils. "Mother, did you know Rhun would die?"

Aderyn frowns.

"Did you know, when you comforted me and said if love could save anyone it would be Rhun? When you gave me the dress and let me be the one to anoint him? Did you know you were making me into the instrument of certain death?"

"Mairwen—"

Mair backs up, out of the glow of candlelight. "Did you lie to me? You've always known the saints die, haven't you? I've tried to work out any other way, and can't. They always die, and always have. Do we kill them? The Grace witches? Don't lie to me now, not about this. Not when my own father—" She turns her head away, grief cracking across her mouth and wrinkling her nose.

Silence beats between them, and several sheep wander over, nuzzling at the fence. Mairwen scrunches her eyes so tightly shut she sees pinprick stars. "You're the Grace witch. You know how it all works," she whispers. "You didn't tell me everything. You knew it's real death. You knew there was no hope for Rhun."

Aderyn grabs her shoulders. "Be calm." She takes Mairwen's chin and forces her daughter to look at her. "We are the Grace witches, and we protect this valley and this bargain. It's what we do and always have done. We *made* the bargain with the devil, and now we uphold it. The anointing oil contains our blood. It ties them to the Bone Tree, because a Grace witch's heart is buried there too. We do not kill them or drag them back inside. They return to the tree because they are anointed. It's fixed by the time the saint accepts his crown. I would have told you everything afterward, passed this full burden on to you. Shared it between us. You could've understood then, calm in your grief and understanding of true sacrifice, what it means to maintain the bargain. It is the only way to be a Grace witch."

"Oh God, Mother!" Fury coats her whisper now. She tears free, knocking into the fence, startling a few sheep. The stars overhead waver exactly like the candle at her elbow.

Her mother tries to touch her again, but Mairwen says, "No," deeply and furiously.

"You'll understand when you think on it long enough. Listen. You'll see you've always known in your heart, because of who you are. You've always understood the forest. It is life *and* death! Both. You love it, long for it. And I've always allowed you that, never tried to take it away, because you were preparing yourself. The only lie we perpetuate is hope, because hope is the thing that lets the saints do what they must. By destroying the hope, you've destroyed the entire bargain. Everyone will suffer for it."

"But Rhun is alive," Mair says.

Aderyn sighs. "If only I believed you love him so much and everything else so little that you would sacrifice everything else for him."

"Have you ever loved anything at all?"

"How can you ask me that?"

"Do you know what my father's bones feel like?" She says it through clenched teeth, growling, desperate as a monster.

Her mother folds her hands before her. "I love you. I have only ever allowed you to be free, to do what you must for yourself and the town."

"I don't believe you. How could you let him be the saint

if you loved him and knew? If I'd known I'd never have let Rhun run."

"You'd have let some other boy do it?"

"I . . ." Mairwen shakes her head, stunned, furious, and even afraid. "I don't know. No! It's wrong to trick them. It's always been wrong! Everyone should know the full truth and then if they still would be a saint, or still be willing to live the way we do, they should know the real price. What our bargain is truly built on. How dare you keep this secret!"

Whirling, Mairwen makes to go, but her mother grabs her arm.

"You've broken it now, yourself, and you will not be thanked for revealing the truth, Mairwen. People don't want the truth."

Mair jerks free and stares, horrified, at Aderyn. Her mother stares back, just as angry.

The moonlight shines all around, and Mairwen feels the forest tugging at her.

She says, "Mother, do you know what happened to the old god of the forest when the first Grace died?"

Aderyn plucks the candle off the fence, leaving behind a cooling ring of wax. "You already know everything I know about the bargain, Mairwen. I'm going to stay with Hetty again tonight, but tomorrow I will take back my house."

When Mairwen is alone in the darkness, pressed near the dozing sheep, she sinks to her knees and hugs her stomach, mouth open in a silent scream.

It hurts too much: her burning eyes, the sting of the charm at her wrist, the sharp pulse of her collarbone, and oh, her heart, her heart! Her toes press into the cold earth and she bows her head. All those ragged, short brambles of hair tickle her neck and ears, a reminder of how she's changed, and she huddles there in the dark and silence. She snaps her jaw closed, grinding her teeth, lips back, shoulders hunched. There is such a blaze across her chest, stabbing with persistence.

Her skin splits, and she feels the birth of hooked thorns, flaring up from her bones.

Trickles of hot blood slip down her skin, running below the scarf and under the collar of her wool shirt to pool in a thin line along her breasts where her bodice presses tight.

R HUN IS SURROUNDED BY SAYERS. THEY'VE OVER-taken an entire long table, with Baeddan in the middle, Arthur at his side, and Rhun at Arthur's. Then the rest: cousins and uncles and aunts, gathered around and pressing near, sharing bowls and drinks. Brac, his most recently married cousin, shares a mug of beer with him. So encircled, Rhun almost manages to feel normal. The lying is over, and it's peeled a few of the hardened layers away from his heart. Three Graces knows what he knows, and even though nothing's been decided, the folk need time to accustom themselves to the revelations.

But he can't quite relax into his great clan. He's unsettled and keeps catching himself looking north, toward the forest. Like that's where he belongs, not here with his family. The Bone Tree waits for him, reaching cold and white against the darkness. *Saint*, it whispers.

"I'm proud of you." Rhun the Elder places a hand on his shoulder, as if sensing it's better not to hug his son.

Rhun the Younger can't respond. If he opens his mouth, the voice of the forest might spill out.

Elis, his little brother, carefully creeps up behind Baeddan, leaning on Arthur's back so his short, tight curls flatten against Arthur's borrowed shirt. Arthur shifts to make better room for Elis, but the boy won't get closer to Baeddan.

"Elis," Rhun says softly, and holds out a hand. His brother leaps at the chance, and climbs up onto the bench with Rhun. Half of Elis's gangly nine-year-old body sprawls on Rhun's lap. Grounding him here. So long as somebody sits on him, Rhun can't get up and run back in.

It didn't feel like this when the sun was up.

He looks to the moon in the east. It rose late, no longer quite full.

"Do you remember what you told me before the Slaughter Moon?" Elis whispers.

He does, and nods. *I love you, and I love all of this, and that's what you should remember,* Rhun said, before going home to collapse in bed, at peace with his own death. It's close to what Baeddan told him ten years ago.

Elis puts his head back against Rhun's shoulder and says,

"I probably will remember this more, dinner with the forest devil."

"Me too," Rhun confesses, managing a smile. Out of nowhere, he thinks he'd like to see what Elis is like in seven years, or ten, or go to Elis's wedding.

Brac is telling a story about missing boots, and Uncle Finn interrupts constantly to correct him, in a familiar pattern. They've told this story a hundred times before. Baeddan suddenly slams his hand down on the table and says, "But the dog was under the bed!"

Silence crushes down the Sayer table in a long wave. It was the final revelation of the story, told a minute too soon.

Baeddan breathes hard, the tips of his sharp teeth showing.

Then Brac laughs, and so does Arthur, and along down the lines of benches the rest of the family joins in.

"That's right," Finn drawls. "The dog was under the damn bed."

Sayers move on to a new memory, and Rhun closes his eyes and tries to ignore the forest moaning in his head. He'll never sleep tonight. Is this what it's like for John Upjohn, always? Not fitting, afraid of what he'll face in his dreams? If Rhun goes to Mairwen and the Grace house, will the hearthstone and Mair's embrace quiet the Bone Tree?

When he opens his eyes, Gethin Couch is there, slinking out of the shadows toward his son. He says, "Arthur."

Arthur turns, eyeing his father. Rhun braces himself.

Crossing his arms over his chest, Gethin says, "What a man you are, my boy."

Arthur laughs meanly. It's Rhun's favorite laugh, though it shouldn't be. Arthur says, "How can you tell? You've never been a man, Gethin. I know the difference now, between the look of a man and the truth of one."

Shock and anger pull his father's mouth open. "Oh, do you?"

"Someone pretending to be a man clings to the trappings. But if you are one, you don't have to cling. You just are yourself."

His father frowns. "If you say so."

"I do, and that's what matters." He shrugs, casually turning back to the Sayers.

For a moment, Gethin remains, but nobody is paying him much heed. Rhun murmurs to Elis to reach for his beer, watching Arthur's father with the corner of his eye. Finally, Gethin scoffs under his breath and leaves.

Rhun nudges Elis out of the way and says, "Arthur?"

He shoots Rhun a skinning look. Then grimaces. "Sorry. It's him, not you."

"I know."

"Elis, you're in my way," Arthur says, grabbing Elis by the waist and dragging him across his chest to set him down beside Baeddan. Elis's face tightens and his brown eyes go all wide.

Baeddan peers through the dim torchlight. "I don't remember you."

"I wasn't born when you ran," Elis whines.

The smile of delight on Baeddan's face makes Elis—and Rhun—smile a little in return. Baeddan says, "Something new!" reaching to poke at Elis's cheek. Arthur scoots nearer to Rhun, so their arms brush when either moves.

"Do you hear the forest?" Rhun murmurs, head tilted toward Arthur.

"No. You do?" Arthur spits a curse. He grabs Rhun's knee, fingers biting through the wool trousers. "I won't let you go back in."

He studies Arthur's face, his pressed lips and furrowed brow, the certainty in his blue eyes, and remembers—

"Stop it! I'm not letting you die here!"

"I don't want to die, but if it's that or you do, I'd rather die a thousand times."

"So would I, you idiot. Why should you get the satisfaction?"

The devil laughs his high, looping laugh and cries, "Oh, you will both die, for trying to die for each other! The forest is whispering so many things, and your battle tastes so good."

Arthur raises his eyebrows in surprise. Rhun grabs his hand.

The sun is minutes from rising, but the devil blocks their path.

Rhun's throat aches and his chest heaves; beside him Arthur bends, spitting blood onto the dead ground. The Bone Tree rules over this grove, and over the entire forest, like a king crowned with moonlight and robed in the bones of twenty-five dead boys.

Rhun closes his eyes.

Arthur says, "It's the devil's turn to die."

Mairwen bares her teeth. "You aren't helping, Arthur Couch!"

"Baeddan Sayer is already dead," Arthur says. "I'm sorry, devil, but you are."

"Dead, dead, dead and breathing," the devil hisses.

"Stop remembering," Arthur says, shuddering.

Rhun puts his hands on the altar, sweeping dry vines off its surface and flaking blood and ancient black rot. "The forest needs your heart," moans the devil beside him.

"I can't stop," Rhun answers. "It's pressing against me, but if I go inside the forest, it will end."

"Listen to me instead of the forest. Listen to Baeddan with your little brother, and all the family."

"I'll try."

"I'm not leaving your side."

"I'm not leaving your side, now or ever, Rhun Sayer. Do you hear me?"

"I'll hold you to it, Arthur."

Arthur lifts his chin, glaring through a smear of blood staining his eyebrow and dripping into his left eye.

In front of the whole Sayer clan, Arthur puts his pale, strong hand on Rhun's cheek, and Rhun breathes carefully, thinking of nothing but the touch, nothing but the sounds of conversation, someone laughing. It's good, and he's here, alive.

"Let's go find Mair," Arthur says.

THE NIGHT IS COLD, AND MAIR HUDDLES AGAINST THE sheep fence. Her face is sticky from tears, her eyes swollen, but she breathes calmly now. With her eyes closed, she can hear the forest whispering at her, calling her.

Mairwen Grace. Daughter of the forest.

All she smells is her own blood, and sweet manure and dry grass. There is rain on the wind too.

She reaches out, shivering, and grabs the grass. She pulls herself forward, crawling, toward the forest. It's where she belongs. And unlike John Upjohn, it's where she *wants* to be. The heart of the forest, curled against the Bone Tree's roots; they will be her cradle against the wind. There she can sleep, finally relax. She is so very weary.

"Mairwen!"

She stops.

It was not the voice of the forest.

"Mairwen!"

Rhun.

She shudders hard; yes, yes, the saint can go with her into the forest. Together they will put a heart in the—in the—

she lifts the veil and says

"Mair, is that you?"

Arthur's voice, joining Rhun.

Their boots hit the earth hard, as if they're running for her, and she feels the vibration through the valley.

Mairwen climbs to her feet. The forest needs her.

"I'm coming," she whispers.

"Mair," gasps Arthur, and then Rhun touches her hand.

An ache cracks her bones. The thorns on her chest seem to tighten and grow at the same time. The forest whispers such a demanding song that her knees falter and she slips to the ground again, crouching there. She shakes, head lowered, teeth clenched, fighting the forest, bleeding, until arms come around her. She lets herself be lifted off the earth and cradled against Rhun's chest. He walks away from the village, and Arthur is with them the whole way home.

A LL THREE TUCK THEMSELVES UP INTO THE DARK, secluded loft in the Grace house. Mairwen farthest in, against the wall, where the thatched roof meets the limewash. Rhun holds her freezing hands while Arthur piles blankets on her, hovering like a worried old man.

"Do you hear it?" she whispers, eyes closed, for there is little to see but the glint of their eyes and shadowy outlines.

"I do," Rhun says, and Arthur at the same time says, "No."

She clutches Rhun's hands, then frees one to reach for Arthur. "Baeddan?"

Rhun says, "With my mom. She, and the whole Sayer clan, can handle him. He seems calmer, after eating, and after being around them all."

"He told a story he remembers from before the forest," Arthur says as he plays with Mair's fingers, spreading them out, tracing the length of each.

"Good." Mairwen pulls both young men toward her. "I am so tired," she murmurs.

"What happened?" Rhun does not give ground, remaining in his awkward crouch, half on the mattress, half off. "I hear the forest, but it did not do this to me."

Irritated he won't just cuddle against her, let her sleep, she says, "I spoke to my mother, and she knew they all died. She knew you had to die, Rhun! She says Grace witches have always known the saint dies! It's our duty to make sure they're anointed, to hold up the bargain. We lie."

Arthur snorts. "I knew it would be like this."

Rhun slides him a glare, but the darkness swallows it.

"I did," Arthur continues. "We should've set fire to the Bone Tree and then we'd be forced to make a new bargain. One we know all the rules to. We have to break it, even if it can't be remade. Nothing else will stop this hold it has on you. I'll go back in and do it now," he boasts. But he, too, is tired. Drained the way Mairwen is drained. He leans closer to Mair in order to press the back of her hand to his heart.

"We might have to," Rhun says.

"Not tonight," Mairwen murmurs, tugging at them again.

This time Rhun takes a moment to remove his boots and climbs in beside her, opening his arm for her to curl against his side. Arthur hesitates. "Do you think I can stop both of you, if you decide to listen to the forest?"

"I won't leave you," Rhun says, mirroring Arthur's earlier promise.

Mairwen nuzzles her blankets. "It's quieter behind your buzzing. Come closer."

Underneath his spikes, Arthur wants nothing more than to be loved by these two people. Something tells him, though, that a future is as impossible now as it was before.

"C'mon, Arthur," Mairwen murmurs.

He stretches next to Rhun, between both of them and the rest of the world.

MOONLIGHT CRAWLS ALONG THE TWISTED BLACK branches overhead, glowing along shelves of fungus and patches of scarlet lichen. They're all headed toward each other: Arthur and Rhun, muddy and damp, follow a bird woman who shrieked at them, singing songs created of Mairwen's name, until they agreed to follow; Mairwen pants with a heady combination of exhilaration and fear on the heels of a devil who grins at her with sharp teeth, touches her with tenderness, and laughs and laughs and laughs.

"There, there!" crows the devil, throwing his arms out. "I told you, Mairwen Grace, that I could find your saint."

The bird woman flares her wings to turn, fleeing for her life, and Arthur skids to a halt. Rhun puts a hand on a nearby tree, shoulders heaving because of the wound on his thigh slowing him down. "Mair," Arthur says, but all Rhun sees is the devil. He notches his ready arrow.

Even as Arthur and Mairwen slam together in a relieved embrace, the devil lashes out, and Rhun shoots.

His aim is true as always, and the arrow hits the devil's shoulder, piercing his black leather coat.

"Rhun!" cries Mairwen.

The devil roars, tearing the arrow free, only to be hit with another.

Arthur hears the note of distress in Mairwen's voice—he hears her fear not only for Rhun, but for the devil, and anger makes him shove her away to grab his last long knife. He joins Rhun in the attack.

Everywhere the devil's skin breaks, purple blood bursts forth, and green vines, tendrils curling and trailing tiny leaves and tinier petals.

The devil is unhurt by the wounds, though he screams and roars, though he bleeds. The devil stabs Rhun with his own arrow and knocks Arthur back with a hard punch. Rhun brings out his ax, and the devil catches his wrist, squeezing almost hard enough to break bone. The devil grins, dancing in place. "You will taste good, saint. You will fill this forest with life again."

Arthur leaps onto the devil's back, arms around his neck. The devil swings, throwing himself around and against Rhun.

"Stop it, now," orders Mairwen, dragging at the devil's arm.

The devil steps toward her. "Go, get out of here," she says to the boys. "Keep running."

"No," the devil growls, pushing her away to face Rhun again.

"Go!" Mairwen screams.

Rhun barely hears through his focus. The devil is unaffected by blood loss and injury, looming over him and Arthur with smears of blood over his face. There are antlers in his hair and thorns growing from his chest, and his black eyes are impossibly dark, reflecting nothing of life or light back.

"We aren't leaving you," Arthur says.

But Mairwen reaches around the devil and slaps her hand flat against his chest. "Baeddan Sayer. Stop."

Something shifts in the devil, and the devil blinks. Awareness, like a man might have, not a monster, is the thing Rhun sees, and it terrifies him more than anything else, though he does not know why.

The devil shakes like a wet dog. "Mairwen, Mairwen, I cannot stop I will eat them I want their bones I want to be free!"

Mair slips around to the devil's front, nudging Rhun away with her boot. "I know. I know. Take me away from here. Let me help you, Baeddan."

And Rhun hears it, suddenly: The name penetrates his battle rush. His cousin, the saint, his beautiful cousin who taught him to love everything. He sees it in the line of the devil's crooked Sayer nose, the shape of his shoulders. "Oh my God," Rhun breathes.

"God!" echoes the devil in despair.

Rhun twists his wrist out of Arthur's hand. "It's not possible."

Arthur says, "It's a trick. It must be."

"Saint!" cries the devil, and Rhun leaps away. The devil claws at the saint, tearing at Rhun's back.

Rhun's knees give out and he falls through a fire of pain. Arthur barely catches him, and Mairwen slaps the devil's chest again, demanding his attention.

"Go! I'll be fine—I have been these last hours. Trust me," she says to Arthur.

"Damn it," Arthur says, and helps Rhun up, running with him, away from Mairwen.

They crash off, limping and tripping, and Mairwen says, "Baeddan, show me the most beautiful place in your forest."

"You imagine beauty in a place like this?" His voice is grating and low.

"You're beautiful."

Baeddan's eyes catch moonlight, revealing stars in them: endless light, cold and distant. But like the stars, they make her long to be nearer.

He growls, and she feels it under her palms.

The devil moves so quickly she gasps. He's a dozen paces away, crouched, glaring at her. "You're tearing me apart. The forest whispers one thing, you whisper another, and I want—I want to listen to you. But the forest is my devil. The forest is all I am. It is my bones and heart and . . . How can I listen to you?"

"I love the Devil's Forest," Mairwen confesses. "If it is your bones, I love your bones. If it is your heart, I—I love your heart."

"Witch!" he cries, and runs back to her, takes her hand, and pulls her with him. They dash through the forest, and the forest bends out of their way. Trees lean aside, branches curl into an arched corridor, roots withdraw and sink into the earth to clear the path. Mairwen's boots fly over the ground, her heart beats fast as sparrow wings, and the devil holding her hand laughs brightly.

He takes her to a grove of silver trees, naked to the sky, reaching slender branches up and up. There is no scatter of leaves on the forest floor, no ungainly roots, no underbrush. It is empty except for slender white vines, looping lazily among the trees, spiraling up trunks and dripping from the low branches, covering the earth in curls and knots.

"This?" Mairwen says. It is not what she imagined when she asked for beauty, but the starkness is inspiring.

"There is room for me here," the devil says, "and the trees are quiet."

She cannot tell if it is pity or love she feels.

Then the devil—Baeddan Sayer—smiles wickedly. "And also this." He spreads his hands, standing in a cross, and his coat opens over his bloody, strong chest. He leans his head back, and at the tips of his clawed fingers tiny flowers of light bloom.

Mair gasps.

The lights bob in the air, blinking in a heartbeat rhythm. More appear, all around them. Mairwen turns slowly, amazed. When she's made a full revolution, Baeddan is right before her, and he takes her hands. Lifting one eyebrow in charming invitation, he sweeps back and pulls her into a dance.

No music plays; there is only moonlight and vines and a gentle wind shaking the bare trees. There is only their footsteps and the brush of her heavy blue dress against his legs.

It is as beautiful as she'd hoped.

Baeddan's hand is cold around hers, and those wicked thorns hooking out of his collarbones are very near her face as they dance. She smells blood, earthy and thick, like the ground after an autumn rain; cold granite in his breath; a shadowy sweetness she wants to taste again. Her front is colder than her back, just as it was when she stood half in the forest and half out the other day. She leans nearer to him, dancing carefully, but with a lightness she's unused to, as if in this moment nothing else matters.

THE SECOND MORNING

Rhun wakes first, as the sun rises. Mairwen sleeps with her head on Rhun's shoulder, an arm stretched over him to rest on Arthur's sternum. Rhun opens his eyes, warm and comfortable with his two most beloved friends on either side of him. Sunlight creeps in through the small square window, and Arthur's hand is under his own; they curled together in the night. He turns his head. Arthur's face is right there, lashes pale gold and fine on his cheeks. His nostrils flare slightly as he breathes sharp and wakes up, eyes flashing open onto Rhun's.

The spark in them is anger, as always, but Arthur does not look away this time, or pretend he doesn't realize how intimate this situation is. He holds still.

"You grounded me here," Rhun whispers. His mouth is tacky from sleep.

Arthur lifts his eyebrows and turns his hand under Rhun's, clasping it. The thorns of Rhun's bracelet prick Arthur's bare wrist. "I won't let you fade away, Rhun Sayer.

Or transform into a monster. Or turn bitter. You are the best, and—no, listen. You're the best to *me*. I only care for what I care for—you know that—and I care for you. And Mairwen. I know what this valley is now, and who I am, and I know who you are and what *matters*. I know. I won't let go of that, and I won't let go of you."

Rhun nods. He grips Arthur's hand and tries not to show too much of his heart. His life was over, and then he learned everything was a lie, except this is true and always has been true: He loves Arthur Couch.

From his shoulder Mairwen sighs in her sleep. Both he and Arthur glance at her. Her skin is splotched and pale, and the hollows around her eyes are too purple. Her lips blood-less. Her hair lank and messy. He remembers his dream, even the part that wasn't his own memory: She danced with the forest devil as if she belonged there.

"We have to keep her safe too," he says to Arthur. He hugs her tight to his side and grunts at a strange poke where her chest presses to him.

"What?" Arthur asks, leaning up.

Rhun shifts, and though Mairwen clings to him, he gently rolls her over, and as she wakes groggily and with an uncomfortable sneer, he peels off her scarf. It's wound behind her neck, crossed over her chest, and tied around her waist again. Blood smears her skin below it, and is crusted to the scarf.

A row of delicate thorns cut up out of her skin, along the sweep of her collarbones.

Arthur hisses over Rhun's shoulder. Rhun is stunned, frozen, and Mairwen finally wakes fully, stretching. She winces as her skin pulls tight, and one hand flies to the thorns. They're tiny, deep brown but fading to a reddish tip like rose thorns.

"Your eyes," Arthur says.

Rhun looks up and he sees it too: Mairwen's eyes are blacker throughout. As if while she slept pieces of brown were plucked out and replaced with shards of darkness.

"What about my eyes?" she asks with measured calm, too calm, the calm of a person who is anything but.

"They're darker," Rhun says.

Mairwen sits, head barely clearing the low thatched ceiling. She fists her hands in her lap. "I want to see. Your mother has a mirror, doesn't she, Rhun?"

"Are we different?" Arthur asks before Rhun can do more than nod.

Fear twists Rhun up, and he turns to Arthur, despite having just spent several moments gazing into Arthur's eyes. But Arthur looks as fine as always. Except for his wrist.

All three of them lift their wrists with the charm: The bracelets seem to have grown into their flesh. For Rhun and Arthur it's a gentle melding, skin grown up against the braided hair and thorns and bone.

Mairwen's wrist is a gauntlet of hardened skin, several inches wide, reddish and brown like healthy bark. Her fingernails are tinged blue, but she says she's not cold.

"Why is this only happening to you?" Arthur asks, sounding as if he's offended.

"I'm the witch," she whispers. "Our hearts already half belong to the Bone Tree. I was supposed to let Rhun die after I anointed him, but instead I gave the rest of my heart to the forest."

Rhun frowns and holds on to her shoulders, studying her face for more differences. He touches her hair, digging his fingers gently against her scalp. No crown of thorns or antlers that he can find, and he strokes down her neck. Her wide new eyes project uncertainty, which he has never seen in Mairwen Grace before. Rhun kisses her.

Her hands flutter against his chest for a moment, then she settles them on his shirt. He looks, and her eyes have drifted closed.

"Your heart wasn't yours alone to give, Mairwen Grace," Arthur says.

CLOUDS PULL HIGH ACROSS THE VALLEY, PEACEFUL and calm. The gray backdrop brings out gold in the fields. Mairwen puts herself between Rhun and Arthur as they leave the Grace house for the Sayer homestead, her hands in theirs.

She is not afraid, though she senses she should be. She is excited, thrilled even, for the bargain she made must be working better than she thought. Maybe she can hold it, inside of her, the way Baeddan Sayer did, and perhaps it will last seven years without a death. Because Arthur is right: She couldn't give all her heart to the forest. Too much is here, with Rhun and Arthur and Haf and her mother, and even Baeddan. All the people in Mairwen's heart lending it greater strength, grounding it in the valley. Perhaps there will be a way to make this the permanent solution: Every time more than one person could be bound to the Bone Tree, and so no single person must die. Together, their hearts, their love, might be strong enough to overcome the need for sacrifice.

Certainly Mairwen seems to be holding the heaviest portion, but she can take it. She was born for this, born to hold the blessing between life and death. Saints and witches.

She laughs to herself, earning a frown from Arthur and an anxious glance from Rhun.

"You sound like Baeddan," Rhun says.

That makes her stop so fast she swallows air, stumbling.

The young men catch her by her elbows, leaning in protectively. She says, "I feel good, not mad, not confused like him."

It's even true.

Mair closes her eyes, shielded by her friends in a pocket of shade and solidarity. She listens. Her toes brush the grass, and the pulse of her heart thumps gently down into the earth. A cool breeze tickles the fringes of her hair, the tip of her nose, and her lips, her ears. She slides her hands into Rhun's and Arthur's again, and feels the heartbeat spread among them.

From the earth rises a whisper, unlike a sound, more of a sensation thrilling through her blood. It does not whisper in words. It warms her belly and tightens her skin, especially along her spine and breasts. She desires this thing from the bowl of her hips.

"Are you all right?" Rhun asks.

She tilts her face toward his. Yes, Rhun Sayer would do. She would devour him and leave his bones at the altar.

Mairwen gasps, wrenching away from both of them. They start toward her, but she shakes her head. "Stop, please," she says, holding her hands to the sky. Oh, what she would give for a pure, hot beam of sunlight.

"It is like Baeddan," Arthur says. "Isn't it? This binding is turning you more like him. Part of the forest."

"Something like that," Mair admits, unmoving. But still it could work. She can take it. She can survive this.

"Damn it." Arthur strides to her and grips her shoulders, forcefully pulling her toward him. "This can't happen. I'm not going to let it."

"You can't stop it," she whispers.

He glares at Rhun, and Rhun says, "We'll find a way. Mairwen, he's right. We won't let you die in my place."

Arthur's mouth compresses. "Neither of you is dying. What do you eat and drink, what do you dream of, that makes you so willing to give everything for this bargain? Do you think I don't understand how much it matters, that I want to let it take anything from this valley? Do you think I don't care about babies dying or famine or bloody, pus-filled boils? I understand, but I won't let it win. *None* of us is dying. Do you understand me? Or do I have to put it in your own language?"

He kisses Mairwen, and she gasps at the abruptness and heat of it. Arthur's kiss is different from before, not angry, despite his anger, but demanding something from her. Demanding she rise to meet him. If Arthur is fire, his kiss should burn and consume her, but instead it makes her want to live, too. Like he's the powerful sunlight she wished for moments ago, and when his kiss ends, she's standing again in the shade.

Her mouth stays open, but she has no idea what to say. His kisses have always been a challenge or a dare, never their own conclusion.

Arthur turns his eyes to Rhun, who steps back under the force in them. "You did this," Arthur says. "You both made this thing happen, between the three of us. I thought it was only the forest, whatever exactly happened at the Bone Tree, but it was more inevitable than that, wasn't it?" And Arthur grabs the front of Rhun's jerkin and kisses him, too.

Mairwen laughs, delighted. Her hands come together in one ferocious clap, and she folds them under her chin, watching. Arthur has no idea what he's doing, clearly, and knocks his mouth against Rhun's instead of using what he knows from kissing Mairwen. She swells with affection for both of them. Her blood flows smoother, losing a measure of thickness, and the throb in her collarbone feels more like bruises and grinding teeth than pain.

The whispering is gone.

Rhun tentatively puts his hands in Arthur's hair, and Arthur leans away, jaw muscles shifting, pink flaring at the points of his cheekbones. He chews his bottom lip once, and Rhun smiles.

With a huff, Arthur stomps away from them. He waves and snarls, "Just think about *that*, you suicidal idiots."

"Arthur." Rhun starts after him, but Mairwen grabs his arm and turns them in a skipping, happy circle.

"Stay with me, Rhun," she murmurs, singsong. "He'll be back. You know he will. He only has to find a way to gnaw up whatever he's feeling and grow spikes over the top of it again."

"I don't want him to grow spikes over it." Rhun looks after Arthur, whose loping progress is fast taking him over the pasture hills toward Three Graces. His golden hair and skin and dark-brown jacket blend in with the autumn fields, and Mairwen likes thinking he fits in for once, finally.

She says, "You like his spikes—I know you do—or you wouldn't be so in love with him."

And the slow smile Rhun gives her is so full of blossoming joy and acknowledgment, for a moment Mairwen forgets everything else.

THE SAYER HOMESTEAD IS HOPPING WITH SAYERS, LIKE fleas in warm weather, especially when Rhun and Mairwen step off the path and into their goat yard. Rhun is still thinking obsessively about Arthur.

Saint Branwen and Llew bound up, barking, and Mairwen laughs a little. Rhun feels their barking in his chest and goes onto one knee to embrace the dogs. They hit him hard, strong in their welcome, but Rhun holds himself upright, scratching their shaggy necks as their long legs scramble at his thighs. He feels an echo of pain slashing down his thigh, the memory of red-eyed monster dogs, and killing them with bare hands and arrows. Rhun shudders, missing Arthur, who stabbed the dog tearing at Rhun's spine. Arthur, who kissed him, not only inside the forest, but out here in the valley, where it means something different. Who is on fire to save everybody, but especially Rhun. It's a good thing, and Rhun won't let go.

His father, Rhun the Elder, whistles for order, and the hounds obey immediately.

He and Mairwen are surrounded by Sayers, mostly men and boys, for that's some odd trick of the bloodline. "Hello, son," the Elder says, smiling the same easy smile Rhun himself used to so frequently sport. "Mairwen Grace," continues Rhun's father, tentative but warm. For years he kept distant from her, not because she's a witch, but worried it would be too hard to lose her when they lost Rhun at his Slaughter Moon. Now that it's over, he's unsure how to be.

Mairwen puts a hand to her breast, over the hidden thorns. "Mister Sayer," she says.

"Where's Baeddan?" Rhun asks.

"Slept up in the loft with us!" Elis Sayer chirps, tugging Rhun's sleeve.

Rhun the Elder nods his chin up at their outbuilding. "Was still sleeping at dawn. He looked more like himself, you know. Like being at home is healing him."

"I want to see him," Mairwen says.

"Maybe we should let him sleep," Rhun murmurs, glancing toward Mairwen's collar.

"Come eat. Non's got food out still, since this whole lot can't settle," Rhun the Elder says.

"All right," Mair agrees. She firms up her expression and heads for the house.

"Sure, Dad. I'm hungry. I could eat a bear," Rhun says, directing the last toward his little brother. Elis wrinkles his face at such a ridiculous idea.

Rhun the Elder smiles tightly and leads the way.

A wake of Sayer cousins streams after them, pressing behind Rhun and Mairwen, none of whom quite cross the threshold, afraid of Nona Sayer's ire. She's clanging around at the hearth while Delia Sayer, Rhun's aunt, prepares a chicken carcass for the pot. Brac's wife, Sal, is stirring a large bowl of cream, seated on one of the odd Sayer stools.

"Ah, you're here!" Sal says, pushing bright curls off her face with the back of her hand. "We were just talking about who we think killed the surviving saints."

Nona hisses with frustration, slamming a lid onto the savory-smelling pot simmering over her fire.

Mairwen says, "Grace witches."

"You must be joking," Nona says, fists on her hips, though the rest of those present are slower to react, shocked.

"Do you have a mirror Mair can use?" Rhun asks, diverting conflict. Since Arthur kissed him, he's been walking a razor's edge of hope.

"I do," his mother says. "Think of another culprit, Mairwen Grace. Your mother is a witch, not a devil."

Mair shifts into a stance Rhun knows well: stubborn and challenging. She says, "My mother knew our blessing ointment for the saint would tie Rhun to the Bone Tree, dooming him. It creates a binding charm that draws the saint back to the tree even if he survives his night, even if he leaves the valley. That's as good as killing them, to do it knowingly. Rhun's blood would have been on my hands, because I made the charm. That is the Grace legacy."

Nona stares at Mairwen with hard eyes. "My boy isn't dead. That's *your* legacy."

Mairwen opens her mouth but says nothing. She stares at Nona.

"The mirror's upstairs in my trunk, girl. And pick out a nicer shawl if you would like."

With a twirl, Mair heads up.

Rhun's mother sends everyone else away too, so it's only herself and her son. Then Nona turns to the fire like she's nothing to say after all, and Rhun stares at her shoulders. At the strength of them, their broadness, the length of her neck and the curls of black hair sticking to it. "Are you still bound to the tree, son? Is what she said true?"

"Yes," he answers. "Though it's different, because of Mairwen, and everything."

Suddenly, Nona spins faster than Rhun has ever seen her move, and her clenched jaw is so like his own, the car-mine in her eyes sparking like his. "I am so very proud of you for ending it, Rhun Sayer. You ran and you fought and you changed everything. No matter what happens now, whatever the bargain becomes. I couldn't bear to change my life outside the valley, for the risk it would be, so I only ran away. But you do what you know is right, for everyone, every moment. I am so proud of you."

Rhun's knees loosen and he sits. He draws a ragged breath. "It was Mairwen and Arthur who made me, who changed it. Not me."

"I don't believe you. They went into that forest for you: They might have begun the change, but they never would have without you."

"I lived my life expecting to be a saint. It isn't such a great sacrifice, if you never expected to have a future." Rhun shrugs one shoulder. "That's why I'm not better. The best. I didn't really give anything up at all."

"Rhun, you gave yourself up every day, again and again. I watched it constantly. Always choosing other than yourself. My selfless boy. I wish you'd been more selfish. I hope you're learning it now."

"Maybe. I—I love Arthur."

And? her eyebrows ask.

"Mom, I mean . . . I love him like you love Dad, like I love Mairwen, like . . . I kissed him. He kissed me."

Nona presses her mouth into a line and stares at him.

Rhun's stomach finally catches up with his confession, twisting hard.

"Well." Sighing, she slumps down onto the bench beside her son. "Well."

"It's just love, Mom," Rhun whispers. His hands clench because he wants to touch her hand, pat her shoulder, or give her a hug.

"Nothing is *just* love," Nona says almost as softly.

THE SECOND STORY OF THE SAYER HOUSE IS ONE LONG room divided by wood panels into two. The front is Nona and Rhun the Elder's bedroom. Gray sunlight stretches through the large windows, casting the room in cool pastels. Mairwen crouches at the top of the ladder, listening to the painful conversation between Rhun and his mother. Her old, easy love for Rhun grows up again as she listens to Nona reveal how proud of him she is, and it flares hot as the sun when Rhun tells his mother about Arthur. She's ready to fall back down the ladder and get in Nona's face if the woman makes even the slightest move to chastise him.

But Nona doesn't, and Rhun falls quiet, and Mairwen touches the thorns on her chest, pressing hard enough to make them ache. She loves him so very much, and Arthur, too, and she isn't going to let anything happen to either of them, or Haf or her family or the Priddys or Pughs, or to a woman like Nona Sayer, who never will talk about her past but was brave enough to leave it and find a future.

That's what Mairwen has to do: carve a future for *everybody* in Three Graces.

Standing, Mair goes to the small trunk beside the bed, opening it. The mirror rests on a narrow shelf carved into the left side of the trunk. Its handle is made of bone, yellowed with age, and the mirror itself is backed with silver and mother-of-pearl.

Taking a fortifying breath, Mairwen flips the mirror around.

The first thing she notices are the stark lines of her cheeks that never were so blatant before. Her eyes are only slightly sunken with weariness, and the eyes themselves large as ever. Bowed lips plenty pink, and when she bares her teeth, she likes the shine of them. Her chin seems daintier now, because of the raw mess of her hair. It falls in jagged curls and weird layers, a true bramble.

And that blackness in her eyes. It's a spiral pattern in one and random starbursts of black in the other. Mairwen shudders, loving it, even as it scares her.

She holds the mirror closer, at an odd angle, to inspect her hairline, to dig in with fingers to find any hint of more antlers or thorns ready to sprout from her skull. Nothing. Lowering the mirror, she unties her shirt and reveals the collarbone. The base of the small thorns are crusted with blood, for she hasn't washed them well, and her skin tinges bluish.

She traces the path they create across her chest. The skin is so sensitive, like her lips. She wants to know what it feels like to have someone else touch her there, with gentle hands or mouth.

For a moment, Mairwen is lost in a forest growing up through the walls of the Sayer house, vines of thick green, bending branches full of emerald and dark purple leaves. The forest whispers in her ears, tickling her skin from the inside out. Her chest expands, her hips roll, and her head falls back as the forest promises to bring her to its heart, again and again.

The veil slips against her braids, against her shoulders and arms as he gently pulls it away. Through the white lace she sees the black flicker of his eyes, the shimmer of his form, always changing— antlers, fangs, fur, soft skin, four delicate legs, bare feet, hands that grip her waist, tendrils of thin green vines circling his arm, his neck, long hair dripping tiny flowers, feathers spilling along his spine, and wings, even, stretching like the night sky—and she longs to be brought inside all of that, a piece of him, when the veil is gone.

She gasps as it falls finally away, and smiles at the creature. Then a whisper in the wind makes her blood cold. He is gone. She's alone, except no—

Who?

What is this. When is this?

Mairwen faces the girl in the long white veil, and the girl lifts her hand, points at Mair, and says—

A footstep on the stairs startles Mairwen awake, and she is only a young woman holding a mirror, kneeling in someone else's bedroom, staring at herself. Her eyes are blacker now, and her gums ache as if her teeth are loose. She pulls back her lips to see her eyeteeth grown just slightly longer and sharper.

"Haf is here," Rhun says. "She needs to show you something."

ADERYN GRACE STANDS IN THE CENTER OF HER COTtage, hands raised to bring down a dried bundle of yarrow. A persistent memory has caught her midaction, an image from her dream—a dream she's experienced the past three nights.

In the dream, she's pressed flush to the wall, laughing, as a man kisses along the curve of her neck. He smells like rain and summer flowers, and Aderyn opens herself up to him as if nothing in the world belongs inside her as well as he does. When he pulls back, taking both her hands, she sees his face and it is beautiful.

But when she wakes, his features fade to a blur of affection and distant memory. The Grace witch does not enjoy uncertainty, nor muddled memories. She's never been inside the forest—why should her mind be affected as her daughter's is?

"Aderyn?"

Hetty ducks around the kitchen table and pokes the witch in the shoulder. It startles Aderyn from her contemplation. "I'm all right. Only . . ."

"The dream. It's your daughter, stirring up memories of Carey, and the early sacrifice, and all the questions. You know."

Aderyn turns to Hetty and takes the other woman's freckled face in both hands. "I hope it does not hurt you."

"How could it? I'll never resent any part of your life, especially a part that gave you Mairwen."

The Grace witch smiles sadly, but with all her heart, and gently tugs Hetty nearer, turning her own head to allow Hetty's lips access to her neck. She will replace the memory with hotter love.

"Ladies."

The voice thunders through Aderyn's ribs and she stumbles away from Hetty. Her eyes squeeze tightly closed as memories rattle her bones, jerking her heart into stillness. Memories of sex and purple flowers and her thrill at getting away with something terrible.

"Addie, I need something of yours," the voice says, rich and crawling up her spine like a lover's scratch.

Hetty screams.

Framed in the cottage doorway is Mairwen's father.

ARTHUR COUCH STANDS AT THE EDGE OF THE DEVIL'S Forest.

Daylight streams through the canopy, despite the thinly overcast sky, reflecting motes of dust and forest rot hanging in the air. A few remaining brown and gold leaves shiver in the tiny breeze, like the trees are waving to him.

"Arthur Couch!" sings a bird woman, swooping toward him. "Did you miss us?"

"Hello, little thing; no, I did not."

She snaps at him and darts away—past him, out into the gray sunlight.

Arthur spins to watch her. In her wake, two more bird women fly out. They giggle and spin, one lifting high to soar like a hawk. Right out in the open, far beyond where he stands at the forest boundary.

Fear makes his heartbeat flicker.

If they're able to fly free, what else? Next could be a thing like that deer that stumbled out when the bargain was weak before. There are so many worse things hiding deep in the forest, and worser still that he might not even remember.

This must be done, and now, before their binding breaks. Before Rhun or Mairwen answers the Bone Tree's call.

Arthur hefts the ax in his left hand, and fingers the fire steel in the pocket of his coat.

When he was a child, he swore he'd run in and offer his heart to the devil, to prove he was the best. It turns out the devil never wanted him, but not because there's anything wrong with Arthur. All the wrongness in their valley was born in the original bargain itself. Those rules for the sacrifice somebody decided mattered—only a boy and only the best—passed down as traditions, creating a tight web of what it means to be the best boy, and barriers dividing people. That way of life, that system, nearly strangled Arthur and would have murdered Rhun Sayer, the only person in Three Graces who definitely didn't deserve it. Born from the lie that you can be both a saint and a survivor.

If the only way to keep it from happening again, to unravel the story back to the beginning, is to burn it all down, then that's what Arthur will do.

He walks back into the Devil's Forest.

B AEDDAN CROUCHES BETWEEN TWO TALL, HAPPY trees just beyond the Sayer homestead, and listens to the call of songbirds. There are no words in their singing, no longing, no danger. Just two birds. He glances up at the canopy, trying to spy them. Leaves fall gently, drifting in the windless forest air, and beyond them the branches splay against a gray sky, with only hints of the sun. It's quiet, peaceful. Baeddan can hear his own calm breathing, and none of his heartbeat.

He covers his ears to make certain, eyes locked above, slowly crossing the sky for the birds.

There! A flit of a wing, too purposeful to be a fluttering leaf. A flash of rusty brown.

Humming, Baeddan walks on, following the bird. He feels free. Someone or something else has drawn away his burden.

Perhaps he is finally dead, he thinks, except the birdsong is too lovely, too much like home.

He woke this morning in a pile of boys and dogs, surrounded by hay and discarded furniture, wrapped in musty wool and his face pressed to a fur blanket. Little boys and cousins younger than him but seeming older all snored

305

together, mouths open, some sprawled, others curled, and it reminded Baeddan of the roots of the Bone Tree, and all their teeth were flowers and their skulls would soon show through withered, dead skin, their hair twisted into vines.

He pushed free and stumbled down the ladder from the barn loft, out the back, where he knew without thinking a rear door opened to a path leading higher up the mountain before it curved around southwest to join with the Upjohn homestead.

It seemed a good path.

His humming mars the birdsong, but a crow joins in, and Baeddan laughs as loud as it calls. He smells smoke and he's hungry for it, for something—anything. Reaching for a nearby tree, he slips his fingers under a fan of pale-orange lichen. He stops. No. He does not eat such things, not out here. Not . . .

Baeddan squeezes his eyes shut. His hunger fades, replaced by discomfort where his bare feet are growing cold. "Baeddan," he says aloud. Will the name ever stick?

Where is the Grace witch? he wonders, glancing around for a flash of white—no. She has brambled brown hair and dark eyes and—

The heart of the forest suddenly beats in his chest.

Thunderous and abrupt.

Saint.

Saint.

He steps in time with it, turning down the mountain.

The voice of the Devil's Forest is hissing and chaotic, pulling at him and others. . . . Baeddan feels it expand suddenly, its need pushing outward and larger than before. Toward him.

He can't understand, but the shadow inside him grows.

What is his name?

Sighing through his teeth, he thinks he should go back to—to the Sayers. Baeddan Sayer. Yes, he should find . . .

Birds dart overhead; they giggle and laugh. Not birds, or not only birds, but—

No, he should go *this* way.

He does, following his instinct down a slope of conifers. His feet slide through the deadfall and he slows, quieting his progress. This requires silence, the stalking, the slipping behind, coming around, listening, listening for—

Saint, the forest says, in a heavy, demanding dark voice this young devil has never heard before.

Bring me the saint.

HAF WAITS IN THE SAYER KITCHEN, HANDS WRUNG together. For a second, Mair sees the veiled girl standing in Haf's place, but she blinks and her friend is there again. Mairwen lists toward Rhun, who holds her elbow.

She feels so strange, and the memory of the veiled girl hangs in her thoughts. It was not her memory, nor Rhun's, nor Arthur's, but a forest memory. Was it the first Grace and the old god?

"What happened to the old god of the forest?" she asks.

"Mairwen?"

Startling out of her thoughts, Mair focuses on Haf as Rhun sits her down at the table and puts a plate of hot bread in front of her. "Yes," she says, lifting the bread.

Rhun sits beside her, and Haf on her other side. They lean together around Mairwen, conspiratorial. Haf murmurs, "Look," and puts out her light-gold hand, palm-up. A smear of blood mars the delicate skin between her thumb and forefinger, around a puncture wound. "I caught it on a splinter last night, stumbling in the dark, and washed it, bound it, went to sleep. It was like this when I woke."

"The bargain should heal this sort of thing overnight," Rhun says.

Mairwen stares. At the fire, Nona stirs up the coals beneath her cauldron and nestles potatoes along the edges. Sal has returned to stirring her bowl of cream, and Delia is stuffing the chicken she cleaned at the far end of the table. All quiet, all listening.

"I said it was temporary binding," Mairwen says in her normal voice, if a bit tighter for worry.

Sal's eyes flash to Mairwen, then Delia, then Mairwen again. "But so soon?"

"Do you feel all right?" Rhun asks Mair, nudging her plate closer to her hand. "Eat."

Nona stands. "It'll last as long as it lasts. Then we're on our own."

"Unless we make a new bargain," Rhun says. He's looking at Mairwen, not his mother.

"If my binding won't hold it, if my heart won't, like this, then death is the only way," Mair says. "We can't just shove someone into the forest to die."

Rhun puts his hand over hers. "It isn't that simple. If I'd known the truth, I might have volunteered anyway. If I'd been raised that way, knowing what it would mean for everybody else. Without the lie."

"Rhun," whispers Haf.

He glances at her. "Bree wouldn't be alive if it wasn't for the bargain. And when I was small there was a pox that rolled through overnight, and vanished. How many might it have killed otherwise? And Rhos's baby is alive right now, and I touched her little nose. It's the same bargain it always was: one life for all this. Isn't that worth it?"

"Some folk are saying so," Haf says. "That the saint is the saint, and you have to . . . that we should . . . put you back in."

"That is what makes it wrong," Nona says, slamming her hand flat to her hearth. "Any folk who'd try that don't deserve my son's life."

Mairwen nods, and Haf, too. Sal leans on the end of the table. "That's right, Rhun."

Aunt Delia has tears in her eyes, but nods.

"You should stay here a while," Haf says to Rhun. "Keep out of sight. And where's Arthur? He's not the saint, not really, but the way his father talks and some others . . . they might . . ."

"I can't hide," Rhun says. "I'll go find Arthur. The bargain will last a little while longer, and then we'll—"

Mair stands. "I'm going to the manor, to look through Sy Vaughn's books. There might be answers there. I want to know what his ancestors think happened to the old god."

"I'm going with you," Haf says, and Mair nods.

"Rhun, find Arthur, and Baeddan if you can. Hunt, encourage everyone you meet to live as if it's any day, and all is well. Three Graces is the life part of the bargain, so people need to live."

Rhun puts his hands on Mair's waist and kisses her.

The veil slips against her braids, against her shoulders and arms as he

Mair presses her mouth harder to Rhun's, feels the burn of the thorns at her collarbone and the impression of her own sharpening teeth against her upper lip. "Be careful," she whispers.

Just as she lets go, she gasps: Her blood pulls taught suddenly, thick and cold. She shivers and lets Rhun wrap his arms around her. She can feel the forest reaching toward her, all the way here on the mountain. It is desperate, and *strong!* The shadows pierce past the line of trees, up the pasture toward her mother's house. Eyes shut, face pressed to Rhun's shoulder, she sees a flock of birds dart over the valley, and a wind drags out of the Devil's Forest, rolling toward her.

. . .

THE DEVIL STUMBLES ACROSS THE YARD AND AGAINST the door, hard enough it shakes and his shoulder grows a new bruise. His sight is fading, blurred. He hurts everywhere, and the command is all, all, all he hears: *hungry, so hungry bring the saint find the saint the saint saint*

Every step withers the grass at his feet. Every tree he touches shivers and turns black in a mark the shape of his hand.

The devil is dying, and taking it all with him.

Throwing himself against the door again, the devil roars. He pounds and claws at it, and the door gives way.

Inside is warm, a fire in the hearth. He growls at a woman and young girl, blurs of skirts and wide eyes, and they grab on to each other, calling "John! John!"

The forest calls, too, *John! John!*

"John!" the devil bellows, and for a moment his sight clears, his mind clears. Baeddan knows why he's here.

Running, he pushes aside the women and tears into the second large room of this homestead: A man waits for him, half dressed, light hair loose, one-handed. The other arm ends at a pinkish, shining scar of a wrist.

John Upjohn can hardly breathe.

The devil's skin is yellowish and cream; the antlers have fallen from hair and head, and even his thorns are dying, two missing, with wounds left behind, and the hint of black bone beneath. He trembles. He's weak. His eyes are sunken into his face and his lips are dry and cracked as he pulls them open over his sharp teeth.

John steps closer, eyes locked to the devil's chest, where the remaining twenty-odd bones of his hand are sewn with vine and sinew into the devil's flesh. Finger bones and hand bones, strange knuckles and pebble-like wrist bones.

The devil jumps forward to claim his prize.

THE FOREST IS QUIET, BUT NOT SILENT.

Light diffuses through the barren canopy, bright enough, but unnerving, as Arthur picks his way as directly north as he can, toward the Bone Tree. He imagines taking axes and shovels and with a line of men cutting a path through it all. Marking it with red paint as a warning not to stray.

Unlike two nights ago, Arthur cuts a strong, confident figure as he strides between the trees. No ducking aside, no peering uncertainly through the shadows. When he comes across a stream, he recognizes it from a flickering memory and leaps over it, glad to know he's still going the right way. When a dozen bird women shriek and dive at him, he only shoves them away, batting gently with his hands. "I am Arthur Couch, and you know me," he says through his teeth. "Let me be. You may not have my blood." When his path is blocked by three undead bone creatures, one with a raven skull, another a goat, and the final a fox, he smiles his most ferocious smile and brandishes his knife.

They laugh and skip around to join the bird women following him.

It isn't more than a quarter hour before Arthur has an entourage of ghouls and bone boys, all clicking their teeth and giggling. A fanged and claw-footed deer picks behind, and a handful of black wolves with red eyes and razor teeth. Shadows flitter, more shape than form, and nearly invisible in this scattered light.

His stomach growls. Arthur wishes he'd eaten something. Though he passes bright apples and vibrant black berries, he won't risk it.

The song of the wind takes up a more skeletal chime, and Arthur knows he's near the Bone Tree. It creaks and groans even without wind, stretching itself wider and digging deep into the earth below the forest.

He steps into the grove, leaving his creepy entourage huddled at the edges.

All is gray, as if it is the surface of the moon, but for the cage of black trees encircling them. The Bone Tree stands tall, looming over everything with cragged white branches and dark gray scars. Strewn across the bare earth are a hundred dead scarlet leaves. And a few sprinkles of blood, darkened to brown or a deep purple.

Arthur bends over, spits blood onto the ground, then does his best to growl. It's a losing fight. He's weak, but he will not let—

Blinking away the memory—for what good will it do him now? He has a mission—Arthur walks carefully toward the Bone Tree.

The altar waits, cold and pale and empty, stripped of its black vines and gruesome remains. Roots thick and grossly pale, like massive worms rising from the earth, embrace the altar and prop up the Bone Tree itself.

And of course, there are the bones. Arthur clenches his fists, seething at the plain evidence of centuries of deadly sacrifice. Twenty-five skulls, staring and smiling, tied in a spiral pattern to the rough white face of the tree. A flare of scapula and ribs, like wings stretching up and back, and rows of long bones, femurs and arm bones lined into a terrible coat of mail.

Glancing up, Arthur winces at the glare of light; everything is too bright, too silvery-white. At least the conflagration he has planned will warm it all.

Arthur heads for the altar. He grabs old vines and scraps of cloth that remain from the jerkins and trousers and shirts of saints before Baeddan. It is gruesome to think on, but he takes satisfaction that he'll be giving them a massive funeral pyre.

He's got a good pile of leaves, twigs, dried-out strips of bark stacked against, around, and atop the altar, ready to light, when a sound catches his attention.

Turning, he looks at the edges of the Bone Tree's grove, hunting for whatever made it.

Nothing.

Silence surrounds him; even the ghouls and monsters ducked between shadows have gone silent. That stillness puts Arthur's teeth on edge. He pulls out his knife. It cannot be Baeddan. That devil was never silent. But who else? What else?

He slows his breathing with great effort and pulls out his fire steel.

A branch cracks.

Arthur nearly drops the loop of metal.

Something groans; it's the Bone Tree.

Mouth hanging in shock, he glances up at the skeletons and staring skulls, at the higher white branches, laced with deep fissures of age. Is that a splash of color? Violet.

A flower. It floats down and lands at the tip of his pyre. The petals look velvety, teardrop shaped, and one by one they wither into blackness.

More fall. Three there, and then a handful, trembling as they flutter down and down around him.

The Bone Tree shudders, and pale-green tendrils push out from the cracks in its bark.

"What is going on?" Arthur asks aloud.

"I've come home," says a creature behind him, voice low and full of satisfaction.

THE LAST TIME MAIRWEN CLIMBED THIS DIFFICULT mountain path, she was eager and desperate, running on fumes of hope because one of the horses in the pasture was sick and Rhos Priddy went into early labor. She scales it again now, with Haf just behind her, conquering the over-grown trail, grasping boulders and tangled roots to drag up and up. But she is stronger than before, filled with a power that tells her where to grasp, how to step. She can reach back and pull Haf up, assisting where it's needed.

"Mairwen, you're not afraid."

Surprised, she stops. Haf pants lightly. Exertion puts a pretty flush in her lips and brightens her eyes. Long wisps of sleek black hair stick to her tan neck.

Mairwen holds out her arm, showing Haf the gauntlet of forest growing from wrist toward her elbow and the way her ruddy pink skin is tinging violet. "It's power. A manifestation of what I'm becoming."

"Which is?"

"Part of the forest, I think. Like Baeddan was, before we pulled him out."

"Is it because you're a witch?"

"And daughter of a saint. And I anointed myself," Mair confesses with a brief downward flick of her eyes.

Laughing breathlessly, Haf takes Mair's hand. "I always wanted to be a witch, too. Because you are, and you're so . . ."

"Weird?"

"But you don't care."

"I think you'd be a marvelous witch. If you weren't so happy with Ifan, and it wouldn't make Arthur cry, I'd convince you to be my witch partner, like Hetty and my mother."

"Do they . . . ?"

"They do."

Haf squirms. "Well." She grips Mairwen's hand tightly.

"Here," Mair says, grinning with her sharp teeth, "is the first lesson: listen."

Silence stretches. Mairwen nods and continues climbing, Haf's hand still in hers. Mair listens to the slip of pebbles tumbling under their feet, the wind through the trees and tall grass ahead, where the mountain juts up past the tree line. She listens to Haf's breath pick up with effort and expectation, to her own slight grunt of effort, and the throb of blood in her ears. She listens to the voice of the forest, calling, calling, and it's not in her ears. It's in her heart. Since it pushed out, it's gone quieter again, as if it caught something and reeled it back in.

"Listen to what?" Haf finally says, exasperated.

"Just listen!" Mair tugs them a little faster. "To everything. Listen. Mom used to set me somewhere and leave me for an hour, and when she returned asked me to tell her everything I heard, and what I thought of it." The reminder is bitter in the aftermath of Aderyn's confession; Mair thinks if she'd learned the lesson better, she'd have known the truth long ago.

"What is the second lesson?" Haf asks.

"My mother would say learning to steep herbs and make an ointment, or patience. But I think it's seeing between day and night. Learning to find a place between everything. That's the charm. Life, dead, and grace in between. The witch in between."

"Being comfortable there," Haf says thoughtfully. She slips her arms around Mairwen's waist.

Mair nods, hugging back. "I think being a witch means making choices, too. If you can see between day and night, if you see shades between good and evil, then you can act on what others can't, or refuse to, see. Change things."

"I've always admired that you didn't fit anywhere, so you made your own place."

"You do too, Haf. Nobody says who you are but you. It doesn't matter who anybody wants us to be. We choose. We decide."

Haf stops moving. She watches Mairwen carefully for a moment, then nods. "Maybe. I think I'm lucky because I *want* to be what others also want me to be. It's harder for you."

"I make it hard."

"Is Arthur a witch?"

Mair huffs.

"He's lived between," Haf suggests. "I thought he was lucky at first, to get to be both, but he hated it."

"He fights so hard against being undefinable! I love it. He'd rather nobody saw his betweenness. How can he see between light and dark if he's determined to only ever stand in the dark?"

"Maybe he couldn't tell who he wanted to be, when people forced it on him so early."

"No more than the rest of us are dressed as we're born and trained as we're supposed to behave," Mairwen says.

Haf sighs.

"Arthur's problem," Mairwen says, "is he puts more value

on being a boy than on being a girl. As if the fact that the best boy is sacrificed means boys are better than girls. That's not why."

"Why?"

"It's just how the bargain was formed. I think any heart would bind it, but that wasn't a good enough story. To make people believe something deeply enough to hurt other people, the bargain had to be specific, had to create rules the town could ascribe meaning to. Could imbue with value. Trust me; people don't like magic that doesn't make sense, that isn't easy to believe. It was easy to believe a strong, skilled, noble boy could be worthy of sacrifice, especially if he had a chance to survive."

"You want to change the story."

"We have to."

"That will hurt too," Haf murmurs, but not to argue against it.

For a moment, Mairwen listens again to the wind, the distant voice of the forest, and her gently beating heart. She knows Haf is right, or mostly right. It wasn't the girl's name or dresses that hurt Arthur. No, he was happy when they were all children. She remembers how hard Lyn Couch laughed. What hurt him was the rule change. Being forced out of girlhood into boyhood, as if it were only an either/ or, as if to make any other choice was unnatural. He was so little when his world was dragged out from under him, it was no wonder he clung to the rules forever after. His world changed and he wouldn't change with it, until he broke another rule, until he ran into the forest and witnessed for himself the lies. Arthur had to change to survive. Just like Three Graces. The rules of the bargain have changed, and they all have to find a way together to change again. For the better. Mair smiles. "We should all learn to be witches in Three Graces."

"I'll start," Haf says.

Mairwen kisses her cheek, breathing in the wonderful smell of the sweet oil Haf rubs in the ends of her hair to keep it from drying out in the winter. "Let's go."

They finally reach the flat yard of stone and gravel, where no trees grow. There are the remains of the bonfire from the night of the Slaughter Moon, when she was the Grace witch and she anointed the saint and kissed him, not knowing what it was she sentenced him to.

Heading quietly past it, Mairwen pushes through the iron gate. At the heavy front door, she lifts a hand to knock, but discovers the door open a handspan.

"Oh," Haf says, worried.

Mair uses her shoulder to shove the door open. "Hello? Lord Vaughn?" Her voice echoes slightly down the dim corridor. She follows it. "Vaughn?"

There's no reply, and hardly a thing to hear. No crackling fire. No noise besides the shuffle of Haf's feet at the threshold. Mairwen's bare toes make no sound.

The girls wend their way through the manor, past pristine limewash and dark wooden panels, through the library and kitchen, sitting room and a narrow music room full of dusty instruments. They search every room they can find, even shoving aside the tapestries for signs of hidden rooms. Vaughn is nowhere to be found.

A S HE MAKES HIS WAY DOWN INTO THREE GRACES, Rhun's thoughts flit between a pleased anticipation for seeing Arthur again and worry that he won't live up to his mother's expectations. *You do what you know is right.* She's proud of him, and he wants to keep it so, but he's not sure what is right anymore. Haf Lewis says folks are upset—and rightly so—that instead of doing his duty he let Mairwen and Arthur change the bargain, rebinding it in a way that can't last. They're right, too. He did choose to live, to give Mairwen's binding a chance.

There's a moment he remembers now from the forest, when Arthur tried to give himself to the devil and save Rhun, and all Rhun could feel was a desperate need to survive. For *both* of them to walk out of the forest. Together. He forgot it, just as he forgot what is worth saving.

Rhun wants to live, but he doesn't want Three Graces to suffer for it.

Moving as quietly as he does, Rhun startles Judith and Ben Heir, who are taking a turn with the sheep, nudging the herd toward longer grass. They're holding hands, and Judith stretches up to whisper something, tickling behind Ben's ear until he smiles. Last night at the Sayer table, Rhun heard from his cousin Delia, who heard from her sister-in-law, that

Judith's pregnant. The next generation of children to be sacrificed for the forest.

He stops. "Congratulations, you two." It's difficult to tell if he means it.

Judith leans back against her husband, whose hands grip her shoulders. "Thank you, Rhun," she says with a smile.

"I want my child to be safe," Ben says, less happy, but with a look that Rhun knows exactly how to interpret.

"I want that too, Ben. Have you seen Arthur?"

"No," Judith answers. She hesitates before saying more.

Ben says, "How can we just let this all fall apart?"

"We're trying not to. Arthur, Mairwen, and me, and Haf Lewis, and anybody else who wants to can try with us. Mair and Haf are up at Vaughn's manor now, looking for answers. I need Arthur. For . . ." He shrugs.

"Strange birds flew out of the forest this morning," Ben says. "And it's been overcast for hours."

"We need rain," Judith reminds her husband.

"We usually get a perfect amount of it. Now, I don't know. What if it floods?"

"What do you think we should do?" Rhun asks him.

The slighter man runs a hand over his short brown hair. He winces. He shakes his head. "I'm not sure."

"It's hard. I know what some are saying." Rhun starts to walk past, thinking of his mother's words. *Any folk who'd try that don't deserve my son's life.*

"I just want my son to live, or my daughter," Ben presses.

Rhun turns back. "You want me, or some other boy, to

die so yours will live, Ben. I understand that. Until he's fifteen or so, and then maybe it's his turn. Only, you'll know there's no chance that he'll run back out of the forest. If your son is the saint." Rhun steps closer, holding Ben's gaze. "I'm sorry."

"Without it, he might die before he's even born," Judith whispers, holding her small belly.

"I know."

"What are we going to do about it, then?" Ben holds his wife tight.

The bracelet on Rhun's wrist tightens suddenly. He freezes and pushes back his sleeve. The braided hair and vines constrict and crumble, turning to ash.

It's gone. Rhun splays out his hand, then makes a fist, concentrating on the strength in his arm. There's no magic.

Eyes widening, he looks north to the forest. It hasn't even occurred to him the voice has been silent for a long while, asleep or dull or just uninterested in seducing him back to the Bone Tree.

But that's not the problem. Their binding isn't slowly weakening, falling apart.

Something just broke it.

IN VAUGHN'S BEDCHAMBER, MAIRWEN AND HAF DIScover a bed the size of Mair's entire loft. Its posts are built of the solid trunks of trees, dark wood and polished to a shine. The mattress is thick and moves with feathers, not straw, and smells of pine and an earthy fragrance Mair can't quite put a name to besides "autumn." Haf runs her fingers along the edge of a narrow silk pillow and reaches up to touch the fringe decorating the dark-blue curtain.

Though she intended to explore the small pile of letters atop the table in the corner, and the lacquered box beside them, Mairwen stops as she crosses the floor at the foot of the bed. A long gray stone is embedded among the smaller stone tiles, and when she crouches, it's slightly warm to the touch.

Just like the hearthstone in her house, and just like the Bone Tree's altar.

"Mairwen," Haf whispers, though there's nobody around to hide from.

A chill creeping up her spine, Mairwen glances at her friend. She's pointing to the cold hearth, and a small oval painting set against it. It's a painted portrait of a little girl.

Mairwen rushes to it, lifting it carefully. The paint is old, cracking along the border where it meets the thin gold frame. But the gaze of the girl is as intense as looking in a mirror. Round brown eyes, a thin pink smile, blotchy pink skin, and dark hair with hints of sunlight red.

It's her. When she was five or six years old.

Before Mairwen can say anything, her wrist pinches.

Then, with a cry, Mair falls to her knees as fire and night-black coldness both flare in her body: the heat in her blood, the cold in her bones.

She drops the portrait, and Haf crashes down beside her, grabbing her shoulders, calling her name.

Mairwen's tongue is so dry, her throat closed; she coughs, wretchedly, feeling something choking her, tearing up from her stomach. She shudders and tastes it, bitter and sweet both, blood and sugar. She spits out a flower. A tiny purple viola.

From Baeddan's bleeding wounds purple flowers grow, wither, and die, falling in black ashes to surround his bare feet. "I let the last one go, and look what's become of me."

"Oh, Mairwen, is it getting worse?" Haf asks.

"No," Mairwen says from a raw throat, then spits out another tiny purple flower. Her hands are splayed before her on the stone floor: one plain and ruddy, knuckles whitening with tension, the other bluish and splotched, but the gauntlet is flaking off, chipping away in tiny brown scraps. The braided hair shrivels, pinching at her.

Suddenly Mair's chest is on fire. She struggles to kneel back and tears down the shirt, ripping the linen on the edge of a thorn. The thorn falls off with a slick sound, and Mair bites her lip.

The forest is withdrawing from her! Fast and desperate, ignoring her body's need for slower change.

"It hurts," she whimpers. "Help me to my feet."

"Get in the bed, Mair. I'll—"

"No! I have to go to the Bone Tree. I have to—something is very wrong!"

Mairwen uses Haf to climb to her feet, stepping on the

portrait. Her heel snaps it in two and she stumbles, but Haf is there to catch her, and together they run out of the manor.

ARTHUR TURNS SO FAST HE KNOCKS BACK AGAINST the altar.

Emerging from the forest is a man, simply dressed in a fine tunic and trousers, his shirt collar untied around his throat and the cuffs loose at his wrists. He wears no boots or stockings, and his bare feet are strangely pale, mottled like moonlight, as is his face. His smile is wide and curved like a scythe, his hair wild and all the colors of tree bark and earth: browns and grays and blacks and reds, twisted into a riot of curls. His eyes seem to widen and narrow separately from each other, one dark and one light, and it is only that which allows Arthur to put a name to the man.

"Lord Vaughn?" he says, squinting.

The man raises his arms, and several bird women land upon his open palms. "Lord, at least," he says warmly.

Flowers continue to rain gently down upon them, and Vaughn tilts his chin to look up at the Bone Tree.

"Ah, my heart," he says.

Arthur's mind is spinning. He sits on the edge of the altar.

Vaughn enters the grove, moving directly toward Arthur but staring at the Bone Tree. Two bird women clutch his arm, and another settles in his hair. In his wake, a handful of bone creatures crawl after, the raven and two foxes, wide eyes stuck on Vaughn in a way Arthur can only read as awe. All around the grove the trees shift and shiver, with no breeze to cause it, and the shadows reach inward. Arthur hears clicking teeth and the rustle of feathers, footsteps, and the creak of cold branches.

And he sees these same little purple flowers that fall from the tree growing anew where Vaughn steps. They push stems out from the cracked earth, from between the massive roots, from under flat stones; they reach up, curling, and the violet buds burst open.

Arthur presses his bottom to the altar's edge, gripping it too, his body rigid with slow understanding and panic.

"You're the devil," he says as Vaughn passes close by. The lord is taller, and his gait inhuman, as if his—yes, his legs have bent wrong, with an extra joint it seems, the strong rear legs of a horse beneath his trousers, but his feet spread and grow tufts of fur, clawed almost like a wildcat.

Vaughn laughs. His voice is hollow, echoing on itself, and deep within the laugh Arthur swears he hears the ringing of bells.

Thorns push out from the lord's forehead and temples, growing up and hooking in, until he wears a crown of them. They divide and spread like antlers, but flowers bloom, wither, and die, then bloom again, spilling down into his hair and over his cheeks.

The old god of the forest, Arthur thinks, and it's Mairwen's voice whispering the words to him. Then Arthur thinks, *I am doomed.*

If he can find a chance to light his fire, maybe he'll get out. Vaughn seems so enchanted by the Bone Tree, by his own movements and laughter, it might be possible. Arthur slowly reaches in his pocket again for the fire steel. He'll have one chance to catch the sparks. Thank God he's already got the rags and dry grass. A spark and a breath and maybe—

He spins and cracks the ring of steel against the altar. Sparks fly. He bends, cupping his hands around the fodder, and gently blows.

A wide, gnarled hand presses down over the sparks. Smoke coils around the devil's fingers. Arthur grabs his knife and spins, cutting simultaneously.

The blade slashes across Vaughn's chest, through tunic and into flesh. Blood splashes on Arthur's face, and Vaughn grabs him by the throat.

Vaughn lifts Arthur off the ground, holding him high by only the neck. Arthur claws at the devil's wrist, kicks out; his boot connects hard, but it's like kicking a giant oak. He grinds his jaw, seething breaths as best he can, holding himself up with the strength in his arms.

Vaughn contemplates Arthur's struggle. Blood, thick and reddish and brown, drizzles slow and sticky down his chest. Like sap. His eyes are black through and through, with flecks of brown and white, and his mouth bright red, devastatingly red, his teeth sharp. As Arthur stares, eyes bulging, Vaughn's skin continues to transform. It darkens in streaks, down from his eyes, gray and purple as if his veins have all burst and spread under his skin, or like death. He's dying and decomposing before Arthur.

"Why," the creature Vaughn asks, words thick, "did your mother not take you with her?"

Arthur hisses, spit flecking his lips, and stars sprinkle through his vision. Black spots pop in his eyes. Blood roars in his ears. He kicks again and again, twisting, but he can't breathe enough to—to—

He's flying backward, tossed easily back, over the altar. He lands in the mess of Bone Tree roots, hard. His body constricts, and he can't catch a breath.

Then he's sucking in air, gasping, coughing, hands on the roots, turning over to crawl up.

The Bone Tree shakes, and beneath him the earth trembles. Or Arthur is the one shaking, breathing hard.

A ringing in his ears fades to a lower pitch, and he hears giggling all around him.

Glancing up through reddened vision, Arthur sees Vaughn at the trunk of the Bone Tree, leaning in to put his cheek against its rough bark. One of his bony hands grips the lowest skull, fingers curled around the bottom jaw like he's holding on to a skeletal scream.

His back has broadened, tearing the tunic, and he's taller, and bright white again. His hair is more like fur, sleek and black, and he glances over his shoulder at Arthur.

"Alive, still. Well."

"I don't—" It hurts Arthur to speak, but he forces words

through his bruised throat. "Why do you . . . care . . . about my . . . mother?"

"I don't understand how she could leave her child. I nearly destroyed myself for mine, and your mother just . . . left."

"I'd never have left!" Arthur yells.

The devil, whatever he is, crouches, balanced easily on his wildcat legs, and watches Arthur. "Yes. You're too like me. I've always believed that, too."

Arthur shakes his head. "No, no, I'm not."

"Too powerful for the place you're rooted. Wanting more but unable to let go."

"No." Pushing to his knees, Arthur shakes his head again. "I'm not."

A moth bats wings against his cheek, and a centipede the size of a snake slips across the back of Arthur's hand, scurrying toward the tree.

Flowers continue to fall.

What did the devil say? Arthur squeezes his eyes tightly shut. *I nearly destroyed myself for mine.* "What child?" Arthur demands. He coughs, racked with the ache of it from his throat.

"It doesn't matter to you, Arthur Couch. I'll be right there, to snap your neck properly."

Arthur begins to crawl away, carefully getting to his feet, though he sways and stumbles back. "So you, what? You wanted more and so you made a bargain with the Grace witches, to leave your forest?"

"Yes, exactly! A taste of freedom, able to leave these

roots, but the roots had to change, they had to have a replacement god."

"The devils you gave it hardly replaced you."

"Not the devils, not the saints themselves, but the life and death of them. The cycle, you see? Life and death. That is what I am, what has always been the heart of my forest. I tore free by giving the heart a different channel."

Arthur can see now what the devil is doing: He's caressing the Bone Tree, slowly coaxing it to open, so that the heavy white bark draws back from a crevasse. "Are you going back in?"

"Planting a new seed, Arthur Couch."

"With what?"

Then Vaughn smiles again. "Here it comes."

Screams of laughter erupt behind Arthur, and he turns. Something is coming, dragging something else behind it.

Arthur stands, holding on to the altar for strength.

The devil—Baeddan.

Arthur steps closer, but Baeddan doesn't see him. His tattered black coat catches and tears on a scraggly bush, but Baeddan continues on, tugging violently at his prize.

"Baeddan?" Arthur says.

The devil looks up and grins. "I've got the saint, and I've got the saint! He'll be woven into the Bone Tree, Arthur Couch, for now and for ever, and I will be free! Oh, I am hungry."

Panic slices through Arthur, and he runs toward Baeddan. "Rhun?" he gasps, skidding to a stop at the edge of the grove.

"Ha, ha, ha!" says Baeddan, then deteriorates into rasping, devilish laughter.

It is a body Baeddan was dragging behind him. There's a roaring in Arthur's ears as he closes in. Baeddan grabs the saint's hair, jerking his head up.

John Upjohn.

The energy of Baeddan's gesture pulls the man's eyes half open, and his jaw is slack. His arms dangle so that his single hand has scraped bloody and raw against the earth. Dirt and leaves cover his chest, and the front of his jerkin is torn.

"He's dead already," Arthur says softly.

Baeddan snorts and drags Upjohn by the hair. Chunks of blond rip free, and Arthur leaps forward, shoving his shoulder into Baeddan. "Let go. Get off him!" Arthur yells. But Baeddan growls, swings his arm, and backhands Arthur.

Pain blackens his vision and blood bursts in Arthur's mouth as his teeth cut into his cheek. He blinks away dark stars, scrambling for Baeddan again. "Stop, Baeddan." He grabs at Baeddan's bare, scarred chest, hitting hard.

Baeddan grunts.

Arthur crouches over John Upjohn, wincing so the surge of sorrow he feels doesn't appear on his face, but only flows through him, spilling out in ragged, heaving breaths. He spits blood onto the leaves. The old saint is limp. Dead. A great scratch claws across his left eye and down his nose.

"Dead?" whispers Baeddan.

"Dead," says Arthur as if it's a curse.

"Well, then," Vaughn drawls behind them, having watched their drama from the heart of the grove. "I suppose, Arthur Couch, you'll be useful after all."

"THE BARGAIN IS BROKEN," RHUN SAYS TO JUDITH and Ben, both of whom stare at the smoldering remains of his bracelet. He won't hide it. He wonders if Arthur has realized it, if Mairwen feels it, and if they'll all three find each other again.

"What are we going to do?" Ben asks again.

And suddenly, seeing the couple there in the powerful sunlight, silver with clouds, Rhun understands: *We* is right.

Everyone was complicit in the secret, even if they didn't know. So everyone has to be just as complicit in the solution. Not a handful of people making choices for all, not the Grace witches or even just him and Arthur. Everybody who benefits or suffers must decide together. Heat flushes his face, like triumph, and he says, "We're going to fix it together. All of Three Graces."

"How?" asks Judith.

Rhun Sayer smiles. "We're all going to become saints, Judith! Come with me into town."

With that, he moves on, revelation unfurling like wings on his back.

When he reaches the first houses, he slows. He calls out, "People of Three Graces, this is Rhun Sayer! You named me your saint, and by that honor I ask you to listen! Come to the center now, the bonfire. Bring coats and boots. Bring a weapon if you must! But come. This is Rhun Sayer, your twenty-eighth saint, and I'm asking this of you!"

Rhun walks on, curving through three of the side streets, crying out his message again and again. He says the names of the people he sees, calling them with the power of their families and histories.

"This is Rhun Sayer!" he yells from the spiral town square. He plants his feet and cups hands around his mouth. "Listen to me!"

More and more gather, slowly some, but others arriving as if they've waited all their lives to be called. It does not escape his notice that the first to come are children and young people, the runners and their cousins and friends. Rhun nods at them. His chest heaves with effort and sparks of excitement. He's neither afraid nor happy, not delighted nor spinning into panic. He is truly, finally ready, like he's never been, because there is nothing to hide now.

Rhun Sayer wants to live, but more than that, he wants everyone to see him. Not his destiny, not what he's promised, not some fabled quality of goodness that makes him the best. No, he wants them to see the answers to all the secrets in his heart: He loves them so much, and he loves this valley so much, he has to make them all saints. Every last one of them. He's changed, and they all need to change with him. To choose it. Nobody will be lied to, nobody will be innocent. Everyone will choose together.

He sees his mother arrive, and his father. He sees Arthur's father, and Cat Dee, Beth Pugh and her brother Ifan. Sayers pour in. All the young men who wanted to be the saint instead of him.

And then, only then, Rhun smiles.

A few townsfolk smile back, because they always smile at Rhun Sayer. It's instinctive.

"Thank you," he says. "Thank you for putting down your work, or your fear, to listen. You know what the bargain we've lived under for two hundred years truly is. Every saint died, none survived until John Upjohn, and me. We tried to bind the bargain, Mairwen, Arthur, and I. We managed it, but it didn't last." He holds up his bare arm. "The charm is broken. The bargain is gone. Because we didn't bind it with death. There's no balance to the life we're given. How can we expect to live as we do without sacrifice?" Rhun laughs softly and with despair at his former ignorance. Shaking his head, he scans the shifting group of friends and neighbors, his family. They're eyeing each other and eyeing him. Silent. As if they're unwilling to argue but cannot quite step into sync with him.

"We'll die!" someone from the back calls.

"We always die," snaps Beth Pugh.

Gethin Couch shoves to the fore. "Are you going to die, then, Rhun Sayer? Or my son? How will we remake this bargain?"

"I don't know," Rhun says. "But we have to do it, all of us. Everyone who will benefit must agree to the price. Everyone hold the weight together." He holds out his hands. "Come with me into the forest, all of you."

Cries of protest and hushed fear burst out, with a few promising *yays* peppered through.

Rhun nods again, meeting the eyes of all he can reach. "Be brave," he says. "Be your best! Mom, Dad, all you Sayers I know have this running in your blood. And you, Braith Bowen, you're strong and you want to keep your family safe. You, Beth, and all of you women who know what fire feels like. Brothers and sisters who can't imagine any other way, let me show it to you."

"You're not our leader, Rhun Sayer," calls Evan Prichard. "You're young. A saint, to be sure, but you're reckless. You and your friends are the ones who changed it all. It was working! Why should we want anything different?"

"It was working at the price of my life," Rhun says.

"You knew that—you competed for the honor!"

Some are agreeing, but Rhun sees in others how much they want Rhun to dissuade Evan Prichard, how much they'd like him to be wrong. They sense it, they just can't convince themselves.

Rhun says, "I was lied to. I thought I had a chance. Baeddan Sayer didn't walk in to his certain death. And John Upjohn wanted desperately to live! Carey Morgan had a daughter on the way! Who's to say they'd have won the sainthood if they'd known? Would you, Per Argall, have stood at my side and answered the question what makes you best if you'd known?"

The young man's eyes pinch, his hands fist, but he doesn't look away. "I don't know, Rhun," he admits, quiet and sorrowful.

"None of us can know," Rhun says. "But it was our right to make a real choice. To be truly brave, to know! Without that truth, every joy we all have in this valley is built on a broken foundation! A secret that kills us."

Nobody else is leaving; they stare at Rhun, awaiting his next breath like he is a piece of God.

Rhun feels the weight of it. He always has. So he breathes hard and says, "We all have a best self. We only have to choose to let it rule us. Your best selves know what I know: We must to do this together. Let me show you the Devil's Forest."

Just then a woman screams, "The devil took John!"

It's Lace Upjohn, weeping and dragging her daughter behind her.

"What?" Rhun dives toward her, and the crowd parts.

"That devil, who was Baeddan Sayer, who you brought out of the forest, broke into my house and dragged my son away! What will you do about that, Rhun?" Her voice is tight and accusing.

Rhun accepts the blame. He clenches his jaw. "I'll go into the forest and stop it. I'll fight for John's life and the lives of everybody here."

"Maybe you should let the devil take him," says Gethin Couch, and judging by the scatter of nods, he isn't the only one to think it.

"How dare you!" cries Lace.

"You said goodbye to him," Gethin snaps, leaning into her face.

"I'm not willing to let that happen, Gethin," Rhun says.

"Some of us are. That's the bargain, like you say, and we need it."

Braith Bowen calls, "Could you sleep tonight, you heartless bastard?"

Evan Prichard calls back, "I sleep every night, except the Slaughter Moon, always knowing we threw a boy to die in the forest. It's the same."

Too many reply at once. It's a cacophony, and Lace Upjohn wipes tears off her face, snatches a knife from Gethin Couch's belt, and marches away, northward.

"I'm going to the Bone Tree!" Rhun yells as loudly as he can. "Go with me if you want to be the best! If you want to deserve this life we have."

Little Bree Lewis says, "My sister would go with you. I'll go too."

Per and Dar Argall step out, axes in hand. "Lead on, Rhun."

From the side, Rhun the Elder brings a bow and arrow.

When Rhun accepts the weapon, it triggers a landslide of volunteers. Not everybody, not nearly, but Rhun has no time to rally the resistant. He'll accept these, mostly young men and women, who have not lived so long with nothing to fight for they don't know how to risk it all. Some of their parents, some cousins, most of the Sayer clan. Ben Heir, though he makes Judith swear to remain and stay safe.

With him, when he strides toward the Devil's Forest, are all the folk of Three Graces who ever had it in them to be brave.

B RANCHES AND LEAVES SLAP MAIRWEN IN THE FACE as she careens down the mountain, barely staying on her feet. Haf is far behind, though following. Mair can't quite bring herself to slow down for her friend, not when the forest is almost gone from her blood, when she's dizzy with the lack of it, when her heart aches like it's broken in half.

She flies into the sheep fields, cutting north and east, toward the forest. Her lungs burn, but her legs are strong and her arms pump, grasping at the air before her as if to drag her faster. Wind tears at her head, and tiny flower petals flutter behind her, shredded and falling from her hair.

As she runs around the rear of the Grace cottage, she glances at the chimney: no smoke. She comes around, ready to press on to the horse pasture, but someone huddles inside the yard, just next to the front door, which hangs half open.

Though she needs to continue into the Devil's Forest, Mairwen slows, drawn back with an inexorable sense of dread.

The decision is made before she realizes it, and Mair runs urgently to her home and shoves through the gate, cutting her palm on stray gooseberry bramble. It's Hetty kneeling beside the front door, arms over her head, bent in half. Her long fingers are dug into her glossy hair, fisting and relaxing again and again.

"Hetty?" Mairwen says through heavy panting.

The older woman lifts her head: Tears streak the freckled cheeks, and blood has crusted at the corner of her mouth. "Mair, I'm so, so sorry. I couldn't stop him. Your mother . . ."

Sucking air through her teeth, Mairwen darts inside the cottage. The door swings hard against the wall, then shuts behind her.

In the dim light, at first everything appears normal. The kitchen table, the benches, all the bundles of dried herbs hanging from the rafters. Her boots where she left them yesterday—yesterday?—before going into town for the celebration, slouched beside the ladder to her loft.

Except the fire is dead, and ashes and black chunks of charcoal fan out from the hearth as if the fire exploded in a great gust.

And across the hearthstone lies her mother.

Or what is left of the last Grace witch.

Aderyn's eyes are closed, her lips gently parted as if in pleased dreaming. Hands relaxed at her sides, palms up, and her skirts folded at her calves. Like Aderyn simply stretched herself out to sleep.

But her chest is a mass of dark blood and blossoming violas, or something like violas, if those tiny purple flowers ever grew in thick braided vines. The flowers pierce straight out of her heart, erupting through her ribs to knot about her sternum and between her breasts.

Mair falls to her knees beside her mother, breathing hard. She hovers her hands over Aderyn's cheeks, then over the flowers, one finger brushing the tip of a petal. Then she covers her own mouth against a wail.

Aderyn's lips twitch and she draws a breath.

"Mother!" Mairwen shrieks, grasping one cold hand.

"Mairwen," her mother whispers.

"Who did this to you? What happened? How can I help?"

"I'm dying, little bird."

The words are so soft, Mairwen must lean forward. "No. There must be some charm, something for me to say, to banish these flowers. The forest is—it is leaving me. It must leave you, too."

Aderyn's brow creases and she whispers, "This is the death for all Grace witches. The flowers in our heart burst, and we become flowers."

Mairwen frowns. "But you weren't called to the forest. Not yet! You didn't . . ."

trees shake, and moonlight coalesces into figures and faces, pushing free of the trees, gathering light to them as sheer veils. Nine women, with flowers growing out of their chests. They remain before their trees, all but one, who

Shaking the memory away, Mairwen tells herself, *Not yet!*

"The forest came to me. It did not have to call," Aderyn says simply. Her voice is too low, too weak.

"No!" Tears fall from Mairwen's eyes and plop onto her mother's collarbone, and another hits a dark heart-shaped leaf. The vine trembles, tightens, and her mother cries out.

Mairwen grabs one of the vines and says, "*Wither*," with all the insistence in her heart. The vine twists and withdraws, but Aderyn whimpers.

"Stop, stop, little bird, and listen: He is back at the heart of the forest."

"What? Who?" She wipes her tears and clenches her jaw. In her veins, her blood throbs. She needs to do something, to rage or run or find the Bone Tree and demand it obey her.

"Vaughn. Your . . ." Her mother's voice fades; she winces as if confused.

"What? Lord Vaughn? He wasn't at his manor. He was gone? Did he do this to you?"

"Yes."

"Why?" she shrieks.

"I remember him. I remember him when you were small, and before you were born. I've been dreaming of him the past three nights, strange dreams . . . like memories, and I—I remember him."

"So do I. Everyone does," Mairwen whispers. "I remember his—his father, too, because he liked me."

"Not his father. Vaughn has no father. He is no man, little—little bird. He is forest and flowers . . . stones and clay . . . all beasts."

The roaring in Mairwen's ears is suspicion, is a wild guess, a terrible thrill of truth that she does not want. "The old god," she whispers.

"Your father."

"No." Mairwen scuttles away from her mother. "No, no. My father was a saint! Carey Morgan, and his bones are on the—on the Bone Tree. I touched my finger to his moon-white cheekbone and looked into his empty eyes!"

She remembers it with perfect clarity.

"I am the daughter of a witch and a saint!"

Mairwen faces the girl in the long white veil, and the girl lifts her hand, points at Mair, and says—

"No," Mairwen whispers.

the girl lifts her hand, points at Mair, and says, "You are not one of us."

*E*VERYTHING IS SILENT.

Silver trees surround her, laced with white vines and moonlight. Her feet brush rocky earth, with no sign of grass or deadfall, and through the branches stars twinkle against the impossible blackness of the night sky. She cannot see the moon. It must be low. Only two hours until dawn.

She leans into Baeddan's shoulder as they shift and slowly spin, dancing beneath bobbing little lights.

"They're waking," Baeddan whispers. He lets go of her hand, and lets go of her waist.

"Who?" Mairwen glances all around. She is so weary, and so at peace, she could close her eyes and sleep against that nearest tree, with Baeddan's arms around her, and listen to his erratic heartbeat and strange songs. Maybe in her dreams the words would make sense.

He backs away awkwardly, as if he does not know where to look. "Watch, Mairwen Grace. They are so beautiful."

Standing in the center of the grove, Mairwen waits alone.

Filaments of light drip down from the stars, setting aglow the cracks in the tree bark, and all the vines shiver, bursting with violet flowers that turn silver and white and then gray as ash before falling quietly to the earth.

The trees shake, and all the light coalesces into figures and faces, pushing free of the trees, gathering light into sheer veils. Nine women, with flowers growing out of their chests. They remain before their trees, all but one, who walks toward Mairwen.

She holds her breath but does not flee.

The girl drifts nearer, and through the long, white veil Mairwen sees dark eyes, white-violet skin, parted lips, and dark hair falling in fat curls around her face and shoulders.

"Hello," Mairwen says, heart and stomach aflutter because she knows who these women are. Grace witches. Her grandmother, and her grandmother's mother, on and on back to the original Grace witches, and this, here, the youngest, first Grace.

The girl, Grace, lifts her hand beneath the veil to point at

Mairwen. Her lips move, and from all around the wind carries her voice, a whisper of wind. "You're not one of us."

Mairwen shakes her head in denial. "I'm a Grace witch. My mother is Aderyn Grace, daughter of Cloua."

"Grace witches do not come into the forest until they are here to remain."

"I came in because my father was Carey Morgan, a saint, and his bones are here."

The other veiled women murmur, asking each other: A saint? Is that all?

Could that be the answer?

Why her breath bends the trees and her blood gathers wind?

But the first Grace shakes her head; her veil trembles with the movement. "No. The saints are all on the Bone Tree, but your heart is not here for sacrifice. Daughter of the forest."

"My—my blood does not gather the wind," Mairwen says.

"The devil obeys you," says the first Grace, glancing outside their grove to where Baeddan Sayer crouches, clutching his head, rocking himself like a baby.

"But . . ." Mairwen's mouth is dry. "My mother is a witch and my father a saint."

The first Grace presses her lips together. She appears no older than Mairwen, sixteen if not younger. Mair wants to ask about the devil, the old god of the forest. Did she love him? Why did she find him beautiful? Mairwen has always thought the worst things were full of beauty, and perhaps this first Grace knows why. But when she opens her mouth, the first Grace says, "Stop."

Mairwen listens, because she chooses to, not because she is compelled.

Wind gusts, and the trees shiver, and the long veils of light flutter. Baeddan groans.

Before Mairwen realizes what's happening, Baeddan is behind her, holding her shoulders. He bends over and shoves her head to the side with his face, then bites into the flesh at the base of her neck.

She cries out in surprise, then at the flash of pain. "Baeddan!"

"I'm sorry, so, so sorry," he whispers, touching his sharp teeth to her skin again. "Oh, Mairwen Grace, look!"

The first Grace's eyes are locked to the wound and Mairwen tries to see, craning her neck. Warm blood leaks down her collarbone.

"Grow for me," the first Grace whispers.

The little star lights floating in the air begin to drop like rain.

Discomfort blooms in Mairwen's chest, slithering like a worm toward the wound on her shoulder. She struggles again, gasping. Her eyes are so wide, but all she can see is dark blood, nearly black in the moonlight.

The worm reaches the bite, and it grabs the edges of broken skin. Mairwen closes her eyes and feels a surge of energy, a spark.

Baeddan laughs. "Look!"

She does, in time to watch the little purple flower lifting itself out of her flesh, twining up her neck to her cheek. Her eye aches from the effort of focusing on it, and then the flower seems to kiss her cheek and break away, drifting and tumbling down to the ground, where it blackens and dies.

"Look!" Baeddan cries again, releasing her to dance around.

He gouges his chest, and with the spurt of purple blood flowers bloom, curling around themselves and winking bright violet. Then they too break off, die, and land like ashes on the ground.

"The forest is inside you," says the first Grace.

Mairwen touches the smear of blood and looks at it. Red, as blood should be, but so dark.

"You can break it all, or remake it."

"What?" breathes Mairwen, still staring at the glint of blood on her fingers.

"You are a witch and a god, Mairwen Grace. Both a girl and a forest. Or you could be, if you let yourself."

Arms circle her from behind; Baeddan, leaning around her as if he needs comfort. He nuzzles the bite mark, kisses it gently, and licks away some of the blood. Mairwen shudders, but feels stronger with his arms around her than alone with the first Grace.

"Tell me what happened," Mairwen says. "Tell me the truth."

The first Grace smiles grimly. "I fell in love with the forest. And the forest loved me back. And so we traded hearts. Mine is here, larger and stronger than it could have been in the small cavern of my body, and I am only death. His heart is outside, free. And he is only life. The saints bind us together, keeping the charm alive, keeping the forest itself half alive without its god. Because the saint lives and also dies, the saints are always alive and always dead."

Baeddan laughs.

"What happened to the old god of the forest?" Mairwen asks.

"He lives. He walks among you. He ventures far from his tree. But he always returns for the slaughter."

Mairwen clutches at Baeddan's wrists, digging her nails in. He hisses his pleasure and tightens his embrace. But Mairwen looks for the moon, then remembers it's so low, so very, very low. "The old god of the forest left the forest."

"I think, pretty Mairwen," the first Grace says, "he must also be your father."

She's panicking, breath too thin and fast, scratching at Baeddan the way he scratches at himself. It's impossible. Her mother would have told her, or at least would not have lied. "My mother . . ."

"Forgot." Grace shrugs. Her veil hardly trembles. "Or forgot some. Our charm makes sure of it, that the old god is forgotten."

"And I can change it? I can change the bargain? Break it or unmake it, because of who . . . what . . . I am?"

"If you let it change you first. But you won't remember I told you so. We've spoken too much of him."

Mairwen backs away from the first Grace, pushing at Baeddan so he steps back too. Eyes bright and on Grace, Mairwen says, "Baeddan, take me to the Bone Tree."

W HEN SHE OPENS HER EYES, MAIRWEN REMEMBERS. Every step inside the Devil's Forest, every cut and every tree she climbed. She remembers the bird women and bargaining with them to be led to Arthur. She remembers Baeddan finding her instead and kissing her and the moment she recognized him. She remembers the rowan doll, and she remembers fighting with him, screaming at him; she remembers his eagerness, his wild singing, his willingness to take her through the marsh. She remembers the brilliant red apples he fed her and trees grown faces and claws, the ferocious half-dead wolves and rotting bone creatures and tracks in the mud, and when she saw Rhun was in the forest too, and Baeddan was desperate to eat him. She remembers Arthur and Rhun fighting over who would die, who should run. Their misery at how much they wanted the other to live.

She remembers dancing with Baeddan in the perfect grove, his sorrow, his distress, and when the Grace witches woke from their graves.

She remembers what the first Grace said, and leaving the grove to find the Bone Tree, where she was confident she could change the bargain and hold it inside her. She remembers counting the skulls on the tree, and finding Carey Morgan's. When she touched his cheekbone, she was saying goodbye, because she did not share his blood after all.

Mairwen remembers climbing onto the altar with Rhun and Arthur, swearing it would free Baeddan, too, and all of them would go home. *I can change it!* she said. They clasped hands, tied woven charms to their wrists, and cried, "*We are the saints of Three Graces,*" just as the sun rose.

She remembers Sy Vaughn laughing and helping her gather yarrow when she was a little girl. Two dark-brown eyes.

And one is different now, but only since John Upjohn's Slaughter Moon. It went gray as the bargain broke. As he lost hold of himself.

All the memories huddle in her mind, dull and dreadful.

Her mother is barely breathing, and so Mairwen leans over to breathe for her, then kisses her lips and stands.

Her knees shake and Mairwen catches herself against the kitchen table. Her insides squeeze and twist. She coughs; it becomes a gag, and she's retching, her body bent and shaking. Mairwen spits another flower out of her mouth, and pieces of tree bark, chunky and wet. Another spasm catches her and she can't breathe through the strength of the retching this time.

She spits out the small, pebble-like wrist bone that had been part of her binding charm.

Her head spins and sweat breaks out all over her body. She is flushed in the face and cold in the hands.

Mairwen sits.

It's over. Her magic is gone. The charm, the pieces of the forest she bound to her: gone.

ARTHUR RUNS.

He's surrounded not only by bone creatures and bird women, wolves and trees, but two devils. Baeddan leaps gleefully toward him, punching Arthur in the chest. Something cracks as he falls back and into the massive arms of the old god.

Arthur struggles, but his legs and arms are held in grips stronger than steel, and he's carried to the altar. He gasps, and he cannot believe this is the end—bound to the forest, changed like Baeddan, his heart broken and his mind in tatters, without Mairwen and Rhun. *My God*, he thinks, what will Rhun do when he finds out? "No, please," he whispers, then lashes with his entire body; his spine bends, he flails, but he cannot get even an inch of freedom.

The devil and the old god of the forest press him onto the altar, scattering the remains of his fire. Vaughn flattens his wide hand over Arthur's chest and vines explode from the earth, crawling up the altar stone like snakes, winding around and around Arthur's arms, around his bruised throat, too. They pierce his skin, sewing his wrists down.

Arthur screams. Flowers and vines make a web, and the old god leans down to put his bright red lips against Arthur's forehead.

"Will they come for you, Arthur Couch?" the old god whispers.

T HE FOREST REFUSES TO ALLOW RHUN AND HIS COMpany easily inside.

He and his father lead the way at the head of an arrow of folk. They shove aside angry branches, sometimes chopping through vines that snake across their feet, and everyone winces against a constant, freezing wind. They progress, but slowly. Some give up, their courage spent out over the flash of teeth from the hollow of a tree, or a scream that nobody else seems to hear.

Bird women dart about, slashing at eyes, giggling and

chanting Rhun's name, and "Too late! Too late!" and "The god is home!" and "There is a saint on the altar already, Rhun Sayer, Rhun-Rhun-Rhun! What will you do?"

"Cut him free!" Rhun growls at them, imagining John Upjohn tied down, his blood staining the altar. "You'll not have his heart!"

And the bird women laugh, flitting at Bree Lewis and Per Argall, who swipe with a knife and ax respectively.

High in the trees, rodents chitter and sneer, winking red eyes at them, dripping putrescence, and Rhun hears the scurry of spiders, the flap of rotting wings. His heart pounds and he prays there will be no wolves.

There are, of course.

One leaps at Braith Bowen, who grunts in pain, and his cousin Dirk hacks at it with his ax. Three more attack, and Rhun does his best to direct the defense, but it is a melee of blades and screams, until finally all four wolves lie wholly dead. Bevan Heir has his thigh sliced up and can't go on. Many are bleeding from less desperate wounds. They lose three to helping Bevan limp home.

Rhun is tired, more so than he was after only an hour in the forest before. He can't imagine why this resistance is so terrible, when the Bone Tree has Upjohn, when Baeddan must be lost there too, trapped by the heart of the forest.

A woman in a veil appears, flanked by two more, and they shake their heads, holding out hands to stop Rhun's progress.

"We're going to the Bone Tree," Rhun says. "To end this."

The women let him pass, but they reach out to slide chilling touches to the cheeks and hands of every single person who follows him.

WHEN MAIRWEN GRACE WAS TEN YEARS OLD, SHE created a charm to wake up her father's ghost. Made of a tin whistle his sister lent her and braids of her own hair and grass she plucked from the shadows of the Devil's Forest, knotted together with the slender red ribbon Rhun Sayer meant for the Witch's Hand tree, but tied into Mairwen's hair instead.

She chewed her bottom lip as she dragged Haf Lewis with her down the pasture hill toward the Devil's Forest, wondering if the charm was hearty enough, or if she should put a few drops of her blood onto the blessing ribbon. It was already life, death, and blessing in between, but this was big magic she wanted, perhaps too much for a little witch's charm.

"This is so near," Haf breathed, fingers cold with terror and clutched tightly around Mair's.

"Of course it is." Mairwen wrinkled her tiny nose at her friend. "He died inside, so I have to be as close as I can get."

Haf stopped and dug her feet into the dirt and green grass at the base of the pasture hill. "Maybe this is near enough."

"It isn't. But stay here if you must. I'm only going a bit farther."

The tall black trees of the Devil's Forest swayed gently in the pleasant summer wind. Mairwen knelt along the line between sunlight and shadow, placing the charm in her lap.

Haf dashed the rest of the way and knelt behind Mair, so that her knobby brown knees fit onto the soles of Mair's tucked-under feet and pressed against her bottom. Twisting, Mair smiled her thanks. It felt better and right to have her friend's connection to the valley and the sun—Haf was always bright, after all, and full of life. Mairwen decided maybe she herself could be the charm: the Devil's Forest was death, Haf was life, and Mair the thread between them.

But she didn't say so out loud to Haf.

Lifting the charm in her cupped hands, Mair put her lips to the mouth of the whistle and blew gently.

It sang a sweet song, only one note.

Mairwen blew harder, all her breath, and again and again, in an even rhythm. Between the notes she whispered her father's name: "Carey Morgan. Carey Morgan. Carey Morgan."

There was no sensation of warmth or change, nothing to signify the charm worked, but that was the way of magic, her mother always said. It either succeeded or it did not. A witch needed to trust her power and her charm.

Haf touched her forehead against Mairwen's back and slid her hands around Mairwen's waist, huddling nearer. When Mairwen whispered her father's name, Haf whispered it too.

The Devil's Forest swayed. Fallen black leaves fluttered on the ground several feet inside it.

Spare thoughts invaded her concentration: Perhaps she should've used the charm at night, for ghosts prefer night, don't they? She should step inside the forest, kneel in the shadows instead. Or maybe the blessing ribbon was too bound up in her feelings for Rhun Sayer to be the right thread here? Oh, but she wanted to see her father so badly, to ask him where his bones were laid, so she could find a way to gather them up.

A snap of wood deep in the forest startled Mairwen out of focus. The whistle faded. She stared wide-eyed into the layering shadows, at shifting light deep in the farthest reaches she could see.

Haf trembled, fingers digging into Mairwen's sides.

Mairwen breathed carefully, but her hands were shaking too.

A figure appeared far away, only a shadow with bright eyes. Strong, like a saint. Mair leaped to her feet. "Dad!" she cried.

Haf scrambled away, gripping Mair's skirt. "Mairwen," she whispered.

The dark figure crouched. She saw the glint of teeth as it smiled or grimaced or growled. One clawed hand touched the tree beside it.

Mairwen's small heart beat faster and faster, and she bared her teeth too. She was afraid and also refused to be afraid. This was not like the red-eyed squirrels and misshapen rabbits. It was not like the tiny birds flitting between the black branches, whispering songs with human words instead of trilling and chirps.

She knew it was not her father's ghost.

Her charm had brought the devil.

Mairwen stepped back, and back again. "Come on, Haf," she whispered, walking backward, never looking away from the devil's eyes until she was far enough from the edge of the forest he blurred into the trees.

S IX YEARS LATER, MAIRWEN DOESN'T HESITATE TO CROSS the threshold again, though this time she is alone, with no charms to protect her or even offer comfort.

The forest is quiet, refusing her its whisper, ignoring her as if she were so insignificant there's no need to bother.

Mairwen clenches her teeth.

She is not nothing. She is a witch and the daughter of a—of a—

Between. She isn't a god or a girl. She isn't a saint or a witch, not only.

Mairwen runs. Her bare feet find easy footing, and she slips between the trees, just a girl in a tattered gray dress.

Her breathing is strong, her gaze focused ahead. Her heartbeat does not waver.

In no time at all she leaps over the creek, pushes through the hedges of red berries, vaults across flint, and into a marsh.

She knows the way, because she remembers all of it. Directly to the heart of the forest.

On and on she runs, swift and sure as a deer.

The Bone Tree towers over its grove, and she steps quietly in, heart pounding, ears ringing. Exactly as she remembers.

And the ground is littered with tiny purple flowers. Viola blossoms.

Baeddan huddles against the altar, and atop it a person is stretched out, tangled in vines and flowers, dripping blood from wrist and ankle. She steps nearer the altar, fear tightening her throat. Strands of angry blond hair escape the vines, and she knows.

Before she can dash to him, she sees John Upjohn sprawled just in front of her, obviously dead. Tears burn, but she refuses to allow them to spill. No.

"Arthur," she says, stepping over John. "Arthur, can you hear me?"

Baeddan's head jerks up. "Go back, go back, Grace witch!" he hisses.

Too late.

"Mairwen!" calls a warm, delighted voice. "You came!"

He is there: walking around the base of the Bone Tree. Sy Vaughn, his russet hair curled around his face, bright and summery. He smiles, and his skin glows as if suntanned, his eyes bright. His coat is brown and green, leather and rich velvet, and fur at the collar. His black boots are polished.

He is the picture of a man in perfect health and prosperity.

But as he walks down a long, curved root toward her, he changes. His eyes blacken and thorns sprout from his cheeks. His teeth lengthen and his lips turn bloodred. His shoulders widen, his legs grow longer and his clothes hug him, transforming into leathery wings, strips of fur, and thick green moss trailing down his hip and thigh. Antlers rise from his head, forking again and again, then cracking and falling away into scarlet autumn leaves. His hair flowers and his hands turn to claws. Feathers appear down his hard stomach, soft and downy as a young owl's.

Mairwen stares, amazed.

He clomps around the altar on heavy hooves, rounded like a horse's, and he stretches his arms out; feathers sprout and fall away. His nose lengthens to a snout, tusks press out of his mouth, curling and curling before turning into vines that snake back over his shoulders. Lichen grows down his forehead, dark orange.

Then he's bloating and turning ugly purple. Pale blood falls from his nose, and his eyes turn white. His skin shucks away, but instead of meat and bone, there he is perfect again: Sy Vaughn with russet hair and butter-pale skin.

"See, my love?" he says.

It begins again, but this time his skin hardens into gray granite exactly like the altar stone, paling to the white, fissured bark of the Bone Tree. His eyes are perfect purple like the violas.

"You're the god of the forest," she whispers.

"You're my daughter."

She ignores it, pushing it away, under the throbbing of her frightened heart. "Why did you come back into the forest now? Why did you hurt my mother?"

"The magic has been tugging at me for years. It was time to come home and reset the bargain myself. Aderyn . . ." He sighs, making a grating sound like stone on stone. "My darling Aderyn was remembering me finally, because all the charms were fading, and I wish I could let her—I miss her, my witch—but I needed her blood."

"For what?"

Vaughn sweeps his arm toward the altar, and Arthur. "To anoint a new saint."

Mairwen shifts nearer to Arthur, clutching her hands together against her sternum. "Is it too late?"

"For him? He'll take Baeddan's place, and you'll speak with him again."

"That isn't . . . Don't do that." She looks at Vaughn's eyes, black and brown now, and intentionally holds his gaze while she says, "Please."

He laughs: a dark, pleasant rumble that vibrates the ground beneath her bare feet. From all around the laughter echoes in giggles and shrieks. Mairwen's spine stiffens, for she'd not realized they were surrounded by denizens of the forest. "That worked once, to save the life of a saint, but I cannot let it work again."

She frowns, suddenly realizes something that tumbles out of her mouth. "You knew leaving John alive would break the bargain. That it would weaken the magic, and—and yourself."

"It was the only thing you ever asked of me." His voice is tender, awkward around the fangs pressing against pink lips. He never stops shifting, transforming, dying, living again.

Mairwen only stares, stunned.

The old god of the forest adds, "It was worth it, for you."

She blinks, and tears fall down her cheeks in straight lines.

"I didn't know I wanted you until you were here," he says. "I never had a child before you. Yet when you were born, I went to Addie and I held you. It was the first time since I left the forest that I had made life, that I had sown life again. I used to. Here in the forest, I was part of it all. Life and death, stars and rot—"

"Heartbeat and roots," Mairwen whispers with him, shivering.

Her father smiles. "I looked at you and longed for the day you'd be old enough to understand, to *see* me."

Mairwen has no word for the feeling swelling inside her; it is light and gentle, but promising more, like dawn or rising bread. She wants it, to live in its spaces, despite knowing it's not real, or not enough to last. But Arthur is dying. Her mother is dying. This creature—god, father, everything he is—cannot have them.

"You took my magic away," she finally says. "It was changing me, but you sucked it all back in when you came here."

"I'd have died if I did not come and see the heart of the forest reborn. The bargain keeps me free, and it is entirely broken. You broke it."

"I would have seen you better if you'd shown yourself when I had thorns in my bones and flowers in my blood."

Vaughn smiles. "You can have it again. Eat a flower from his heart and take the power back, Daughter."

She looks at Arthur, at the tiny purple flowers blooming from his chest, the lines of blood dripping down the sides of the altar stone. At Baeddan, who trembles, whose skin is sinking against his skull. He is dying too.

"I know you, Mairwen. I know you want this," the god says eagerly, holding out a hand to her. "You are everything I hoped. Brave and bold and powerful, my daughter."

She glances down at the flowers curling around his toes. A thin path of them trails behind him, climbing the roots of the Bone Tree, painting its white bark green and violet.

Vaughn says, "You are bound to this place because my blood makes you part of it, Mairwen. Grace blood and the blood of the forest itself! Ah." He laughs. "We can have all of this, all the power. You and me, a family."

The hand he holds to her urges her to clasp it, with gnarled wood fingers, and a spark of wild joy. "Daughter," he says. She wants him to be earnest. To want her for herself and the possibility in his words, not for power.

Mairwen slides her fingers along his, her thumbs spreading across his palm. She stares at the lines forming in this bark-skin and brings his hand to her face. She presses her cheek into it, turns and kisses the ball of his thumb. It smells like musty roots.

"You and me, Mairwen," the god tempts. "No one in Three Graces will stand against us if we are united."

"No," she murmurs quietly. Her family is Rhun and Arthur and Haf, her mother, yes, and even this devil tempting her. Her toes are cool against the forest floor; she feels vital energy strung through the earth of roots.

"No!" Vaughn is genuinely surprised.

"Mairwen already has a family," Rhun Sayer calls from the edge of the grove.

RHUN'S SHOULDERS RISE AND FALL HARD AS HE PAUSES at the edge of the Bone Tree's grove to collect himself. He heard enough of Mair's and the devil's conversation to know this is the old god, and the old god is both Vaughn and Mair's real father. Her father who is offering her all the power of the forest she's ever longed for.

Somehow, Rhun is not surprised. *No*, he thinks as he watches Mairwen touch her father's hand and consider, he *is* surprised; it's just that he isn't worried. He'll deal with these revelations, but there's no sliver of doubt in his heart what Mairwen will do. He's very likely more sure of her than she is of herself in this moment.

"Mairwen already has a family," he says confidently, emerging fully into the grove.

Mairwen spins to him, and Baeddan growls, stumbling to his feet.

The devil—the god—grins. "Rhun, welcome, and welcome all who've come in your wake. Bree, Per, Rhun the Elder! Nona, I'm not surprised. Braith and even you, Cat Dee! You must be determined, to have made it here on those tired old legs. Welcome to the heart of my forest. Ah, is that you, Lace?"

Sy Vaughn is recognizable by everyone, despite the thorns and flowers twisting into a crown among his curls, despite the sharp teeth and black eyes. His bearing is as noble as they've always been used to, and his voice only slightly more gravelly.

They all remember him now: There was no previous Lord Vaughn, but only this one, young and handsome, for two hundred years.

"Rhun," Mairwen says, but Lace Upjohn pushes into the grove and limps to the body of her son.

"Oh, John, no," she whispers, hands shaking. "You did this, Mairwen Grace."

Mair steps away from her, stricken.

Cat Dee says, "No. It was him. That creature."

The townsfolk who followed Rhun hesitantly join them under the spreading white branches of the Bone Tree.

It's Vaughn who goes to Lace and crouches. "I am so very sorry, Lace. We'll celebrate that he had three extra years to live, to be with you."

She looks up at him with teary eyes, her son's cold hand in both of hers. "What are you?"

"The forest, dear lady. I'm the forest god, and also your lord, whom you've known all your life."

"I remember," Lace murmurs. She blinks at him, seeming unafraid.

Rhun says, "We're here to make a new bargain, or end it forever, Vaughn. All of us."

The devil glances at him, standing up on tall legs. Bree Lewis and Ginny Argall crouch with Lace, helping her hold on to John.

"Well, Rhun Sayer, what makes you think you're in any position to bargain?"

"We won't give you more saints. We're all here to decide what to do together."

The devil smiles, and laughs, a sound like thunder and bells, both. Rhun clenches his jaw.

"Arthur is already on the altar," Mairwen says quietly; the words travel, though, and Rhun jerks his head up.

There *is* a body on the altar, wound in vines and bleeding, too. "No," he says, and runs.

But Baeddan knocks him back with a hard arm. Rhun hits the ground, breath whooshing out of him, and gets up as quickly as he can. His cousin steps near, gripping Rhun's upper arms. He sings, "You can't pass me, saint-saint-saint. This is the only way I'll be free-free-free."

"Baeddan, let me go. You know it's wrong. Arthur isn't a saint. He isn't one of us." Rhun doesn't believe it. He

believes Arthur's heart is so very worthy, but he pleads anyway, whatever he needs to say to move to the altar.

His cousin's eyes are blacker than river muck again, dull
and quiet. Baeddan's skin is sunken to his skull; his breath
comes fast, dry, and smelling of mold.

Distantly, he hears Mairwen say something, and the
devil reply, but Rhun puts his hands on Baeddan's chest.
He shoves, leaning all his weight against Baeddan. "Let
me by."

"I cannot, cousin. Brother." Baeddan shakes his head and
begins pushing Rhun back and back, with the strength of a
mountain. He bares teeth of hard, pointed granite. Black
thorns break through the thin, cracking skin along his jaw-
bone, as if the effort is changing him again.

"I love him," Rhun says.

"I know. It doesn't—I can't fight—the forest. It is inside
me. I'm inside it. I am a flame in a lantern and the glass trapping my own heat, saint. I am—I am roots and earthworms.
They crawl inside my stomach and it tickles, Rhun Sayer. It
tickles." Baeddan giggles, fingers tightening on Rhun's arms,
bruising. "My lungs are dry leaves. My heart—my heart is
flower petals."

At the edges of the grove appear spirits—white-veiled
ghosts. Screams erupt as a hundred bird women dart about
the grove, flapping and chattering curses, followed by running bone creatures who cut at the villagers with hard fingers
and yelling maniacally. Decaying wolves howl, teeth falling
from their mouths, and everyone from Three Graces crowds

together, kicking and reaching out with axes and brooms, defending themselves.

"*Stop!*" roars Sy Vaughn, arms out, flowers catching fire in his hair.

The tiny monsters and little devils flee, and Rhun ignores it all, breathing hard and evenly, staring at his cousin.

Rhun stops struggling. He relaxes. "All right, Baeddan. I understand." And he does. He knows what he must do to save Arthur.

Baeddan's shoulders slump. "Good, good. I'm sorry about Arthur. His heart will last. It will last, and he'll remember you for—for a while. I'll be in the Bone Tree, watching with empty eyes and smiling a bare-boned smile." Baeddan laughs sharply at his own terrible joke. Then he lets go of Rhun.

Rhun grabs the handle of the knife in his boot. Nothing else matters around him except holding his cousin's churning black gaze as he snaps up again and slides the blade deep and fast across Baeddan's neck.

"SEE," THE OLD GOD SAYS AFTER MAIRWEN TELLS everyone Arthur is on the altar and Rhun is stopped by Baeddan. "See, everyone, there already is a saint sacrificed, and I will tend the transformation. You have seven more years, and all you need do is return to your lives."

"I won't leave without Arthur," Mairwen says to Vaughn, then turns her gaze onto all the people of Three Graces brave enough to come with Rhun. She is proud of them. "We can't leave him to die, to become what Baeddan became."

"It is the only way to put life back into the forest, Mairwen. See all these poor creatures, neither alive nor dead, like Baeddan. Would you have the forest fester and perish?"

Haf bursts out of the trees. "Mair! There . . ." She bends over, panting, and leans her hands on her knees. "I saw your mother! I saw Hetty."

Mairwen clenches her jaw.

"You cannot stop the sacrifice, Mairwen," Vaughn says. Somehow he's slowed his constant cycle of changing, fixed himself as the summery Vaughn, with only hints of wildness: thorns, antlers, flowers. Mairwen understands he doesn't wish to frighten the people. He looks like a god from a story: beautiful and strange, but not monstrous.

"I'll stop you."

"Not like this," he says with a smile. "Not unless you eat a flower from his heart and take up your power again."

She shakes her head.

Braith Bowen says, hands in fists at his sides, "Lord Vaughn, I . . . We came with Rhun because we want to know the truth. We want to be part of the decisions."

"Yes, we must!" says Bree Lewis from beside John Upjohn's body; she's holding on to Lace's arm.

"Let us all bargain with you," Nona Sayer demands. She's flanked by Alis Sayer, Delia Sayer, her husband and a dozen Sayer men and boys.

The devil rolls his shoulders and feathers burst from them, trailing down into massive wings. "Yes," he says through a mouth of curved fangs, "bargain with me. What would you offer for peace and prosperity in the valley? If not one of your hearts?"

Mairwen crouches, puts her hands to the earth. "Forest," she whispers. "I need you to wake again in my blood."

Daughter of the forest. Mairwen Grace.

The ghosts of all the Grace witches appear around the boundary of the grove. Mairwen sucks in a quiet breath just as bird women shriek and the forest denizens leap in to fling rocks at the ghosts, to tear at the skirts and boots of the men and women who do not belong here in the Devil's Forest.

"Stop!" commands Vaughn, and the goblins, bone monsters, and bird women dart away, dashing and slipping into the shadows again. "Hello, Grace," he says, turning to the youngest girl, who smiles beneath her veil.

"My *heart*," the first Grace says. "*It is too long since you visited me here.*"

"I could not come back inside once the charm was done, my love."

"How can you love her?" Mairwen says. "You used her for your freedom."

"I love her *and* I used her, little bird. Most things in this world are more than one thing."

Gasping with understanding, Mairwen stands and goes to the first Grace. "Give me my power back."

"*Take it,*" Grace murmurs, lips hardly moving.

A guttural sound distracts her, and Mairwen spins to Rhun just in time to see him cut Baeddan's throat.

Dust and motes of light splatter from the wound. No blood.

The wound burns in Mair's gut, as if she had been stabbed. "No," she says, rushing to the dying devil.

Vines crawl out of Baeddan Sayer's flesh, pulling him apart, and smoke puffs out of his lips, rises from the corners of his eyes like upside-down tears. He bares his sharp teeth and they're falling out, spinning as they tumble to the ground. Baeddan continues to laugh, throws back his head and grasps Rhun's shoulders again. Rhun throws his arms around his cousin, loving him, and afraid.

They collapse together. It smells like fire and sharp metal, and Baeddan crumbles in Rhun's hands, turning to embers and ash, dirt and cutting brambles, hooked thorns and even flowers, desiccated and colorless.

The vines on the altar twist and tighten, and three more flowers burst open.

Tears fall from Rhun's eyes.

Mairwen, crying too, kneels beside Rhun and digs into the flowers, into the brittle bones, to find the chunk of thorns that was Baeddan's heart. She pries the knife from Rhun's hand. She slices it across her chest and throws it down, then presses the heart to the long, fiery line of blood. It crumbles, and Mairwen licks the ashes from her palm.

Thorns and brambles explode up from the earth, surrounding her in a violent nest.

Rhun stumbles away from the thorns, gasping her name, then runs for the altar.

While most are fumbling back, a few follow Rhun, and the Sayer women surround Vaughn, arrows out like swords, an ax in each of Nona's hands. The spirit women drift nearer; the first Grace smiles at Vaughn, widening to a grin as the feathers of his wings shrivel to ashes. His life and death cycle begins again.

Inside her cocoon of thorns, Mairwen shivers and cries at the slick, heavy dragging of her blood, as vines and flowers push free, as they knot in her stomach and crack her bones. Her collar burns as thorns grow again, all at once, and her nails darken.

At the altar, Rhun begins sawing at the vines, ripping as best he can. Haf helps, as do his father and Braith. There is Arthur's throat, and there his mouth, open, flowers spilling out.

"It can't be too late," he whispers, touching Arthur's cheeks, his lips. "Arthur, wake up! Baeddan is dead. You cannot be too." He kisses Arthur's eyebrow, as the others continue dragging the vines free. Blood splashes when they cut free the thorny vines about his wrists, tearing them from his flesh.

Arthur jerks, back bowed. He opens his mouth and screams silently.

Mairwen, still inside the nest of brambles, grasps a vine, cutting open her palms. Where her blood falls, flowers blossom in tiny white clusters like yarrow. She tears open a way through the briars and emerges.

"Arthur, I'm here. It's all right," Rhun is saying. "I won't let the forest have your heart. It's *mine*."

"Let that saint on the altar go," Mairwen commands the Bone Tree.

Vaughn says, "You cannot defeat me, Daughter. Your power is only life, not death. You have to be both. You have to let it change you completely. That is real power: change."

"Stopping you is enough," she says. The forest pours out of her mouth, burning her eyes until they are black coal, and her lips crack. Yarrow blooms and falls, and her hair is a briar, too, curling over itself as tender green shoots emerge and twine into the thorns.

Arthur Couch sits up, coughing blood and petals. He spits and falls off the altar, against Rhun's chest. He cannot focus his eyes, but hears roaring and bells all around him. His body is weak; Rhun holds him up. Every beat of his heart thumps through his bones.

The Bone Tree creaks and shudders, bursting with scarlet leaves: the signal for a Slaughter Moon.

"There," Mairwen says through the flowers on her tongue. "The bargain is broken again. The tree needs a heart, and you will not have any of ours."

"Your crops will fail, the rain will not come, then, and your babies will die," the old god says. Fur grows down his cheeks, antlers from his head. His back bends and he sinks to the four delicate legs of a stag, transforming completely.

This is my heart tree. You will all suffer without me! Locking me here again, he says as the fur falls away in chunks and the stag's antlers become naked branches, as he rots and is only bones, then covered in new flowers again and rises

371

onto two legs: a bear, a man, a creature of lichen and mud and clay, a beautiful man again, with leathery bat wings and a mouth of heavy molars. "Make me a bargain," he says through the rocks. "Daughter. They'll hate you if you do not, if their children die. If you all starve. You won't be welcome in your valley, and you will not be welcome here, where your heart is."

Mairwen stares, exhausted already, aching and barely holding tight to the flaring edges of the magic that courses through her veins, bulging them, overwhelming her heart.

"You're a witch, Mairwen!" screams Haf Lewis. "Be a witch!"

She looks at Haf, whose cheeks are marred by tears, and she looks at the first Grace, who is smiling. Then she looks at Rhun Sayer and Arthur Couch, holding on to each other against the altar. Arthur catches her eye, and she sees that circling the first three fingers of his right hand is his fire steel.

She told Haf being a witch was being in between: seeing both sides, all sides, seeing what others cannot and using that power to choose. To change the world.

Your power is only life, not death. You have to be both. You have to let it change you completely. That is real power: change.

"Arthur," she says. "Do what you came here to do."

The old god cries out, half in fury, half laughter. The forest leans in, grabbing at the people. Bone creatures attack, and the bird women shriek.

Mairwen does not wait. She runs for the Bone Tree, scrambling up its roots to the black hollow her father coaxed open. Diving in to the sticky, cold womb, she turns and looks down at Arthur.

Steadying himself against Rhun, who fights at his back, keeping the monsters away, Arthur lifts the fire steel. His lips make the shape of her name.

"I love you," she says, though nobody can hear it. "Both of you, and all of you. Hold on to my heart and I'll be fine. Now do it."

His nostrils flare as he takes a furious breath, and Arthur Couch strikes a spark.

THE ALTAR IGNITES. THE DRY AND CRACKED VINES, fueled by blood and crisp flower petals, light, and the old god laughs.

He laughs because a fire is not enough to hurt him. The Bone Tree will be born again after it dies.

But the first Grace, his Grace, appears before him and smiles. *"Your daughter is in the heart of the tree."*

The old god looks and there Mairwen is, pressed to the dank inner wood, digging her claws into its heart, letting the flowers from her mouth twine against the flaking white bark of the tree.

Arthur picks up a burning branch, nudges Rhun, and takes the fire with him as he climbs nearer to Mairwen, then plunges the flames into the roots. Rhun says, "No!" but Arthur answers, "Trust me. Trust *her*," so Rhun lifts a thick vine snaking with fire and drapes it at the foot of the Bone

Tree. Haf Lewis helps, and her little sister. The rest battle the desperate creatures of the forest, the half-living, half-dead bone creatures, the monstrous birds and rodents, the bending, shifting trees.

The old god warns, "This will ruin you all," still thinking he can stop them and also never afraid of death and inevitable rebirth. "Mairwen, I'll go with you. We'll be reborn together."

"No," she whispers, thinking of her mother. Mairwen Grace *pulls* on her heart, and the old god falters. He falls to his knees.

"Mairwen."

"Father," she whispers, but he hears it. Deep in his flesh and beyond his bones, he hears her voice.

As the Bone Tree burns, Mairwen closes her eyes and presses her palms to the angry wound on her breast, to the ruins of Baeddan's thorny heart, the dying heart of the forest, the key to the bargain. She makes it grow.

Flowers burst from the old god's mouth. His hands grow into the roots and earth, trapping him.

Fire flickers around the god and his daughter, licking at both, casting a web of shadows across Mairwen's face.

The old god coughs, dying again, and Mairwen says, "It will be mine now. My heart, my forest."

She weaves briars across the hollow mouth of the Bone Tree, and she is alone in the darkness.

Except, she will never be truly alone, because her heart belongs to more than one.

WHEN MAIRWEN, ARTHUR, AND RHUN CLIMBED onto the altar together, in the final moments of their Slaughter Moon, they put still-bleeding bone bracelets around each other's wrists and held hands. They cried out the words of their charm, holding tight, eyes closed, heads thrown back. *We are the saints of Three Graces!*

It felt like drowning, painful and desperate. It felt like waking from the worst nightmare. It felt like fire, and it felt like their hearts beat so fast they hummed.

When the Bone Tree is consumed by flame, it feels the same.

THERE IS ONLY FIRE. NO BALANCE, NO PEACE, ONLY THE burning destruction, reaching in every direction out and down and even up, up, up toward the sky.

Wind swirls, dragging sparks from the Bone Tree, and flash fires break out, lighting up a tree here and there. Bird women fly too near and go up in a burst of lightning flame.

Rhun and Arthur hold on to each other, and Haf Lewis puts her hand on Arthur's back. Her little sister holds her hand, and Per Argall holds Bree's, and on and on until every person from Three Graces still in the grove links themselves together.

"We are the saints of Three Graces," Rhun says too soft for anyone to hear over the fire. But it's his prayer and the forest knows.

Mairwen opens her eyes in the center of the firestorm. It

hurts. She pushes out with her magic and wonders if she can die faster, but no—she has to be with the tree if she wants to transform. If she wants to take all her power.

That is what she clings to: transformation.

In the forest, life to death to life is the spark, the seed of magic.

Life and death, and Grace in between.

Mairwen, in between. Both. She *will* survive.

She grinds her teeth as the heat overwhelms her and she cannot breathe at all. She gasps, coughs, cannot stop coughing. Her muscles spasm and she bends in half, falling, cracking her shape and losing all sight and hearing, all feeling but for the fire.

T HE BONE TREE EXPLODES, FIRE AND ASHES, FLAMING branches and billowing streaks of smoke.

It flings the people back and away, out in an arc.

Smoke and wind swirl, and nine columns of silvery moonlight stretch up and up, dissipating against the dark twilight sky.

The moon has yet to rise.

The altar itself is cracked in two: atop it a pile of bones and fur and sinew slowly falling to pieces. All that's left of Sy Vaughn, an ashy mirror of the ruined Bone Tree.

Between the altar and the tree, Rhun and Arthur prop each other up.

Behind them, the grove is empty of everything but human

beings. Haf Lewis and her sister clutch tight to each other. Nona Sayer and her husband embrace. Lace huddles over her son's body. Braith and Cat Dee and Ifan Pugh and Beth Pugh stare at one another, holding hands. They are covered in ashes and flower petals stick in their hair.

Except for the small grunts and muttering of people slowly picking themselves up, and the creak of the forest stretching itself up again, there's little sound. The Bone Tree smolders, split in three.

"Mairwen!" Rhun cries, and it comes out hoarse and empty. Arthur turns, lungs raw as if he sucked down all the fire.

Neither cares for anything in that moment but her, and they shove around, pulling apart the ashes and hot chunks of roots, hunting. Haf joins them, tears tracking through the spray of ashes on her cheeks. Then others, too.

A few moments of fruitless hunting bring Rhun and Arthur together again. Rhun looks thrashed, near tears, and Arthur wants to pull out a knife and gouge his skin off as if it would be a welcome distraction. Instead, he just puts his arms around Rhun, holding him close and tight. Rhun's head falls against Arthur's, and his shoulders tremble.

Nobody knows what Mairwen did. Nobody knows if the charm is back in place, if there's a new bargain, or if their valley is like any other valley now.

"What story will we tell?" murmurs Haf.

Arthur brushes his fingertips on Rhun's sleeve. "Look."

Spring-green vines are curling up the remains of the

Bone Tree, winding and spiraled. They shoot up, growing unnaturally fast, covering the blackened bark, chipping it away. Soon the entire three splayed pieces of the tree are more emerald than black, more living than charcoal. Tiny white yarrow blossoms.

Rhun takes Arthur's hand. Arthur grabs Haf's, and they pick their way over crumbling roots and new tangles of vines.

They help each other up the massive base of the tree, to where the three broken pieces of the trunk converge. It's empty of all but ash, yarrow flowers, and thin, moon-bright bones.

EVERY MORNING
AFTER

Every morning as the sun rises, Rhun Sayer and Arthur Couch wait at the edge of the Devil's Forest. Sometimes Haf Lewis joins them with a basket of bread.

It's been twelve days since the Bone Tree burned. No other tree caught fire. John Upjohn is buried in the cemetery under the saints' memorial. Too little was left of Baeddan, though Rhun picked up a few teeth and a curving rib bone. Haf and Hetty led them to the Grace cottage, where Aderyn Grace's body was grown straight into the hearthstone, and from her chest a small gray sapling reached up toward the ceiling. Rhun and Arthur climbed onto the roof and pulled apart enough thatching to shed light on the little tree.

Rain came, just enough, and Rhos Priddy's baby isn't doing well, but lives. They've finished the harvest, and a dozen people left the valley, including Arthur's father. Without a bargain, they said, why remain where they cannot achieve greater things? Arthur shrugged and moved his meager belongings from the Sayer barn up into Sy Vaughn's manor and pointedly took a pair of Rhun's boots with him. Rhun hasn't been ready to move out of his family home yet. Not while he doesn't know. When the sun shines on a patch of fallen red leaves he thinks of Mairwen.

Twice he and Haf climbed up to the manor house at night and sat around the fire pit where the saints were named, three fat candles burning, just to watch the moonlight against the pale green, flowering branches of the Bone Tree. Arthur always makes them come inside and tell stories to the few other kids who live with him already. Per Argall, for one, and seven-year-old Emma Howell, who says she wants to be a saint. Arthur tells her she can't, but only because there are no more saints. He'll still teach her to skin a rabbit and make a fire and whatever else would help her survive alone in the wilderness.

It takes three days for the burns on Rhun's and Arthur's and Haf's hands to heal completely. Slower than with the bargain, but they wonder if it's still magic-fast. None in the valley know or remember how long it should take.

Arthur stares at Rhun one afternoon, when they're setting a series of rabbit traps. Rhun starts to sweat under the intensity of the look, and backs up against a tree. Arthur pushes off his hunter's hood and kisses Rhun.

Closing his eyes, Rhun accepts the kiss, letting Arthur work through it. After an uncooperative moment, Arthur's mouth softens and he brushes his lips against Rhun's cheek, too. His eyelashes flutter, teasing Rhun's skin.

It breaks some barrier that had been keeping Rhun from demanding what Arthur had been doing at the Bone Tree alone.

"I went to burn it down," Arthur says, not moving away. There's only a handspan of air between them.

"You shouldn't have."

Arthur shrugs and touches his own lips.

Rhun can't let it go, despite his gaze locked on Arthur's fingers and Arthur's lips. "We all had to decide together! It doesn't matter what you learned or how you changed. If you were just going to make a choice alone, make the decision alone, it's as bad as all the secrets and lies that came before. You don't get to choose for other people."

"There wasn't really a choice to *make*. The bargain was wrong. You know it."

Reluctantly, Rhun nods. Regret and sorrow drag down at him. He frowns. He misses Mairwen so much. She'd know what to snap at Arthur to make him understand he can't change people by taking everything over, even if he's right.

Arthur sucks in a sharp breath. "I want her back."

"Even though she was the devil's daughter?"

"We always knew that," Arthur says with a wry smile.

Most of Three Graces doesn't hold anything against Rhun or Arthur, though some continue to give Arthur sideways glances, but likely because Arthur is as quick to sneer as ever. Arthur thinks the first time someone dies of illness there'll be a hard few weeks for the former saints. Rhun promises they'll get through it. Rhun the Elder and Braith Bowen and Cat Dee create a few plans for storing more food over the winter and ask for better records of the animals and crops in the valley, just in case they need, in the spring, to send someone into a city for supplies or more chickens or something. They'll figure it out.

This morning it's two weeks since the Slaughter Moon, and as the sun rises, so does an impossibly tiny sliver of a smiling moon.

Rhun crouches at the edge of the Devil's Forest, hands covering his bowed head. Light spreads over Arthur beside him, stretched out in uncertain sleep.

A bird trills at the dawn, hesitant in the frosty breeze. Not a cloud mars the sky, so dawn rings the valley: pink and gold in the east, gentle cream in the west. Stars cling to their last in the dark apex. Rhun presses his fingers into his scalp, releasing fractions of the gentle ache that's haunted him the past hour or so.

Arthur is not asleep, but unready to open his eyes. His back is cold where he's lain for hours, flattening the yellow grass, and the tip of his nose, too. Only his hands are warm, folded under the front of his jacket. He's tired of this dawn vigil, impatient for Mairwen to either prove herself alive or be dead. If she's dead he'll want to die too, but Rhun will need him. The not knowing is making his stomach crawl constantly.

Then he can taste the light on his lips.

Rhun puts his hand on Arthur's waist, and the heat of the touch through his shirt opens Arthur's eyes. He squints and sits smoothly, taking Rhun's hand and holding on to it by the wrist. He stares at the smear of bright pink burn scar, shining perfectly parallel to one of the lines across Rhun's palm.

"It's been too long," Arthur murmurs.

Rhun's fingers curl protectively around his palm. "She told me she would marry you."

Arthur laughs merrily. "She doesn't even like me."

Rhun only watches, quietly amazed at how beautiful Arthur is when he forgets to be cranky. Dawn brightens the sharp line of Arthur's jaw, and the ragged layers of his hair, and flares along his eyelashes.

The hungry look on Rhun's face reminds Arthur their hands are folded together and his easy laugher fades into a suspicion. "You mean she said she'd marry me if you died."

"No. She promised either way. And if I survived, I could live with you both."

"Oh God." Arthur is laughing again, thinking what a disaster it would be, but liking it.

Rhun shrugs, over-aware that Arthur is holding his hand, thumb stroking the delicate skin of his palm. He shivers. There's still some magic here, and perhaps throughout the valley.

Suddenly Arthur goes rigid. "Rhun," he whispers. "Flowers are blooming in the forest."

. . .

S HE WANDERS.

There is a smile in her heart that has yet to translate onto her mouth, for her body is new, transformed, less a girl than yesterday. Or the day before. She isn't sure. Where she steps, the forest roots rise to poke and caress, and branches reach out for her where she passes. Her touch encourages brightening leaves, despite the approach of winter. The beat of her heart is strong, pumping cool blood, like forest streams that never see sunlight, through her veins.

If she pauses to close her eyes, she can feel all of it: the entire valley. Her feet connect through the earth, her hands through the trees she strokes. She tastes it on her tongue and hears the quiet song of it. Her heart throbs and the valley echoes it back. A hundred, no a thousand and more lives flicker with her. People. Little creatures, clicking their teeth. Birds, hounds, rabbits and foxes and a few white deer. Some are hungry, some asleep. Some hunting and others stretching wings against the cold breeze. Alive. They're all alive.

She's not stuck between light and dark, or valley and forest. She isn't a thread of magic or a piece of a charm. She's not one of three. She's the center of it all.

The sun rises and she approaches the edge. A forest devil, a witch, a young woman, with eyes like a starry night and teeth like cats, and thorny, flowering brambles tangled in her hair, littering white petals behind her.

They're waiting for her. Two of the hearts: one burning, one perfectly in tune.

She smiles, lips parted over sharp but not too-sharp teeth.

Instead of slowing, she leaps forward. She dives at them, throwing arms around both together. One hisses as some sharp piece of her body slices at his skin, and the other grunts because he catches most of her weight. Neither of them lets go.

❖ THE END ❖

ACKNOWLEDGMENTS

Thanks to everyone who's ever listened to me talk about how suspicious I am of magic while at the same time longing for it, or argued with me about witches and forest gods and gender. This book was born during those bonfire conversations.

Natalie, my wife, bears the brunt of my magic and gender anxieties, followed closely by Robin Murphy, who I have yelled at about b.s. gender essentialism in modern paganism for twenty years. I'm only a little sorry, and I love you both.

Thanks to:

Lydia Ash for hooking me up with resources on bone cleaning, and Gretchen McNeil for horror recommendations that I basically did not use at all.

My dad and brothers for not flinching when I texted

them asking very specific questions about sewing somebody's hand bones into somebody else's chest.

And thanks to my mom for putting up with all of us.

My agent, Laura Rennert, who refuses to give up on me or any of the weird things I send her.

My editor, Ruta Rimas, who not only helped me make the book better, she identified some of my worst writing habits and didn't let me get away with them. That is worth my weight in gold. And thanks to the unsung heroes at McElderry Books who copyedit, design, produce, and sell my work.

I got incredibly helpful feedback from the following readers: Miriam Weinberg, Jordan Brown, Laura Ruby, and Justina Ireland. I owe you!

To all the friends who've supported me and my family throughout the past two rough years, thank you. When someday I take to the sea, you can all come. Maybe.